PRAISE FOR

LARA ADRIAN'S

New York Times and #1 internationally best-selling vampire romance novels

MIDNIGHT BREED SERIES

NOVELS IN THE
MIDNIGHT BREED SERIES
By Lara Adrian

The
MIDNIGHT
BREED
Series Companion

☾

LARA ADRIAN

ISBN: 1939193923
ISBN-13: 978-1939193926

THE MIDNIGHT BREED SERIES COMPANION: The ultimate insider's guide to the New York Times and #1 internationally best-selling vampire series

www.LaraAdrian.com

Available in ebook and print editions.

ACKNOWLEDGMENTS

This book has been a work-in-progress for a couple of years now—much longer than that, if I am to count all of the thought and planning that went into the development of the Midnight Breed series from the time I first began writing it and adding pages of notes to my series "bible."

At first, I expected my notes would remain as background material whose only purpose was to help me remember my own series lore and character stats. But along the way, as the series gained popularity and readers started emailing me with thought-provoking questions about one thing or another, or asked me at book signings to explain things about the Ancients or the Breed or the Breedmates that wasn't necessarily in the text of the books, I realized that it could be fun to share all of my "insider info" with the fans of the series who had grown to love the Midnight Breed perhaps as much as I do.

I've had a lot of help from my husband and support staff at various times in compiling and editing the material contained in this Companion book, but no one has been more instrumental than my awesome Facebook admin and assistant (who also happens to be my lovely step-daughter and the mother of my first grandchild!) Heather Rogers. Thank you, Heather, for all of your effort, creativity and patience. I love you!

Of course, neither this book nor any of the others I've written would be possible without the love and encouragement of my husband, or the enthusiasm and support from you, my dear reader.

This book is for all of you, with love and gratitude.

CONTENTS

INTRODUCTION
BY LARA ADRIAN

For as long as I can remember, I've had a deep love of books. Although neither of my parents are avid readers, they made sure my siblings and I had library cards in elementary school and a couple of dollars to spend when the Bookmobile came around to our small hometown in Michigan. I can still remember the wonder I felt—and the agonizing indecision—every time I wandered the aisles of the public library or perused the tables of brand-new books set out for consideration in the traveling Bookmobile. It was always so hard to choose just one or two!

Other kids saved their pennies for candy or the latest cool toys. I could never get enough books. I could never get enough of the mysteries that books showed me, the magic they created, or the many incredible worlds they opened up in my mind's eye.

Books were my escape from all the things that troubled me. They were my passage into amazing, sometimes terrifying places I never dreamed might exist. Books were my home port, their pages a comfort and companion, no matter my age or where life took me.

They still are.

The fact that I now make my living writing books—telling stories I hope will give my readers some of the same kind of escape and wonderment that other storytellers have given me throughout my life—is a privilege I never take for granted.

I worked hard, but I also got lucky early on, landing a publishing contract with Random House for the very first book I'd ever written—a medieval romance that released in 1999 under my first pen name, Tina St. John. I wrote six more historical romances over the next six years, books that received nice reviews and won awards, but never found a large enough audience to keep a publisher happy.

And so it was, in the summer of 2005, that I found myself at a crossroads. My publisher didn't want any more medieval romances from me. The proposal for the book I was working on had been rejected and I was without a contract—news I received just after my husband and I had signed a mortgage on the first home (a condo) that we'd ever owned.

Fortunately, my editor believed in me and invited me to send in something totally different for consideration. Even though I was reeling from the fact that my Tina St. John career had just ended without notice, my mind was already leaping forward to the folder of story ideas I'd been gathering and playing with over the years—ideas that included everything from gritty thrillers and psychological suspense stories, to small-town, feel-good romances. I also had a couple of concepts sketched out for dark, sexy vampire novels.

My agent wasn't very enthusiastic when I told her I wanted to propose a vampire romance. She cautioned me that editors had been predicting the death (the true death?) of vampires for quite some time. She worried that, as with my historical romances, I might be coming in on the downward curve of the trend. Little did anyone know that in just a few months' time, a certain phenomenon called *Twilight* would breathe all-new life into romances with blood and bite!

A couple of weeks after that bad news call from my agent, I submitted a rough outline and first three chapters for a book I'd tentatively titled, *Kiss of Darkness*. Feeling I had nothing to lose, I packed my story with all the things that entertain me most as a reader: action, suspense, urban fantasy, and, of course, scorching sensuality and romance featuring a dark, absolutely lethal, drop-dead gorgeous, uber-alpha male.

My agent read the material, and she loved it. She loved it so much, she asked if I could possibly expand the outline to cover three books, so she could shop the proposal to a handful of publishers as a trilogy. I worked out brief plotlines for another two books (one story that stuck pretty much as I'd pitched it, and another that, well, didn't—which I'll explain further on in this Companion). My agent sent out the proposals and told me she hoped we'd have some nibbles of interest shortly.

Not even a week later, we had offers from almost all of the top publishing houses in New York. An auction took place between several of them, and within a few days I went from being an unemployed historical romance writer to a brand-new, dark contemporary vampire romance author with a new name and multiple offers in hand.

In the end, I remained with Random House and the wonderful Shauna Summers, the editor who plucked me out of the slush pile with that very first medieval romance manuscript. Random House released the first three Midnight Breed books in rapid succession— two of them back-to-back in the summer of 2007, and a third later that year. To my total amazement, the series was an instant success, landing on major best-seller lists since the beginning.

There are now a total of eleven Midnight Breed novels in print through Random House USA (with a twelfth coming soon!) and one ebook novella. This Companion to the series covers the first ten books—*Kiss of Midnight* through *Darker After Midnight*—which comprise the original story arc of the series. You'll find background information on the story world and each of the first ten novels, a complete character reference guide, a Q&A with readers, fun trivia questions and more.

This Companion volume also includes Gideon and Savannah's story, something I've been promising Midnight Breed fans for what seems like forever. *A Touch of Midnight* is an all-new, never-before-published novella of around forty-thousand words—a big "short" story, almost half the size of one of my typical novels. It finally answers all the questions you have about Gideon, how he and Savannah met, why he no longer runs combat missions, and even a couple extra surprises that shed light on other things you've asked me about through the years.

My intent for the Companion had been to release it as something of a bridge between *Darker After Midnight* and *Edge of Dawn*, the book that begins the current, second story arc of the series featuring the offspring of the Order and a powerful new enemy on the horizon.

But things don't always work out as planned, and for a number of reasons, this Companion almost didn't happen at all. Instead, with options opening up to authors through self-publishing, I decided not to wait any longer and instead release it myself in ebook and trade paperback.

If there is reader interest, I'd love to release a second Companion volume in the future to cover all of the exciting things and interesting new characters you'll encounter as the series continues with *Edge of Dawn* and the other books still to come.

In the meantime, I hope you enjoy revisiting Lucan, the Order, the Breedmates, the story world, the behind-the-scenes tidbits and all the rest, in this, *The Midnight Breed Series Companion.*

Lastly, a word of caution: ***This book is full of spoilers!***

You'll find no warnings (other than the one you're reading now) so if you haven't yet read the Midnight Breed Series, this may not be the best place for a new reader to start. Unless you're like me, that is—frequently peeking at the last page of a book first, and taking no less enjoyment in the journey despite knowing how everything will end.

Either way, enjoy! And thank you for being part of this journey along with me.

With big hugs and much love,

Lara Adrian

THE STORY WORLD

ANCIENTS

Why Aliens?

If I'm going to talk about the world of the Midnight Breed series, I suppose I need to start at the beginning. I have always loved vampires, from the time I was a kid. From the creepy, sometimes campy, Dracula movies on the Saturday afternoon "Creature Feature" on TV, or films like *The Lost Boys* and *'Salem's Lot*, to Anne Rice's mesmerizing novels featuring sophisticated, lethally seductive Lestat, vampires were—and still are—my #1 monster of choice. What other supernatural creature inspires fear and desire in such equal measure? He is death and sex and limitless power, all rolled into one insatiable (usually gorgeous) package. Vampires represent the ultimate dark, erotic fantasy.

There's just one problem with this picture. The corpse thing. I don't know about you, but for me it's not exactly a turn-on. Hard to imagine getting up-close-and-personal with a lot of cold, dead flesh. And no heartbeat means no blood flow. Which also means…well, *no blood flow*. And in a romance novel, especially the kind I like to write, that's a leap of logic that really can't be overlooked. But beyond that consideration, I suppose I just prefer my book boyfriends to be breathing.

So, when I got the green light from Random House and began creating my own race of vampires—my own mythology—the "undead" issue was the first thing I had to resolve. When I mentioned to John (my husband and most-valued plotting partner) that I needed to come up with a plausible origin for the Breed, he quipped, "Maybe they're aliens."

It seemed kind of crazy—vampires from outer space—but also kind of brilliant. All the pieces started coming together in my mind as soon as he said it. I couldn't jot down my thoughts fast enough—everything from the Ancients' arrival on Earth, what they looked like, what kind of planet they came from, how their offspring would look, how they would live and love and sometimes die…all of it.

Not everything has made it into the books themselves. Maybe it never will. But when it comes to research and world-building, I think it's important for a writer to know the answers to questions that might not ever get asked in any particular work. It helps give a firmer foundation to the characters and to the universe they inhabit, even if that foundation remains just below the surface of the actual stories.

Here are my world-building notes, taken from my story "bible" as I was writing the book that became *Kiss of Midnight* and the start of the Midnight Breed series:

What life is like on the Ancients' planet

The planet is mostly dark, with about four hours of sunlight during which the inhabitants sleep in order to avoid getting smoked by UV rays. The planet is chilly due to the lack of light, but the aliens' blood runs faster than human/mammals so they are not affected. There isn't a lot of plant or animal life on the planet (also due to lack of light), but there is a lot of water and hilly, rocky terrain. The aliens live in technologically advanced cities and dwellings, made from metals excavated from the hills.

Because of the lack of natural animal life, the alien society eats its own—they are cannibals, except they don't consume meat or muscle, only blood. They have farms that raise "crops" of blood hosts for the masses. The powerful in alien society purchase private stocks of blood hosts, rather like slaves, who exist only to nourish and entertain their masters.

The race is cruel and aggressive: Males enjoy the sport of hunting and often arrange predator parties for their elite friends; females sometimes are permitted to organize gladiator-style spectacles of the choicest male slaves, who are typically forced to "service" their mistresses. The male hunting fervor has also spread to the "street" crowd, but it resembles more gang-style murder than organized sport. This underground form of hunting among the lower classes is illegal, and punishable immediately by death.

As far as laws and government, a few powerful individuals control an entire society. There are no elections, no rights of the individual, only those of the strong and the elite. The work force is in business to serve rich masters. There are no schools for general population; they are kept ignorant of everything except what the government deems they need to know. Reproductive rights are nonexistent; general civilians are bred like cattle, with most offspring being taken away to serve the rich. There is only one religion, and powerful priests dictate to the masses how they should live.

There are no marriages, only reproductive matings among the powerful and selective, and clinical breedings (generally IVF, or stud servicing if the owners prefer more hands-on supervision) among the masses. Females are viewed as valuable only so long as they can breed—whether that's on the demand of an elite male (if the female is of a highborn bloodline) or in the farms and in servitude. Barren females, which are rare, and those who can no longer bear offspring, are euthanized—if they're lucky. Basically, you don't want to be born female on this planet!

The race has its own complex language, but they can also communicate telepathically and read one another's mind. The masses are prohibited from telepathic communication by the implantation of stunting chips at birth, which cut off that part of their brain. Individuals raised on the farms are basically lobotomized in vitro, since they will not need any of their faculties in their dim existence.

The army of this planet is immense, and brutal. This is a race of beings that thrives on violence and conquest, which has bred an entire class of gladiatorial warriors in service to powerful generals, as well as the generals themselves, who relish blood sport. From time to time, pods of these warriors are sent out to scout neighboring planets for possible inhabitation and/or resources. They love bringing home trophies from "exotic" places—usually skulls or other evidence of the carnage left in their wake.

Physical description of the Ancients

Humanoid in form, but typically 6'5" and often taller. Immensely strong. Eyes are greenish-topaz, with elliptical pupils—very much like cats' eyes. Optimum nocturnal and predatory vision.

Bodies and heads are completely hairless, with unusual skin markings ("dermaglyphs") that serve as camouflage and ultraviolet ray protection (meager) as well as indications of their lineage and social rank. These markings are henna-like and intricate, but change colors (brown, gold, green, blue, red) and iridescence based on the individual's emotional state. The markings cover their bodies, often even into their faces and the tops of their heads.

Psychic abilities of the Ancients

- Mind reading and telepathy between their own kind
- Mind control of humans
- Ability to create "Minions" (mind slaves) of bled humans
- Ability to move at speeds beyond human sensory detection
- Telekinesis
- Heightened sensory perception (like predator animals)

The crash-landing on Earth

Thousands of years ago, a group of eight warriors from the Ancients' planet set out on a conquest and crashed on Earth. Immediately following their arrival, two of their crew died of UV exposure. They learned quickly that Earth has long days of sunlight, and, vulnerable during this time, they had to seek shelter deep underground.

The aliens were highly evolved intellectually, so they picked up on human languages with relative ease, aided by the ability to read simple human minds. They communicated with Earth's inhabitants when needed, if mainly to taunt them with threats and verbal domination, which provided a basis for some of the alien and vampire folklore that spread through countless human generations.

Hunger was an immediate factor in the survival of the aliens on Earth. At night, they would sweep in on quiet villages to feed and kill without discrimination. They actually wiped out entire civilizations in this fashion (Atlantis, the Maya, others of less note). Because of Earth's harsh climate, the aliens required more blood than on their own planet, so they consumed in vast quantities, spreading mass fear and superstition through humankind for centuries.

Other hungers needed to be sated as well. The aliens relished hunting humans and razing peaceful settlements, but they also craved sex. Rapes were commonplace in the raids and attacks. Human females didn't always survive the brutality of their alien conquerors, but some did. And some—a rare few—actually proved fertile to the alien seed. These women were the first Breedmates, and would become the unwilling mothers of a new race of vampire on Earth...a hybrid race that would come to be known as the Breed.

The Ancients' demise on Earth

Those Ancients who didn't perish in the first few centuries after they arrived were later brought down (Post-Black Death era, so mid-1300s) by their own descendants—those who would become the first Breed warriors of the Order—who joined forces under Lucan's leadership to rise up to overthrow the remaining Ancients for the good of mankind and the entire Breed nation around the world.

None of the original eight Ancients are known to have survived Lucan's war on them, however, rumors persist about one Ancient who escaped and now hibernates in a hidden location. It's likely that Rogues have information about this slumbering Ancient that the Order could pursue. [*Author's note: I later decided to keep the hibernating Ancient a secret, not a rumor, and put the alien under the charge of one individual, Dragos, rather than involving Rogues.*]

Methods for killing a vampire

- Sunlight exposure (typically within minutes)
- Starvation (slow death)
- Decapitation (instant)
- Complete or massive body trauma (effectiveness depends on damage)
- Severe injuries inflicted with weaponry or explosives (less effective)

THE BREED

The Breed

The Breed are the hybrid offspring, and subsequent direct descendants, of an Ancient and a Breedmate. Through the genetic dominance of their Ancient fathers, Breed infants are born exclusively male. Breed males share the huge size and strength of their alien fathers, and when agitated (either by hunger, anger, or lust—any extreme emotion) their eyes take on an alien, amber glow and their pupils turn thin like a cat's eye.

The most powerful of the Breed are those born of the first generation (Gen One), however with their physical/mental strength comes fiercer hungers and an added vulnerability to the things that can kill one of the Breed, such as sunlight exposure and blood addiction. Later generations of the Breed must deal with these issues too, but Gen Ones bear the hardest burdens.

All vampires need to drink blood from a fresh, flowing human (or Breedmate) vein in order to live. No blood bags, transfusions, animals or synthetics. Blood is essential, but where their Ancient sires have no limits on how much their systems can absorb, for all members of the Breed, there is a dangerous tipping point where survival and excess meet. If a Breed consumes too much, or too frequently, he risks developing Bloodlust, an addiction to blood.

Much like a human addiction to a powerful narcotic, Bloodlust is destructive and lethal. The addict swirls deeper and deeper into the void, until all that was good in him is gone. For one of the Breed, once Bloodlust claims him, he is very often a lost cause. Without intervention, his blood system will corrupt and his sanity will soon follow, turning him into a killing machine with no hope of recovery. At that point, he is considered Rogue, the closest a human/vampire can get to his savage alien roots.

How the Breed compares to classic vampires

Likenesses include: Must consume blood in order to survive; long lifespans of many centuries, but not true immortality in that they can be killed by various methods (see Ancients); photosensitivity, both the eyes and the skin; ability to move at great speeds, beyond the detection of human senses; mind control in varying degrees; telekinesis in varying degrees.

Differences include: No aversion to garlic or holy water; no need to be invited into a place before entering; no problems with sacred ground or churches, as they are not the undead or the damned; no trouble seeing their own reflections, as they are real flesh and blood individuals; no ability to disappear or dematerialize; no shapeshifting ability; cannot be killed by a wooden stake to the heart.

Physical traits of the Breed

While Breed males inherit their Ancient fathers' vampiric thirsts and strengths, physically, in terms of hair, skin, and eye color, a Breed male's appearance is influenced by his Breedmate mother's looks. Breed males are also tall and muscular, like their alien fathers, with flawless health and physical fitness.

Dermaglyphs: Colors and meanings

Also inherited from their alien fathers are the camouflaging and mood-influenced skin markings called "dermaglyphs." Gen Ones have the most elaborate and extensive glyphs. Later generations, as the purity of their alien genes are diluted with those from their maternal side, Breed males display less markings in fewer places on their bodies. Dermaglyph hues change according to the emotional state of the vampire:

- contentment/normal state: a shade darker than his skin color
- satiation from recent feeding: deep russet-bronze
- general hunger: pale scarlet and faded gold
- fierce, spasmodic hunger: deep purples, reds, to black
- desire: burgundy, indigo, and gold

Extrasensory powers and abilities

Every Breed male has a unique ability (or a curse, weakness) passed down to him from his Breedmate mother. For some individuals, it is a tangible gift, such as the ability to heal or to kill. In others it is an extrasensory power, such as precognition or a psychic bond with animals.

With the exception of trancing, telekinesis of small objects, doors, locks, etc., and high-speed movement, most of the Breed's psychic abilities exist only in the oldest or most powerful individuals. They can, with limited results, influence the minds of humans, but it is a taxing exercise for generations later than Gen One and is rarely put to use. It is considered dishonorable for any Breed male to mind control a Breedmate.

The most powerful Breed males, Gen Ones in particular, have the ability to create Minions, but Breed law prohibits the practice (as does Breed honor).

Weaknesses

Like their Ancient fathers, the Breed is vulnerable to ultraviolet sunlight. Gen Ones can withstand no more than ten minutes of direct exposure and their skin begins to burn in less time than that. Later generations fare slightly better, but no member of the race would dare stay out in the sunlight for more than a half hour's time.

In much the same way an Ancient is hard to kill, so are the Breed. Decapitation is the fastest, most certain means of killing one of the Breed (but good luck trying!). Other methods include massive or complete body trauma, catastrophic injury, or starvation (rare occurrence).

The Breed is always susceptible to blood addiction (Bloodlust), and if he should turn Rogue, a Breed can then be killed relatively easily, and surely, with a wound inflicted via titanium blade. Rogues' blood systems are diseased, corrupted in such a way that titanium becomes poison to them. One laceration can send the poison into their bloodstream, which devours the Rogue from the inside out. Should a Rogue evade capture and killing, very often his madness drives him to suicide, usually via death by sunlight.

Breed society

Vampire society at large resides in civilian communities called

Darkhavens. They are located in cities, towns, villages, on farmlands and islands—virtually anywhere, with the exclusion of the tropics or high UV areas. Each Darkhaven, from the toniest high-rise to the quaintest berg and hollow, has one thing in common: access to a secured room or bunker where the Breed vampires can escape the daylight, for long durations, if needed. A Darkhaven is usually home to a single or extended family unit, with a head of household known as the Darkhaven leader. This Breed male, very often the eldest, or highest-born, Breed male of the family or unit, is responsible for ensuring the security and general wellbeing of the Darkhaven's residents.

Breed civilian society is protected, by and large, by an organization called the Enforcement Agency. They are a cross between a police force and a governing body, with all the corruption and political empire-building to go along with it. The Agency began with good intentions centuries ago, but over time has decomposed internally into an ineffective, often dangerous, organization.

Existing outside of the Darkhavens sanctuaries and the Enforcement Agency is another, smaller cache of vampire society: the warriors of the Order. These guys are the strongest, fittest, most lethal members of vampire society. Usually outsiders for one reason or another, and far too alpha to pussy around in some nicey-nice commune, they have dedicated their lives to the true protection of their kind, even if that means running up against—or in the face of—the Agency. The Breed warrior is the vampire equivalent of US military special forces and assassin/snipers. They operate outside of regular vampire law enforcement, often covertly, always deadly.

Across the proverbial tracks from all three of the above, are the Rogues. These guys are the outlaws, gangbangers, boneheads and other low-lifes of the vampire world. They are addicts living in anarchy, acting on impulse, whether that's to feed or rape or kill. Rogues skulk like vermin around human settlements, mainly larger cities, where the hunting is plentiful. Like human narcotic addicts, Bloodlusting Rogues have no personal pride, no care for how they live. Consequently, they generally live in filth and decay. They also kill humans openly, just one of their most unforgivable offenses, as this behavior could jeopardize the security of the entire Breed nation.

Breed life events: Birth, blood bonds and death

Breed gestation is nine months, similar to a human pregnancy. Unlike humans, however, Breed newborns feed on their mother's blood, not milk or formula. The infant is born with tiny fangs and can nurse from his Breedmate mother's blood (wrist, generally, not breast) until the time he is old enough and strong enough to hunt for a blood Host on his own—typically around four or five years old.

At puberty, a Breed male's feeding habits become more complicated. Now, feeding from a Breedmate will result in a blood bond to that female—a physical and psychic connection that, once initiated, cannot be broken except by death.

A Breed male can live an almost immortal lifespan, often many centuries. If he takes a Breedmate, his blood bond will allow her to live as long as him—barring any incident or accident that could kill her. An injured Breed male (or Breedmate) can be aided dramatically in healing, sometimes even brought back from the brink of death, if he or she drinks from the other at the time of injury.

BREEDMATES

Breedmates

A Breedmate is a mortal female with unique blood and DNA properties that allow for reproduction between her eggs and vampire sperm. Breedmates are distinguishable physically by the small teardrop-and-crescent-moon birthmark they are each born with somewhere on their bodies. Breedmates are also naturally physically fit and immune from illness in all stages of life, although on their own, they are not immortal. A Breedmate requires a blood bond with one of the Breed in order for her aging to cease.

Breedmates typically exhibit varieties of extrasensory abilities, but these abilities are often sporadic and/or difficult for her to control or master unless and until she forms a blood bond with one of the Breed. These females are also very often gifted artistically or creatively in some fashion.

Physical traits of the Breedmate

Breedmate physical appearances are as varied as human women all over the world. Breedmates can be born in all corners of the world, so ethnically they represent many kinds of women and cultures. What Breedmates share in common is their birthmark, and the presence of a blood scent that is unique to each woman.

Breedmate blood scents are detectable by members of the Breed, but generally not distinguishable to less-developed human olfactory senses. Breedmate blood scents are attractive to the Breed, sometimes even aphrodisiacal.

Although Breedmates can and do bite their Breed lovers to drink their blood, Breedmates do not have fangs or blood thirst, nor do they develop either after the blood bond with a Breed male. They do not have dermaglyphs or elliptical pupils.

The Breedmate mark

The Breedmate birthmark is a small red symbol, present somewhere on the body of every Breedmate. The mark itself is in the shape of a teardrop falling into the cradle of a crescent moon.

The Breedmate mark represents the blood bond (teardrop is actually a blood drop) and the fertility cycle of a Breedmate, which is the period of the waxing and waning (crescent) moons. The symbol is also representative of the act of conception, when the Breed male's blood and seed are accepted by the chalice of the Breedmate's body.

Breedmate talents

Breedmate ESP talents range from simple mind-reading and emotive perception, to more powerful gifts such as sonokinesis, pyrokinesis, and the ability to either restore life or rescind it with a touch. A Breedmate's talent will strengthen, along with her ability to wield and control it, once she is blood-bonded to a Breed male.

During pregnancy with a Breed offspring, a Breedmate's talent will diminish and not resume until the birth of her child. Whatever unique talent a Breedmate possesses, it is inherited by her Breed offspring.

Breedmate origins

[Author's note: The following is another example of world-building and background information that hasn't (yet?) made it into any of the novels themselves. I decided to include it here because it helps paint a picture of the dark, early days of the Breed's genesis on Earth.]

In the early ages, human females who bore the spawn of their alien rapists often routed out the gestating seed, or, on their own or at the pressing of worried family, made sure the infant abominations did not survive their births. The first Gen Ones were considered devil babies, and treated as such. The few Gen Ones who were spared maternal slaying, were often abandoned in the wild to be consumed by their first sunrise, or if sheltered in dark caves, by slow starvation for blood.

Stories of these "demonic" rapes and resulting cursed births were passed down as warnings from woman to woman, until, finally, a small number of pregnant Breedmates found each other and formed a pact to protect themselves—and their children—from the superstitions of humankind and the monstrous savagery of their babies' then-presumed demon fathers. These women loved their babies regardless of their origins, and banded together in secret, hidden enclaves.

Circa 1000 CE. One rare exception to the aliens-as-rapists dynamic was Lucan's own parents. His Breedmate mother and Ancient father actually came to care for one another. Narok (the father) separated himself from the rest of his kind and, for a time, made a home with his lover (Etain). Tragically, Narok's alien genes proved too strong, and he ended up killing Etain while feeding from her in a state of severe physical injury following a battle. *[Author's note: This incident was referenced more than once in the novels, however, in compiling this Companion, I realized I never specifically mentioned Lucan's parents by their names in the novels. I've included it here because I thought readers might find it interesting to have this info.]*

As the series evolved, it has been revealed that Breedmates are not merely human women born with inexplicable genetic properties and true ESP talents. They are, in fact, the daughters of mortal, *Homo sapiens* women and men from a hidden, immortal race of beings popularized in human mythology as Atlanteans.

Breedmate life events: Blood bonds, child-rearing and death

A Breedmate's life expectancy is equivalent to a human female's, unless and until the Breedmate forms a blood bond with one of the Breed. Then, she will cease aging at her prime (roughly the age of thirty) and remain youthful for the duration of her blood bond.

A blood bond provides all the nourishment a Breedmate needs to live, although they can (and do) continue to enjoy human food when they wish, unlike the Breed, who cannot consume human food except in extremely small quantities and only in rare instances.

Breedmates nourish their young with blood, not by breastfeeding or synthetics. A Breed child will drink from his mother's vein (usually the wrist) from the moment of his birth until around the time he is four or five years old and able to hunt and feed on his own. If a Breedmate mother should die before the child is ready to be weaned, a Breedmate surrogate can feed him.

If a Breedmate's partner should be killed, her blood bond is broken and her body will resume aging unless she takes another Breed male as her mate. A widowed Breedmate never loses her place in the vampire community, even if she loses her mate.

As the widow of a Breed male, she has a couple of options. She can choose to continue to live without taking another mate from within the community. This will mean that her human biology will kick back into gear, and she will begin to age normally (and eventually die) like any other human. Alternatively, a widowed Breedmate can decide to take another mate at some point in time. She would then begin a new blood bond with that Breed male. Her aging process would again slow and cease, reverting back to her youthful prime, should she be advancing in physical age at the time of the new bond.

RITUALS

Mating and fertility

There is no true "wedding" among Breed males and their Breedmates. The blood bond and the binding ceremony are the closest they have to the human equivalent of a wedding. There are no papers, religion, or legalities involved; only a heartfelt commitment and a pledge to share the rest of their lives together—a sacred, eternal vow sealed with blood. This is an intensely private, intimate affair between the mated pair only. It isn't until after a formal binding is complete that the couple announces to friends and/or family. The binding is a cause for celebration, and, given its intense sexual nature, a cause for ruthless ribbing amongst the Breed males of the community.

The binding ceremony is a symbolic and literal declaration that the mated pair intends to live for each other from this night forward. The ceremony is conducted during the eve of a crescent moon, with the mated pair sneaking off to some undisclosed location where they will make love beneath the crescent moon, exchange blood (may or may not be for the first time) and pledge their undying devotion.

[Author's note: Lucan and Gabrielle's binding ceremony was shown in Chapter 34, the closing scene of Kiss of Midnight.*]*

Infant presentation ceremony

Breed tradition dictates that by the eighth night after an infant's birth, he should be formally named and presented by his parents to the members of their Darkhaven. In contrast to the binding ceremony and blood bond, the infant presentation ceremony is a public affair and great cause for celebration. Godparents are designated and present for this ritual, as they will be responsible for the upbringing of the child, should anything happen to his mother and father before the infant is old enough to feed and support himself.

As part of the ritual, the baby is presented to the gathering by an officiant who asks, *"Who brings this child before us tonight?"*

The parents reply that they do, and announce the baby's name. They then take the infant and hold him up for all to see, with the couple reciting in unison:

"This babe is ours. With our love, we have brought him into this world. With our blood and lives we sustain him, and keep him safe from all harm. He is our joy and promise, the perfect expression of our eternal bond, and we are honored to present him to you, our kin."

To which, the gathered reply, *"You honor us well."*

From there, the officiant then asks, *"Who pledges to protect this child with blood and bone and final breath should duty call upon it?"*

The godparent (or godparents) come forward and reply, *"We do."*

To conclude the ceremony, the officiant places the infant in a cloth cradle made of strips of white silk, woven together at the start of the ceremony and now held suspended by the child's parents. The Breed godparent then bites his own wrist (and that of his Breedmate, if he has one) and let their blood drip onto the baby's naked body, signifying their commitment to surrender their lives for the protection of his.

[Author's note: The presentation ceremony for Xander Raphael, Dante and Tess's son, was shown in Chapter 28 of Darker After Midnight.*]*

Breed funerals

When it comes to paying respects to the fallen, Breed tradition dictates that the deceased be given up to the sun the first morning after his death. To prepare for this solemn event, the body of the dead is anointed with eight ounces of perfumed oil, wrapped from head to toe in eight layers of white silk, then taken outside by an appointed honor guard who will attend the body for eight minutes in full morning sunlight, before leaving the dead to burn to ash.

Prior to the release of the body, a ceremony is held, where the dead's kith and kin, and his Breedmate if he had one, gather to pay their last respects. If the dead was not mated, his parents or siblings will speak to the gathering of his honor then say their good-byes.

If the dead was mated, his Breedmate will wear a hooded scarlet tunic, representative of her blood bond with the deceased. She will go to the body on the altar and speak the following words: *"This male was mine, and I was his. His blood sustained me. His strength protected me. His love fulfilled me in all ways. He was my beloved, my only one, and he will be in my heart for all eternity."*

To which the gathered reply, *"You honor him well."*

The Breedmate will then accept a ceremonial blade from the officiant and carry it with her to the body of her mate. Private words of good-bye are spoken, not meant for outside ears, then the Breedmate scores her lip with the knife and places a bloodred kiss on the white silk covering the mouth of her beloved.

When she is ready to let him go, she moves aside and the Breed male appointed to carry the dead up to the daylight steps forward to begin his sober duty.

[Author's note: Funeral rites were first depicted in Kiss of Midnight, *Chapter 12, after Conlan's death, and again in* Shades of Midnight, *Chapter 31, following Kade's brother, Seth's demise.]*

Breedmate funerals

Breedmate funerals follow the ritual for those of the Breed, with the exception of how the body is released following the ceremony. Breedmates do not turn to ash under direct sunlight, so their remains must be cremated. Ritual dictates that a Breedmate's ashes be kept by her mate until his death, if she has a mate, or with her Darkhaven family, if she dies unmated. The practice of keeping ashes is very old, and is usually followed only by the most traditional of Breed males.

Significance of Eight

The number eight, the symbol for infinity, is present in Breed rituals and in other aspects of Breed life throughout the series. In addition to eight factoring into birth and death rituals, it is also no accident that the Ancients arrived on Earth as a group of eight, or that the Order first formed with eight Gen One sons.

THE ORDER

The founding of the Order

In the mid-1300s in Europe, violent attacks by the Ancients and Rogues were on the rise. A Gen One Breed named Lucan (Thorne) refused to stand by and let it go unmet. His mission took on a firmer, more resolute shape when his father, an Ancient, murdered Lucan's mother in a fit of blood hunger gone too far. Lucan took his alien sire's head that same night, then razed the family castle and declared all-out war on the remaining Ancients.

Original members

Joined with Lucan in this fight were seven other Gen One Breed males including Lucan's eldest brother, Marek, a deadly individual named Tegan, and another of the original eight named Dragos (the elder). They succeeded in obliterating the last of the Ancients...all, save one, that is. But it was not until hundreds of years later—in modern times—that the secret of that hidden, surviving Ancient came to light.

Of the original founding members of the Order, four remain unnamed in the series, their current whereabouts unknown. Dragos the elder and Marek are both dead, the former having been killed during the time of the old war; the latter meeting his end at Tegan's hand during the timeline of the series. Lucan and Tegan are both current members of the Order in present day.

Establishment of the Boston headquarters

The original eight members of the Order disbanded after the war with the Ancients had ended. They drifted apart, seeking their own paths in life, some never to be heard from again.

Lucan and Tegan were at odds following the abduction and death of Tegan's first Breedmate, Sorcha, during the Middle Ages. The thread of friendship—of a brotherhood forged by war—stretched thin, then severed. Tegan wandered for many long years, spending some time in Germany and elsewhere, before resurfacing in the late 1890s to seek out Lucan once again.

As for Lucan, his personal mission following the war with the Ancients had been to combat Rogues wherever he found them. That goal eventually brought him to America, and in 1898, he decided to reform the Order with new members and establish a Boston headquarters, joined by a younger Breed male from London named Gideon. Tegan came on soon afterward, followed eventually by several other courageous modern-day warriors: Conlan, Dante, Rio, Nikolai, Kade, Brock, Hunter and Chase.

The secret, underground Boston compound thrived for more than one hundred years, until finally being compromised by one of the Order's chief adversaries.

GLOSSARY OF TERMS

GLOSSARY OF TERMS
(alphabetical order)

Ancient   Term used to describe one of the eight male vampire-like conquerors from another world who crash-landed on Earth thousands of years ago and eventually sired the race of alien/human hybrid beings known as the Breed. The Ancients are not Breed, and vice versa.

Atlantean   Term used to describe the race of male and female immortals who formed a secret, highly advanced colony on Earth thousands of years ago. This colony eventually came to be referred to in human mythology and legend as Atlantis. It was destroyed by the Ancients, in a catastrophic offensive strike that sent the Atlantean queen, her legion and subjects into hiding, where they remain to this day. A small number of Atlanteans defected from their colony over the years. It has recently been revealed that these defectors went on to father children with human women, creating the genetically and extrasensory gifted female offspring known as Breedmates.

blood bond   The deep, unbreakable physical and emotional connection that forms between a Breed male and a Breedmate upon the exchange of ingested blood. A blood bond gives a Breed male added strength and healing power, and in a Breedmate, the bond enhances and stabilizes the power of her ESP talent, provides healing and nutritive strength and also gives her near immortal longevity. Blood bonded couples can sense heightened emotion in each other, and can sense their mate's presence and proximity in their veins. A blood bond initiates upon the first drink (whether it's a Breed male drinking from a Breedmate, or vice versa) and is sealed when the other member of the pair drinks from the other, completing the connection. A blood bond is severable only by death, even if only half of the bond has been initiated. For example, if a Breed male drinks from an unbonded Breedmate, he is inextricably connected to her, until one or the other of them dies. He cannot bind himself to another, and will sense this Breedmate in his blood for the duration of that bond. This same rule applies if a Breedmate drinks from an unbonded Breed male. Further, only blood bonded pairs are capable of conception.

blood club   An illegal hunting sport, whereby Breed vampires collect a group of humans to be used as live game (see Renata, Mira) in a chase to the death. Blood clubs have long been outlawed, but there is still an element of the Breed who feel entitled to indulge their predator natures. The Order has broken up blood clubs during the course of the series.

Bloodlust   An addiction in one of the Breed to drinking blood. Bloodlust is generally irreversible, but depending on the severity or length of the addiction, there have been rare instances of rehabilitation and cure (see Tegan, Sterling Chase). Once a Breed's Bloodlust passes the tipping point, where his blood system is fully corrupted by the disease and he can no longer control the transformation of his eyes or the presence of his fangs, he is considered to have gone Rogue and is beyond saving.

blood reader   The ability to siphon thoughts or memories from the blood of the individual from whom one is drinking. This talent can work on humans, Breed, or Breedmates, in combination or exclusively one or the other (see Hunter, whose ability works on Breed and Breedmates, but not humans).

Breed   The resulting offspring of an Ancient and a Breedmate. Like their alien forebears, the Breed lives on blood, possesses superhuman strength and speed, and can only be killed by prolonged sunlight exposure, decapitation, or catastrophic bodily injury. On the distaff side, a Breed male inherits his mother's eye, hair and skin coloring, as well as her unique Breedmate ESP talent. Breed offspring have always been born exclusively male due to the genetically dominant DNA of their Ancient fathers, however, experiments conducted in private by an individual named Dragos have resulted in the first laboratory-created Breed females (see Tavia Fairchild).

Breedmate   The resulting offspring of an Atlantean male and a human woman. Called Breedmates because of their unique genetic and blood properties that make them capable of reproducing with one of the Breed, these women typically demonstrate flawless health and are psychically gifted in some unique way, and usually artistically gifted as well. Breedmates are born exclusively female due to the genetically dominant DNA of their Atlantean fathers.

Breedmate mark   A small red birthmark present somewhere on the body of every Breedmate. The mark is a teardrop falling into the cradle of a crescent moon. This mark is also a significant symbol to the Atlantean culture. It has recently been revealed that Atlanteans bear this hidden symbol in their palm, an indication of their life's energy, which extinguishes with their death.

Crimson   A club narcotic created and distributed by a human named Ben Sullivan (see Kiss of Crimson). This red powder drug had unfortunate side effects when taken by members of the Breed, inciting a fevered blood thirst that in many cases resulted in a swift spiral into Bloodlust, and, in some cases, turned individuals Rogue (see Camden Chase).

Darkhaven   A civilian Breed residence or commune. Dark-havens exist in most cities around the world and in some rural areas. Each Darkhaven has a leader, usually the senior member of the family or head of household. This Breed male is responsible for the safety and wellbeing of all who live under his roof.

dermaglyphs   A pattern of skin markings appearing on an Ancient or one of the Breed, which change colors according to the individual's emotional or physical state of being. Dermaglyphs present in swirling, flourish and arc patterns and can be plentiful, covering an individual from skull to ankle (as seen in Ancients and some Gen One Breed vampires) or more sparsely distributed (as seen in subsequent generations of the Breed).

dreamwalk   The ability to enter the dreams of another person and "walk" through what the dreamer is doing, seeing, etc. (See Claire Reichen)

Enforcement Agency   The Breed's self-governing law enforcement arm. The Enforcement Agency is mired in political jockeying, personal empire building and corruption, often resulting in ineptitude and ineffectiveness in protecting the Breed's civilian populations. The Enforcement Agency usually runs counter to the Order, and while animosity on both sides is common, there have been instances of alliances and helpful partnerships between the two organizations (see Mathias Rowan, Sterling Chase).

First Dawn   The morning that followed the night the Breed's existence was exposed to mankind around the world, after Dragos freed scores of bloodthirsty Rogues from incarceration to terrorize human civilians.

Gen One   A Breed of the first generation, born of an Ancient and a Breedmate. Gen Ones' dermaglyphs are more plentiful than on later generations of the Breed. Gen Ones are not necessarily the oldest members of the Breed, depending on when they were born and to whom, but they are the strongest of the race, physically and otherwise. However, Gen Ones are also the most susceptible to Bloodlust.

Host   A human, male or female, from whom a Breed vampire feeds.

hypnotic manipulation   The ability to make someone see or believe something that's not there (as Lucan did to Gabrielle when he showed her a non-existent police badge in Kiss of Midnight).

Master   The term used by Minions to refer to the Breed vampire who made them.

mind-blast   The ability to temporarily cripple someone by psychically delivering debilitating pain in their skull (see Renata).

mind scrub / memory scrub   The process used by one of the Breed to erase memories from a human or Breedmate, though the latter is frowned upon as disrespectful and seldom done. Mind scrubs are typically done to prevent the subject from exposing the Breed to mankind following the witness of something unexpected or potentially damaging to the Breed nation.

Minion   A human or Breedmate who has been bled to the very brink of death by one of the Breed, but ultimately kept alive. At that point, the person becomes a Minion, his or her will completely and permanently enslaved by the Breed vampire who drank from them. There is no cure for a Minion, except death. Minions are seldom good interrogation subjects, as they will readily take their own lives to avoid betraying their Master's trust or commands. Only the most powerful members of the Breed (Gen One and second generation, typically) are capable of making Minions.

Order, the   A cadre of Breed warriors founded and led by Lucan Thorne. The Order was formed in Europe in the mid-1300s as a group of eight Gen One warriors who rose up against their fathers, the Ancients. In 1898, Lucan reformed the Order in Boston along with Gideon and others, all united in the mission of keeping both humans and Breed civilians safe from Rogue violence. The Order remained headquartered in Boston for decades, but since First Dawn has been based in Washington, D.C., with command centers and warrior teams located around the world.

psychometry   The ability to read the emotional past or actual history of an object, usually with a touch (see Savannah).

pyrokinesis   The ability to ignite fires or explosions with one's mind (see Andreas Reichen).

Rogue   A Breed individual who's become irrevocably addicted to blood. Rogues display permanently extended fangs and eyes present solid, glowing amber with vertical pupils fixed in a constant state of constriction (like a cat's eye). Once a Breed vampire has gone fully Rogue, there is no hope for recovery. Rogues' blood systems become corrupted and weakened, in a fatal allergy to the metal titanium. Most Rogues eventually go insane with their disease and attempt, or succeed, to commit suicide.

shadow bend   The ability to gather shadows around oneself and manipulate them into a concealing mass (see Sterling Chase).

sonokinesis   The ability to manipulate and amplify sound waves with one's mind (see Corinne, Nathan).

suckhead   Derogatory word used to refer to a Breed individual who's addicted to blood and gone Rogue.

talent   A term used interchangeably with ESP ability in regard to the unique extrasensory gifts of Breedmates and the Breed.

trance   The act of inducing a temporary state of unconsciousness in a human or Breedmate by one of the Breed. All members of the Breed are capable of trancing someone. Trancing a Breedmate for any reason is considered rude and is generally done only as a last resort.

THE NOVELS

Kiss of Midnight

BOOK 1

Romantic Leads
Lucan Thorne
Gabrielle Maxwell

Plot Summary
A gifted young art photographer gets caught in the crosshairs of a growing war within the Breed, thrusting her into the arms of the darkly sensual leader of the race's warrior Order.

Primary Story Locations
Abandoned old asylum outside Boston, Massachusetts
La Notte night club in Boston's North End
Gabrielle's apartment on Willow Street in Boston
Order's compound headquarters in undisclosed location in Boston
Various other locations in and around Boston

Playlist
Save Yourself by Stabbing Westward
Tourniquet by Evanescence
Falling by Lacuna Coil
Lunatics Have Taken Over the Asylum by Collide
Predator by Collide
Too Sick to Pray by A3
Possession by Sarah McLachlan

Story Background

As much as I enjoyed writing historical romances, I have to admit I was getting a little bored with the restrictions inherent to the genre—particularly the limitations on character types and settings. So, when I first sat down to put together a formal proposal for Lucan and Gabrielle's story, which at the time I was calling, *Kiss of Darkness*, I felt an incredible sense of freedom. I could set my book anywhere. I could populate it with a diverse cast of characters from all walks of life. My heroes—hell, even my heroines—could carry badass weapons, drive cool cars, carry a cell phone, even use the f-word if the situation called for it!

Of course, I also wanted to write something that would interest a publisher, as I'd just received word that I was out of a contract at the same time I'd just become a first-time homeowner. But even that setback fueled my enthusiasm to throw off all of the old restraint I'd learned from writing historical romances and write the kind of book I would want to read but wasn't finding in the romance genre at the time. A gritty, dark, scary-sexy vampire story set in Boston, a city I love.

Less *Dracula* and more *Underworld.*

Better yet, an erotically charged blend of *Predator* meets *Blade.*

The story poured out of me fast and furious, and I realized it had been a very long time since I'd had so much fun writing. By this point, I had an amazing three-book contract in hand from one of the top publishers in New York, and a twisty plot that would carry me through the trilogy and bring everything to a big finish.

But then I got to the last page of Lucan and Gabrielle's story and I realized that the ending I plotted out for this book...well, it sucked. The bad guy (Marek) needed to get away so he could come back again, bigger and badder, in the next two books. But the way I orchestrated his escape—a very lame "exit, stage left" kind of thing, where he dashed out the back door of a warehouse while Lucan ran in to save Gabrielle—read like a lazy cop-out.

I sent the draft in to my editor and told her I wasn't satisfied with the ending in particular and that I wanted to take another crack at it. She read the manuscript and agreed with me—the ending needed some work. Then she did what never seems to happen in tight publishing schedules anymore: She gave me more than a full month to work on the revisions.

I tend to write a clean first draft, and I'm even better with revisions and polishing. So a month to fix a shaky ending was an invitation for me to take a good look at the entire manuscript and really make it shine as best I could.

Now, it's at this point that my husband would tell you he rode in to save the day. And maybe he did. John has been my best friend for nearly three decades. He's also my best plotting partner (and my sanity checker when it comes to writing believable men). So when I complained to him that my ending was weak and I needed the villain to escape in a big way, John nodded and said, "You need a helicopter."

Um, okay. Together we sketched out a better escape plan for Marek, and I went back to write in a helicopter to another scene in the book so it wouldn't seem totally convenient that at the pivotal moment the bad guy happened to have one handy.

I fleshed out a lot of other things too, including more "getting to know you" scenes between Lucan and Gabrielle, and I layered in more details about upcoming characters that I could use in the other two books.

I also changed the ending from a simple, "I love you, let's make a life together" type of closing, to one where we get to see Lucan finally show Gabrielle a more vulnerable side of him than he had allowed thus far in the book. Not the smoldering powder keg, but the tender lover he was promising to be for her in asking her to take his blood, to bond with him, and be his mate forever.

I sent in the revised manuscript and was stunned to hear back from my editor just a couple of days later. She loved it! Actually, she said something along the lines of, "This book was great the first time I read it, but you've taken it to a whole new level." Wonderful words. Almost eight years later, I still remember them and smile.

It wasn't too long afterward that I got another call from Shauna. Everyone at the publishing house was really excited about the revised book, so instead of releasing it by itself in 2006 as planned, they wanted to hold it until I had the second book ready to go too, and they would release them as a back-to-back marketing event in the first half of 2007.

The series was off to a great start!

Kiss of Crimson

BOOK 2

Romantic Leads
Dante
Tess Culver

Plot Summary
A reckless act of need binds the fiercest of the warriors to a mortal woman who arouses his most primal hungers and desires...a woman who just might be in league with his enemies.

Primary Story Locations
Tess's veterinary clinic in South Boston
Order's compound headquarters in undisclosed location in Boston
Chase family Darkhaven in Back Bay, Boston

Playlist
Razorsharp by Collide
Weak and Powerless (Tilling My Own Grave) by A Perfect Circle
Wicked Game by H.I.M.
Uninvited by Alanis Morrisette
Morning After by Chester Bennington
Welcome to the Jungle by Guns n Roses
Killing Loneliness by H.I.M.

Story Background

Creatively, I was on fire when I began writing *Kiss of Crimson*. I'd just turned in Lucan and Gabrielle's story, and I had a lot of publisher and agent enthusiasm behind me, the only outside feedback I had on the series at the time. Let me tell you, knowing that you have a team of experienced industry professionals genuinely excited about something you created—especially after failing in another genre—is incredibly motivating.

Plus, I just couldn't wait to write Dante and Tess's story.

While Gabrielle was my wounded, tormented artist, Tess was a scrapper and a survivor. I'd had the opening chapters from *Kiss of Crimson* in my head for a long time—from Dante biting her in a state of desperation, to her stabbing him with the syringe full of animal tranquilizer.

Their courtship was dark and aggressive, unconventional (to say the least!) but, of course, Dante wouldn't have it any other way. Dante is the kind of character who's most interesting when he's pushed into a corner, so forcing the smartass, street-fighter of the Order into a blood bond with a mate he didn't plan on having made sparks fly right away.

Dante also runs up against a source of conflict in his work with the Order—a source of conflict by the name of Sterling Chase, Special Investigative Agent with the Enforcement Agency. ('Scuse me, I mean, *Senior* Special Investigative Agent.) I like a good bromance almost as much as I like a good romance, so pairing these two up as unwilling partners in a joint investigation between the Order and the Enforcement Agency was one of my favorite parts about this book.

So, about Sterling Chase. When I was writing this book, I didn't realize I would be developing his character or storyline beyond what we see in *Kiss of Crimson*. As far as I knew, I was writing a trilogy, and I already had the plot and characters for Book 3 sketched out. I loved Chase, but he was going to fade into the background after this book (along with Elise, who, by the way, was never meant to end up with him).

But in the middle of writing this book, we had something terrible happen in real life. John's eldest daughter, who'd been battling leukemia and the aftereffects of treatment since late 2001, passed away in January of 2006.

All along, in the third book, I had been planning to match Tegan up with a human woman who was a world-famous concert pianist, but who was also dying from a mysterious blood cancer. Tegan was going to abduct her from the hospital and find a way to cure her with his blood. *[Author's note: This is now against the series lore; Breed males cannot heal human disease with their blood, and they don't take human women as their mates.]* I suppose I thought it would be therapeutic or romantic in some way to write a happy ending for a heroine battling what seemed to be a terminal disease.

But as Leslie became sicker, and after she eventually passed, I knew there was no way I wanted to live that kind of story for the months it would take for me to write it. Nor did I want to minimize what Leslie went through, and it seemed out of the question to make that kind of story a part of my household when everyone was so raw with grief.

Which meant I had to come up with an entirely different romance for the heart of Book 3.

It didn't take long for me to realize that widowed Elise Chase would make a wonderful mate for Tegan. Perhaps even better than what I'd originally envisioned for him. So, I reworked a few scenes to bring the two of them together, and what do you know? I found what is arguably one of Midnight Breed readers' favorite pairings from the entire series thus far.

I completed *Kiss of Crimson* and before I wrote the first word on the new outline for Tegan and Elise's story, I received word from my agent that Random House had made an early offer for three more books in the series. Hurray!

Except…my overarching plot was ending with Book 3.

It *had* to end there. I had already altered so much of the storyline for the book, but one thing that had to remain was the death of Marek and the way it was all supposed to go down with the final confrontation between Tegan and him.

So, while I celebrated the opportunity of being able to write about more characters in this new story world, I also knew I needed to come up with a suitable villain to carry the torch after the end of Book 3. And he needed to be a bigger threat than Marek, because we'd been there and done that.

The pressure was on in many ways as I set out to begin Tegan and Elise's story.

Midnight Awakening

BOOK 3

Romantic Leads
Tegan
Elise Chase

Plot Summary
An unlikely alliance is formed when a beautiful Darkhaven widow enlists the help of the Order's deadliest vampire warrior in her personal vendetta against the Rogues.

Primary Story Locations
Chase family Darkhaven in Back Bay, Boston
Order's compound headquarters in undisclosed location in Boston
Andreas Reichen's Darkhaven in Berlin, Germany
Aphrodite erotic club in Berlin, Germany
Rogue rehabilitation facility in Germany
Bohemian mountains in Czech Republic

Playlist
Cat People by Gosling
Iris by Goo Goo Dolls
The Sacrament by H.I.M.
Man in The Box by Alice in Chains
Hand That Feeds by Nine Inch Nails
Stripped by Shiny Toy Guns
Lithium by Evanescence

Story Background

I got off to a wobbly start when I began writing *Midnight Awakening*. I was trying to adjust to a new romance storyline and a new heroine, while at the same time working to wrap up the overarching plotline of the first three books and begin a new external plotline that could carry me through another three, but potentially more, if things went well with the back-to-back debut of the first two in May and June of 2007. Everything about this book seemed up in the air for a long time, including the title, which during the first draft phase was called *Kiss of Temptation*. (I know, blech!)

But there were a lot of good things happening too.

The series had been acquired by an exciting new German publisher that was looking to start a paranormal romance imprint called LYX. They wanted my series to be their launch title, which was a thrill for many reasons, not the least of which being that Germany is my mom's home country. I wanted to do something to show my appreciation to my new German publisher, and to the readers there whom I hoped would enjoy my books. So as I was recasting and re-plotting *Midnight Awakening*, I decided to write in a brand-new character, Andreas Reichen, a charming, sophisticated Breed male who led a Darkhaven in Berlin.

I also decided to bring on more members of the Order in this book. I had three more books to write, after all, and if I wasn't careful, I'd run out of Breed warriors pretty quick! Thus, enter Kade and Brock—a wolfy-looking Alaskan, and a smooth-talking Rogue-killer who hailed from Detroit. The pair of new recruits provided some comic relief in an otherwise dark book, and they also brought out more interaction between the rest of the Order's members who would soon be on deck with their own books.

As originally planned, *Midnight Awakening* puts to bed the bad guy plot involving Lucan's brother, Marek, as the villain. In the final showdown with him, readers also learn more about Tegan's first Breedmate, Sorcha, and the truth behind her abduction and eventual death—events first referenced in *Kiss of Midnight*.

Marek was an evil man, no doubt about it. But I was about to introduce an even bigger threat in the series—and begin sowing the seeds of a larger story arc that had the potential to expand over more than just the next three books.

To make this transition to a greater evil, it was important to me that it feel organic to the first three books somehow. I didn't simply want to shoehorn it in, I wanted a clean dovetail. So I went back to the beginning to see if there was some creative portal I'd left open and could make use of now. I found it in *Kiss of Midnight*. Specifically, I found the answer I needed in the medieval tapestry hanging in Lucan's study at the Boston compound.

In *Midnight Awakening*, we discover that one of the original members of the Order, back in the Middle Ages, helped conceal the last remaining Ancient—his alien father—instead of killing the creature as Lucan's edict demanded. That Order member, Dragos, had an infant son also named Dragos. And between the separate actions of the two of them, the hidden hibernation chamber where this last Ancient slept remained sealed for centuries. Until the close of *Midnight Awakening*, when the Order uncovers the betrayal and finds the chamber empty.

Midnight Awakening was a challenging book, but one I'm ultimately very proud of. It took a bit longer for me to write than the first two books had. Of course, 2006 had been a long, difficult year on the personal side. I finally wrapped up Tegan and Elise's story in 2007, around the same time that *Kiss of Midnight* (the formerly titled *Kiss of Darkness*, until it was discovered that an established *New York Times* best-selling author was releasing a vampire book by that same title in 2007) was about to publish.

Kiss of Midnight debuted on May 1, 2007, and immediately hit the USA Today best-seller list. On May 29, *Kiss of Crimson* released. This book hit the USA Today best-seller list too, but it also hit the New York Times list! Not long after the books came out, I noticed readers online were beginning to call the series the "Kiss" series. At this time, Random House was not printing the series title on the front covers, only inside on the title page (for what reason, I have no idea).

In an effort to root some part of the actual series name in readers' minds, I decided to begin putting the word "Midnight" in every title. So, for those of you who wonder why *Kiss of Crimson* is the only oddball title in the series without the word "Midnight" in it, now you know!

Midnight Rising

BOOK 4

Romantic Leads
Rio (Eleoterio de la Noche Atanacio)
Dylan Alexander

Plot Summary
After surviving a savage betrayal, Rio has given up hope of redemption...until he finds himself craving a fiery tabloid reporter who's in pursuit of a sensational story that's closer to the truth than she could ever imagine.

Primary Story Locations
Bohemian mountains in Czech Republic
Andreas Reichen's Darkhaven in Berlin, Germany
Various locations in New York City
Order's compound headquarters in undisclosed location in Boston
Croton Dam in New York

Playlist
Who Will Love Me Now by Sunscreem
The Undertaker by Puscifer
Apologize by OneRepublic
Dance with the Devil by Breaking Benjamin
Savin' Me by Nickelback
Make Me Believe by Godsmack

Story Background

Midnight Awakening came out in late November, 2007, to lovely reviews and further appearances on national bestseller lists. I had a contract to write the next three books in the series, and based on the success of the first three that year—and the amazing response from readers in just a few months' time—I had the feeling that Random House was probably going to allow me to run with the series even beyond books four through six.

To avoid writing myself into another corner with my next overarching plotline, as I began working on *Midnight Rising*, I decided to sketch out basic story premises for all of the main characters I knew I wanted to write. And I also came up with the Big Finale for the series (which, by some miracle, played out in *Darker After Midnight*, Book 10, right down to the final scene, just as I'd planned it).

But back to *Midnight Rising*. Poor Rio! When I nearly blew him to pieces in *Kiss of Midnight* and killed off his duplicitous Breedmate, Eva, I had no idea I'd need to put him back together again and find him a suitable heroine. But as I was writing Tegan and Elise's book, I already had my eye on the sexy Spaniard, and had begun trailing breadcrumbs that would lead to a hidden cave in the Czech mountains—the place where Rio's second chance at a happy ending was to begin.

One of my first hurdles with Rio was his name. What kind of name is that, anyway, for a hundred-something-year-old vampire? Frankly, things went so quickly on the initial publication side with these books, I hadn't done much homework on the characters beyond the first three heroes of my "trilogy." So, in addition to plotting for the overall action thread of the series, I also went back to the drawing board and fleshed out character profiles for the rest of the cast going forward.

For Rio, coming up with his true name, Eleuterio de la Noche Atanacio (or, loosely translated from Spanish, "he who is free and of the night everlasting") inspired his entire background and the dark circumstances of his youth. It also gave me the answer to what Rio's unique Breed ability was—his *"manos del diablo,"* (devil's hands), which allowed him to kill with a touch.

I don't recall how Rio's heroine in *Midnight Rising*, tabloid reporter Dylan Alexander, came to me initially. I knew he needed someone fiery and forthright, someone whose own personal goals—to find a juicy story that would hopefully save her loathed, but necessary, job—came into direct conflict with his. And at the time that Dylan stumbles upon Rio, his primary goal is to be left alone to die in peace.

Of course, Dylan didn't merely stumble upon Rio's hiding place; she was led there by Eva in ghost form. I felt bad for the way things ended between Eva and Rio. I knew Eva wasn't a horrible person, just a selfish one who let her possessiveness become a disease, one that made her do something so reprehensible, there was no turning back. But I wanted to redeem her, even if only in some small way. Using her as the conduit for bringing Rio out of the dark place he'd retreated to after Eva's betrayal felt right to me. I like things that come full circle, and letting Eva atone for what she did by guiding Dylan into his life—and later, for allowing Eva to assist Rio in saving Dylan when she was in mortal danger—is one of my favorite parts of *Midnight Rising*.

In addition to the emotional, romantic side of this book, we also get our first glimpse at the new villain of the series—Dragos. I wanted him to come on scene in a big way, demonstrating right up front that if Marek seemed dangerous, this guy was diabolical. Hiding behind assumed names and secret alliances that wormed deep into the highest ranks of the Enforcement Agency, Dragos was going to give the Order a real run for their money.

Midnight Rising came out in April, 2008. John and I were driving home to Michigan to visit my parents when my editor called late in the afternoon, as we were approaching Buffalo, New York (yes, I remember where I was!). The *New York Times* bestseller list had just come in. *Midnight Rising* had debuted at #6!

Rio and Dylan's story stayed on the *New York Times* list for another four weeks. It spent two weeks on the *USA Today* bestseller list, and was my first appearance on the *Publishers Weekly* bestseller list. Later, *Midnight Rising's* German translation, *Gebieterin Der Dunkelheit*, would be my first bestselling title there, debuting on *Der Spiegel*.

Veil of Midnight

BOOK 5

Romantic Leads
Nikolai
Renata

Plot Summary
A mission to stop an assassin that's targeting Breed elders calls warrior Nikolai to Montreal, where he crosses paths with—and finds an unlikely ally in—the one woman capable of bringing him to his knees.

Primary Story Locations
Various locations in Montreal, Quebec, Canada
Sergei Yakut's lodge outside Montreal
One of Dragos's labs outside Montreal
Order's compound headquarters in undisclosed location in Boston

Playlist
Bring Me to Life by Evanescence
Ghostflowers by Otep
Time of Dying by Three Days Grace
REV 22:20 by Puscifer
The Bird and The Worm by The Used
Woman by Wolfmother
Closer by Nine Inch Nails
Personal Jesus by Marilyn Manson

Story Background

I can still recall the surge of excitement I felt when I was jotting down the preliminary concept for *Veil of Midnight*. I'd never written a truly kickass heroine before—one who dressed in black leather and spike-heeled boots, and who bristled with as many deadly weapons as any one of my vampire alpha heroes of the Order. So much the better, that this Breedmate was also gifted with an extrasensory ability that could take down even the most lethal Gen One Breed.

Dear reader, meet Renata.

Naturally, a woman like that needs an equally strong partner. I couldn't think of anyone more suited to go toe-to-toe with Renata than the adrenaline-junkie, combat-loving, gear-head of the Order, Siberian-born Nikolai.

As you can probably tell from the playlist of music I listened to while working on *Veil of Midnight*, Niko and Renata's story was hard-driving, fast and gritty, full of action. It was also sexy and dark, at times very tender. I strive to make each Midnight Breed book feel new and different from the others, while still maintaining a sense of cohesion within the series. *Veil of Midnight* was certainly different from the others, but it also marks a turning point in the series. One that set the second half of the series into motion, but also laid the groundwork for what I didn't know at the time—that the ending I'd plotted for Book 10 would actually be the beginning of a whole new generation of characters and a further arc in the series as a whole.

Which brings me to Mira.

Now, I'm not really into kids. I never had any of my own, whether that was the result of too many teenage years of babysitting jobs or something else, I don't know. But as I was plotting this book, I realized that for all of Renata's toughness and almost superhero invincibility, she needed to have a soft underbelly. She needed something to make her vulnerable, and I mean something aside from the reverb migraines she suffered after using her mind-blasting ESP talent. Renata needed to care about something, about some *one*.

And that someone was an eight-year-old orphan girl (a young Breedmate with the gift of precognition) whom Renata had rescued from a Montreal blood club run by Renata's future employer, the nefarious Gen One, Sergei Yakut.

It was Sergei Yakut who brought Nikolai to Montreal on a mission for the Order, but it was the child-seer Mira who showed Niko that his future was tied to the hot female bodyguard who handed him his ass the first time they met.

Writing this book was a hell of a good time, and I hope it shows in the text. It was also a challenge, because in addition to the romance and the action plot of Niko and Renata's story, I was also introducing new characters and weaving external suspense threads that would continue into the rest of the series.

It is in *Veil of Midnight* that the storyline of my next book, *Ashes of Midnight*, starts to unfold. Since the arrival of Berlin Darkhaven leader Andreas Reichen in *Midnight Awakening* and his further involvement in *Midnight Rising*, I knew I wanted to include him in the series in a more meaningful way. This goes back to my own German roots, and to my awareness of how unusual it is to find German characters in American commercial fiction—romance, in particular—who are not straight-up Nazis or some other brand of bad guy. Plus, I really loved Reichen!

It was difficult tearing his world down so completely. I loved the relationship he had with his long-time human lover, Helene. I loved his Darkhaven family in Berlin, such as the young mated couple with the new baby who'd only recently named Reichen godfather. I loved the life he had in Berlin, and I loved his easy-going, charming personality.

But there's a popular saying among writers: *Kill your darlings.*

The fact was, the way I'd written it so far, Reichen's life was perfectly settled. His storyline thus far did nothing to move the series forward. Reichen had no conflict, had made no mistakes in life, had no enemies...*or did he?*

I realized that to give him a compelling story of his own, I needed to first destroy everything I loved about him. It sounds really cruel, but one thing I've learned as a writer is that happy characters make for boring fiction. So I set out to make Andreas Reichen very, very unhappy. And very, very angry. By the time his story takes place, Andreas Reichen is a man on fire—in more ways than one!

Other introductions taking place in *Veil of Midnight* include the first on-page appearance of the Ancient, no longer in hibernation but imprisoned in Dragos's breeding lab. We also meet for the first time, golden-eyed Hunter, one of Dragos's homegrown assassins. Hunter is one of an unknown number of Gen Ones bred from the captive Ancient and raised to be emotionless killers, loyal to Dragos not only out of duty and training, but also because of the unremovable ultraviolet collar that keeps these lethal soldiers under his total control.

By the end of *Veil of Midnight*, Hunter is no longer shackled to Dragos's command. Thanks to the Order—and a vision glimpsed in Mira's prophesying eyes—Hunter leaves Montreal to join the Order in the fight against his creator and villainous master.

Veil of Midnight released in late December, 2008. It was my first book to stay on both the *New York Times* and *USA Today* bestseller lists for four weeks straight!

Ashes of Midnight

BOOK 6

Romantic Leads
Andreas Reichen
Claire (Samuels) Roth

Plot Summary
Consumed by revenge for the murder of his kin, Darkhaven leader Andreas Reichen embarks on a quest of fiery retribution...a quest that leads him to the woman who once owned his heart, but who now belongs to his most treacherous enemy.

Primary Story Locations
Wilhelm Roth's Darkhaven estate outside Berlin, Germany
Wilhelm Roth's office in Hamburg, Germany
Danika's little farmhouse in Denmark
Order's compound headquarters in undisclosed location in Boston
Claire's grandmother's estate in Newport, Rhode Island

Playlist
Broken by Seether and Amy Lee
Close to the Flame by H.I.M.
Going Under by Evanescence
All of This Past by Sarah Bettens
Dreamsleep by Collide
Falls on Me by Fuel

Story Background

So, I'd left poor Andreas Reichen in quite a state at the end of *Veil of Midnight*. As his story picks up in *Ashes of Midnight*, he is a man with a plan. And that plan is the total annihilation of his newly recognized enemy, a Breed male named Wilhelm Roth. A Breed male who's been mated to Claire Samuels, the woman Andreas once loved—and lost—a long time ago.

Claire is one of the gentlest heroines in the series. But don't mistake her calm exterior for weakness. True, she's made some mistakes in her life—chief among them, doubting Andreas's love for her and choosing another mate, the powerful Wilhelm Roth, after Andreas leaves her without a trace or a word of good-bye. Once she realizes the depth of her mistake many years later, after Andreas strides back into her life on a tide of fire and ash and bloody-minded vengeance over what Roth has done to Andreas's loved ones, Claire is prepared to march into battle right along with him.

After writing *Veil of Midnight* and spending time on the page with a kickass heroine like Renata, I came to *Ashes of Midnight* still very much on a "I am woman, hear me roar" kind of high. It is in this book that the women of the Order—who now included newcomers Renata, Dylan, Elise, Tess and Gabrielle, in addition to Gideon's longtime mate, Savannah—first step in to lend their own skills to the Order's rising war against Dragos and his followers.

Although Lucan and his cadre of Breed warriors are strong, none of them paired up with a woman who would be willing to stand by and let her man fight alone when she has unique talents to lend to their missions. For Claire, that talent is dreamwalking, which she uses in *Ashes of Midnight* to help Andreas and the Order locate one of Dragos's breeding labs and defeat one of his most dangerous lieutenants, Wilhelm Roth.

In the end, Dragos wins this round. His escape—and the hasty relocation of the captive Ancient—sets the stage for big things yet to come in *Shades of Midnight* and the books to follow. As for Andreas Reichen and Claire, while they do not come into the Order's fold officially in *Ashes of Midnight*, they remain an integral part of the series.

Another character we meet again in this book is Danika, the widowed Breedmate of Conlan, who was killed in action in *Kiss of Midnight*. During the events in *Ashes of Midnight*, I needed a safe house for Claire and Andreas to elude Roth's men. With Germany being so close to Denmark, it only seemed logical that the Order would call upon Danika for this special favor.

What I hadn't expected was the response from readers after *Ashes of Midnight* released. So many people were thrilled to see Danika again! Apparently, they'd been wondering how the Breedmate, who'd been pregnant with Conlan's son at the time of his death, was faring since leaving Boston to deliver her child back home in Denmark. Readers emailed, asking if I would write a story for Danika and give her a happy ending. Although I didn't have plans to expand on her future at that time, the ideas started percolating, and eventually I got the opportunity to revisit Danika again.

Ashes of Midnight published in May, 2009, spending three weeks on the *New York Times* bestseller list, two weeks on the *USA Today* list, debuting at #31, my highest showing on that list at the time. And still another high spot, Claire and Reichen's book hit #6 on the *Publishers Weekly* bestseller list its first week out as well.

Shades of Midnight

BOOK 7

Romantic Leads
Kade
Alexandra Maguire

Plot Summary
A mission to Alaska to investigate a string of savage vampire attacks sends Breed warrior Kade to the frozen land of his birth, where he encounters a sexy female bush pilot whose own quest for answers forces him to confront his darkest secrets, and an even greater evil that could destroy all he holds dear.

Primary Story Locations
Small (fictional) town of Harmony, Alaska
Kade's family Darkhaven outside Fairbanks, Alaska
Order's compound headquarters in undisclosed location in Boston

Playlist
The Fear by Trust Company
Shame by Stabbing Westward
So Cold by Breaking Benjamin
Crashed by Daughtry

Story Background

Since the introduction of black-haired, silver-eyed Kade to the series in *Midnight Awakening,* I couldn't wait to set one of the books in Alaska. Naturally, it had to be his!

I'd had it in my head for a while that Kade had left his family Darkhaven outside Fairbanks for a reason he didn't really want anyone to know. And I'd also had it in my character notes that he was an identical twin—although whether Kade should be the "good" twin or the "bad" one, I wasn't yet sure.

I began plotting *Shades of Midnight* from the external side of things: The Ancient's escape from the cargo train at the end of *Ashes of Midnight*, and the subsequent slaughter of the Alaskan family, which prompts the Order to send Kade north—far north—to investigate. It was this same slaying that would bring female bush pilot, Alexandra Maguire, into the middle of the Order's business and, soon afterward, into Kade's bed.

The first big lesson I learned in plotting *Shades of Midnight* was that Alaska is unlike any other state in the country. I mean, I knew that, of course. But I had no idea just how vast and wild and undeveloped the place was until I started studying maps, buying reference books, and Googling for general information on living conditions, temperatures, bush piloting, law enforcement and various other details I wanted to get right in the book.

Alaska is harsh, primitive frontier in many places; in others, it's absolute, forbidding wilderness. It was actually perfect for the kind of story I wanted to tell.

And the perfect place to have produced someone like Kade—not to mention, his twin brother, Seth.

Given their shared Breed ability to connect psychically with predator animals, the subplot of Kade's backstory and the dark secret he'd been running from both fell into place as an integral part of *Shades of Midnight*. It would also form the wedge that would eventually come to stand between Kade and Alexandra.

It is in this book that the Ancient eventually meets his end. I planned for it upfront, knowing the way the Ancient would die, although I hadn't decided on the specifics of who would ultimately take him over that ledge until a little farther into the actual writing of the story.

I also knew that before the Ancient died, he would leave behind a piece of himself—a biotechnology "key" that would unlock secrets about his kind and their time on Earth. The Ancient leaves this biotech chip (along with some of his DNA) embedded in the nape of a human warrior—former Alaska State Trooper, Jenna Tucker-Darrow, Alex's best friend.

When I first sketched out the premise of the Ancient wanting to ensure part of him lived on as he faced a certain death, I had a vague notion that in addition to the chip creating a transformation in Jenna on a genetic level—turning her into something far more than human—it could also become a tool the Order could use in their efforts to defeat Dragos. That part of the equation changed once I started refining the plot for *Taken by Midnight*, Jenna and Brock's story.

And for the readers who've asked whether there was a reason for the Ancient forcing Jenna to choose "life or death" before he embedded the chip inside her? Yes, there is a reason! I promise, I'll answer that question fully before the series is over.

Shades of Midnight released in late December, 2009. It hit the *New York Times* bestseller list higher than ever, in the #5 spot, and it stayed on the list for three weeks straight. Kade and Alex's story also spent three weeks on the *USA Today* and *Publishers Weekly* bestseller lists. And, for the first time, I broke the top ten at Barnes & Noble, with *Shades of Midnight* debuting there at #7 out of all books on sale.

Meanwhile, in Germany, the series was doing very well too. So well, in fact, that my publisher, Egmont LYX, invited me to come for a multi-city book tour that following summer, when Kade and Alex's story was due to arrive in bookstores over there. I'd never been on book tour. My U.S. publisher has never arranged for me to tour here in the States, so this invitation to travel overseas and meet readers in Germany was incredible. Of course, I said yes!

And so it was that in June of 2010, I found myself on a whirlwind "mini-tour" of several cities, including Dortmund, where a crowd of more than 150 warm and welcoming German Midnight Breed fans came out to have their books signed and hear passages from *Shades of Midnight* read to them by me (in English) and by the wonderful narrator of my German audiobooks.

While I was in Germany, I received more amazing news: *Shades of Midnight (Gezeichnete des Schicksals)* debuted in the highest spot for the series so far, #3 on *Der Spiegel*!

Taken by Midnight

BOOK 8

Romantic Leads
Brock
Jenna Tucker-Darrow

Plot Summary
Tasked with the protection of a beautiful human female who's brought from Alaska to the Order's Boston headquarters, Breed warrior Brock soon finds himself entangled in an impossible passion—one that challenges him to confront the mistakes of his past, and to risk his heart for the one woman he can hold, but can never truly possess.

Primary Story Locations
Order's compound headquarters in undisclosed location in Boston
FBI office in New York City
Dragos's secret prison for captive Breedmates from his breeding labs
Andreas Reichen and Claire's Darkhaven in Newport, Rhode Island
Cemetery outside Harmony, Alaska

Playlist
Home by Daughtry
Give Me a Sign by Breaking Benjamin
Fade Into You by Mazzy Star
All That I'm Living For by Evanescence
Angel by Sarah McLachlan

Story Background

Here we arrive at *Taken by Midnight*, eight books into the series. Looking back now, it's astonishing to me how far the overarching storyline has come from its beginnings in those first three novels. I often tell people that had I known when I first pitched Lucan and Gabrielle's story that I was embarking on an adventure that would span ten books and counting, I might not have had the guts to start.

I'm a plotter. I like to know where I'm heading before I put the first word on paper. But I'd never attempted anything this expansive. It's been a great experience for me to grow as a writer, as a storyteller. I'm learning to trust my instincts, and in *Taken by Midnight*, those instincts were put to the test.

This book takes the series a big leap forward with the introduction of a heroine who's a human female undergoing a genetic transformation that's more than a little on the freaky side of science fiction. I wasn't sure how readers would react to Jenna, frankly. But the decision to move her in this direction was one of those instinct moments. I had to do what I felt was best for the character, the current book, and for the series as a whole. And I've been relieved to find that by and large, Jenna is a curiosity that most everyone seems to like.

So, just what is she becoming, anyway?

That's the question I hear all the time whenever the subject of Brock and Jenna comes up. And it was a question many of you asked in one form or another through the Q&A contest we held at my website a while ago.

I'll tell you what Jenna isn't becoming. She won't be turning into one of the Breed. She's human at her core, remember. The Breed's genetic makeup is otherworlder (Ancient) and Breedmate (which we now know to be—I don't think this is a big secret anymore—half Atlantean). So, while Jenna's body now contains Ancient DNA, she is missing the other piece that would turn her into one of the Breed.

Jenna's alien DNA gives her many of the strengths of an Ancient: self-healing, prolonged life, superhuman strength and speed, enhanced cognitive and language skills. As she later discovers, the biotech implant has additionally given her access to the Ancient's memories. And let's not forget, she's also got a pretty cool *dermaglyph* growing at the back of her neck.

What Jenna doesn't have is a fatal allergy to sunlight, like both the Breed and the Ancients do. Nor does she have fangs or a need for blood in order to sustain her, although she has been known to eye Brock's carotid with more than a passing interest.

Jenna is human with a big serving of alien. She is unlike anyone else we've seen so far in the series. And she'll be key to events still to come as the second arc of the series continues.

But let's get back to *Taken by Midnight*.

Brock and Jenna's romance was about second chances, and about learning to let your walls down in order to let love find you again. They both came together from places of pain—Jenna following the loss of her husband and young daughter in a car accident, and Brock still weathering the guilt of his failure to protect an innocent young Breedmate who'd been placed in his charge as her bodyguard when Brock lived in Detroit.

Theirs was a tender romance, perhaps the most tender of the entire series so far. Neither of them came into their relationship as wide-eyed innocents or reckless people easily caught up in a hot passion that might burn out just as quickly as it started.

Brock and Jenna had been knocked down before. They'd been wounded. They both carried their own burden of guilt from their pasts, telling them they weren't good enough to be loved by someone. So, when they finally came together—when their unwilling partnership in Order business began to ignite into irresistible attraction and true, deepening affection—their bond was such that it didn't require blood to seal it.

While Brock and Jenna's romance smolders at a slow burn, the action in *Taken by Midnight* ratchets up the threat of Dragos and his determination to strike hard at the Order for their hand in the death of the Ancient in *Shades of Midnight* and the destruction of one of Dragos's secret lab facilities in Alaska.

With Dragos growing bolder, the warriors and their mates begin working together in earnest to stop him. While the warriors pursue Dragos and his secret lieutenants on night patrols, the women of the Order strive to locate the Breedmates being held captive in his breeding labs. They come upon clues that lead them to a former runaway shelter worker, and, through a mix of cunning and courage,

Jenna, Renata, Dylan and Alex eventually unmask the Minion in charge of holding the prisoners. With the warriors and their women working as a true team, the captive Breedmates are freed—including Corinne Bishop, the young Breedmate who'd been entrusted to Brock's protection decades past in Detroit.

Other new characters enter the series in this book as well: Mathias Rowan, an Enforcement Agent in Boston and a former friend and associate of Sterling Chase; and the Archer family, Lazaro, the Gen One patriarch of a Boston Darkhaven, and his son Christophe, who come to the Order requesting help in recovering Christophe's teenage son, Kellan, who's been abducted from their home by unknown captors.

This abduction—and the recovery of Kellan Archer—set into motion events that would alter the Order's future in the next book to come, and would change the landscape of the series forever.

Taken by Midnight spent the most time on the U.S. bestseller lists after its release in September, 2010. It stayed four weeks on the *New York Times* and *USA Today* bestseller lists, and three weeks on *Publishers Weekly*. It also made the Indiebound bestseller list—another career first for me.

Around this time, I started hearing from my agent that Random House wanted to take the series into hardcover soon. Hard to believe that just five years earlier, I thought my career was over. I suppose the lesson here is not unlike the underlying theme of Brock and Jenna's romance: Just because you felt like a failure in the past, doesn't mean you can't get back up again and make something better of your future.

Deeper Than Midnight

BOOK 9

Romantic Leads
Hunter
Corinne Bishop

Plot Summary
After years of captivity and torture by malevolent vampire Dragos, beautiful Corinne Bishop finds safety and passion in the arms of Hunter, the most lethal of the Order's warriors—a Gen One Breed born and raised to kill on Dragos's command. Now Hunter's loyalty to the Order will be tested when duty to his new allies forces him to risk breaking Corinne's tender heart.

Primary Story Locations
Bishop family Darkhaven in Detroit, Michigan
Various places in and around New Orleans, Louisiana
Amelie Dupree's bayou home at Atchafalaya, Louisiana
Massachusetts senator Bobby Clarence's North Shore residence
Order's compound headquarters in undisclosed location in Boston

Playlist
Through Hell by We Are The Fallen
This Night by Black Lab
Breathe Me by Sia
Empty Bed Blues by Bessie Smith

Story Background

I really felt the momentum of the overall series arc coming to a head as I wrote *Deeper Than Midnight*. On the external storyline side of things, events were in motion that would lead to the final, big showdown between the Order and Dragos.

Lucan and the warriors were soon to discover that the kidnap of Kellan Archer had been a calculated move by Dragos—a strike intended to prompt the Order to break one of their cardinal rules: admitting a civilian into the Boston compound. A secret, hidden location for more than a hundred years, the Order's headquarters is suddenly compromised to their greatest enemy when Kellan spits up a tracking device placed inside him by his abductors.

Lucan has never been one to run from danger. Yet he knows that a swift relocation is the only responsible choice if he wants to keep the compound's residents safe—his family, as he's reluctantly come to think of them all over the course of the series. Kellan's Gen One grandfather, Lazaro Archer, offers one of his properties in the Maine woods as a temporary base of operations, but just as the Order begins making plans to move to safer ground, Tess, who's been pregnant since *Midnight Rising*, goes into labor.

But I'm getting ahead of myself.

Deeper Than Midnight is Hunter and Corinne's story. Hunter, the emotionless Gen One assassin born and raised to be a soldier in Dragos's personal army, and Corinne Bishop, the Breedmate kidnapped from under Brock's watch in Detroit decades ago and recently freed from imprisonment in Dragos's breeding lab. Both victims of Dragos's evil, Hunter and Corinne are thrust together in an unexpected alliance, when he's tasked with escorting her home to her family, only to discover that Corinne had been secretly surrendered to Dragos all those years ago by her Darkhaven father.

And Corinne is keeping a secret of her own too. A thirteen-year-old secret, born to her in the breeding labs and snatched away from her when he was just minutes old to become the same kind of expert killing machine that Hunter is. As soon as she was released from captivity by the Order, Corinne's driving purpose is to find her son and rescue him from Dragos's control.

I thought it would be interesting to pair up Hunter (my first virgin hero!) with a woman who shared his background of abuse and manipulation by Dragos. Even more interesting, a woman whose personal quest will bring Hunter face-to-face with his own history— revelations that tear down the walls he's had to build around his emotions in order to survive.

As a writer (and a woman) I'm fascinated by a stoic, strong, fearless man who comes from a background so destructive and poisonous that it would reduce most other men (rightly so) to quivering pools of weakness and self-pity. As the saying goes, the strongest steel is forged in the hottest fire. That certainly sums up Hunter, but it also sums up Corinne as well.

While Hunter and Corinne set out to uncover more of Dragos's lieutenants and find her son, Nathan, back in Boston the Order has its hands full too. Aside from the sudden vulnerability of the compound to Dragos and the birth of Dante and Tess's son, Xander Raphael, another of the Order's inner circle is caught in a downward spiral that threatens to have catastrophic consequences.

Sterling Chase, once the uptight, by-the-book Enforcement Agent, has over time begun to slip perilously toward Bloodlust. But despite the grip of his consuming disease, he uncovers a stunning link to Dragos through an ambitious human senator who's somehow allied with the Order's chief adversary. And in Chase's quest to learn more, he crosses paths with the senator's assistant, Tavia Fairchild, a beautiful young woman whose very existence will change the course of the series and alter Chase's own future with a single gunshot.

So, about that cliffhanger ending....

I've never written a cliffhanger before. While I don't mind them as a reader, so long as the book doesn't end mid-sentence or without wrapping up the main story I've been invested in for the past four hundred pages, when I chose to end *Deeper Than Midnight* with Chase's voluntary surrender to human law enforcement in an effort to spare his friends at the compound, I did so with the intention that the next book, *Darker After Midnight*, would be coming out very soon afterward. As in a few months afterward.

But *Darker After Midnight* proved to be a bigger book than I anticipated. It took longer for me to get it just right. When I finally turned it in to my editor, she told me it was the best one in the series so far. It was a big book, she said, with a big book feel. And because of that, Random House was going to release it in hardcover. Which meant an even further delay in publication than if the book had come out as a mass market original.

Deeper Than Midnight released at the end of June, 2011. It debuted on the *New York Times* at what remains my highest showing on that list, the #3 spot. Since my last release, the *Times* had recently begun tracking ebook sales in addition to print, and *Deeper Than Midnight* also placed high on the ebook/print combined, coming in at #5. It stayed for two weeks on the *New York Times, USA Today* (peaking at #12) and *Publishers Weekly* bestseller lists.

It was around this time that Random House also made an offer for my next two books. I had already decided I was having too much fun with the Midnight Breed world to let go now—and I also had this germ of an idea for a second story arc that could feature an all-new generation of Order warriors in a near-future setting.

As we went to work on a contract for what would become Books 11 and 12 of the series, I also pitched the idea of the series Companion you're reading now. My editor liked the concept—and the plan to include Gideon and Savannah's story as an original novella—but ultimately Random House and I could not agree on how to publish the book. They wanted to do it ebook only, with the potential of a limited-run hardcover release if, and only if, sales of the ebook were robust enough.

I was adamant that the Companion release in both print and ebook formats. And besides, with the industry changing so rapidly, giving authors more and more freedom to publish their work independently, I decided to decline their offer and table the Companion until I could do it on my own.

A Taste of Midnight

BOOK 9.5
(novella)

Romantic Leads
Danika MacConn
Malcolm MacBain, aka Brannoc

Plot Summary
A widowed Breedmate of the Order, raising her infant son alone after the death of her warrior mate in action, seeks the solace of a Christmas in Edinburgh, Scotland—her beloved's homeland—never dreaming the holiday escape would bring her face-to-face with a deadly Breed crime boss and the dark, mysterious henchman who serves to protect him...someone she once knew—and could have loved—a long time ago.

Primary Story Locations
MacConn family Darkhaven estate outside Edinburgh, Scotland
Various places in and around Edinburgh, Scotland

Playlist
Who Wants to Live Forever by Queen
Wherever You Will Go by The Calling
I Will Stay by We Are The Fallen

Story Background

This ebook original novella came about quickly and unexpectedly. I'd recently completed the manuscript for *Darker After Midnight*—which was to be my first hardcover release, in January 2012—and I'd just unsuccessfully pitched the concept of a Midnight Breed Series Companion featuring a novella for Gideon and Savannah.

As we were in the midst of contract negotiations for Books 11 and 12, my editor asked about the possibility of me writing an ebook original novella to be used to fill the time gap between *Deeper Than Midnight* and *Darker After Midnight*, the idea being the new novella would also help promote the upcoming hardcover. They wanted to include an excerpt from *Darker After Midnight* at the end of the novella, and later on, after the book was reissued in mass market paperback, the novella would then be included as bonus material in that release.

It all sounded great to me…until they mentioned they wanted me to give them Gideon and Savannah's story to use as the ebook original novella.

Well, no way. Out of the question. As longtime readers of the series know, Gideon and Savannah met and fell in love thirty years before the timeline of *Kiss of Midnight*. To release their story on its own toward the big finale in Book 10 would make no sense in the fabric of the series. And on top of that, I wasn't about to pull their story—a true series prequel—out of the Companion, which is where I felt it belonged for many reasons.

I said no, and I figured that was the end of the ebook original conversation. But Random House really wanted me to write something to fill that void, so I started thinking about secondary characters and storylines that could exist if not within the overarching plot already in progress, then running parallel to it.

My first choice was Danika. And since the ebook novella would be coming out in early December, I decided to write a holiday story and set it somewhere other than where the series had been so far. Naturally, that sent my imagination to Conlan MacConn's homeland of Scotland. Edinburgh, to be specific.

In *A Taste of Midnight*, I wanted to craft a story that I hoped would respect the relationship Danika and Conlan enjoyed while he was alive, yet introduce a passion that readers could believe in, especially considering the short storytelling timeframe a novella dictates. Danika had to fall in love fast and deeply, so I decided to give her Malcolm MacBain, a Breed male she and Con both knew very well, a very long time ago. Both Danika and Mal had lost people they loved, so giving them a happily-ever-after together seemed fitting to me.

In *A Taste of Midnight*, we also meet a new and intriguing Breed male from the Enforcement Agency named Thane. Although I don't have a storyline in mind for this black-haired, ruggedly handsome and mysterious man, I have a feeling we haven't seen the last of him.

A Taste of Midnight released in ebook December, 2011. It is the only Midnight Breed story not available in print on its own in the United States. Readers can only find this story in ebook, and in the back of the mass market paperback of *Darker After Midnight*. Danika and Malcolm's story is available as a standalone in Germany through Egmont LYX in both paperback and ebook.

Darker After Midnight

BOOK 10

Romantic Leads
Sterling Chase
Tavia Fairchild

Plot Summary
Separated from his brethren of the Order and struggling with an addiction that threatens to consume him, Sterling Chase has fallen far from grace—but he soon finds his best hope for redemption in beautiful, mysterious Tavia Fairchild, a woman unlike any other the world has ever seen.

Primary Story Locations
Order's compound headquarters in undisclosed location in Boston
Lazaro Archer's Darkhaven in northern Maine
Dragos's island lair off coast of Maine
Various locations in and around Washington, D.C.

Playlist
Down with the Sickness by Disturbed
One Last Breath by Creed
Awakening by The Damning Well
Bodies by Drowning Pool
In Your Eyes by Peter Gabriel

Story Background

After plotting out the bones of this story, the tenth of the series, back around the time I was writing *Midnight Rising*, when I finally approached the first chapter of *Darker After Midnight* it was with a mix of excitement, pride, trepidation, and even a bit of sadness.

As Lucan, Gideon and Tegan—the Order's longest-standing members of the cadre based in Boston—began to detonate the explosives that would seal the compound forever, I was right there with them, knowing it had to be done, yet not really sure what the future would hold for the Order and their world once this chapter closed.

I knew the series would continue because I had just signed with Random House for the next two books, but I didn't know if readers would be interested in a new generation of characters and a twenty-year leap into the future where the Breed no longer hid from mankind, but was struggling to find a place of peace among them. Nevertheless, the first arc of the Midnight Breed series was drawing to a close right here and now, and I had a lot of threads to finish off in *Darker After Midnight*.

Chief among them was the resolution of Sterling Chase's fall from grace and his ultimate redemption and healing. Things with Chase had gone from bad to worse as his story opened here. Through his bad attitude and reckless behavior, he had lost the respect and friendship of his brethren in the Order. His spiral toward blood addiction was dancing him closer to the edge of going full Rogue. And of his own volition, he was now in human police custody, being charged in a shooting at a prominent Massachusetts senator's private residence.

The very last thing Chase needed was to race to the rescue of a beautiful young woman who had stepped into the crosshairs of Dragos's escalating war against the Order. Then again, maybe that's just what he needed. And I'd been waiting all this time—six books' time—for Chase to come face-to-face with Tavia Fairchild and the big secret that her very existence would finally bring to light.

One thing I felt had been sorely missing from the Midnight Breed series from fairly early on was the possibility of a female Breed. Going into the series as first a trilogy, then a sextet, it wasn't long before I started chafing against my own world rule that all of the Breed were born exclusively male. But I'd also had a world rule stating that the race as a whole forbade biological and technological interference when it came to conception and birth. Aha!

So natural births produced male babies every time, but had anyone ever attempted to fiddle with biology? Certainly someone like Dragos would not be opposed to breaking Breed law to further his own mad plans....

So, back at Book 4, when I took a leap of faith and assumed the series might run as long and as far as I wanted to take it, I decided that one of the final twists in the overarching story arc would be the existence of a female vampire. But not just a female Breed, a genetic splicing of Ancient and Breedmate DNA, which would give this first-of-her-kind female the ability to blend in among humans—so long as she maintained strict medical monitoring and treatments.

She would be as strong and as powerful as any Gen One, yet have the ability to walk in the daylight and consume human food. And if she reproduced, it opened up the very real possibility of more females among the Breed—perhaps even a daywalker or two in the future.

Introducing Tavia to the series—writing the scene where Chase first realizes what she is—was one of my favorite parts of *Darker After Midnight*. And it was awfully fun introducing Tavia to the other members of the Order in all her hissing, vampiric glory, when Tegan, Hunter, Niko and Renata arrive at Mathias Rowan's Darkhaven in Boston to haul Chase in for some Breed-style intervention back at headquarters.

But Tavia wasn't the only big surprise in store as the series rolled toward its climax.

In *Darker After Midnight*, Jenna reveals through her link to the Ancient's memories that the otherworlders were not the only preternatural beings on Earth at the time of their crash-landing thousands of years ago. There was another powerful race of immortals—Atlanteans—with whom the Ancients had been fighting in a private war of their own. Some of these Atlanteans, despite being forbidden by their queen to mate with humans, had produced hybrid offspring of their own on Earth....

Daughters born with the Atlantean symbol of a teardrop falling into the cradle of a crescent moon.

This explanation of the Breedmates' origins was, I'll freely admit, an afterthought that came to me only when a reader at one of my events in Germany during my first book tour there pointed out the lack of logic in this part of the series. It bothered her, the fact that Breedmates were somehow, inexplicably *special* and could be born with different genetic makeup than any other human female. This reader wanted the "why" of it, and I came home determined to find an answer that not only made sense, but that would fit within the already established lore and text of the series.

Now, you might be scratching your head and thinking, Altanteans?

But go back to *Kiss of Midnight*. You'll find a line in the book mentioning the various civilizations that the Ancients wiped out after their arrival on Earth. One of them was Atlantis. All I had to do was find a way to connect Atlantis to the Breedmates, make sure I hadn't written myself into any corners with the histories of the Breedmates already introduced in the series, and also figure out why no one in the story world thus far would know about this connection.

The answers to all of those questions finally came to light in *Darker After Midnight*. Even more exciting to me, as I was putting those pieces together a few books back, I realized I also had the basis for some intriguing new characters and storylines—even a powerful new enemy, once Dragos was given his just desserts. I imagined all kinds of possibilities for the continuation—the evolution—of the Midnight Breed series, taking it in a whole new, exciting direction.

Which brings me to what I feel is the biggest twist in *Darker After Midnight*: the outing of the Breed to mankind.

This is another of those events in the series that I'd been writing toward since around the fourth book. One of the worst things to happen to a long-running series is stagnation. While I hadn't gotten bored writing Midnight Breed books yet, and certainly not when I was just halfway through the eventual ten-book storyline, I didn't want to fall into the trap of keeping my series on artificial life support just because it was a success and readers wanted more.

So, I started planning early for a way to shake things up. I wanted to give the series a finite resolution, while still leaving the door open in case I did want to take it further. One way to do that was to *kill my darlings*. No, not literally. But remember how I said in another section that happy characters make for boring fiction? The same can be said of your story world.

Granted, removing such a large piece of what made the Midnight Breed series popular with readers—the secret, hidden aspect of life among the Breed—was a risk. But I believe it was the most authentic way to close the original story arc. After all, Dragos wouldn't go down without one hell of a fight. And he'd given plenty of evidence for anyone to assume he would be just mad enough to orchestrate a retaliation so awful and irrevocable.

Although the world they once knew no longer exists, at the end of *Darker After Midnight*, the Order and their mates have made it through the fire, a little battered perhaps, but unbroken. There is new life already arrived, and still more on the way.

And in the end, for all the darkness, there is also hope.

Darker After Midnight released in hardcover at the end of January, 2012, debuting on the *New York Times* hardcover fiction bestseller list at #9, and on the ebook and print combined list at #8. It remained on the *New York Times* list for two weeks, and on the *USA Today* bestseller list for two weeks as well, where it reached a career high for me of #17.

A TOUCH OF MIDNIGHT

NOVELLA

DEDICATION

For every reader who asked me to share this story.

Thank you for loving Gideon and Savannah. I hope this glimpse into their past will make you love them even more.

CHAPTER 1

Boston University
October, 1974

S avannah Dupree turned the silver urn in her gloved hands, studying its intricate engravings through the bruise-colored tarnish that dulled the 200-year-old work of art. The floral motif tooled into the polished silver was indicative of the Rococo style of the early and mid-1700s, yet the design was conservative, much less ornate than most of the examples shown in the reference materials lying open on the study lab table in front of her.

Removing one of the soft white cotton curator's gloves meant to protect the urn from skin oils during handling, Savannah reached for one of the books. She flipped through several pages of photographed art objects, drinking vessels, serving dishes and snuff boxes from Italy, England and France, comparing their more elaborate styles to that of the urn she was trying to catalogue. She and the three other freshman Art History students seated in the university's archive room with her had been hand-picked by Professor Keaton to earn extra credit in his class by helping to log and analyze a recent estate donation of Colonial furnishings and artifacts.

She wasn't blind to the fact that the single professor had selected only female students for his after-hours extra credit project. Savannah's roommate, Rachel, had been ecstatic to have been chosen. Then again, the girl had been campaigning for Keaton's attention since the first week of class. And she'd definitely gotten noticed. Savannah glanced toward the professor's office next door, where the dark-haired man now stood at the window, talking on the phone, yet staring with blatant interest at pretty, red-haired Rachel in her tight, low-cut sweater and micro-miniskirt.

"Isn't he a fox?" she whispered to Savannah, a row of thin metal bangle bracelets clinking musically as Rachel reached up to hook her loose hair behind her ear. "He could be Burt Reynolds' brother, don't you think?"

Savannah frowned, skeptical. She glanced over at the lean man with the shoulder-length hair and overgrown moustache, and the mushroom-brown corduroy suit and open-necked satin shirt. A zodiac sign pendant glinted from within a thick nest of exposed chest hair. Fashionable or not, the look didn't do a thing for Savannah. "Sorry, Rach. I'm not seeing it. Unless Burt Reynolds has a brother in the porno business. Plus, he's too old for you. He must be close to forty, for crying out loud."

"Shut up! I think he's cute." Rachel giggled, crossing her arms under her breasts and tossing her head in a move that had Professor Keaton leaning closer to the glass, practically on the verge of drooling. "I'm gonna go see if he wants to check my work. Maybe he'll ask me to stay after school and clean his erasers or something."

"Mm-hmm. Or something," Savannah drawled through her smile, shaking her head as Rachel waggled her brows then sauntered toward the professor's office. Having come to Boston University on a full academic scholarship and the highest SAT scores across twenty-two parishes in south central Louisiana, Savannah didn't really need help bolstering her grades. She'd accepted the extra credit assignment only out of her insatiable love for history and learning.

She looked at the urn again, then retrieved another catalogue of London silver from the Colonial period and compared the piece to the ones documented on the pages. Doubting her initial analysis now, she picked up her pencil and erased what she'd first written in her notebook. The urn wasn't English in origin. *American,* she corrected. Likely crafted in New York or Philadelphia, if she were forced to guess. Or did the simplicity of the Rococo design lean more toward the work of a Boston artisan?

Savannah huffed out a sigh, frustrated by how tedious and inexact the work was proving to be. There was a better way, after all.

She knew of a far more efficient, accurate way to resolve the origins—all the hidden secrets—of these old treasures. But she couldn't very well start fondling everything with her bare hands. Not with Professor Keaton in his office a few feet away. Not with her other two classmates gathered at the table with her, working on their own items from the collection. She wouldn't dare use the peculiar skill she'd been born with.

No, she left that part of her back home in Acadiana. She wasn't about to let anyone up here in Boston think of her as some voodoo freak show. She was different enough among the predominantly white student body. She didn't want anyone knowing how truly strange she was. Aside from her only living kin—her older sister, Amelie—no one knew about Savannah's extrasensory gift, and that's how she intended to keep it.

Much as she loved Amelie, Savannah had been happy to leave the bayou behind and try to make her own path in life. A normal life. One that wasn't rooted in the swamps with a Cajun mother who'd been more than a shade eccentric, for all Savannah could recall of her, and a father who'd been a drifter, absent for all of his daughter's life, little better than a rumor, according to Amelie.

If not for Amelie, who'd practically raised her, Savannah would have belonged to no one. She still felt somehow out of place in the world, lost and searching, apart from everyone else around her. For as long as she could remember, she'd felt...*different.*

Which was probably why she was striving so hard to make her life normal.

She'd hoped moving away to attend college right out of high school would give her some sense of purpose. A feeling of belonging and direction. She'd taken the maximum load of classes and filled her evenings and weekends with a part-time job at the Boston Public Library.

Oh, shit.

A job she was going to be late for, she realized, glancing up at the clock on the wall. She was due for her 4PM shift at the library in twenty minutes—barely enough time to wrap up now and hurry her butt across town.

Savannah closed her notebook and hastily straightened up her work area at the table. Picking up the urn in her gloved hands, she carried the piece back into the archive storage room where the rest of the donated collection's catalogued furniture and art objects had been placed.

As she set the silver vessel on the shelf and put away her gloves, something caught her eye in a dim corner of the room. A long, slender case of some sort stood propped against the wall, partially concealed behind a rolled-up antique rug.

Had she and the other students missed an item?

She strode over to get a better look. Behind the bound rug was an old wooden case. About five feet in length, the container was unremarkable except for the fact that it seemed deliberately separated—hidden—from the rest of the things in the room.

What was it?

Savannah moved aside the heavy, rolled rug, struggling with its unwieldy bulk. As she leaned the rug against the perpendicular wall, she bumped the wooden case. It tipped forward suddenly, about to crash to the floor.

Panicked, Savannah lunged, shooting her arms out and using her entire body to break the case's fall. As she caught it, taking the piece down with her onto her knees, the old leather hinges holding it together snapped apart with a soft *pop-pop-pop.*

A length of cold, smooth steel tumbled out of the case and into Savannah's open hands.

Her bare hands.

The metal was a jolting chill against her palms. Heavy. Sharp-edged. Lethal.

Startled, Savannah sucked in a breath, but couldn't move fast enough to avoid the prolonged contact or the power of her gift, which stirred to life inside her.

The sword's history opened up to her, like a window into the past. A random moment, fused forever into the metal and now exploding in vivid, if scattered, detail in Savannah's mind.

She saw a man holding the weapon before him as in combat.

Tall and menacing, a mane of thick blond waves danced wildly around his head as he stared down an unseen opponent under a black-velvet, moonlit sky. His stance was unforgiving, the air about him as grim as death itself. Piercing blue eyes cut through the tendrils of sweat-dampened hair that drooped into the ruthless angles of his face and square-cut jaw.

The man was immense, thick roped muscles bulging from broad shoulders and biceps beneath the loose drape of his ecru linen shirt. Smooth, fawn-colored trousers clung to his powerful thighs as he advanced on his quarry, blade poised to kill. Whoever the man was who'd once wielded this deadly weapon, he was not some post-

Elizabethan dandy, but a warrior.

Bold.

Arrogant.

Magnetic. Dangerously so.

The swordsman closed in on his target, no mercy whatsoever in the hard line of his mouth, nor in the blazing blue eyes that narrowed with unswerving intent, seeming almost to glow with some inner fury that Savannah couldn't comprehend. A dark curiosity prickled inside her, against her better instincts.

Who was this man?

Where was he from? How had he lived?

How many centuries ago must he have died?

Through the lens of her mind's eye, Savannah watched the warrior come to a halt. He stared down at the one he now met in mortal combat. His broad mouth was flat, merciless. He raised his sword arm, prepared to strike.

And then he did, driving home the blade in a swift, certain death blow.

Savannah's heart raced, pounding frantically in her breast. She could hardly breathe for the combination of fear and fascination swirling inside her.

She tried to see the swordsman's face in better detail, but his wild tangle of golden hair and the shadows of the night that surrounded him hid all but the most basic hints of his features.

And now, as so often happened with her gift, the vision was beginning to fracture apart. The image started to splinter, breaking into scattered shards.

She'd never been able to control her ability, not even when she tried. It was a powerful gift, but an elusive one too. Now was no different. Savannah struggled to hold on, but the glimpse the sword gave her was slipping...fading...drifting out of reach.

As Savannah's mind cleared, she uncurled her fingers from their grip on the blade. She stared down at the length of polished steel resting across her open palms.

She closed her eyes and tried to conjure the face of the swordsman from memory, but only the faintest impression of him remained within her grasp. Soon, even that was slipping away. Then it was gone.

He was gone.

Banished back to the past, where he belonged.

And yet, a single, nagging question pulsed through her mind, through her veins. It demanded an answer, one she had little hope of resolving.

Who was he?

CHAPTER 2

Broken glass and debris from the rotting rafters rained down in the dark as three members of the Order patrol team dropped through a filth-clouded skylight of the abandoned clothing factory in Chinatown. The surprise attack from above sent the group of feral-eyed, blood-addicted squatters in the old ruin of the building scrambling for cover.

For all the good it would do them to run.

Gideon and his two comrades had been tailing one member of this Rogue nest most of the night, waiting for the opportune moment to strike. Waiting for the suckhead to lead them to his lair, where the Order could take out not just one Bloodlust-crazed predator, but several. Half a dozen, by Gideon's quick count, as he, Dante and Conlan dropped in unannounced just after midnight.

Gideon was on one of the Rogues as soon as his boots hit the rubbish-strewn floor. He leapt after the suckhead, grabbing a fistful of the vampire's dirty trench coat as it flew out behind him like a sail. He took the Rogue down in a hard tackle, pinning it with his forearm braced against the back of the rabid male's neck. With his free hand, Gideon reached for the shorter of the two blades he wore in combat. The twelve-inch length of razor-sharp, titanium-edged steel gleamed in the scant moonlight shining in from the open roof overhead.

The Rogue began to fight and flail, snarling through its fangs as it struggled to get loose. Gideon didn't give the suckhead a chance to so much as hope it might escape him.

Shifting his hold, Gideon clutched a hank of the Rogue's unkempt brown hair and wrenched its head back. The vampire's amber eyes glowed wild and unfocused, its open maw dripping sticky saliva as it growled and hissed in the mindless fury of its Bloodlust.

Gideon plunged his dagger into the hollow at the base of the Rogue's exposed throat.

Death from the blade might have been certain enough, but the titanium—fast-acting poison to the diseased blood system of a Rogue—sealed the deal. The vampire's body convulsed as the titanium entered its bloodstream, began devouring its cells from the inside out. It wouldn't take long—mere seconds before there was nothing left but bubbling ooze, then dried-up ash. Then nothing left at all.

As the titanium did its worst on Gideon's kill, he wheeled around to gauge the situation with his comrades. Conlan was in pursuit of a suckhead who'd fled for a steel catwalk above the factory floor. The big Scot warrior dropped the Rogue with a titanium dagger shot from his hand like a bullet.

A few yards away, Dante was engaged in hand-to-hand combat with a Rogue who'd had the bad sense to think he could fight the dark-haired warrior up close and personal. Dante calmly, but swiftly, eluded every careless strike before drawing a pair of savage, curved blades from their sheaths on his hips and slicing them across the attacking Rogue's chest. The suckhead howled in sudden agony, collapsing in a boneless heap at the warrior's feet.

"Three down," Con called out in his thick brogue. "Another three to go."

Gideon nodded to his teammates. "Two heading for the back loading dock now. Don't let the bastards get away."

Conlan and Dante took off on his direction without question or hesitation. They'd run Rogue-hunting missions under Gideon's command for years, long enough to know that they could rely on his direction even in the thickest of urban combat.

Gideon sheathed his short blade in favor of his sword, the weapon he'd mastered back in London, before his travels—and his vow—brought him to Boston to seek out Lucan Thorne and pledge his arm to the Order.

Gideon swiveled his head, making a swift, sweeping search of the shadows and gloom of the old building. He saw the fourth Rogue in no time. It was fleeing toward the west side of the place, pausing here and there, ostensibly seeking a place to hide.

Gideon focused on his quarry, seeing it with something more than just his eyes. He'd been born with a much stronger gift of sight:

The preternatural ability to see living energy sources through solid mass.

For most of his long existence—three-and-a-half centuries and counting—his gift had been little more than a clever trick. A useless parlor game, something he'd valued far less than his skill with a sword. Since joining the Order, he'd honed his extrasensory talent into a weapon. One that had given him new purpose in life.

His sole purpose.

He used that ability now to guide him toward his current target. The Rogue he chased must have decided better of its notion to look for cover. No longer wasting precious seconds out of motion, the feral vampire veered sharply south in the building.

Through the brick and wood and steel of the sheltering walls, Gideon watched the fiery orb of the Rogue's energy shift direction, pushing deeper into the bowels of the run-down factory. Gideon trailed its flight on silent, stealthy feet. Past a chaos of tumbled sewing stations and toppled bolts of faded, rodent-infested fabric. Around a corner into a long, debris-scattered hallway.

Empty storage rooms and dank, dark offices lined the corridor. Gideon's target had fled into the passageway before making a hasty, fatal mistake. The Rogue's energy orb hovered behind a closed door at the end of the hallway—just a few scant feet from a window that would have dumped him onto the street outside. If Bloodlust hadn't robbed the vampire of his wits, he might have eluded death tonight.

But death had found him.

Gideon approached without making a sound. He paused just outside the door, turned to face it. Then kicked the panel off its hinges with one brutal stamp of his booted foot.

The impact knocked the Rogue backward, onto its back on the littered office floor. Gideon pounced, one foot planted in the center of the feral vampire's chest, the blade of his sword resting under its chin.

"M-mercy," the beast growled, less voice than animalistic grunt. Mercy was a word that had no meaning to one of the Breed lost to Bloodlust as deeply as this creature was. Gideon had seen that firsthand. The Rogue's breath was sour, reeking of disease and the over-consumption of human blood that was its addiction. Thick spittle bubbled in its throat as the vampire's lips peeled back from enormous, yellowed fangs. "Let me...go. Have...mercy..."

Gideon stared unflinching into the feral amber eyes. He saw only savagery there. He saw blood and smoke and smoldering ruin. He saw death so horrific, it haunted him even now.

"Mercy," the Rogue hissed, even while fury crackled in its wild gaze.

Gideon didn't acknowledge the plea. With a flex of his shoulder, he thrust the sword deep, severing throat and spinal column in one thorough strike.

A quick, painless execution.

That was the limit of his mercy tonight.

CHAPTER 3

Savannah arrived early at the Art History department that next afternoon. She couldn't wait for her day's final class to let out, and made a beeline across campus as soon as English Lit 101 ended. She dashed up the three flights of stairs to the archive room outside Professor Keaton's office, excited to see she was the first student to report in for the after-class project. Dumping her book bag next to her work table, she slipped into the storage room containing the items yet to be catalogued for the university's collection.

The sword was right where she'd left it the day before, carefully returned to its wooden case in the corner of the room.

Savannah's pulse kicked as she entered and softly closed the door behind her. The beautiful old blade—and the mysterious, golden-haired warrior who'd once used it with lethal skill—had been haunting her thoughts all this time. She wanted to know more. Needed to know more, with a compulsion too strong to resist.

She tried to ignore the little pang of guilt that stabbed her as she bypassed the bin of clean curator's gloves and sank down, bare-handed, in front of the container that held the sword.

She lifted the lid of the long box, gently laying it open. The length of polished steel gleamed. Savannah hadn't had the chance to really look at its craftsmanship yesterday, after it had fallen so unexpectedly into her hands.

She hadn't noticed then how the tooled steel grip was engraved with the image of a bird of prey swooping in for a brutal attack, its cruel beak open in a scream. Nor had she paid attention to the blade's gemstone pommel, a blood-red ruby caged by grotesque metal talons. A cold shiver ran up her arms as she studied the weapon now.

This was no hero's sword.

And still, she couldn't resist the need to know more about the man she'd watched wield it in her glimpse from before.

Savannah flexed her fingers, then gently rested them on the blade.

The vision leapt into her mind even faster than the first time.

Except this was a different peek at the weapon's past. Something unexpected, but equally intriguing in a different way.

A pair of young boys—tow-headed, identical twins—played with the sword in a torchlit stable. They could be no more than ten years old, both dressed like little seventeenth-century lords in white linen shirts, riding boots and dark blue breeches that gathered at the knee. They were laughing, taking turns with the sword, stabbing and lunging at a bale of straw, pretending to slay imaginary beasts.

Until something outside the stable startled them.

Fear filled their young faces. Their eyes went to each other, dread-filled, panicked. One of them opened his mouth in a silent scream—just as the torch on the wall of the stable went out.

Savannah recoiled from the blade. She let go of it, shaking, gripped with a marrow-deep terror for these two children. What happened to them?

She couldn't walk away. Not now.

Not until she knew.

Her fingers trembled as she brought them back over the blade again. She set her hands down on the cold steel, and waited. Though not for long.

The window to the past opened up to her like a dragon's maw, dark and jagged, an abyss licked with fire.

The stable was ablaze. Flames climbed the stalls and rafters, devouring everything in their path. Blood bathed the rough timber posts and the bale of yellow straw. So much blood. It was everywhere.

And the boys...

The pair of them lay unmoving on the floor of the stable. Their bodies were savaged, broken. Barely recognizable as the beautiful children who'd seemed so joyous and carefree. So alive.

Savannah's heart felt trapped in a vise, cold and constricted, as this awful glimpse played out before her. She wanted to look away.

She didn't want to see the terrible remains of the once-beautiful, innocent twin boys.

Ah, God. The horror of it choked her.

Someone had killed those precious boys, slaughtered them.

No, not someone, she realized in that next instant.

Some *thing*.

The cloaked figure that held the sword now was built like a man—an immense, broad-shouldered wall of a man. But from within the gloom of a heavy wool hood, glowing amber eyes burned like coals set into a monstrous, inhuman face. He wasn't alone. Two others like him, dressed similarly in hooded, heavy cloaks, stood with him, parties to the carnage. She couldn't make out their features for all the shadows and the flickering, low light of the flames twisting up the walls and support beams of the stable.

Not human, her mind insisted. But if not human, then what?

Savannah tried to get a better look as the image of the boys' attackers began to waver and dissolve.

No. Look at me, damn you.

Let me see you.

But the glimpse started splintering, visual shards that broke into smaller pieces, turning this way and that. Slipping out of her grasp. Distorting what she saw.

It had to be a trick of her unsteady hold on her gift.

Because what she was seeing from this vision of the past couldn't possibly be real.

From within the deep hood of the one now holding the sword, the pair of glowing eyes blazed bright amber. And in the instant before the image vanished completely, Savannah would have sworn on her own life that she saw the bone-white glint of razor-sharp teeth.

Fangs.

What the...?

A hand came down on her shoulder. Savannah shrieked, nearly jumping out of her skin.

"Take it easy!" Rachel laughed as Savannah swung her head around. "Don't have a damn heart attack. It's just me. Jeez, you look like you just saw a ghost."

Savannah's pulse was hammering hard, her breath all but gone. She had no voice to answer her roommate, could only stare up at her mutely. Rachel's gaze went to the sword. "What are you doing in here by yourself? Where did that come from?"

Savannah cleared her throat, now that her heart had finally vacated the area. She pulled her hands away from the blade, hiding them so Rachel wouldn't see how they shook. "I...I found it yesterday."

"Is that a ruby in the handle of that thing?"

Savannah shrugged. "I think so."

"Really? Far out!" She leaned in for a better look. "Let me see it for a second."

Savannah almost warned her friend to be careful, that she wouldn't want to see what Savannah had just witnessed. But that gift—a curse, today—belonged solely to her.

Savannah watched as Rachel picked up the blade and admired it. Nothing happened to the girl. She had no inkling of the horrific past secreted in the centuries-old weapon.

"Rach...do you believe in monsters?"

"What?" She burst out laughing. "What the hell are you talking about?"

"Nothing." Savannah shook her head. "Forget it. I'm just kidding."

Rachel gripped the sword in both hands and pivoted on her heel, taking on a dramatic combat pose. Her wristful of thin metal bangle bracelets jingled together musically as she mock thrusted and parried with the blade. "You know, we shouldn't be handling this thing without gloves on. God, it's heavy. And old too."

Savannah stood up. She plunged her hands into the pockets of her flared jeans. "At least two hundred years old. Late 1600s would be my guess." More than a guess, a certainty.

"It's beautiful. Must be worth a fortune, I'll bet."

Savannah shrugged. Gave a weak nod. "I suppose."

"I don't remember seeing this on the collection's inventory list." Rachel frowned. "I'm gonna go show it to Bill. I can't believe he would've missed this."

"Bill?"

Rachel rolled her eyes. "Professor Keaton. But I can't very well call him that tonight on our date, now, can I?"

Savannah knew she was gaping, but she didn't care. Besides, it was nice having something else to think about for a moment. "You're going out with Professor Keaton?"

"Dinner and a movie," Rachel replied, practically singing the words. "He's gonna take me to that scary new one that just came out. *The Chainsaw Massacre.*"

Savannah snorted. "Sounds romantic."

Rachel's answering smile was coy. "I'm sure it will be. So, don't wait up for me at the apartment tonight. If I have anything to say about it, I'm gonna be late. If I come home at all. Now, hand me the case for this thing, will you?"

Savannah obliged, giving a slow shake of her head as Rachel donned a pair of curator's gloves and gently placed the awful weapon back inside the slim wooden box. Tossing Savannah a sly grin, the girl turned and left.

When she had gone, Savannah exhaled a pent-up breath, realizing only then how rattled she was. She reached for her own pair of gloves and the notebook she'd filed on the shelf the day before. Her hands were still unsteady. Her heart was still beating around her breast like a caged bird.

She'd seen a lot of incredible things with her gift before, but never something like this.

Never something as brutal or horrific as the slaughter of those two children.

And never something that seemed so utterly unreal as the glimpse the sword had given her at a group of creatures that could not possibly exist. Not then, or now.

She couldn't summon the courage to give a name to what she witnessed, but the cold, dark word was pounding through her veins with every frantic beat of her heart.

Vampires.

CHAPTER 4

For almost a hundred years, the city of Boston had played unwitting host to a cadre of Breed warriors who'd sworn to preserve the peace with humans and keep the existence of the vampire nation—its feral, Bloodlust-afflicted members in particular—a secret from mankind. The Order had begun in Europe in the mid-1300s with eight founding members, only two of which remained: Lucan, the Order's formidable leader, and Tegan, a stone-cold fighter who played by his own rules and answered to no one.

They, along with the rest of the cadre's current membership—Gideon, Dante, Conlan and Rio—sat gathered at a conference table in the war room of the Order's underground headquarters late that afternoon. Gideon had just reported on his team's raid of the Rogue lair the night before, and now Rio was relaying the results of his solo recon mission on a suspected nest located in Southie.

At the head of the long table to Gideon's left, the Order's black-haired Gen One leader sat in unreadable silence, his fingers steepled beneath his dark-stubbled chin as he heard the warriors' reports.

Gideon's hands were not so idle. Although his mind was fully present for the meeting, his fingers were busy tinkering with a new microcomputer prototype he'd just gotten a hold of a few days ago. The machine didn't look like much, just a briefcase-sized metal box with small toggle switches and red LED lights on the front of it, but damn if it didn't get his blood racing a bit faster through his veins. Almost as good as ashing a Rogue. Hell, it was almost as good as sex.

Not that he should remember what that was, considering how long it had been since he'd allowed himself to crave a woman. Years, at least. Decades, probably, if he really wanted to do the math. And he didn't.

While Rio wrapped up his recon report, Gideon executed a quick binary code program, using the flip toggles to load the instructions into the processor. The machine's capacity was limited, its functions even more so, but the technology of it all fascinated him and his mind was forever thirsty for new knowledge, no matter the subject.

"Good work, everyone," Lucan said, as the meeting started to wrap up. He glanced at Tegan, the big, tawny-haired warrior at the opposite end of the table. "If Rio's intel shakes out, we could be looking at a nest of upwards of a dozen suckheads. Gonna need all hands on deck down there tonight to clear the place out."

Tegan stared for a moment, green eyes as hard as gemstones. "You want me to go in, take the nest out, say so. It'll be done. But you know I work alone."

Lucan glowered back, anger flashing amber in the cool gray of his gaze. "You clear the nest, but you do it with backup. You got a death wish, deal with it on your own time."

For several long moments, the war room held an uneasy silence. Tegan's mouth twisted, his lips parting to bare just the tips of his fangs. He growled low in his throat, but he didn't escalate the power struggle any further. Good thing, because God knew if the two Gen One warriors ever went at each other in a true contest, there would be no easy victor.

Like the rest of the warriors gathered around the table, Gideon knew about the bad blood between Lucan and Tegan. It centered on a female—Tegan long-dead Breedmate, Sorcha, who'd been taken from him back in the Order's early days. Tegan lost her first, tragically, to an enemy who turned her Minion and left her worse than dead. But it was by Lucan's hand that Sorcha perished, an act of mercy for which Tegan might never forgive him.

It was a grim but potent reminder of why most of the warriors refused to take a mate. Of those currently serving the Order, only Rio and Conlan had Breedmates. Eva and Danika were strong females; they had to be. Although the Breed was close to immortal and very hard to kill, death was a risk on every mission. And worry for Breedmates being left behind to grieve was a responsibility few of the warriors wanted to accept.

Duty permitted no distractions.

It was a tenet Gideon had learned the hard way. A mistake he couldn't take back, no matter how much he wished he could.

No matter how many Rogues he ashed, his guilt stayed with him.

On a low, muttered curse, Gideon yanked his thoughts out of the past and entered the last string of his programming code into the computer. He flipped the switch that would execute the commands, and waited.

At first nothing happened. Then...

"Bloody brilliant!" he crowed, staring in triumphant wonder as the red LED lights on the front panel of the processor illuminated in an undulating wave pattern—just as his program had instructed them to. The warriors all looked at him with varying expressions, everything from confusion to possible concern for his mental wellbeing. "Will you look at this? It's a thing of fucking beauty."

He spun the processor around on the table for them to see the technological miracle taking place before their eyes. When no one reacted, Gideon barked out an incredulous laugh. "Come on, it's remarkable. It's the bloody future."

Dante smirked from his seat across the table. "Just what we needed, Gid. A light-up bread box."

"This bread box is a not-yet-released tabletop computer." He took the metal lid off so everyone could see the boards and circuitry inside. "We're talking 8-bit processor and 256-byte memory, all in this compact design."

From farther down the table, Rio came out of a casual sprawl in his chair and leaned forward to have a better look. There was humor in his rolling Spanish accent. "Can we play *Pong* on it?" He and Dante chuckled. Even Con joined in after a moment.

"One day, you'll stand in awe of what technology will do," Gideon told them, refusing to let them dampen his excitement. No matter how big of a geek he was being. He gestured to an adjacent closet-like room where years earlier he'd begun setting up a control center of mainframes that ran many of the compound's security and surveillance systems, among other things. "I can envision a day when that room full of refrigerator-sized processors will be a proper tech lab, with enough computer power to keep a small city up and running."

"Okay, cool. Whatever you say," Dante replied. His broad mouth quirked. "But in the meantime, no *Pong*?"

Gideon gave him a one-fingered salute, smiling in spite of himself. "Wankers. Bunch of hopeless wankers."

Lucan cleared his throat and brought the meeting back on track. "We need to start ramping up patrols. I'd like nothing better than to rid Boston completely of Rogues, but that still leaves other cities in need of clean-up. Sooner or later, things keep going like they are, we're gonna need to evaluate our options."

"What are you saying, Lucan?" Rio asked. "You talking about bringing on new members?"

He gave a vague nod. "Might not be a bad idea at some point."

"The Order started with eight," Tegan said. "We've held steady at six for a long time now."

"Yeah," Lucan agreed. "But things sure as hell aren't getting any better out there. We may need more than eight of us in the long run."

Conlan braced his elbows on the edge of the table, sent a look around to everyone seated with him. "I know of a guy who'd be a good candidate as any, I reckon. Siberian-born. He's young, but he's solid. Might be worth talking to him."

Lucan grunted. "I'll keep it in mind. Right now, priority is taking care of business at home. Six Rogues ashed last night and another nest in our crosshairs is a decent place to start."

"Decent, yes," Gideon interjected. "But not nearly enough for my liking."

Rio gave a low whistle. "Only thing sharper than your mind, amigo, is your hatred for Rogues. If I ever fall, I'd not want to find myself at the end of your blade."

Gideon didn't acknowledge the observation with anything more than a grim look in his comrade's direction. He couldn't deny the depth of his need to eradicate the diseased members of their species. His enmity went back about two centuries. Back to his beginnings in London.

Dante eyed him speculatively from across the table. "Counting the suckheads you took out last night, how many kills does that make for you, Gid?"

He shrugged. "Couple hundred, give or take."

Inwardly, Gideon did a quick tally: Two-hundred and seventy-eight since coming to Boston in 1898. Another forty-six Rogues lost their heads on the edge of his sword, including the three who slaughtered his baby brothers.

He could no longer picture the boys' faces, or hear their laughter. But he could still taste the ash from the fire as he tried desperately to pull them out of the burning stable the night they were killed. Gideon had been hunting Rogues ever since, trying to douse his guilt. Trying to find some small degree of redemption for how he'd failed to protect them.

So far?

He wasn't even close.

CHAPTER 5

Savannah took the T in to the university campus from her apartment in Allston, still groggy and in dire need of coffee. She'd had a restless night's sleep, to put it mildly. Too many disturbing dreams. Too many unsettling questions swirling in her head after what she'd witnessed by touching that damned sword. She'd been more awake than not for most of the night.

It hadn't helped that Rachel never made it home from her date with Professor Keaton. Of course, that had been her intention. Hadn't she said as much yesterday? Nevertheless, Savannah had lain awake in her bedroom of the cramped little apartment, listening for her roommate to return. Worrying that Rachel was getting in over her head with a guy like Professor Keaton, a much older man who made no secret of his willingness to play the field. Or, in his case, a large part of the female student body.

Savannah didn't want to see her friend get hurt. She knew firsthand what it felt like to be played by someone she trusted, and it was a lesson she hoped never to repeat. Besides, Rachel would probably only laugh off Savannah's concern. She'd call her a mother hen—too reserved and serious for her age—things Savannah had heard before from other people throughout her life.

Truth be told, part of her was a little envious of Rachel's free spirit. While Savannah had fretted and worried the night away, Rachel was probably having a great time with Professor Keaton. Correction: *Bill,* she amended with a roll of her eyes, trying not to imagine her roommate gasping out Professor Keaton's name in the throes of passion.

God, how she was going to get through class today without the involuntary—totally unwanted—mental picture of the pair of them naked together?

Savannah rounded the corner onto the university campus on Commonwealth Avenue, still considering the potential awkwardness of it all when the sight of police cruisers and a parked ambulance with its lights flashing in front of the Art History building stopped her short. A pair of reporters and a camera crew jumped out of a news van to push their way through a gathering crowd outside.

What on earth...?

She hurried over, a heavy dread rising in her throat. "What's going on?" she asked a fellow student toward the rear of the onlookers.

"Someone attacked one of the Art History profs in his office late last night. Sounds like he's in real bad shape."

"At least he's alive," someone else added. "More than you can say for the student who was with him."

Savannah's heart sank to her stomach, as cold as a stone. "A student?" *No, not Rachel. It couldn't be.* "Who is it?"

The reply came from another person nearby. "Some chick in his freshman Antiquities class. Rumor is they were engaged in a little extracurricular activity up in his office when the shit went down."

Savannah's feet were moving underneath her, carrying her toward the building entrance, before she even realized she was in motion. She ran inside, dodging the cops and university officials trying to keep the growing crowd outside and under control.

"Miss, no one's allowed in the building right now," one of the police officers called to her as she dashed for the stairwell. She ignored the command, racing as fast as she could up the three flights of steps and down the corridor toward Professor Keaton's office.

The news crew she saw arrive a few minutes ago hovered in the hallway, cameras rolling as the police and paramedics worked just inside the open door. As she drew nearer, a stretcher was wheeled out into the corridor with a patient being administered to by one of the ambulance attendants.

Professor Keaton lay unconscious as they pushed his gurney toward the elevators, his face and neck covered in blood, his skin bone-white above the blanket that covered him up to his chin. Savannah stood there, immobile with shock, as Keaton was whisked off to the hospital.

"Coming through!" a gruff Boston accent shouted from behind her. She jolted back to attention, and took a step aside as another gurney was pushed out of the professor's office.

There were no medics attending this patient. No urgency in the way the emergency responders wheeled the stretcher into the hallway and began an unrushed march toward the second bank of elevators. Savannah brought her hand up over her mouth to hold back the choked cry that bubbled in her throat.

Oh, Rachel. No.

Her petite body was draped completely in a sheet mottled with dark red stains. One of her arms had slid out from under the cover to hang limply over the side of the gurney. Savannah stared in mute grief, unable to tear her gaze away from that lifeless hand and the dozen-plus bangle bracelets gathered at Rachel's wrist, sticky with her blood.

Reeling in disbelief and horror, Savannah stumbled into the professor's office, her stomach folding in on itself.

"Outta here now, everybody!" one of the police detectives working inside ordered. He put a hand on Savannah's shoulder as she slumped forward and held her midsection, trying not to lose her breakfast. "Miss, you need to leave now. This is a crime scene."

"She was my roommate," Savannah murmured, tears choking her. Nausea rose at the sight of the blood that sprayed the wall near Professor Keaton's desk and sofa. "Why would someone do this? Why would they kill her?"

"That's what we're trying to find out here," the cop said, his voice taking on a more sympathetic tone. "I'm sorry about your friend, but you're gonna have to let us do our work now. I'd like to talk to you about when you last saw your roommate, so please wait outside."

As he spoke, the news crew seemed to think it was the opportune time to crowd in with their camera. The reporter inserted himself between Savannah and the officer, shoving his microphone at the detective. "Do you have any indication of what happened in here? Was it a random break-in? Robbery? Or some kind of personal attack? Should the campus be concerned for the safety of its students and faculty?"

The cop narrowed his eyes on the vulture with the mic and heaved an annoyed sigh. "Right now, we have no reason to believe anyone else is in danger. There are no signs of forced entry, nor any obvious evidence of a struggle beyond what occurred here in this office. Although it doesn't appear anything was stolen, we can't rule out theft as a motive until we've had a chance to fully review and process the scene...."

Savannah couldn't listen to any more. She drifted out of Keaton's office and into the adjacent study lab where she, Rachel and the other students had been working less than twenty-four hours ago. She dropped into a chair at one of the work tables, feeling outside her own body as the discussion of Rachel's murder and Professor Keaton's narrow escape continued in the blood-splattered office.

Savannah's gaze roamed aimlessly over the reference materials stacked on the lab tables, then over toward the archive storage room. The door was wide open, but no cops or university officials were inside.

She stood up and approached numbly, walked into the darkened room.

And even through her fog of shock and grief, she realized immediately that something wasn't right.

"It's not here."

She pivoted, a sudden surge of adrenaline sending her back to Professor Keaton's office at a near run. She made a quick visual search of the room, looking past the disheveled desk and well-worn sofa. Past all the blood.

"It's gone." The police officers and news crew went silent, everyone turning to look at her now. "Something *was* taken from here last night."

~ ~ ~

Eva had set off the compound's kitchen smoke alarm again.

The high-pitched beeping brought every warrior in the place running at full tilt to shut the bloody thing off.

Gideon abandoned his morning's work on the microcomputer—his new obsession—and hot-footed it up the serpentine corridor of the underground headquarters to the kitchen installed specifically for Eva and Danika, the only two residents biologically capable of eating anything that came out of it. Even that was questionable, when it was Rio's Breedmate's turn at the stove.

The Spaniard arrived in the kitchen mere seconds before Gideon got there. Rio had silenced the alarm and was pulling Eva into an affectionate embrace, chuckling good-naturedly as she tried to make excuses for what happened.

"I only turned away for a minute to watch something on the news," she protested, waving her hand toward the small television set on the counter as Lucan, Dante and Tegan shook their heads and returned to what they'd been doing. Conlan stayed, going over to put an arm around his mate, Danika, who stood nearby, trying to hide her smile behind her hand.

"Besides," Eva went on, "there was only a little bit of smoke this time. I swear that alarm hates me."

"It's all right, baby," Rio said around rich laughter. "Cooking has never been your best quality. Look at the upside, at least no one got hurt."

"Tell that to their breakfast," Gideon said wryly. He picked up the skillet of charred eggs and sausage from the stove and dumped the mess into the trash.

As he walked past the TV, he was struck by a pair of chocolate-brown doe eyes, fringed with feathery, thick lashes. The young woman was being interviewed outside one of the local universities. Short black curls haloed her face, a lovely, gentle face. Its soft features graced a perfect oval of smooth coffee-and-cream skin that looked like it would be as soft as velvet to the touch.

But the young beauty's mouth was tense, bracketed with stress lines on either side. And now that Gideon was looking closer, he realized tears were welled in those pretty dark eyes.

"Tell me more about the artifact you say appears to be missing," the news reporter pressed, shoving a microphone up toward her face.

"It's a sword," she answered, a voice to match her beautiful face, despite the tremor that made her words shake a bit. "It's a very old sword."

"Right," said the reporter. "And you say you're certain you saw this sword just yesterday in Professor Keaton's classroom?"

"What's this about?" Gideon asked, his gaze riveted to the young woman.

"Someone assaulted a professor at the college last night," Danika explained. "He's been taken to Mass General, critical but stable. The student who was with him was killed. Sounds like they suspect it may have been a robbery gone bad."

Gideon grunted in acknowledgment, wondering what the student being interviewed had to do with the situation.

"The sword was part of a collection of Colonial furnishings and art objects that were donated to the university recently," she told the reporter. "At least, I believe it was part of the collection. Anyway, it's missing now. It's the only thing missing, far as I can tell."

"Uh, huh. And can you describe for our viewers what the sword looks like?"

"It's English. Mid-seventeenth century," she replied with certainty. "It has an eagle or a falcon engraved into the handle."

Gideon froze, his blood running suddenly cold in his veins.

"There's a ruby in the pommel," the young woman went on, "held in place by carved steel talons."

Ah, Christ.

Gideon stood there, wooden, immobilized by the words that sank into his brain.

The weapon this student was describing in such unmistakable detail...he knew it all too well.

He'd held that very sword in his hand, a very long time ago. It vanished the night his twin brothers were murdered, taken, he assumed, by the Rogues who'd slaughtered them with it while Gideon had been away from the Darkhaven. Not there to protect them, as he should've been.

He never thought he'd see the sword again, never wanted to see it. Not after that night.

He never imagined it might end up here, in Boston.

For how long? Who had it belonged to?

More to the point, who would want it badly enough to kill for it?

The need to find answers to those questions lit his veins up with fire. He had to know more.

And as Gideon watched the pretty coed on the television screen, he knew exactly where to start looking.

CHAPTER 6

"T hat's the last of today's returns, Mrs. Kennefick." Savannah replaced the checkout card in the back of a popular new horror novel about a social misfit named Carrie. She eyed the book, sympathetic to the fictional high school girl from Maine who possessed some kind of frightening power. She was half-tempted to sign the novel out herself. Maybe she would have, if her day hadn't already been horrific enough.

Her supervisor, old Mrs. Kennefick, had offered to let Savannah take the night off, but the sad fact was, the last thing Savannah wanted to do was spend any more hours than necessary back home at her apartment alone. Her evening shift at the library was a welcome distraction from what happened at the university.

Rachel was dead. God, Savannah could hardly believe it. Her stomach clenched at the thought of her friend and Professor Keaton being attacked by an unknown assailant. Her eyes prickled with welling tears, but she held them back. She couldn't allow herself to cave in to her grief and shock. She'd had to excuse herself from the book return desk twice already tonight, barely making it to the ladies' room before the sobs had torn out of her throat.

If she could get through the remaining forty minutes of her shift without losing it again, it would be a miracle.

"All set then, dear?" Mrs. Kennefick patted her neat gray bun, then smoothed her similarly colored cardigan as she ambled around from her desk in the processing room.

"All set," Savannah said, adding the worn-out copy of *Carrie* to the wheeled book cart with the rest of the returns she'd handled that evening.

"Very well." The old woman took the cart and began rolling it away before Savannah could stop her. "No sense in you waiting around any longer tonight, dear. I'll go shelve these returns. Will you lock up behind you on your way out?"

"But, Mrs. Kennefick, I really don't mind—"

The woman dismissed her with a little wave and kept going, hunched over the cart, her drab-skirted behind and soft-soled shoes retreating into the quiet labyrinth of the library corridor.

Savannah glanced at the clock on the wall, watching the second hand tick slowly. She looked for something more to do there, knowing it was just an excuse to keep from returning to the reality that awaited her outside the library. She took advantage of the opportunity to organize Mrs. Kennefick's pencil cup and paperclip dispenser, even going so far as to use the edge of her long sleeved turtleneck sweater to sweep away the nonexistent dust from the pristine surface of her supervisor's desk.

Savannah was busy straightening the patron files when she felt the fine hairs at the back of her neck rise with a odd sense of awareness. A warmth prickled over her skin, strange and unsettling.

Someone was in the library's delivery room outside.

Although the adjacent room was silent, she closed the file drawer and walked out to investigate.

Someone was there, all right.

The man stood in the center of the room, facing away from her, dressed in a long black trench coat, black pants and black, heavy-soled boots. A punk, from the look of him. A very large punk.

Geez, the guy had to be six-and-a-half-feet tall and built of solid muscle. Which made it all the more incongruous to find him standing there in silent meditation, his head full of thick, spiky cropped blond hair tipped back on his broad shoulders while he perused the mural of paintings that circled a full 360 degrees around the ornately paneled, medieval-styled room.

Savannah strode toward him, cautious yet intrigued. "The library is about to close soon. Can I help you find something?"

He slowly pivoted around to face her, and, oh, wow....

The punk description might have fit his clothing style, but that's where it ended. He was handsome—devastatingly so. Under the crown of his golden hair, a broad brow and angular cheekbones combined with a square-cut jaw that would have seemed more in place on a movie screen than standing in the middle of the Abbey

Room in the Boston Public Library.

"Just looking," he said after a long moment, a tinge of Britain in his deep voice.

And so he was looking, though no longer at the art. His piercing blue eyes met her gaze and held fast, so sharp and cool they seemed to read and process everything about her in an instant.

Savannah's skin felt tighter under his attention, making the soft knit of her ivory-colored turtleneck feel like sandpaper against her throat and breasts. She felt too warm, too noticed, and too aware of the sheer size and masculinity of this stranger before her.

She tried to project an air of calm and professionalism, despite the weird chaos going on with her central nervous system in reaction to this man. Striding up beside him, if only to escape his scrutiny, she glanced up at the series of fifteen original works depicting King Arthur and his Round Table Knights, painted for the library at the turn of the century by the artist Edwin Austin Abbey. "So, which are you more interested in: Abbey's work, or Arthurian legends?"

He followed her gaze up now. "I'm interested in everything. *The mind is not a vessel to be filled, but a fire to be kindled.*"

Savannah registered the statement, knew she'd heard it in class somewhere before. "Plutarch?" she guessed.

She was rewarded with a sidelong grin from the gorgeous non-punk standing next to her. "A student of philosophy, I take it."

"It's not my strongest subject, but I get by all right in most of my classes."

His smile quirked a bit at that, as if he mentally scored a point in her favor. He had a nice smile. Straight white teeth framed by full, lush lips that made her pulse kick a little. And that English accent was doing funny things to her heart rate too. "Let me guess," he said, studying her in that unnerving way again. "Wellesley? Or maybe Radcliffe?"

She shook her head at the mention of the two prestigious, private women's colleges. "BU. I'm a freshman in the Art History program."

"Art History. An unusual choice. Most of the colleges are turning out high-priced doctors and lawyers these days. Or mathematics whiz kids hoping to be the Einsteins of the future."

Savannah shrugged. "I suppose you could say I'm more comfortable with the past."

Normally, that would be one hundred percent true. But not lately.

Not after what she'd seen reflected in the sword's history yesterday. Now, she wished she could go back in time and undo the touch that showed her the horrors inflicted on the pair of young boys from the past. She wished should could deny the other horror she witnessed in the blade's history too—the monsters that simply could not exist, except in the darkest kind of fiction.

She wished she could turn back the clock to the moment Rachel told her about her date with Professor Keaton, so she could warn her not to go.

Right now, after everything that had happened recently, Savannah could find no comfort in the past.

"I'm Gideon, by the way." The deep, rich voice pulled her back to the present, a welcome life line, even offered by a stranger. He held out his hand, but she couldn't muster the courage to take it.

"Savannah," she replied quietly, clasping her bare hands behind her back to resist the temptation to reach out to him, even though her gift didn't work on living things. The idea of touching him was both compelling and unsettling. She felt as if she should know him somehow, perhaps saw him at the library or around the city somewhere, yet she was certain she'd never seen him there before. "People don't generally spend a lot of time in this area of the library. The Bates Reading Room and Sargent Hall are more popular with patrons."

She was rambling, but he didn't seem to notice or care. Those arresting blue eyes watched her, studied her. She could almost sense the machinery of his mind analyzing everything she said and did. Searching for something.

"And what about you, Savannah?"

"Me?"

"Which room is your favorite?"

"Oh." She exhaled a nervous laugh, feeling stupid around him, a feeling she wasn't accustomed to. As if none of her studies or schooling could have ever prepared her for encountering someone like him. It was crazy to think it. Made no logical sense. And yet she felt it. This man—Gideon, she thought, testing the name with her mind—seemed ageless and somehow ancient at the same time. He held himself with a confidence that seemed to say little to nothing could surprise him. "This room is my favorite," she murmured dully. "I've always liked hero stories."

His mouth quirked. "Men who slay dragons? Rescue the princess in the tower?"

Savannah slanted him an arch look. "No, the quest for truth by someone who isn't afraid to pursue it, no matter the cost."

He acknowledged her parry with a slight lift of his chin. "Even if it means risking the Seat Perilous?"

Together, they glanced up at the panel depicting that part of Arthurian legend, the chair at the Round Table that would spell death to anyone taking his place there who proved unworthy of seeking the Holy Grail.

Savannah could feel Gideon studying her, despite that his gaze was fixed on the painting overhead. The heat from his big body, nearer to her than she'd noticed, seemed to burn through her clothing, imprinting itself on her skin. Her pulse ticked a bit faster as the seconds stretched out between them.

"Freshman," he said after a while, an odd pensiveness in his tone. "I didn't realize you were so young."

"I'll be nineteen in a few months," she replied, inexplicably defensive. "Why? How old did you think I was? How old are you?"

He gave a slow shake of his head. Then he brought his gaze around to look at her beside him. "I should go. As you said, the library's closing. I don't want to keep you from your work."

"It's all right if you want to stay awhile. I won't need to kick you out for another fifteen minutes, so until then, feel free to enjoy the art." She took one last look at Sir Galahad being led to the chair that would either confirm his honor or spell his doom, and couldn't help reciting another of Plutarch's quotes: *"Painting is silent poetry, and poetry is painting that speaks."*

Gideon's answering smile threatened to steal her knees out from under her. "Indeed, Savannah. Indeed it is."

She couldn't hold back her smile either. And for the first time all day, she felt relaxed. She felt happy. She felt hopeful, as odd as that seemed. Not weighted down with grief and numb with shock and confusion.

All it took was a chance meeting with a stranger, some unexpected conversation. A few moments of kindness from someone who had no inkling of what she'd been through. Someone who wandered into her workplace on a whim and ended up making the worst day of her life seem less awful simply by being in it.

"Nice to meet you, Gideon."

"Likewise, Savannah."

This time, she was the one who held out her hand. He didn't hesitate to take it. As she expected, his grip was warm and strong, his long fingers engulfing hers easily. As they broke contact, she wondered if he felt the same jolt of awareness that she did. God, their brief connection went through her like a mild electrical current, heat and energy zinging into her veins.

And she couldn't escape the fact that something about him seemed so vaguely familiar...

"I should go," he said for the second time tonight. She didn't want him to leave so soon, but she couldn't very well ask him to stay either. Could she?

"Maybe I'll see you around again sometime," she blurted, before she had the bad sense to let impulse take over her brain.

He stared at her for a long moment, but didn't respond one way or the other.

Then, like the mystery he'd been the moment she first saw him, he simply turned and strode away, out the door and into the waiting night.

~ ~ ~

Gideon waited, crouched low like a gargoyle on the rooftop corner of the library, until Savannah exited the building a few minutes later.

He meant to leave, as he'd said he would. He'd decided after talking with her for just a few minutes—after learning that she was an eighteen-year-old college freshman, for crissake—that his quest to find out more about whoever had that damned sword would need to unfold without involving a bright, innocent young woman.

He couldn't use Savannah for information.

He wouldn't use her for anything.

And he sure as hell didn't need to be lingering around her place of work, following her in stealthy silence from one rooftop to another, as she made her way from the library to the T station. But that's just what he did, telling himself it was a need to see a vulnerable female home safely in a city rife with hidden dangers.

Never mind that she might rightly count him among those

dangers, if she had any idea what he truly was.

Gideon leapt down to street level to slip into the bus station a healthy distance behind her. He boarded a different car, watching through the crowds to make sure she was unmolested for the duration of the commute. When she got off at Lower Allston, he followed, tracking her to a modest five-story brick apartment building on a side street called Walbridge. A light went on behind a curtained window on the second floor.

He waited some more, keeping an unplanned vigil from the shadows across the way, until the dim glow of Savannah's apartment light was extinguished an hour and a half later.

Then he melted back into the darkness that was his home and battlefield.

CHAPTER 7

Art History class was cancelled that next day, of course.

The department building was quiet, no students inside today. Just professors working privately in their offices. Rumor around campus had it that Professor Keaton was expected to make a full recovery. He was still in the hospital, but someone had heard another of the professors mention that Keaton could be discharged and back to work in a couple weeks or less. It was the only good news to come out of the whole, awful situation.

Savannah only wished Rachel had been as fortunate too.

It was her friend's death that brought Savannah back to the Art History department that morning, even though there was no class to attend. She slipped inside the building, inexplicably drawn to the scene of the terrible crime.

Why had Rachel and Professor Keaton been attacked? And by whom?

The antique sword was valuable, certainly, but was it enough to warrant such a heinous, lethal assault?

As Savannah climbed the stairs to the second floor of the building, she felt a bit like she was heading for her own Seat Perilous, on a quest for a truth she wasn't certain she was prepared for, or equipped to face.

The police detectives were long gone, the barricades and tape removed from the scene. Still, simply being there put a chill in Savannah's veins as she neared Professor Keaton's office door down the hallway. But she needed to see the room again. She hoped to find something inside that she'd overlooked, something that would provide some sense of understanding of what happened, and why.

Keaton's office door was closed and locked. So was the archive and study room next door.

Shit.

Savannah jiggled the doorknob, for all the good it did. There would be no getting past the locks. Not unless she wanted to head downstairs and try to persuade one of the department professors to let her in.

Even though she made it a practice to avoid lying and manipulation, her mind started working on a host of excuses that might win her access to the rooms. She accidentally left one of her books for another class inside and needed it for an upcoming exam. She lost her student ID and thought it might be with her notebook in the study room. She needed to finish cataloguing one last item in the archive collection to make sure she got her extra credit for the project once Professor Keaton returned to school.

Right. One idea more lame than another.

Not that the honest answer would be any more convincing: She wanted to go through Professor Keaton's office and touch everything in sight with her bare hands, to see if she could pick up any clues that the police might have missed.

Deflated, Savannah started to pivot away to leave. As she turned, something caught her eye farther down the hallway on the floor. A thin circle of metal.

Could it be what she was thinking?

She hurried over to look, feeling both excited and sickened to see the delicate bangle at her feet. She recognized it immediately. One of Rachel's bracelets. It must have fallen off her wrist when they were wheeling her body away.

Savannah's whole being recoiled at the sight of the bloodstained evidence of Rachel's suffering. But she had to touch the bracelet. Whatever the tragic memento had to tell her, Savannah had to know.

She picked it up off the floor, closed her fingers around the cold metal ring.

Her extrasensory gift woke up immediately. The jolt from the bracelet overwhelmed her, the memory housed in the metal so horrifically fresh.

She saw Rachel in Keaton's office. Her face was twisted in stark, mortal terror.

And it didn't take long for Savannah to understand why....

Without warning, she was suddenly looking into the face of

Rachel's attacker as the beast closed in.

And it was a beast. The same kind of fiery-eyed, fanged monster that Savannah had been trying to forget since she touched the old sword. Except this monster wasn't dressed in a hooded cloak like the group that killed the little boys. This beast wore an expensive-looking dark suit and crisp white shirt. A gentleman's refined clothes and richly styled, brown hair, but the face of a nightmarish monster.

The creature lunged for Rachel, its razor-toothed jaws open as it went for the girl's throat.

Oh, my God.

Impossible. She couldn't be seeing this, not again. It could not be real.

Was she losing her mind?

Savannah couldn't breathe. Her lungs constricted, burned in her chest. Her heart slammed hard, drumming in her ears. She couldn't find her voice, even though her entire body seemed to be screaming.

She gaped down at the bracelet now resting in her upturned palm. Every instinct told her to throw it away, as fast and as far as she could. But it was all that remained of her friend.

And the fragile ring of metal contained what might be the sole evidence of Rachel's killer.

She had to tell someone what she saw.

But who?

Her psychometry ability was outlandish enough, but to expect anyone to believe her when she tried to explain the monsters she's seen—not once, but twice—through her gift?

They would think she was crazy.

Hell, maybe she was.

Savannah's sister, Amelie, had long said their mama was a little touched in the head. Maybe Savannah was too. Because right now, that was the only thing that made sense to her. It was the only way she could explain what she had witnessed over the past couple days.

She didn't know what to do, or who to turn to.

She needed time to think.

Needed to get a grip on herself, before she lost it completely.

Savannah dropped Rachel's bracelet in her book bag and dashed out of the building.

~ ~ ~

Gideon rapped a second time on Savannah's apartment door, not at all convinced it was a good idea for him to be there.

Then again, it also hadn't exactly been stellar logic to detour from his first hour of patrol tonight and swing past the Boston Public Library in the hopes of seeing her. Nevertheless, he'd done that too, and had been troubled to learn that Savannah was absent from her shift. Bad judgment or not, he couldn't keep his boots from carrying him across town to her modest apartment.

As his knuckles dropped against the door for a third time now, he finally heard movement from inside. He'd known she was home; his talent had betrayed her to him, even though she seemed determined to ignore whoever was at the door. The peephole shadowed as she moved in front of it now to look out. Then, a soft inhalation from the other side of the door. One lock tumbled free. Then another.

Savannah opened the door, her face slack with mute surprise. Gideon drank in the sight of her in an instant, from her pretty, dark eyes and sensual mouth, to her lovely curves and lean, long limbs. Tonight she was dressed for comfort in flared jeans that hugged her hips and thighs, and white rock band tank top under an unbuttoned, faded denim work shirt.

God's balls, she was braless beneath the bright red Rolling Stones logo. The unexpected sight of her perky little breasts almost made him forget why he was there.

"Gideon." Not exactly a welcoming greeting, the way her fine black brows were knit on her forehead as she looked at him. She sent a quick glance past him to the second floor landing behind him, seeming distracted and edgy. When her attention came back to him, her frown deepened. "What are you doing here? How do you know where I live?"

He knew that bit of recon would pose a problem once he arrived, but it was a risk he'd been willing to take. "I swung past the library tonight, thought I might see you again. Your supervisor told me you had called in sick today. She seemed very concerned about you. I hope you don't mind that I came around to check in on you."

"Mrs. Kennefick gave you my address?"

She hadn't, but Gideon neither confirmed nor denied it. "Are you unwell?"

Savannah's creased brow relaxed somewhat. "I'm okay," she said, but he could see that she was flustered, nervous. There was a pale cast to her cheeks, and her face was tense, lines bracketing her mouth. "You shouldn't have come. I'm fine, but this isn't really a good time for me right now, Gideon."

Something was very wrong here. He could feel her anxiety pulsing off her in palpable waves. Savannah's fear hung heavily in the two feet of space between them. "Something happened to you."

"Not to me." She gave a weak shake of her head, crossing her arms over herself like a shield. Her voice was quiet, small. "Something happened to my friend, Rachel, the girl I was rooming with here. She was killed a couple nights ago. She and one of the professors at BU were attacked. Professor Keaton survived, but Rachel..."

"I'm sorry about your friend," Gideon said. "I didn't realize."

It was the truth, or close enough. He hadn't known Savannah had been close to either of the victims. He could see that she was hurting, but there was something more going on too, and the warrior in him was suspicious of what else he didn't yet know about the situation.

"I did hear something on the news recently about a robbery at the Art History building on campus," he said casually. "Your friend and the professor were attacked during a break-in and theft of some type of relic, wasn't it?"

Savannah stared at him for a long moment, as if she couldn't decide whether to answer. "I'm not sure what happened that night," she finally murmured. She uncrossed her arms and moved one hand to the edge of the door. She took a step backward. The hand braced on the door now began to close it by fractions. "Thanks for checking in on me, Gideon. I'm not much in the frame of mind for talking right now, so—"

With her retreat, he advanced a pace. "What's wrong, Savannah? You can tell me."

She shook her head. "I don't want to talk about it. I can't..."

Gideon's gut tightened with concern. "You lost someone you cared about. I know that's not easy. But last night at the library, you seemed different. Not visibly upset, the way you are now. Something's scared you, Savannah. Don't try to deny it. Something happened to you today."

"No." The word came out choked, forced past her lips. "Please, Gideon. I don't want to talk about this anymore."

She was trying desperately to hold herself together, he could see that. But she was really shook up, dealing with something more visceral than simple grief or fear.

She was terrified.

He studied her closer, seeing the depth of her fright in the trembling that raked her from head to toe where she stood. Good God, what the hell could have put her in such a state?

"Savannah, did someone threaten you somehow?" His blood seethed at the thought. "Did someone hurt you?"

She shook her head, silent as she withdrew into her apartment and left him standing at the open door. He followed her inside, uninvited, but he wasn't about to walk away and leave her alone to cope with whatever had her so stricken with terror.

Gideon closed the door behind him and strode into the cramped living room. His gaze strayed toward the bedroom to the left, where a suitcase lay open on the bed, a few articles of folded clothing tossed inside.

"Are you going somewhere?"

"I need to go away for a while," she said, still drifting ahead of him into the small living space, keeping him at her back. "I need to clear my head. The only place I know where I can do that is back home in Atchafalaya. I called my sister this afternoon. Amelie thinks it's best if I come home too."

"Louisiana?" he said. "That's a bloody long way to go just to clear your head."

"It's my home. It's where I belong."

"No," he said, a clipped denial. "You're panicked about something and you're running away. I figured you to be stronger than this, Savannah. I thought you liked heroes who stood fast and pursued the truth, no matter the cost."

"You don't know the first thing about me," she shot back, and pivoted to face him. Her dark brown eyes pierced him with a hot mix of fear and anger. She crossed her arms over her chest again, a wounded, self-protective stance.

He walked toward her with unrushed strides. She held her ground, watching him approach. She wasn't retreating now, but she kept those arms braced tight against herself, barring him—maybe barring anyone—from truly getting close.

Gideon took one of her hands in a firm, but gentling, grasp. "You don't need to protect yourself against me. I'm one of the good guys."

He took hold of her other hand too now, and drew her arms down to her sides. Her breast rose and fell with each shallow, rapid breath she took as he reached up to cup her delicate jaw in his palm. Her skin was creamy smooth under the pad of his thumb, her plump lips soft as satin, the color of a dusky wine rose.

He couldn't resist the need to taste her—if just this once.

Curling his fingers around her warm nape, he brought her toward him and brushed his lips over hers. She was sweeter than he'd imagined, the heat of her mouth and the tenderness of her kiss awakening a need in him the way a thirsting man must crave cold, clear water.

Gideon couldn't keep from dragging her deeper against him, testing the seam of her lips with the hungered tip of his tongue. She let him in on a pretty moan, her hands coming up to his shoulders, clinging to him in delicious surrender.

He swept her denim shirt off so he could feel the bare skin of her arms. A mistake, that. Because now the pebbled peaks of Savannah's unbound breasts were crushed against his chest, an awareness that burned right through his black leather jacket and T-shirt, arousing him as swiftly as if she'd been standing fully naked before him.

He felt the sharp tips of his fangs elongating as desire swept through him like a wildfire. Good thing his eyes were closed, or the heated glow of his irises would betray him to her in an instant as something other than human.

Gideon growled against her mouth, telling himself this swift, dangerous passion was simply the result of a long, self-imposed drought.

Right. If only he believed that.

What he felt was something far more surprising. Troubling, too.

Because it wasn't just any woman he wanted in that moment. It was this one only.

Maybe she sensed the dark strength of his need for her. God knew, she had to feel it. His cock was a ridge of steel between them, his veins pulsing with a drumming demand to take her. To claim her.

"Gideon, I can't." She broke away and sucked in a hitching breath. Her fist came up to her mouth, pressing against her glistening, kiss-swollen lips. "I'm sorry, I can't do this," she whispered brokenly. "I can't start wanting something that feels so right when everything else around me feels so terribly wrong. I'm just so confused."

Hell, he was too. Confusion was a wholly unfamiliar feeling for him. This woman had knocked him off his axis the moment he met her, from her quick-witted comebacks at the library, to the intense attraction she stirred in him, just to be near her.

He hadn't come to her apartment looking to seduce her, but now that he'd kissed her, he wanted her. Badly. Their kiss left a fierce desire pounding through him for the first time in more years than he cared to recall. It took all his self-control to cool the hammering of his pulse, to make sure the amber was extinguished from his eyes before he met her gaze. To coax his fangs back to their human-like state before he attempted to speak.

Savannah heaved a sigh. "I've never been so confused in all my life. And you're right, Gideon. I am scared." She looked so vulnerable and sweet. So alone. "I'm scared that I'm going crazy."

He stepped closer, gave a mild shake of his head. "You don't seem crazy to me."

"You don't know," she replied, her voice quiet. "Nobody knows, except for Amelie."

"Nobody knows what, Savannah?"

"That I...see things." She let the statement hang between them for a long moment, her gaze searching his eyes, watching his face for a reaction. "I saw the attack on Rachel. I saw how she was murdered. I saw...the monster that did it."

Gideon held himself still at her mention of the word *monster*. He kept his expression neutral, a carefully schooled show of outward calm and patient understanding, despite that inside his Breed instincts were on full-alert, alarm bells clanging. "What do you mean, you saw your friend's killing? You were there?"

She slowly shook her head. "I saw it afterward, when I found one of Rachel's bracelets outside Professor Keaton's office. She was wearing it that night. I touched the bracelet, and it showed me everything." Her lips pressed together, as though she wasn't sure she should go on. "I can't explain how or why, but when I touch an object...I can see a glimpse of its past."

"And when you touched her bracelet, you saw your friend's death."

"Yes." Savannah stared at him with a gaze that was far too wise.

Bleak with a dark, unswerving knowledge. "I saw Rachel being murdered by something inhuman, Gideon. It looked like a man, but it couldn't have been. Not with sharp fangs and hideous glowing yellow eyes."

Holy. Bloody. Hell.

Forgetting the fact that she had just confessed to having a powerful extrasensory ability—something many mortals faked but very few genuinely possessed—it was Savannah's other revelation that had Gideon's veins going tight and cold as she spoke.

When he didn't answer right away, Savannah blew out a humorless laugh. "Now you do think I'm crazy."

"No." No, he didn't think she was crazy. Far from it. She was intelligent and beautiful, a hundred years of wisdom in those soft brown eyes that hadn't even seen twenty years of life yet. She was extraordinary, and now Gideon wondered if there was something more to Savannah that he had yet to understand.

But before he could pose the questions—questions about her ESP talent and whether her body bore any unusual birthmarks—she turned away from him and the answer was right there in his line of sight. A small red mark on her left shoulder blade, only partially visible beneath the thin strap of her white tank top. It was unmistakable: a teardrop falling into the cradle of a crescent moon.

Savannah wasn't merely human.

She was a Breedmate.

Ah, fuck. This wasn't good. Not good at all. There was a protocol to be observed when it came to the discovery of women like Savannah living among the *Homo Sapiens* public at large. That protocol certainly didn't include seduction or duplicity, two things Gideon was currently teetering between like a man on a high wire.

"Since I've obviously rendered you mute with my mental instability," she went on, as his uncharacteristic loss for words or a quick solution eluded him, "then I might as well tell you about the other glimpse I saw. There was a sword in the Art History's collection, a very old sword. The one item that went missing the other night. I touched that sword recently too, Gideon." She turned back to look at him. "It showed me the same kind of creature—a group of them, in fact. Using that sword, they slaughtered a pair of little boys a long time ago. I'd never seen anything so awful. Not until I saw what happened to Rachel. I know you probably don't believe any of this...."

"I believe you, Savannah." His mind churned on the implications of everything he was hearing, everything he was seeing in this frightened, but forthright, female. "I believe you, and I want to help you."

"How can you help?" He heard the desperation edging into her voice now. She was exhausted, emotionally drained. She drifted over to the sagging sofa and dropped down onto it Bent over her knees, she held her head in her hands. "How can anyone help with something like this? I mean, there's no possible way that what I saw is real. It doesn't make any sense, right?"

God help him, he nearly blurted out the truth to her, right then and there. He wanted to explain away her confusion, help her make sense of everything that had her so distressed and uncertain now.

But he couldn't. He didn't have that right.

The Order needed to be informed of Savannah's existence. As a warrior—hell, like any other member of the Breed race—Gideon was duty-bound to see this female gently introduced to their world and her place within it, should she choose to take part. Not plunged carelessly into the worst of it.

"What I saw doesn't make sense," she murmured. "But maybe I should go to the police and tell them anyway."

"You can't do that, Savannah." His words came out too quickly, too forcefully. It was a command, and he couldn't take it back.

Her head came up then, her brow creased in a frown. "I have to tell someone, don't I?"

"You did. You told me." He walked over, sat down beside her on the sofa. She didn't flinch or withdraw when he put his hand on her back and slowly caressed her. "Let me help you through this."

"How?"

He reached up with his free hand to stroke the velvet curve of her cheek. "For now, I just need you to trust me that I can."

She held his gaze for a long moment, then gave a nod and curled into his embrace. Her head rested over his heart, her slender body nestled close, warm and soft in his arms. It was a struggle to hold his desire in check with Savannah pressed so sweetly against him.

But she needed comfort now. She needed to feel safe. He could give her that, at least for the moment.

Gideon held her as she fell into a hard sleep in his arms.

Sometime later, easily hours, he lifted her off the sofa and carried her tenderly to her bed so she could rest more comfortably.

He stayed until the hour before dawn, watching over her. Making sure she was safe.

Wondering what the hell he was getting himself into.

CHAPTER 8

Tell me this is some kind of fucking joke."

Lucan Thorne wasn't at all pleased to hear that Gideon had gone AWOL from the night's patrol. He'd been even less enthused to learn where Gideon had spent those off-grid hours.

"A goddamn Breedmate? What the hell were you thinking, man?" The Gen One leader of the Order blew out a nasty curse. "Maybe you weren't thinking. Not with your brain, anyway. That alone is cause for serious concern, if you ask me. You've never lost sight of your duty to the Order, Gideon. Not once in all these years."

"Nor have I lost sight of it now."

He was seated in the war room with Lucan and Tegan, the former radiating fury and pacing the room like a caged cat. The latter was sprawled in a conference chair at the other end of the table, showing less than passing interest in Gideon's morning-after ass-chewing while idly spinning a pen around on top of a mission review notebook.

"My interest in this woman has nothing to do with Order objectives. I told you, it's personal."

"Exactly my point." Lucan's stormy gray eyes narrowed on him. "Personal agendas have no place in this operation. Personal agendas make people sloppy. You get sloppy, you get people killed."

"I can handle this, Lucan."

"Not your choice, Gid. You know the protocol. We have to let the Darkhavens know about her, let them step in on this. We don't do diplomatic work. For damn good reason."

"She witnessed a Breed assault on a human," Gideon blurted. "The coed who ended up in the morgue after the attack on her and

123

one of the professors over at the university the other night. The dead girl was Savannah's roommate. She was killed by one of our kind."

Lucan's jaw went even more rigid. "You're certain of this? You're saying this Breedmate—Savannah—was there when it happened?"

"Her talent, Lucan. It's psychometry. She touches an object and can see a bit of its past. That's how she saw her friend's killing."

"She tell anyone about this?" Tegan drawled from his seat at the end of the table.

"No. Only me," Gideon replied. "I'd like to keep it that way—for her own sake and that of our entire race. And that's not all she's seen with her gift."

Both Gen One warriors stared at him now.

"This shit is about to get even worse?" Lucan growled.

"During the attack, there was a sword taken from the university's Art History archives. A sword I'm very familiar with, because it was the one a band of Rogues turned on my young brothers the night they were slaughtered outside our family Darkhaven in London." Gideon cleared his throat, still tasting the smoke that lingered for months after the stable was torched. "Savannah touched this sword too. She saw the Rogues and what they did to my kin. I never gave that damned sword another thought, until now. Until I realized it had surfaced in Boston, some three hundred years later."

Tegan grunted. "Surfaced, only to disappear again."

"That's right. I need to know who has that blade now."

Tegan gave a vague nod, his overlong tawny hair falling over his eyes, but not quite masking the intensity of his gem-green gaze. "You think there's a connection between the sword being here in Boston and the murders of your brothers centuries ago."

"It's a question that needs to be answered," Gideon said. "And I can't do that unless Savannah can identify the Breed male responsible for the attack at the university."

"What about the other victim, the one who survived?" Lucan said. "That's another potential witness who was actually there and lived to tell."

Gideon shook his head. "He's still hospitalized, critical. In the time it takes him to come around enough for some private questioning and the requisite memory scrub afterward, Savannah could have already given me everything I need."

Although Lucan didn't say as much, Gideon could see the

suspicion in the Gen One's keen eyes. "You're risking too much, letting yourself get close to this female. She's a Breedmate, Gideon. That might be all right for guys like Con and Rio, but for any of us?" He glanced to Tegan, then back to Gideon. "We're the longest-standing members of this operation now. We're the core. We've each been through enough shit to know that relationships, blood bonds, don't mix well with warfare. Someone always gets hurt in the end."

"I'm not looking for a mate, for fuck's sake." Gideon's reply was sharp, sounding too defensive, even to his own ears. He exhaled a ripe oath. "And I have no intention of hurting her."

"Good," Lucan said. "Then you'll have no problem when I arrange to have one of the Darkhavens meet the female at her apartment and take her into their protective custody while she's being brought up to speed on the Breed and her place in our world."

Gideon bristled, coming up out of his chair to face off with his old friend and the Order's commander. "Trance her and dump her with one of the Boston Darkhaven leaders? Not a chance. She's just a scared, confused kid, Lucan."

"You're not acting like she's just a kid. You're acting like you're responsible for this female. Like you've already got more than a passing interest."

Christ, did he? Gideon wanted to refute the accusation, but the words sat like cold lead in the back of his throat.

He hadn't intended to feel anything for Savannah. He sure as hell didn't expect to feel the sudden, violent spike of possessiveness over her at the mere idea of walking away now, leaving her safety and wellbeing in the care of the Breed's civilian arm.

Nor could he ever have imagined the day when he'd be standing off against Lucan Thorne over any direct command, let alone a command that Gideon knew in his gut was the right call for Lucan to make. For Savannah's sake, if nothing else.

Lucan fixed Gideon with a grim stare. "She's out there right now, walking around with the word vampire on the tip of her tongue. How many people do you think she'll tell before we have the chance to contain her? She told you, for crissake. What if she tells the police next?"

"She won't," Gideon said, wishing he believed it. "I told her I would help her sort everything out. I told her she could trust me."

"Trust you? She just met you," Lucan pointed out. "She's got friends she could tell this tale to, classmates. Family?"

Gideon nodded. "A sister in Louisiana. I don't know about anyone else. But I can find out. I can take care of any loose threads. I want to be the one to explain everything to Savannah. After last night, I owe her that."

Lucan grunted, his expression stony, unconvinced.

Gideon pressed on. "I want to know what the sword that was used to slay my brothers is doing here in Boston. I want to know who has it, and why. I should think the Order would like that answer too, seeing how the son of a bitch in question murdered one human to get it and left another near death."

"We can't leave her out there on her own, Gid. Her knowledge is a threat to the entire Breed nation. It's also a threat to her, if the one who killed her roommate somehow learns there was a witness and turns his sights on Savannah."

Gideon's veins turned to ice at the thought. He would eviscerate any Breed male who so much as touched her with intent to harm. "I'm not about to let anyone hurt her. She needs to be protected."

"Agreed," Lucan said. "But that means day and night, something we can't enforce so long as she's living among the human population. And we sure as hell aren't bringing a civilian female here to the compound." Lucan stared, a tendon ticking in his square jaw. "You want to initiate her about the Breed and our world, fine. I'll give you that. You want to see if her talent can help us ID the bastard who attacked those humans the other night, that's yours too."

Gideon nodded, grateful for the chance and more relieved than he should have been at the prospect of Savannah being entrusted to his care.

Lucan cleared his throat pointedly. "You bring her up to speed. You question her. But you'll do all of this inside the secured shelter of a local Darkhaven. It's the best place for her right now, Gideon. You know that."

He did. But that didn't mean he had to like it.

And he didn't like it.

At the moment, he didn't see any better options.

"I'll make some calls," Lucan said. "This plan goes into motion tonight."

Gideon remained standing, his molars clamped together, fists curled at his sides as the Order's leader left the room. Tegan got up from his chair a moment later. He prowled toward Gideon, studying him with those unreadable eyes. He held something in his hand—a folded piece of paper, torn from the notebook that lay on the table alongside the pen he'd been toying with during the impromptu meeting.

"What's this?" Gideon said as the big Gen One offered the square of note paper to him.

Tegan didn't answer.

He strode out of the war room and headed down the corridor without a word.

~ ~ ~

The university campus was crowded with students that next day at noontime, people seated in small groups under tall, leafy oaks, eating packed lunches, others playing sports on the broad, green lawns. It seemed practically everyone was taking advantage of a sunny and warm October day. A pretty snapshot of a world that seemed so innocent. So...normal.

Savannah strolled past her chattering, laughing, carefree classmates, her steps hurried on the concrete sidewalk, her arms wrapped tightly around her book bag.

She had just left a meeting with her academic advisor, who'd given her clearance for a short leave of absence from her classes. She was going home soon, leaving in several hours. Although she'd told the advisor she expected to return to class in a couple of weeks, after she dealt with some "personal issues," Savannah wasn't sure there was enough time in the world to come to terms with everything she'd seen over the past few days.

She still wondered if she were somehow losing her mind. Gideon hadn't seemed to think so last night. It had been incredibly sweet of him to check in on her, concerned that she had called in sick from work. His comfort, although totally uninvited and unexpected, had been just what she needed.

His kiss hadn't been half bad either. More like, incredible. She hadn't been prepared for how good it felt to be in his arms, her mouth under his control. If she concentrated, she could still feel the heat of his lips on hers. And her body remembered too, every nerve ending going tingly and warm at just the thought of being wrapped up in him.

If Gideon were a lesser man, he might have used her shaky emotional state to his advantage last night and tried to get into her pants. God knew, after the kiss they shared, she likely wouldn't have needed much convincing to let him take things further.

She had actually dreamt he stayed with her most of the night. But there was no sign of him when she woke up alone this morning in her bed, still dressed in her tank top and jeans.

Would she see him again?

Probably not very likely. She had no idea how to reach him. No idea where he lived, or what he did for a living. She didn't even know his full name. Somehow, since their first chance meeting, he had managed to avoid revealing her a single thing of significance about himself, other than the facts that he was obviously well-read and well-educated.

Not to mention endlessly patient and understanding when it came to hysterical women going off about woo-woo ESP abilities and supernatural creatures that couldn't possibly exist outside slasher films and horror novels.

Gideon had been more than patient or understanding, in fact. He'd been a source of calm for her, more supportive than she ever could have hoped. Some part of her believed him when he said he could help her figure everything out. That he wanted to help her make sense of what she'd told him, even though inwardly he had to suspect she was more than a little touched.

There was a part of her that believed Gideon to be capable of anything he said, anything he promised. He simply projected that air of total, unswerving command. He filled any room he was in, radiated an indefinable power. His intelligent blue eyes told anyone who looked in them that he possessed the wit and experience of a man twice his age.

Just how old was he, anyway?

Savannah had mentally placed him around thirty, but she couldn't be certain. He never did answer when she asked him his age that first night in the library. He seemed too worldly, too wise somehow, to be older than her by just a decade-plus. He had to be much older than she had assumed, yet his face had no lines, no scars or blemishes to betray his years.

And his body...it felt built of solid muscle and strong,

unbreakable bone. Ageless, like so much else about him.

And now that she was thinking about it, there was something distantly, oddly familiar about Gideon too. She looked at him and felt a niggling of her senses, as if they'd met somewhere before, impossible though it was.

Despite the enthusiasm of her instincts—or other parts of her anatomy—she was positive the first time she'd ever met Gideon was two nights ago in the Abbey Room of the Boston Public Library. Until two nights ago, he'd been a stranger to her. A stranger who didn't deserve to have her problems, real or imagined, dumped on him.

Which is why, when Amelie called early that morning to tell Savannah she'd purchased a bus ticket home for her and had it waiting at the station for her later that evening, Savannah had agreed it was probably best for her to return to Louisiana for a while.

She had one more appointment to take care of on campus, then she would be going back to her apartment to finish packing. She wished there was a way for her to see Gideon before she left, say goodbye at least. But short of camping out at the library in the hopes that he might show up there again this afternoon, she had no means of locating him before she had to leave for the bus station tonight.

Maybe Mrs. Kennefick knew more about him? She'd worked in the library records room all her adult life; if Gideon was a patron, maybe Mrs. Kennefick could give Savannah his full name or address. It was a place to start, anyway. Savannah could call and ask as soon as she wrapped up at the English department.

The thought put such a current of hope through her veins, Savannah hardly noticed the white Firebird rolling up behind her at a slow crawl on the street parallel to her on the sidewalk. The passenger side window was rolled down, disco music sifting out from the car.

Annoyed, Savannah glanced over, squinting in the sunlight as the driver reduced his speed even more to keep pace with her.

He was the last person she expected to see today. "Professor Keaton?"

"Savannah. How are you?"

"Me?" she asked, incredulous. He braked to a stop and leaned across the seats as she bent and peered to have a closer look at him. "I'm okay, but what about you? What are you doing out of the hospital? I heard you weren't expected to be released for a week or more."

"Been out for the past hour. Thank God for the miracle of modern medicine." His smile seemed weak, not quite reaching his eyes. He appeared pale and wan, his tanned skin kind of waxy against the dark color of his moustache and heavy brows. He looked haggard and exhausted, like a clubber coming off a rough weekend bender.

And no wonder—two nights ago the man had been hauled away unconscious to the ICU. Now he was behind the wheel of his muscle car with Barry White crooning through the speakers. She walked toward the car and leaned down to talk to him through the passenger window. "Are you sure you should be driving this soon? You were almost killed the other night, Professor Keaton. It just seems like after everything you've been through..."

He watched her fumble , his expression sober now. "I shouldn't be here at all, is that what you mean, Savannah? I shouldn't be alive when your friend is dead."

"No." She shook her head, embarrassed that he misunderstood her clumsy choice of words. "I didn't mean that. I would never think that."

"I tried to protect her. I tried to save her, Savannah." He heaved out a deep sigh. "There was nothing I could do. I hope you believe me. I hope you can forgive me."

"Of course," she murmured. "I'm sure you did everything you could. No one could blame you for what happened to Rachel."

As she spoke to reassure him, she couldn't keep the image of the monster's face from forming in her mind's eye. The horrible fangs. The fiery coals that were its eyes. Her skin went cold at the memory, sending a bone-deep shudder racing up her spine.

And yet Keaton seemed strangely unaffected. He seemed somehow removed from the terror of what he'd endured that night. Calmly accepting of the miracle of his survival following an attack by something inhuman, hellish. Either he truly didn't know the depth of the horror he endured, or he was hiding it from her.

Unless it was Savannah's gift that couldn't be trusted. It had never been fully in her control, but maybe it was becoming unreliable. Maybe she wasn't going crazy after all. Maybe she was simply losing her grasp of the ability she'd tried for so long to keep a secret from the rest of the world.

"I can't imagine how awful the experience must've been for you, Professor Keaton. You and Rachel both." She looked at him closely, searching for any cracks in his demeanor. "When you were trying to save her life, were you able to get a look at the attacker?"

"Yes," he replied, not so much as blinking. "I got a brief look, just before I was knocked unconscious."

Savannah's breath froze in her lungs. "Have you told anyone?"

"Of course. I told the police this morning, when they came to see me in the hospital as I was being discharged."

Savannah swallowed, not at all certain she wanted to hear her terror voiced by another person. "What did you tell them, Professor Keaton?"

"I told them what I saw. A vagrant who likely wandered in off the street, looking for something of value to pawn for his drug money. Rachel and I surprised him, and he attacked us like a wild animal."

Savannah listened, unable to speak for a moment. It didn't make sense. Not that what she saw in the glimpse from Rachel's bracelet made more sense, but she could tell Keaton was lying. "Are you sure about that? You're sure it was a vagrant, not...someone else?"

Keaton laughed then, a short bark of humor. He turned the radio off abruptly, his movements too quick. "Am I sure? I was the only one there to see what happened. Of course, I'm sure. What's this all about, Savannah? What's going on with you?"

"Nothing." She shook her head. "I'm just trying to understand what happened."

"I told you." He leaned farther across the cockpit of the Firebird, reaching for the door handle on the passenger side. "Where are you heading, anyway?"

"English Department," she replied woodenly, an inexplicable sense of unease spreading through her. "I have to meet with my professor about taking some coursework home with me on my leave of absence."

"You're leaving school?" He sounded surprised, but his face remained oddly unchanged, blank and unreadable. "Is it because of what happened?"

"I just need to go." She backed away from the door, careful to keep her steps subtle and her voice light as she hurried to formulate a protective lie. "There are some problems at home right now, and my family needs me there."

"I see." Keaton nodded. "I'm sure you've heard that Rachel's funeral is in Brookline later this week. I know you're all alone in Boston, so if you'd like, I could take you—"

"No, thank you." She had heard about the service, of course, and had already given her condolences and regrets to Rachel's mother when the distraught woman called to let her know the date and time of the gathering. "I'm leaving tonight for Louisiana. I've already got my bus ticket reserved and waiting for me."

"So soon," he remarked. "Well, then, at least let me give you a ride over to the English Department now. We can talk some more about all of this on the way."

Savannah's unease around him deepened. There was no way in hell she was getting near him the way he was acting. "I'm late as it is. It'll be faster if I cut across campus on foot." She forced a casual smile. "But thanks for offering, Professor Keaton. I really gotta go now."

"Suit yourself," he said, then turned the radio on again. "See you around, Savannah."

She gave him a bright nod as she retreated backward to the safety of the sidewalk and the hundreds of students still milling around on their lunch break. Savannah watched as Keaton drove away.

When he was out of sight, his white car disappearing around a corner onto another part of campus, she let out the breath she didn't realize she'd been holding. Then she pivoted in the opposite direction and ran like the devil was on her heels.

CHAPTER 9

Savannah sat on the edge of her hardside suitcase at the South Station bus terminal, her right knee bouncing with nervous energy. Her bus was late. She'd gone to the station a couple hours ahead of time that evening, eager to be on her way back home. Desperate, even.

Her troubling encounter with Professor Keaton had her rattled enough on top of everything else, but it was her phone call to the library after she'd gotten home to her apartment that had really compounded Savannah's state of confusion and mounting unease.

Mrs. Kennefick hadn't been able to help Savannah locate Gideon. Oh, she recalled the big blond man in black leather who'd come around the other night inquiring after Savannah.

"Hard not to notice a man like him," she'd said, understatement of the year. "He's not exactly the library's typical clientele."

No, there was nothing typical about Gideon at all. Except the fact that he was male, and apparently adept at lying to a woman's face. Because when she'd asked Mrs. Kennefick if she'd told Gideon where Savannah lived, the older woman had balked at the very idea.

"No, of course not, dear. One can never be too careful these days, sad to say. But he did tell me he was a friend of yours. I hope I didn't overstep when I informed him you'd called in sick."

Savannah had reassured her kindly old supervisor that she'd done nothing wrong, but inwardly she was awash in doubt about everything. Now she had to put Gideon in that number too. If Mrs. Kennefick hadn't sent him to Savannah's apartment, how had he found her? And why did he let her think he'd come across her address through honest means?

Nothing was making sense to her anymore. She couldn't help

feeling suspicious of everything and everyone, as if her entire world was veering off the path of reality.

She needed a good dose of home to set her right, put her life back together. Help her put everything in its proper place again. She was eager for Amelie's good cooking, and her warm, soft shoulder to lean on.

If only the damn bus would get here.

Twenty minutes delayed now. Night had recently fallen outside the station. Evening rush hour commuters filled the place, hurrying to their trains and buses as exhaust fumes belched in through open doorways and garbled public address announcements squawked virtually unintelligibly from the ceiling speakers overhead.

No sooner had they come, the commuters were gone again, leaving Savannah and a few straggling others to wait a seemingly indeterminable time for some sign that they might actually make it out of the station tonight. She stood up on a deep yawn, just as the station speakers crackled to life and croaked out something indecipherable about the bus to Louisiana.

Savannah picked up her suitcase and hoofed it over to one of the counter attendants. "I missed the announcement just now. Did they say how long it will be before the bus to New Orleans begins boarding?"

"Ten minutes."

Finally. Just enough time to find a restroom and then she would be on her way at last. Savannah thanked the attendant, then headed off for the ladies' room farther up the terminal, luggage in hand. The bulky suitcase made for awkward walking. So awkward, that as she neared the bank of restrooms and payphones, she nearly tripped over the big, booted foot of a homeless person seated in the shadowy alcove just outside the ladies' room door.

"Excuse me," she murmured when she realized she'd bumped him.

He didn't seem to care. Or maybe he wasn't even aware of her at all, passed out or sleeping, she couldn't tell. The man in the tattered navy hoodie sweatshirt and filthy work pants didn't even lift his head. Savannah couldn't see his face. Long, dirty hair hung over his heavy brow and down past his chin.

Savannah attempted a better hold on her suitcase and skirted around his unmoving bulk to head into the restroom.

~ ~ ~

Gideon knew Savannah wasn't home, even before he knocked on her door. No lights on inside. No sound from within. No telltale glow through the walls as he searched for her with the gift of his sight.

"Shit."

Maybe he should have tried the library first, instead of checking for her at home. But even as he considered how quickly he could make it across town to look for her there, he was gripped with a sinking feeling of dread.

Savannah wouldn't have left Boston...would she?

That had been her intent last night, after all. He thought he might have convinced her to stay and let him help her, but what had he given her to hold on to? A heated kiss and a vague promise that he could somehow, miraculously, make everything better?

Fuck. He was an idiot to think she'd stick around on that flimsy incentive. He couldn't blame her if she finished packing her bag and took off for Louisiana as soon as he crept out of her bed twelve hours ago.

He couldn't have lost her so easily.

He *wouldn't* let her go so easily, damn it. And that claim had less to do with the Order's objectives or Darkhaven protocol than he cared to admit, even to himself.

If Savannah left, he was going after her.

Gideon took hold of the doorknob in death grip. Locked.

He was strong enough; he could have torn the damn thing off in his fist. But he was also Breed, and that meant he didn't have to resort to caveman tactics when he had more stealth tools at his command.

He mentally freed the two deadbolts from their tumblers. The door sprang open, and Gideon slipped inside the apartment. A quick scan of her bedroom told him his worst suspicions were correct.

Savannah's suitcase was gone. In the cramped little closet, a bunch of empty hangers.

"Damn it," he growled, stalking out to the living room where he'd kissed her just last night, held her in his arms while she slept against him on the sofa. He sent his gaze all over the place, looking for anything—a clue that might lead him to her.

He zeroed in on a memo pad lying next to the kitchen phone. He flashed across the room, more than walked, to pick up the note. In loopy, vibrant cursive handwriting, someone had jotted down *South Station*, followed by a number and a time. A bus schedule.

Savannah's departure for New Orleans.

She was leaving.

And if the schedule was accurate, she was already on her way.

Gone, more than twenty minutes ago.

Gideon flew out of there anyway, determined to catch her. He took off on foot, his Breed genetics carrying him much faster than any manmade vehicle could.

He was nothing but cold air on the humans he passed, his feet flying over pavement and through clogged traffic in the streets, speeding toward South Station.

~ ~ ~

Savannah parked her suitcase next to the paper towel dispenser in the empty restroom and stepped into the middle stall. She slid the wobbly lock into place, hearing the soft whoosh of the swinging entry door as someone came into the ladies' room a few seconds behind her. Hopefully someone who wouldn't think her battered American Tourister suitcase looked worthwhile to steal.

She was about to unzip her jeans, until the room echoed with the sudden sound of metal scraping heavily on concrete. As though someone were dragging the overflowing trash bin across the restroom floor. Was it the janitor coming in to clean?

"Hello? Someone's in here right now," she called out.

And then wished she'd kept her mouth shut because no one answered.

The room went very still, nothing but the soft trickle of water dripping into one of the clogged white sinks outside the stalls. Savannah froze, every animal instinct she had going taut with alarm.

She listened, hoping for the sound of someone's voice—an awkward apology for the intrusion, a request that she leave soon so the restroom could be maintained. She heard nothing. She was in there alone.

No, not alone.

There was a rasp of open-mouthed breathing from somewhere on the other side of the shaky metal door. Heavy boots scuffed on the filthy concrete floor. They stopped in front of her stall.

Savannah recognized them instantly.

It was the homeless man who'd been sleeping in the terminal outside.

A wash of fear swept over her, leaving her skin prickled with goosebumps, but she summoned the most threatening tone of voice she possessed. "You'd better get out of here right now, asshole, unless you want to spend the night in jail."

Through the soughing of his breath, a chuckle. Low and malicious. Not quite sane. Maybe not quite human.

Oh, God.

Savannah swallowed hard. She was trapped in the stall, didn't know whether to scream and bring someone else into her nightmare, or remain silent and pray that this was just another trick of her fracturing mind.

At least the threat was on the other side of the door. The metal panel wasn't the most sturdy, but it was locked from the inside. So long as she kept that door barred between them, she was safe.

But for how long?

She had her answer a second later.

While she stood there, trembling between the toilet and the door, the lock started to jiggle loose all on its own.

~ ~ ~

South Station was packed with passengers from a newly arrived bus when Gideon skidded to a halt inside the terminal. Weaving between the sea of incoming humans, some striding with impatient purpose, others wandering aimlessly, Gideon searched out the schedule board and scanned the departures for Savannah's bus to New Orleans.

Delayed.

Which would have been excellent news, except the board was showing the bus had left the station. Departed just two minutes ago.

Gideon could hardly curb the need to put his fist through something. "Damn it."

He considered running after the bus. If he didn't catch up to it en route, odds were good that he'd find it at its first stop along the way. Then what? Hop on board and search Savannah out among the other passengers?

What would be the better tack once he found her: Trance her and carry her off the bus while attempting to avoid the notice of a few hundred witnesses? Or plop his ass into the seat next to her and give her a quick rundown on Breedmates, Rogues and other alien-spawned vampires right there on the Amtrak Number 59 to New Orleans?

Christ, what a disaster.

Not that he had a lot of choices here.

Gideon headed deeper into the terminal, mentally calculating potential outcomes of both less-than-ideal scenarios. As he stalked toward a corridor leading to the departure gates, he caught a whiff of something sickly sweet in the hallway.

Unmistakable to his Breed senses, the stench of a Rogue somewhere nearby.

Gideon glanced around, looking for the source of the odor. Nothing but humans in the station around him. Still, his nape prickled with certainty. His gaze slid to a yellow maintenance cone blocking the door to the ladies' room across the hall. He strode closer, and the foul scent of a feral vampire strengthened.

His talent penetrated the wood and steel swinging door, locking on to a pair of heat sources inside. One was massive and hulking. The other, tall and slender, frozen in place before the threat facing her.

Ah, fuck.

Savannah.

Gideon's entire body ignited in hot, ferocious rage. One second he was in the terminal hallway, the next he was in the closed public restroom, shoving past the overturned rubbish can and leaping on the Rogue—just as the suckhead was about to crowd into the stall to attack Savannah.

On a low growl, Gideon heaved the vampire away from Savannah. He drove the Rogue's spine into the wall of white sinks and dirty mirrors on the opposite side of the room. On impact, one of the old basins crashed to the floor, shattering on a heavy thump at Gideon's feet. Water sprayed from the broken spigot, hissing almost as fiercely as the feral vampire struggling to free itself of Gideon's unyielding hold.

The suckhead grunted and snarled, gnashing its yellowed fangs. It reeked of Bloodlust and the soured evidence of a recent feeding, but its amber eyes and thin, slitted pupils held the look of a ravenous beast still thirsting for blood.

That this beast had gotten so close to Savannah—mere seconds away from touching her, biting her, close enough to kill her—made Gideon's veins throb with the need to punish.

To eviscerate the son of a bitch who intended her harm.

And he would have, had Savannah not been in the room to witness it.

Her stricken face was reflected in the cracked glass of the mirror behind the Rogue's struggling bulk. Savannah's dark doe eyes were wide with terror, her pretty mouth dropped open in a silent scream as she stared at Gideon and the beast pinned between him and the restroom wall.

"Get out of here," Gideon told her, ready to end the suckhead and loath to do it in front of her. "Wait for me outside, Savannah. You don't want to see this."

But she didn't move. Maybe she couldn't. Or maybe it was the sheer tenacity of the woman, her sharp, curious mind, that would not give in to fright when the need for answers was stronger.

The Rogue bucked and thrashed, trying to throw Gideon off. There was little time to hesitate. The din of the terminal outside the restroom door would mask most of the sounds of struggle, but he had to end this quickly, before they drew unwanted attention. Gideon pulled one of his long daggers from the sheath beneath his black trench coat.

The suckhead's amber eyes rolled toward the movement. Awareness of his impending death flashed across the open-mawed sneer. He roared, one filthy hand shooting out to the side of him, grabbing for some kind of weapon of his own.

He didn't get the chance.

Gideon shifted his hold and brought his dagger up between their bodies. With a hard thrust, the blade sank deep, plunging into the center of the Rogue's chest. The suckhead froze, panting rapidly, the twin coals of his eyes fixed on Gideon, hideous face sagging in defeat.

Gideon held the dagger in place as the diseased Breed vampire shuddered around the killing length of titanium-edged steel.

Death was immediate. Gideon dropped the big corpse as the titanium began to feed on the Rogue, dissolving it from the inside out. In mere minutes, the lump of dying flesh and bone would be nothing more than ash, then all evidence of its existence gone altogether.

Gideon turned to face Savannah. "Are you hurt?"

Mutely, she shook her head. "Gideon...who was he? What was he?" She drew in a ragged breath. "My God, what the hell is going on?"

Gideon stowed his bloodied blade and went to her. He pulled her trembling body under his arm and gently lifted her face. "Did he touch you?"

"No," she murmured. "But if you hadn't been here..."

He kissed her, a brief, tender brush of his mouth against hers. "I'm here. I will keep you safe, Savannah. Do you trust me?"

"Yes," she whispered. "I trust you." She peered around him, to where the dead Rogue was swiftly disintegrating, clothing and all. "But I don't understand any of this. How can any of this be real?"

"Come on." He took her hand in his. "There could be more where that one came from. We have to go now."

He led her out of the restroom, back into the bustle of the station. It wasn't until they were standing at the curb in the cool night air that Gideon realized he was at a loss as to where to go.

Savannah's apartment was across town, several miles away. Not that it seemed like a smart idea to take her there. He doubted very much that the Rogue going after her at the bus station was a random thing. Whoever put the suckhead on her trail would no doubt have her apartment under watch too. And as much as Gideon wanted to know who that someone was, Savannah's wellbeing was his sole concern now.

Which should have been cause enough to send him with her to the nearest Darkhaven.

To be sure, that would be the most logical, pragmatic choice. But logic and pragmatism could get fucked right about now, for all he cared about that.

He wasn't ready to yank Savannah away from harrowing situation and a thousand questions in need of answers, only to turn her over to the diplomatic arm of the Breed nation. In fact, he was finding it hard to imagine a scenario where he'd ever be ready to hand her over to someone else and walk away. He felt her soft fingers tighten around his broad palm as she stood beside him in the dark, waiting for him to make his choice.

Trusting him to keep her safe, as he promised he would.

Gideon glanced into her velvet brown gaze and knew a sudden, fierce protectiveness surge through him. Sending her away now was out of the question. It was his duty to walk her into his world gently. He bristled at the thought of letting some stranger out of the Enforcement Agency or civilian ranks step in where this woman was concerned.

His woman.

The claim swept up on him from somewhere deep in his subconscious, a sharp, primal thing. It throbbed in his veins, drumming hard in his ears with every beat of his heart.

And he needed her too.

After seeing her so close to danger back in the station—after realizing how quickly he might have lost her tonight—Gideon wanted nothing more than pull Savannah against him and never let her out of his sight again.

He wasn't going to push her off on the Darkhavens or the Enforcement Agency, even if that meant willfully ignoring Breed protocol.

Even if that meant blatantly defying Lucan's orders.

Gideon reached into the pocket of his black fatigues and withdrew the scrap of paper Tegan had given him back the compound earlier that day. He read it for a second time. Just an address, nothing more.

An address that was only a few blocks away from where he stood now.

He wasn't sure what to expect when they got there, but at the moment it seemed to be his best and only option.

"Let's go," he murmured, brushing his mouth against the warmth of her temple.

And with Savannah tucked under the shelter of his arm, clinging to him like a life line, Gideon guided her away from the busy bus terminal.

CHAPTER 10

W hat is this place?"

Savannah stood beside Gideon on a quiet, historic residential street little more than a mile from South Station, by her guess. Before them loomed a slim, three-story redbrick townhouse. It was stately, but unremarkably so next to its handsome, welcoming neighbors.

No lights glowed from within this house, no sounds emanated from within its walls. Its windows were dark, shuttered tight with black slatted panels. The iron-and-glass porch light was cold, leaving the walkway and stoop unlit as she and Gideon had made their way up to the heavy wood door.

The house, for all its seemingly deliberate effort to blend in with the others on the street, stood forbidding in its utter stillness.

Savannah rubbed off the chill that raced up her arms as she took in the stoic slab of brick and darkness. "Does anyone live here? It's as quiet as a tomb."

"I've never been here before," Gideon said. Head down, he stared with steady intent on the deadbolt drilled into the thick oak door. Although she didn't notice if he had a key, in mere seconds, the lock was freed and Gideon opened the door for her. "Come inside."

She followed him, pausing in the unfamiliar place, uncertain. Still shaken from what happened at the bus station. "It's so dark in here."

"Stay where you are." His deep voice with its soothing accent was a low rumble beside her, his blunt fingertips warm where he stroked the side of her face. "I'll find you some light."

She waited while he ably crossed the room and turned on a small lamp several feet away from her.

The soft illumination revealed a nearly vacant living space. One lone chair—a rough-hewn relic from the turn of the previous century, at least—sat beside the simple wooden table where the lamp now glowed. On the other side of the room, the cold, black mouth of a fireplace seemingly long out of use laced the stale air with the acrid tinge of old wood smoke.

Savannah cautiously trailed Gideon as he left the main living area to enter an adjacent room. She crossed her arms in front of her, tucking her bare fingers in to her sides to avoid the inadvertent touch that would wake her extrasensory ability. She suspected this house had never been filled with family or laughter. She didn't need to rouse her gift and confirm it.

No, she'd had enough darkness to last her a good long while.

"We'll be safe here, Savannah." Gideon turned on another lamp in the space where he stood now. He removed his black leather trench coat and laid it on the bed. Fastened around the hips of his black combat fatigues, he wore a thick belt studded with all manner of weapons—a pair of pistols, an array of knives, including the savage blade that he'd wielded back at the station. He took off the belt and placed it on top of his coat. "Savannah, I give you my word, I'm not going to let anything happen to you. You know you can trust me on that, yeah?"

She nodded and stepped into the modest bedroom, noting immediately the lack of decoration or personal effects. The bed was made, but fitted in plain sheets and a single pillow.

The kind of bed one might expect to see in a soldier's barracks, more so than a home.

There was a sadness in this place.

A deep, mournful sorrow.

And rage.

Black, raw...consuming.

Savannah shuddered under the weight of it. But it was the memory of what she witnessed earlier that night that threatened to take her legs out from under her.

"Gideon, what happened back there?" God, just speaking of it now made her head reel all over again. She had so many questions. They spilled out of her in a rush. "How did you know to look for me? How could you have known where I was—that I was in trouble behind that closed door of the restroom? How were you able to do what you did to that...that *monster*? I saw what happened. You stabbed him, and he—" She exhaled a shaky breath, wanting to deny what she witnessed, yet certain it was real. "You stabbed him and he disintegrated. You killed him as if it was no big thing. As if you'd seen that kind of monster a hundred times before."

"More times than that, Savannah." Gideon strode over to her, his handsome face sober, alarmingly so. "I've killed hundreds like him."

"Hundreds," she murmured, swallowing past the staggering word. "Gideon, that man...that creature...it wasn't human."

"No."

Savannah stared at him, struggling to process his calm reply. She had hoped he'd offer some kind of logical explanation for what was going on, some kind of reasonable denial that would soothe the panic rising inside her.

But the quick wit and reassuring confidence that usually glinted in his blue eyes was nowhere to be found. His expression was filled with a quiet gravity that made him seem both tender and lethal at the same time. Two qualities she had seen firsthand in him during the short time she'd known him.

She drew in breath, tried to tamp down the hysteria that threatened to climb up her throat and choke off her air. "That same kind of monster killed Rachel. And those little boys I saw when I touched that old sword in the Art History collection—they were slaughtered by a group of that same kind of monster. I tried to tell you that when you came to check in on me at my apartment last night. I didn't want to believe it then. I still don't."

"I know." He reached out and gently smoothed his hand along her cheek. "And as I told you last night, I'm here for you, Savannah. I want to help you make sense of it all."

She stared up into his gaze. "Vampires," she said quietly, her voice threadbare, fear still raw and ripe in her breast. "That's what we're talking about, isn't it. That man at the bus terminal. The ones I saw when I touched the sword and Rachel's bracelet...they were vampires."

Something flickered in his gaze now. There was an uncharacteristic hesitation in his steady voice. "By the most basic definition, yes. That's what they were."

"Oh, my God." It had been hard enough to come to grips with the idea when it only lived in her head. But to hear him speak it now—to have witnessed Gideon gutting one of the creatures right in front of her—made the reality crash down on her like a suffocating wave. "You're telling me vampires are real. They're real, and you somehow know how to kill them."

"I, along with a few others like me, yes." He was studying her now, measuring her in some way, as if he wasn't sure she could handle his answers. "Not all of the Breed are like the one who came after you at the station. Or the one who killed your friend. Or the ones who murdered those innocent boys. Only Rogues do that, Savannah. The most depraved, diseased individuals."

"This is madness, Gideon. I don't want to hear any more right now. I can't."

"Savannah, you need to understand that there are dangers in this world. Dangers that few people truly comprehend. After tonight— after everything you've seen—you can't go back to your old life. Maybe not ever. You're part of something darker now, and there are things you need to know if you're going to survive—"

"No." She shook her head and drew away from Gideon's soothing touch. Everything was happening too fast. She was confused and shaken, too overwhelmed to process anything more. "I've heard enough for now. I don't want to hear any more about monsters or danger or death. I'm trying to hold it together, Gideon, but I'm just so fucking scared."

She put her face in her palms, struggling not to lose it in front of him, but failing miserably. A sob shook her. Then Gideon's arm wrapped around her and drew her up against his strong, warm body. He didn't say anything, simply held her close and let her regain herself for a moment.

"I'm so confused," she murmured against his chest. "I'm terrified."

"Don't be." He caressed her back, his touch a welcome comfort, easing her anxiety. His body felt so powerful around her, solid and sheltering, engulfing her in his steady strength. "The last thing I want is for you to be confused," he whispered against her temple. "I don't want you to be afraid of anything. Least of all me."

"Afraid of you? No." She gave a slow shake of her head, then pressed her brow to the center of his chest, feeling the hard drum of his heartbeat against her. "You're the only thing that feels real to me, Gideon. Of everything that's happened the past few days, the only thing I know for sure right now is the way you make me feel."

His answering growl was low, vibrating from somewhere deep inside him. She felt his muscles twitch as he continued to hold her, his strength coiled and deadly, yet wrapped around her with utmost tenderness.

Savannah lifted her head to meet his gaze. His eyes had gone darker in the dim lamplight, yet in the depths of all that stormy blue, a mesmerizing fire seemed to crackle. The heat in him was a palpable thing, radiating into her everywhere they touched.

"You felt right to me last night, Gideon, when you kissed me. I was scared then too, but you felt so right." She reached up to catch his rigid jaw in the cradle of her hand. "How is it you came into my life just when I needed you most?"

He said her name, a thick whisper that leaked from between his clenched teeth. A torment seemed to sweep over him, every sinew growing taut and still as they stood together in the meager sanctuary of the bedroom.

"If anything scares me when it comes to you," she confided softly, "it's how much I need to feel your arms around me like this. You make me feel safe, Gideon. In a way I never knew before. You make me feel as though nothing bad can touch me so long as I'm with you."

"It can't. I won't allow that. Not so long as I am breathing." His voice was thunder, deep and rumbling. "You'll always be safe, Savannah. I'll stake my life on that."

She smiled, moved by the ferocity of his vow. "Spoken like one of Arthur's noble knights. I've never had my own hero."

He blew out a low, strangled curse. "No, not noble. And most certainly not anyone's hero. Just someone who cares about you. A man who wants to know you're never in harm's way. A man who wants you to find the happiness you deserve. A man who wants...ah, fuck." His gaze burned as he looked at her. "I'm a man who wants too damn much where you're concerned.."

Savannah watched the tension play across his lean, angular cheeks and the broad line of his mouth. It deepened when his hot gaze locked on to her unflinching stare. "What do you want, Gideon?"

His searing eyes drank her in, and when he spoke, his answer came in the form of a guttural, almost animal snarl. "I want this," he said, and brought her deeper into his embrace with only the faintest twitch of the muscles that held her caged against him. Power coursed through him with barely an effort, his pulse points drumming against her skin everywhere their bodies connected.

"And this." He softly skated his fingertips along the side of her face, then brushed the pad of his thumb across her lower lip. Lowering his head to hers, he descended on her until their mouths were less than a breath apart. "And I want this."

He kissed her.

Not the slow meeting of their lips from the other night, but a hungered kiss that claimed her mouth without apology, his tongue pushing past her teeth in fevered demand. He growled something indiscernible as he crushed her against him, his breath coming fast and hard, hot against her face.

His mouth consumed her. Drank her in with a ferocity that both startled and enflamed her.

Gideon's hold on her tightened. His arousal was unmistakable, a hard, heavy presence that called to the most primal part of her. Savannah's body answered, pooling with warm need at her core. She moaned as Gideon's kiss deepened, passion-filled, questing. So naked with desire, it sucked the breath from her lungs.

He dragged her body flush against him now, catching her nape in his big hand. His fingers burned where they wrapped around the side of her neck, branding his touch on her skin.

And his kiss owned her too.

Her pulse throbbed everywhere he touched her, building to a roar that filled her ears as his lips and tongue consumed her. She gave it back to him, meeting his tongue with hers and drawing him deep. Pleasure rumbled through him, low like thunder, vibrating against her breasts and belly.

Savannah arced into him as his free hand found the hem of her sweater and slipped inside. His hard, hot fingers ran up her ribs and over the thin lace of her bra. She groaned with pleasure, lost to his touch as he kneaded her breasts and continued to wreak havoc on her senses with his kiss.

"I have to have you, Savannah," he rasped against her lips, breathless, his voice oddly thick. "Ah, Christ...I've never wanted anything more than I want this with you now. I want *you*. All of you."

He didn't wait for permission. Stripping off her sweater and bra and tossing them aside, he bent to lavish her bare breasts with the delicious heat of his mouth. Her nipples were taut and achy under his attention, the wet need in her core turning to fiery lava with every lap and nip and suckle of his mouth.

Desperate to have her hands on him, she reached down to the zippered fly of his black fatigues and felt the steely bulge of his cock swell even fuller under her palm and fingers. His sex was raw power beneath her hand, pulsing with carnal demand.

She was on fire for him too. Hungry with the same need, the same urgency to feel his hard body up against her, inside her. She gripped him through the fabric, and he tore away from her breasts on a ragged growl. Head down, he kissed a descending trail of fire across her ribs and abdomen, sinking to his haunches before her. His questing mouth went lower then, teasing her sensitive skin above the low-slung waistline of her hip-hugging jeans.

"Gideon, yes," she panted, trembling with sensation, her own words little more than a gasp of sound. "Oh, God, yes. I need this too. I need you now."

She sucked in a shallow gasp as he unfastened the buttons and tugged both jeans and panties down with one swift, unswerving motion. Cool air hit the naked tops of her thighs and the exposed thatch of curls between them. Then a moment later, it was all heat, as Gideon pressed his face to her mound and kissed that most private place.

Savannah dropped her hands to his shoulders, holding on for dear life as his mouth closed down on her sex. His tongue cleaved into the seam of her, wet and hot and wicked. He suckled her, taking her tight little pearl between his teeth, toying with it, swirling the tip of his tongue over her flesh and making her mewl with mounting pleasure.

"You taste so sweet, Savannah," he told her between those erotic, sensual kisses. "I wanna eat you up. Lick every sweet inch of you. Hear you scream my name."

Oh, God, it wouldn't take much more, she thought, closing her eyes and dropping her head back on her shoulders as he gripped her bare ass and buried his face between her parted legs. He teased her clit with his mouth, tantalizing strokes as he gently spread the swollen, wet petals of her core with fingertips made slick from her body's juices.

"So tight," he murmured, penetrating her slowly with just one finger. Her body clung to him instantly, greedily, her thighs quivering as he lapped at her and worked his finger inside the core of her sex. "God, Savannah...I knew you were extraordinary, but damn. I never would've been ready for this. You're so sweet the way you respond to me. So fucking beautiful."

She moaned at his sensual praise, the only reply she could manage as her blood rushed feverishly through her veins, setting every nerve ending on fire.

And Gideon gave her no quarter whatsoever. His fingers played her with masterful skill. His mouth was relentless, his tongue so very, very good.

Her legs were going boneless beneath her. She clutched his head, buried her fingers in the short blond silk of his hair as her pleasure built and crested, about to crash into her. "Gideon," she gasped. "I can't take anymore. Please...you have to stop..."

"Never," he growled. "Let go, baby. Let me take you there."

Her knees were jelly, the muscles of her thighs quaking as the rush of orgasm roared up on her.

"Mmm, that's it, Savannah," he coaxed. "Come for me. Let me hear you."

Her voice was a strangled cry as he suckled her harder, driving her higher as her climax raced for its peak. She couldn't slow it down. Couldn't hold it back another moment.

And then she did scream his name. It tore out of her on a ragged gasp as her entire being shattered against Gideon's mouth. She was still quivering with aftershocks as he rose up from his crouch and quickly shed his pants.

"Shirt too," she murmured, drowning in pleasure but wanting to feel his naked skin against her. He hesitated for a moment, his face averted—a strange pause that might have registered more fully, had she not been wrapped in the fog of the most incredible orgasm she'd ever had.

Gideon pulled off his shirt and she caught only a fleeting glimpse of intricate, tribal-like tattoos on his chest in the instant before he swooped down on her with a fevered kiss. "I need to be inside you," he growled, sounding dark and hungered, the rough scrape of his deep voice virtually unrecognizable. "Now, Savannah."

"Yes," she agreed, needing to feel more of him too. "Now."

He claimed her with a kiss so savage and carnal, it rocked her. She felt herself moving backward swiftly, her feet hardly touching the floor. She came up hard against the wall of the bedroom, Gideon's big body covering her. His mouth still locked on hers, his strong hands drifted down to cup the cheeks of her ass. He squeezed her possessively, his erection rising hot and proud against her hip. He shifted his weight on his feet, catching her in a different hold now. Then he lifted her as though she weighed no more than a feather, guiding her legs around him.

He felt so good against her, warm and hard and hungry.

So real.

In the midst of so much terror and confusion, being with Gideon was the only place she felt safe.

She'd never known anything that felt so right.

"Take me now," she murmured. "Take all that you want, Gideon."

He didn't answer. Not in words, that is.

Holding her aloft in his hands, he thrust his pelvis forward and seated her to the hilt on the thick spear of his cock. He moved with urgent strokes, in and out, deeper and then deeper still, pistoning her on his length.

Savannah felt tension rack him as his tempo increased to a fevered pitch. His shoulders were granite under her curled fingers, his muscles bunched and knotted as she clung to him and let him chase his own climax.

He found it swiftly, his hips bucking wildly, pushing farther inside with every claiming pound of his flesh against hers. Savannah was already breaking apart again, splintering with pleasure, as Gideon roared a wordless, reverent-sounding oath and filled her with the hot rush of his release.

CHAPTER 11

Bill Keaton knew he had company at his house in Southie that night, even before the tall, impeccably suited man peeled away from the shadows inside the front door. He'd been expecting this visit, forbidden to ever seek the man out, but to wait always for his instructions. To carry them out without question or failure. Keaton was loath to disappoint, and he knew the news he had to impart tonight would not be welcome.

He got up from his recliner and left his half-baked frozen dinner sitting untouched on the TV tray to greet his visitor. Behind him in the living room, the television blared with sirens and gunshot sound effects. One of those cop dramas he watched every week, but now couldn't recall why. Like the salisbury steak and mashed potatoes he'd warmed up for dinner more than an hour ago, he found he no longer had the taste for any of the things he once enjoyed.

He was different since the incident at the university a few nights ago.

He was a changed man.

And the cause of that change now stood before him in expectant silence inside Keaton's house. Keaton gave a deferential nod of greeting, as respectful as a bow.

"Did the individual sent to deal with the girl show up as planned tonight?"

"Yes," Keaton replied, eyes remaining downcast, subservient. "Everything was in place, just as we discussed."

"So, the girl is dead?"

"She is not," Keaton answered, anxious now. He hazarded to lift his eyes and meet the hard stare of the one he served. "She lives. I saw her leave the station with a man."

The shrewd gaze narrowed on him, sparking with deadly fire. "What man?"

"Big," Keaton said. "Tall. A blond thug in a black leather trench coat. I saw weaponry belted at his waist, but he was no police officer or law enforcer. And he was not mortal."

This Keaton understood with full certainty, just one of the new senses he'd acquired a few nights ago, when his eyes were opened to a dark, hidden new world. The world this man showed him when he made Keaton all over again.

"Did they see you—the girl and her companion?"

Keaton gave a slow shake of his head. "No. I realized what he was, and so I made sure not to be noticed. He is one of your kind."

A grunt of acknowledgment, while the fire in those predator's eyes crackled even more coldly. "Of course, he is one of my kind. All the worse, he's one of the Order." Then, more to himself, he mused, "Could he possibly know about me? Does he realize I have that sword, after all this time?"

The sharp gaze came back to Keaton now. "You saw them leave the station together. Where did they go?"

"I don't know," Keaton answered, supposing that he should feel fear to admit that, yet compelled only to speak the truth to the one who owned him now. "I saw the girl and her companion exit the terminal, but then they vanished. I don't know where they've gone. I went to her apartment in Allston to wait, but they never arrived there."

A growl erupted from between gritted teeth. "I need to find that girl before she tells the Order what she knows. Fuck, it may be too late for that already."

"Shall I locate the individual we sent to the station tonight and have him stake out her apartment?" Keaton offered, eager to provide a solution.

His suggestion earned only a dismissive wave. "That particular weapon is of no use now. Gideon will have killed the Rogue for certain. Then again, maybe this setback can work to my advantage." A dark smile broke over his ageless, unlined face. "To think, I nearly killed my Breedmate when she stupidly gave away a number of my private mementos to the university. She didn't know, of course. She couldn't know. I never told her about that sword or how I came to have it."

"And now you have it in your possession again," Keaton said. "I am pleased to have served you in retrieving what belongs to you."

The answering bark of laughter was sharp-edged, humorless. "As I recall," he muttered, "I gave you no choice, Keaton. Once you saw what I did to that slut you were fucking in your office, you broke easily enough."

Keaton felt no reaction to the reminder of his cowardice. He was detached from the whole event, freed of all the weaknesses of his former self. All that mattered to him now was doing what was needed, what his Master commanded of him.

"I will see to it that the task is carried out as you wish, Sire. Savannah Dupree will die."

"No. I think not." The vampire who owned Keaton's life and mind now—his soul itself—paused with unrushed deliberation. "I have a better plan. Find her. Bring her to me. Since she obviously is of some interest to the warrior, Gideon, she can help me finish a score he started centuries ago."

~ ~ ~

Take all that you want.

Savannah's tender offer pounded in Gideon's temples—in his blood—hours after they'd made love. He'd left her satiated and softly sleeping in the bedroom a short while ago, while he slipped out to the main room of the empty old house to work off some of his restless energy.

Shirtless, dressed only in his black fatigues, he went through a series of quick, sweeping combat maneuvers with the long dagger from his weapons belt. He kept his hands and body in much-needed motion. His mind churned on vivid recollections of the passion he'd shared with Savannah, earth-shaking passion that still had his veins lit up and electric. Other parts of his anatomy were running on a short leash too.

But undercurrent of the incredible pleasure he'd taken from Savannah was the guilt he felt for having hidden himself—his true self—from her, even while she had surrendered everything she had to him.

Take all that you want, Gideon.

"Fuck," he muttered, low beneath his breath. If she only knew how much he wanted.

He pivoted on his bare heel to make a savage swipe at an invisible opponent. Himself, or the Rogue who accosted Savannah tonight? He wasn't sure who was the bigger villain tonight.

He needed to tell her what he was. It would have to be Savannah's choice how she chose to think of him, after he gave her the truth she rightfully deserved a few hours ago.

The truth she deserved from the moment he first realized the pretty, innocent young student was a Breedmate, not a simple *Homo sapiens* female. Savannah deserved a hell of a lot more than he'd given her so far.

And if he was being honest with himself, she deserved more than he could ever hope to offer her as the mate of a male whose past was steeped in bloodshed and failure. A warrior whose future was pledged in full to the Order.

He needed to explain all of that and more to Savannah. Damn it, he'd meant to before things had gotten so far out of hand tonight. He'd let himself get too entangled, and now he was caught in a trap of his own making.

It would take time and some doing to make things right now. Time alone with Savannah being a luxury he didn't expect he'd have for much longer.

After what happened at the bus terminal, it was imperative that Savannah be given the full protection and sanctuary the Breed nation had to offer. Before the danger that pursued her came any closer than it had earlier tonight.

As much as Gideon wanted to deny it, it was no coincidence that the Rogue just happened to go after Savannah at the station. He had stalked her there. Not through blood thirst or basic opportunity. Gideon would bet his sword arm that someone had sent the suckhead after her.

More than likely, the same someone who had killed her roommate and left her professor for dead. The same someone who was now, apparently, in possession of the sword used to slaughter Gideon's kin.

He needed to find the bastard and bring him down.

Before Savannah ended up any further into the crossfire.

They couldn't stay here forever. Wherever they were. Tegan had never mentioned this place before. Even though the warrior had offered the old house up to Gideon, he had no misconceptions that Tegan meant it to be a very temporary shelter. Frankly, Gideon had to agree with Savannah that the place felt more like a neglected tomb than a home.

As much as Gideon hated to admit it, she needed to be moved to a more suitable, more permanent, arrangement. And unless he had lost his mind and meant to defy Lucan Thorne's edict for a second time in so many days, he couldn't very well bring Savannah to the compound. Gideon could just imagine how the Order's unyielding Gen One leader would react to a civilian being brought there against long-standing Order protocol.

But if she went there as Gideon's mate?

The notion hit him hard. Not because it was a fucking crazy, bad idea. But because of how sane and right it felt to him.

Savannah at his side, bonded together in blood and life for somewhere close to forever.

Take all that you want, Gideon.

Savannah, his Breedmate.

Holy hell . . . .

The thought opened up something hot and deep in his chest. A longing. A yearning so total, it rendered him motionless, unbreathing.

Ah, Christ.

The bloody last thing he needed was to let himself fall in love with Savannah.

He cursed roundly, making a vicious stab at the air with the long dagger he'd used to gut the Rogue who'd gone after Savannah. Pivoting on his bare heel, he lunged into another mock strike, this one intended for the unknown enemy he was determined to unmask—right before he would force that Breed male to swallow the same steel that killed his Rogue errand boy.

It was at that moment Gideon heard a soft stirring in the other room.

Savannah was out of bed. She drifted into the open doorway of the adjacent room where he stood, the long dagger gripped in his hand, his motion suspended in the stance of a man poised to kill.

"Savannah."

She stared at him, her big brown eyes still drowsy, her beautiful, lithe body utterly naked. So stunning.

Gideon drank in the sight of her with a greedy gaze, his pulse kicking with swift, fierce arousal.

But she wasn't looking at him the same way.

She seemed stricken somehow. Wooden with silent shock.

"Oh, my God," she murmured after a moment. Her voice was small and breathless, though not from sleep or desire. She gaped at him in a mix of shock and hurt, her pretty face twisted with confusion. "Oh, my God...I knew you looked familiar. I knew I'd seen you somewhere before—"

"Savannah, what's wrong?" He set the blade down on the fireplace mantel and headed toward her.

"No." She shook her head, held out a hand as if to bar him from getting any closer. "I saw you before, Gideon. When I held the old sword, I saw the murder of those two little boys all those years ago...but I also saw you."

His blood ran cold in the face of her fear. "Savannah—"

"I saw you, like this, with a blade in your hand—the way you looked just now," she said, talking over him. "Except it wasn't you. It couldn't be you."

He didn't speak, couldn't refute what she was saying. What she saw with her Breedmate's gift.

"I mean, how could it be you, right?" she pressed, a raw edge to her words. "The man I saw should be a couple of centuries dead by now."

"I can explain," he offered lamely.

He stepped closer toward her, but she flinched away. She crossed her arms over herself as if she were naked in front of a stranger now. "You're not human," she murmured. "You can't be."

He cursed softly. "I don't want you to be afraid of me, Savannah. If you would just hear me out now—"

"Oh, God." She barked out a sharp laugh. "You're not even going to try to deny it?"

He felt a tendon tick heavily in his jaw. "I wanted to explain everything to you, but not while you were upset. You said yourself tonight you weren't ready to hear more."

She staggered back a pace, shaking her head in mute denial. Her stare had gone distant, turning inward. He was losing her. She was pulling away from him as something to be mistrusted, feared. Maybe even reviled. "I have to get out of here," she murmured flatly. "I have to go home. I have to call my sister. She was expecting me to be on the bus tonight, and I..."

She broke away then, turning to rush back into the bedroom. She made a frantic circuit of the room, started retrieving her clothing.

Gideon followed her. "Savannah, you can't run away from this. You're in too deep now. We both are."

She didn't respond. She grabbed her panties off the floor and hastily stepped into them, flashing the dark thatch of silk between her legs and giving him an intimate glimpse of her long, satiny thighs and creamy mocha skin.

Skin he'd tasted everywhere and longed to savor again.

Without speaking to him or looking at him, she searched for her bra. Her small breasts swayed with her movements as she shrugged into the little scrap of lace.

Arousal stirred inside Gideon, too powerful for him to hold back. He couldn't curb his swift physical reaction to the sight of her, so pretty and disheveled from his lovemaking of a few hours ago. His *glyphs* started to churn to life on his skin. His gums tingled with the awakening of his fangs.

Hastily, she grabbed up her sweater and jeans, holding them to her as she rushed past him, head-down, out of the bedroom.

He followed swiftly, stalking behind her.

"Savannah, you can't leave. I can't let you go home now. It's too late." His voice was gravel, roughened by his rising desire and the fierce need to make her understand the full truth now.

He flashed over to where she stood, faster than she could possibly track him. He put his hand on her shoulder where the small scarlet teardrop-and-crescent-moon Breedmate mark stamped her flawless skin. "Damn it, stop shutting me out. Listen to me."

She whirled around, her eyes wide. His own gaze felt hot in his skull, must have blazed back at her in that moment as bright as lit coals. By some miracle of deception and desperate will, he'd been able to conceal his transformation from her earlier tonight, but not now. Nor did he try.

"Oh, my God," she moaned, fear bleeding into her voice. She struggled in his hold, turned her head askance on a strangled gasp of horror.

Gideon took her chin and gently guided her face back toward his. "Savannah, look at me. See me. Trust me. You said you did."

Her eyes fell slowly to his open mouth and the tips of his fangs, which stretched longer every second. After a long moment, she looked back up into his fiery stare. "You're one of them. You're a monster, just like them. A Rogue—"

"No," he denied firmly. "Not Rogue, Savannah. But I am Breed, like they are. Like they were, before they lost themselves to Bloodlust."

"A vampire," she clarified, maybe needing to say the word out loud. Her voice dropped to something less than a whisper. "Are you undead?"

"No." He resisted the urge to laugh off the crude misconception as ridiculous, but only because she was so obviously horrified at the thought. "I'm not undead, Savannah. That's where myth and reality differ the most when it comes to my kind. The Breed is otherworldly in origin. Big difference."

She gaped at him now, studying him. He didn't mind her blatant inspection, since the longer he stood still before her, the calmer she seemed to become. "You have nothing to fear from me," he told her, speaking the words as a promise. A solemn vow. "You need never fear me, Savannah.."

She swallowed hard, her gaze flicking over every inch of his face, his mouth, his *dermaglyph*-covered chest and shoulders.

When she hesitantly lifted her hand then dropped it back to her side again, Gideon took her fingers in a loose grasp and gently brought her palm to his mouth. He kissed its warm center, giving her none of his sharp edges, only the soft, warm heat of his mouth. Then he guided her hand to his chest, resting it over the heavy beat of his heart. "Feel me, Savannah. I'm flesh and blood and bone, just like you. And I will never harm you."

She kept her hand there, even after he let go. "Tell me how any of this is possible," she murmured. "How can any of this be real?"

Gideon smoothed his fingers along her cheek, then down along the pulse point of her carotid, that fluttered like a caged bird against the pad of his thumb. "Get dressed first," he instructed her tenderly, more for his own good than hers. "Then sit down and we'll talk."

She glanced over at the lone wooden chair in the living room of Tegan's desolate house. To Gideon's relief, she looked back at him not in terror or revulsion, but with the arch wisdom and keen wit of a woman better than twice her young age. "Time for me to risk my own Seat Perilous?"

"I doubt there's ever been anyone more worthy," he replied.

And if he wasn't already half in love with her, Gideon reckoned he fell a little harder in that moment.

CHAPTER 12

Gideon had paced in front of her the entire time he spoke. Now that he had finished, he finally paused, watching her with an expectant, oddly endearing kind of silence as Savannah worked to absorb everything she'd just heard.

"Are you all right?" he asked carefully, when the weight of her new education rendered her speechless. "Still with me, Savannah?"

She nodded, trying to make all the pieces fit together in her mind.

The whole incredible history of his kind and where they came from, how they lived in secret alongside humans for thousands of years. And how Gideon and a small number of like-minded, courageous Breed males—modern-day, dark knights, from the sound of it—worked together as a unit right there in Boston to keep the city safe from the violence of Rogues.

It was all pretty mind-boggling.

But she believed him.

She trusted him at his word that the fantastical tale he'd just told her was the truth.

It was, whether she was prepared to accept it or not, her new reality.

A reality that seemed a little less terrifying having Gideon in it with her.

She glanced up at him. "Vampires from outer space, huh?"

He smiled wryly. "The Ancients were otherworlders, not little green men. Deadly predators unlike this planet has ever seen. The very top of the food chain."

"Right. But their offspring—"

"The Breed."

"The Breed," she said, still testing everything out in her mind.

"They're part human?"

"Hybrid progeny of the Ancients and Breedmates, females like you," he clarified.

Savannah reached up to her left shoulder blade, where a small birthmark declared her the other half of Gideon's kind. She exhaled a soft laugh and shook her head. "Mama used to say it was a faerie's kiss."

Gideon stepped toward her where she sat on the old wooden chair. He gave a mild shrug. "Something made you and those others born with that mark different from other women. Who's to say it wasn't faeries?" His mouth curved in a tender, intimate smile. "It makes you very special, Savannah. Extraordinary. But you would be both those things and more, even without your mark."

Their eyes met and held for a long moment. Savannah watched, mesmerized, as the fiery sparks in his bright blue irises glittered like stars. His pupils had thinned to slender, vertical slits—inhuman, like a cat's eye. Maybe she should have been alarmed or repulsed; instead she was transfixed, astonished to see the change coming over him in so many intriguing, fantastical ways.

She reached out to him, invited him closer. He stepped between her knees and sank down on his haunches. His big body radiated a palpable heat. Where her knees and thighs touched him, she could feel the hard hammer of his pulse. Her own heartbeat seemed to answer it, falling into his rhythm as though they were one and the same being.

Savannah couldn't resist touching him.

His bare chest, shoulders, and powerful, muscled arms were alive with a tangle of intricate arcs and swirls that covered him, just a shade darker than his golden skin.

Dermaglyphs, he'd explained, along with the rest of what he'd told her.

She traced one of the patterns over his firm pectoral with her fingertip and marveled at how its color deepened at her touch. She followed the graceful swell and dip of the *glyph*, watching it come to life and flood from tawny gold to dark jewel tones.

"They're beautiful," she said, and heard his low rumble of approval deep in his chest as she teased more color into other places on his velvety skin. He had fascinated her from the moment she first met him under the Abbey murals at the library. But she was curious about him in a new way now. She wanted to know him better, wanted to know everything about her lover who was something much more than a man. "I could play with your *dermaglyphs* all day," she admitted, unable to hide her wonder and delight. "I love how the colors change to wine and indigo when I touch them."

"Desire," he rasped thickly. "That's what those colors mean."

She glanced up and saw a growing hunger in his handsome face, heard it in his low, rough-edged voice. "Your eyes," she said, noticing how the sparks had multiplied, now more of an amber glow, slowly swamping the blue of his irises. "When we made love earlier, I felt the heat of your gaze. I saw there was a fire coming to life in your eyes. This kind of fire. You hid it from me."

"I didn't want to frighten you." A flat, unabashed admission.

"I'm not afraid now, Gideon. I want to know." She reached out to him, cupped his rigid jaw in her palm. "I want to understand."

He stared at her for a long moment, then growled her name and covered her mouth in a long, slow kiss.

Savannah melted into him, swept up in the heat and pleasure of his lips on hers. She hungered for a deeper taste, testing the seam of his mouth with her tongue. He didn't give way to her at first, groaning as if to refuse her.

She wouldn't let him hide from her. Not now. Not again, not ever when they were together.

She scooted to the edge of the chair and wrapped her hands around the back of his head, spearing her fingers into the silk of his short hair. She traced her tongue along his mouth, insistent, pressing her body to his.

He gave up with a low curse and she pushed inside, thrilling to the feel of his hungered mouth. The sharp tips of his fangs scraped her tongue as she kissed him deeper. When she could hardly take it any longer, she drew back to look him full in the face.

There was little left to confuse him with a mortal man. His eyes were blazing, fangs enormous and razor-sharp. His *dermaglyphs* were livid with dark color, churning like living things on his skin.

He was magnificent.

And she felt no fear as she drank in his full transformation.

"Take me to bed, Gideon. Make love to me again, now, like this. I want to be with you just the way you are."

With an otherworldly snarl of agreement, he swept her roughly off the seat and into his strong arms.

Then he rose and carried her into the bedroom as she'd commanded.

~ ~ ~

Gideon had never seen anything lovelier than the look of pleasure on Savannah's face as she climbed toward orgasm, her dark eyes locked on his gaze while she rode him in an unrushed, but slowly increasing, tempo.

They'd left the bed sometime before morning had dawned outside the sealed-up townhouse. Now, they sat face to face in a tub of warm bathwater, Savannah straddling him, his cock buried deep inside her tight sheath, her breasts dancing in tantalizing motion in front of his thirsting eyes and hungry mouth. He couldn't resist pulling one of the pert brown nipples between his teeth, rolling his tongue over the tight little peak and gently grazing the tip of his fangs along the supple curve of her flesh.

She drew in a sharp, shivery breath when he closed his mouth down on her a bit harder, just enough to remind her what he was and to torment himself with the want he felt to take things further with her—to make her his in every way.

Making love to her openly, without fear or concealment of his true nature, had been amazing. Mind-blowingly good. They had exhausted each other last night, sleeping for a short while in each other's arms before waking more than once to kiss and caress and make love all over again.

Gideon knew he should have broken away at some point to report in to the compound, but he hadn't been able to find the will to leave the bed he'd shared with Savannah. The way things were going this morning, he might never make it back. Savannah rocked on him, their eyes locked, her face aglow with the amber light of his pleasured gaze.

He stroked her face and throat as she moved on him in a deeper, faster rhythm. The bathwater lapped around them noisily, the sound of their lovemaking wet and erotic. She started to come then, soft moans slipping through her parted lips.

Gideon gripped her ass in a firmer hold and moved his pelvis in time with her undulations. His cock felt like hot steel inside the tight clutch of her body, pressure building to a fever pitch at the base of his spine. His fangs filled his mouth. His gums throbbed with the urge to taste the graceful column of Savannah's neck as she threw her head back and cried out with her climax.

Gideon followed her over the edge a moment later, his orgasm racking him in a full-body heave and a coarse shout of release. He shuddered inside her, wave after wave of scalding heat shooting out of him. He swore her name, prayer or curse, he didn't know.

She smiled as he filled her, her dark eyes drinking him in, even though he knew he must look savage and unearthly. She didn't shrink away. Not his Savannah, not now.

She slumped against him, limp and satiated. Gideon held her close, smoothing his hands along her back. Her breath was warm against the side of his neck, her lips soft and moist on the pulse point where she rested, making his carotid jump and pound in response.

"I can't get enough of you," she murmured. "Are you working some kind of Breed mojo on me that makes me want you so bad?"

He chuckled. "If only I had that kind of power. I'd never let you out of my bed. Or my bathtub."

"Or off the chair in the other room," she added, a reminder of yet another location they'd made use of in the past few blissful hours.

Gideon's arousal woke anew at the thought, and he wondered how intense their lovemaking would be if they were mated, sharing a blood bond. One little bite and she would be his forever. Dangerous thinking. Something he wasn't prepared to consider, no matter how much his body seemed to feel otherwise.

"I can't get enough of you, either," he told her, pressing a kiss to her temple. "It's been a long time since I've been with someone. I've had to remember all over again how it's done. Although I can't think of anything better than studying your body and learning all the ways to please you."

He felt her smile against him. "Well, you're doing everything right."

"I'm a fast study."

Savannah laughed and nestled in closer, mostly on top of him in the cramped, Victorian-era tub. Her long leg was draped over him, her arms wrapped around his chest. Gideon stroked her arm. "For a long time, I've been putting all of my energy and focus into the Order's missions. I'm definitely slacking there now. I'll likely have hell to pay—and rightly so—when I report back about where I've been."

Savannah lifted her head, studying his face. "How long?"

"How long since I've wanted anyone the way I want you?"

She nodded.

"Never," he said. "You're a first in that regard. I've had my share of liaisons. Thoughtless dalliances that meant nothing to me."

"How long since you've made love?" she pressed.

"The last time?" He shrugged. "Eighteen or nineteen years, if I had to guess." The span of her whole lifetime, which seemed somehow fitting to him now. "It wasn't memorable, Savannah. None of them were, compared to this. Compared to you."

She grew quiet, tracing a *glyph* on his chest. "I've only been with one guy before—Danny Meeks, a boy from my hometown. High school jock, varsity quarterback, homecoming king...the boy every girl in school dreamed of being with."

Gideon grunted, feeling a surge of bald possessiveness. He wanted to make a smartass comment about steakhead athletes with IQs smaller than his boot size, but he could sense Savannah holding back as she spoke.

"What did he do to you?" he asked, his possessiveness darkening toward fury with his suspicion that the stupid boy-man had wounded her somehow.

"I thought he really liked me. He had his pick of anyone he wanted in school, and he'd just broken up with the prettiest, most popular girl in my class. But there he was, pursuing me." She sighed softly, still moving her finger along the curve of Gideon's *dermaglyphs*, whose color was rising not in desire again, but anger for her pain. "We went on a few dates, and after several weeks, he started pressuring me to take things further with him. I was a virgin. I wanted to wait until I met the right one, you know?"

Gideon caressed her arm, letting her talk, while inside he knew where this was heading and he didn't like it.

"Finally, I gave in," she said. "We had sex, and it was awful. It hurt. He was clumsy and rough."

Gideon growled. He didn't want to imagine her with another man, let alone one who would be so careless with her.

"We dated for a couple of months afterward," she went on. "Danny never treated me any better. He just took what he wanted from me. After a while, I started hearing rumors that he had been calling his old girlfriend again. That he was only with me to make her jealous. They got back together, and I didn't even know about it until I saw them making out at one of his games. He never cared about me at all. He pretended to be one thing with me, but the whole time we were together, he was only using me to get something he really wanted."

"Bastard," Gideon snarled. He was pulsing with fury, wanting nothing better than to teach the little asshole a lesson. Throttle the human son of a bitch for hurting her. "Savannah, I'm sorry."

"It's okay." She shook her head where it rested against his chest. "I learned from it. It made me more careful. More protective of myself, of my heart. And then you came along..."

She looked up into his eyes. "I've never imagined I could feel all the things I feel with you, Gideon. I never understood how lost I've felt—all my life—until I found you. I think it must've been fate that brought us together at the library a few nights ago."

A pang of guilt stabbed him at the mention of how they'd first met. Only he knew it hadn't been fate at all that sent him to her that night. He'd first sought her out as a warrior on a private mission to gather intel on the sword and whoever had it now.

That mission had soon changed, once he came to know Savannah. Once he came to care about her so swiftly, so deeply. He should have come clean about their initial meeting before now. He should have done it right then—would have—but before he could summon the first word, she covered his mouth in a tender kiss.

It was all he could do not to end her sweet kiss and blurt out the other damning words that were on the tip of his tongue: *Be with me. Bond with me. Let me be your mate.*

But it wasn't fair to ask so much of her, not when she was just entering his world and he still had unfinished business to attend.

He still had hidden enemies to eliminate. And he wouldn't assume for one moment that killing the Rogue who'd accosted her at South Station removed the whole of the threat that was stalking Savannah.

Recalling that encounter made him go tense and sober. She must have felt the change in him, for Savannah drew back from him now. "What is it? What's wrong?"

"Last night, at the bus terminal," he said. "Did you notice anyone following you? Watching you, before or after you arrived? I don't mean the Rogue that cornered you, but someone else. Someone who might have been aware that it was happening."

"No. Why?" Apprehension flickered in her searching gaze. "Do you think the Rogue was with others? Do you think I was targeted somehow?"

"I think it's a very real possibility, Savannah. I'm not willing to assume otherwise." Gideon didn't want to alarm her unnecessarily, but she also had to understand how dangerous the situation could be for her outside. "I think the Rogue was sent to find you for someone else."

More than likely, sent to silence her, a thought that made his blood go icy in his veins.

Savannah stared at him. "Because of what happened to Rachel and Professor Keaton? You mean, you think the one who attacked them is now after me? Why?"

"The sword, Savannah. What else did you see when you touched it?"

She shook her head. "I told you. I saw the Rogues who killed those two little boys. And I saw you, striking someone with the blade. You killed someone with it."

Gideon gave a grim nod. "In a duel, many years ago, yes. I killed the Breed male who made the sword. His name was Hugh Faulkner, a Gen One Breed and the best sword maker in London at the time. He was also a prick and a bastard, a deviant who took his pleasure in bloodshed. Particularly when it came to human women."

"What happened?"

"One night in London, Faulkner showed up at a Cheapside tavern with a human female under his arm. She was in bad shape, pale and unresponsive, nearly bled out." Gideon couldn't curb the disgust in his tone. There were laws among his race meant to protect humans from the worst abuses of Breed power, but there were also individuals among their kind like Faulkner, those who regarded themselves above any law.

"Few of the Breed males in the establishment would consider rising up against a Gen One, especially one as nasty as Faulkner. But I couldn't abide what he had done to the woman. Words were exchanged. The next thing I knew, Faulkner and I were outside in the darkness, engaged in a contest to the death over the fate of the woman." Gideon recalled it as if the confrontation had just happened yesterday, not some three-hundred years in the past. "I had earned some renown for my skill with a sword, more so than Faulkner, as it turned out. He lost his blade almost immediately and stumbled. It was a fatal misstep. I could've taken his head then and there, but in an act of mercy—stupidity, in hindsight—I stayed my hand."

"He cheated?" Savannah guessed.

Gideon gave a vague nod. "The minute I turned to walk away and retrieve his fallen blade, Faulkner began to rise up to come at me. I realized my mistake at once. I recovered quickly—and before Faulkner could get to his feet, I rounded back on him and cleaved him in half with his own damned sword."

Savannah sucked in a soft breath. "That's what I saw. You, killing him with the sword I touched."

"I won the contest and sent the human woman away to be looked after until she was well again," Gideon replied. "As for Faulkner's sword, I wish I'd left it where it lay that night, next to his corpse."

Understanding dawned in Savannah's tender eyes. "The twin boys I saw playing with the sword before they were attacked in the stable by Rogues..."

"My brothers," he confirmed. "Simon and Roderick."

"Gideon," she whispered solemnly. "I'm sorry for your loss."

"A long time ago," he said.

"But you still feel it. Don't you?"

He released a heavy sigh. "I was to blame for not protecting them. Our parents were dead. The boys were my responsibility. Several weeks after the confrontation with Faulkner, I was out carousing in the city. Simon and Roddy were young, not even ten years old, but old enough to hunt on their own as Breed youths. I took it for granted that they'd be safe enough on their own for a few hours that night."

Savannah reached over and pulled his fisted hand up to her lips, kissed the tightly clenched knuckles with sweet compassion. He relaxed his fingers to twine them with hers. "My brothers were the reason I came to Boston. I joined the Order t hunt Rogues, after killing the three who murdered the boys, as well as dozens more for good measure."

"Hundreds more," Savannah reminded him.

He grunted. "I thought killing Rogues would make the guilt about my brothers lessen, but it hasn't."

"How long have you been trying to make it better, Gideon?"

He exhaled a low oath. "Simon and Roddy were killed three centuries ago."

She lifted her head up and stared at him. Gaped at him. "Exactly how old are you?"

"Three-hundred and seventy-two," he drawled. "Give or take a few months."

"Oh, my God." She dropped her head back down on his chest and laughed. Then laughed again. "I thought Rachel was nuts for lusting after Professor Keaton, and he was only in his forties. I'm falling in love with a total relic."

Gideon stilled. "Falling in love?"

"Yes," she replied quietly, but without hesitation. She glanced up at him. One slender black brow arched wryly. "Don't tell me that's all it takes to scare a three-hundred and seventy-two-year-old vampire."

"No," he said, but he did feel a sudden wariness.

Not because of her sweet confession; he would come back to that tempting pronouncement another time.

Right now, his warrior instincts were buzzing with cold alarm. He sat up in the tub, frowning.

"Keaton," he said flatly. "When is he due out of the hospital?"

"He is out," Savannah replied. "I saw him yesterday on campus. He looked awful, but he said he'd made a full recovery and the hospital released him earlier than expected. He was acting kind of odd—"

Gideon tensed. "Odd in what way?"

"I don't know. Weird. Creepy. And he lied to me when I asked him about the attack."

"Tell me."

She shrugged. "He told me he saw who killed Rachel and attacked him that night. Keaton said it was a vagrant, but the glimpse I got from Rachel's bracelet showed me a man in a very expensive suit. A man with amber eyes and fangs."

"Holy shit." Why he didn't see it before, Gideon had no idea. The attacker killed Savannah's roommate, but left the professor alive. That was no accident. "What else did Keaton say to you?"

"Nothing much. Like I said, he was just acting strangely, not like himself. I didn't feel safe around him."

"Did Keaton know you were going to the bus station last night?"

She paused, thinking. "I told him I was going home to Louisiana. I might have mentioned I was taking the bus—"

Gideon snarled and got out of the tub. Water sluiced off his naked limbs and torso. "I need to see Keaton for myself. It's the only way I can be certain." He thought about the hour of the day—probably just past noon—and cursed roundly.

Savannah climbed out too, and stood beside him. She put her hand on his shoulder. "Gideon, what do you need to be certain of?"

"Keaton's injuries the night of the attack," he said. "I need to know if he was bitten."

"I don't know. I didn't see that much when I touched Rachel's bracelet." She stared at him in confusion. "Why? What will it tell you if Keaton was bitten?"

"If I see him, I'll know right away if he's still human or if he's been bitten and bled by his attacker. I need to know if he's been made a Minion to the vampire who took that sword from the university."

"A Minion." Savannah went quiet now. "If Keaton was bitten, that will tell you what you need to know?"

"Yes." He raked a hand over his scalp. "The problem with that is, I'm trapped indoors until sundown."

"Gideon," she said. "What if I see Keaton now?"

"What do you mean?" He bristled at the thought of her getting anywhere near the man. "You're not going anywhere without me. I won't risk that."

She shook her head. "I mean, maybe I can tell you if Keaton was bitten during the attack." At his answering scowl, she said, "I still have Rachel's bracelet."

"Where?"

"Here, with me. It's in my purse in the other room."

"I need you to go get it, Savannah. Now."

CHAPTER 13

Savannah woke up from an unusually heavy doze, in bed alone.

How long had she been asleep? Her head felt thick, like she was coming out of a light anesthesia.

Where was Gideon?

She called out to him, but the empty house was silent. Pushing herself up from the mattress, she made a bleary-eyed scan of the dark bedroom. "Gideon?"

No response.

"Gideon, where are you?"

She sat up and tossed the sheet away from her. Turned on the bedside lamp. On the pillow next to her lay a piece of paper. A note scribbled on the back of the unused bus ticket that had been in her purse. The handwriting was crisp, precise, forward-tilting and bold— just like him.

Sorry had to do it like this. You're safe here. Back soon.

Savannah looked around the bedroom. Gideon's clothes were gone. His boots and weapons. Every last trace of him, gone.

She knew where he went.

Through the fog of whatever he'd done to her, she recalled his explosive reaction when she'd used Rachel's bracelet for another glimpse of the vampire attack that night in Professor Keaton's office.

Keaton had been bitten, just as Gideon suspected.

No longer the man he was, but a slave to the command of his vampire Master.

An individual Gideon seemed hellbent to find.

He had nearly climbed the walls with restless energy as the afternoon dragged on outside the house. He couldn't wait to get out of there. He'd paced anxiously, waiting for the chance to head out and confront Keaton, then hunt for the Minion's Master.

Savannah had wanted to go with him, but his refusal had been harsh and unswerving. He'd been adamant that she stay right where she was, leave him to deal with the situation as he saw fit—alone. Or with his brethren of the Order, if necessary.

It wasn't until she had insisted she wouldn't stay behind, digging her heels in with determination equal to his own that he finally gentled.

He'd kissed her tenderly. Brought her into the shelter of his arms, and carefully touched his palm to her forehead. Then...

Then, nothing.

That's all she could remember of the past couple of hours at least.

Sorry had to do it like this, he'd written in his note.

Damn him!

Savannah vaulted off the bed. She threw on her clothes, ran to the front door. She yanked on the latch. It wouldn't budge.

He'd locked her inside?

Pissed now, she went to the windows and tried to open them. Sealed permanently shut, each of them shuttered from outside. The whole house was locked down, she realized, making a frantic perimeter check of the entire place.

She finally came to a rest in the small, empty kitchen, breathless with outrage.

There was no way to get out.

She was imprisoned here, and Gideon was somewhere out there, looking to face off with a powerful enemy on his own.

She knew she couldn't help him—not in the kind of battles he was used to fighting. But to leave her behind like this to wait and worry? To strong-arm her into complying with his will by flexing his Breed power over her? If she wasn't so worried about him, she'd want to kill him herself the next time she saw him.

She choked back a panicky breath. *God, please, let me see him again.*

She sagged down to the rough plank floor on her knees...and noticed something in the far corner of the kitchen that she hadn't seen in her search for a means out of the house.

There was a door in the floor.

Hardly visible, fashioned out of the planks and perfectly level with the rest of the flooring.

With a mix of curiosity and foreboding, Savannah crept toward it and felt around for its seams. She pried her fingers between a couple of the planks and found the hidden, square panel was unhinged and unsecured. She lifted it, slid it aside, and sat back as a draft of cool, damp air breathed out of the dark opening.

Savannah peered down into the space, trying to see if it the gloom led out of the house somewhere, or merely down to an old cellar. A prickle at her nape told her it was neither, but now that she had opened the door, she couldn't simply close it again without having the answer.

A crude ladder was built into the earthen wall below. She slipped down into the hole and carefully climbed about twenty feet to the bottom.

It was a deep pit, lightless, except for the scant illumination spilling in from the kitchen above.

Had she thought the house felt like a tomb last night, when she and Gideon first arrived? This hand-hewn chamber in the cold, dark earth brought the feeling back tenfold.

Who made this?

What was it for?

Savannah peered around the forlorn space. Nothing but dank walls and floor, a place of sorrow and isolation. A place of forgetting.

No, she thought, seeing the purpose of the hidden room only now—a niche carved into the far wall, created to hold the crude wooden box that had been carefully placed within the nook.

This hole in the earth was a place of remembrance.

Of penance.

She drifted closer to the alcove and the aged box it contained. Even without touching it, she could feel the anguish that surrounded the reliquary.

Where had the box come from? Why was it here? Who had set it so deliberately in this place?

She had to know.

Savannah ran her bare hand lightly over the top of the ancient box.

Grief swamped her, seeping straight to her marrow.

A young woman's remains were inside from long, long ago. Ash and bone, anointed in tears. A man's tears.

No, not a man.

A Breed male, unfamiliar to her, mourning his dead mate. Blaming himself for her demise.

Savannah saw him in a flash of her extrasensory gift: A massive warrior with shaggy, tawny hair and piercing gem-green eyes. Eyes that burned hot with rage and sorrow and self-loathing.

His pain was too much, too raw.

Too wrenching for her to take any longer.

She drew her hand away in a hurry and backed off, putting as much distance as she could between herself and the terrible past contained in the box.

Shaken, wanting no more knowledge of this house's hidden rooms or secrets, she ran back upstairs to wait for Gideon's return.

~ ~ ~

After pulling a B&E on the Faculty Administration building at the university as soon as night had fallen, Gideon headed into the working-class neighborhood of Southie, his sights set on the home of one Professor William Charles Keaton.

The run-down, turn-of-the-century New Englander didn't exactly scream swinging bachelor pad, but there was a flashy white Firebird parked on the side driveway that was advertisement enough for a coed skirt-chaser like Keaton.

Or rather, a skirt-chaser like he had been.

After hearing Savannah confirm that afternoon what Gideon had suspected—that Keaton had, in fact, been bitten by the Breed male who attacked him—Gideon was pretty sure the only thing that interested Keaton now was obeying his Master's orders.

Gideon needed to know who Keaton served.

He needed to know who wanted Hugh Faulkner's sword bad enough to kill for it, and why.

He wasn't holding out much hope that Keaton would give up those answers easily, if at all. Interrogating Minions wasn't often the most productive effort. A mind slave's allegiance belonged totally to its Master.

Still, Gideon had to try.

For Savannah's safety, if nothing else.

He'd hated like hell to have to resort to trancing her just before sundown, but he didn't see where he'd had much choice. He never would have gotten out of that house without her. Locking her inside probably wasn't going to win him any hero awards, either.

Shit.

He'd have to add another apology to the rest he owed her—starting with the one he planned to open with as soon as he saw her again.

The one about how he'd let her go on thinking all this time that the way they first met had been simple serendipity. Fate, as she'd christened it, just before her sweet confession that she was falling in love with him.

She needed to know that despite his reasons for seeking her out in the beginning, what he felt for her now—immediately after meeting her, if he were being honest with himself—was real.

She needed to know that she mattered to him, even more than his personal quest for answers about the damned sword and the Breed male who'd been willing to kill for it.

She needed to know that he loved her.

He didn't know a better way to prove that than removing the threat of anyone who sought to do her harm.

Starting with the Minion inside this house.

Gideon entered stealthily, the feeble lock on the old front door no contest at all for the mental command he gave that opened it. A television blared unattended in the living room just off the entryway. A day-old dinner sat dried out in its foil container on the TV tray next to a cushioned brown recliner. Spread open on the seat was a state map of Louisiana.

Son of a bitch.

Gideon had to clamp down hard on the fury that began to boil in his gut as he noted the penciled line tracing down to the south central region of the state.

He swept his gaze all around him, searching for the bodily energy of the house's occupant with his ESP talent. He found Keaton's faint orange glow beneath the floorboards at his feet. The Minion was in the cellar.

Gideon stalked toward the hallway stairwell leading to the basement below.

A dim light was on down there.

Sounds of vague rummaging filtered up the steps...then, abrupt silence.

The Minion had just clued in to the presence of a Breed male other than his Master.

Gideon had one of his guns in hand as he descended the stairs into an open area of the basement. Keaton was gone, fled somewhere to hide, no doubt. Not that he could get far.

Gideon walked down, his gaze straying to a rough-hewn workbench and wallboard hung with home improvement tools and small containers of supplies. A dark duffel bag sat open on the bench. Inside it were coils of rope, a hunting knife, a roll of silver duct tape.

Gideon's blood seethed at the sight of an obvious abduction kit.

Keaton's Master had apparently changed his mind about siccing Rogues on Savannah and now wanted her taken alive. The thought didn't sit any better with Gideon.

He swung his head around the cluttered basement, looking for the Minion.

Found him lurking in a back room of the space.

Gideon strode forward, toward a connected room separated by a beaded curtain. He swept it aside and entered a room decorated in what could only be described as Assorted Early Warfare. The walls sported an extensive collection of muskets and maces, rapiers and powder horns. Evidently, Keaton preferred his history with a dash of bloodshed.

Gideon stalked toward the glow of Keaton's form, concealed behind a closet door at the far end of the room. Gideon wanted to blast a hole in the bastard through the wood panel, but he needed the Minion breathing so he could wring the name of his Master from him.

"Planning a road trip, Keaton?" he asked.

No reply. The Minion made small, urgent movements inside the closet, movements Gideon saw as slight shifts of the human's energy mass. He couldn't kill Keaton outright, but taking off a limb at a time might prove his point.

"We need to have a talk, Keaton. You need to tell me who you serve."

The Minion snickered now. Gideon blew out a curse and shook his head. "You can come out now, or you can come out in pieces."

Again, no response. So Gideon fired a shot into the door.

The Minion grunted upon the impact, but hardly reacted to the pain. Then he started chuckling. Tittering maniacally.

Gideon realized his mistake only a fraction of a second too late.

Keaton opened the closet door. He was smiling, holding two World War II-era grenades in his hands. The pins were already gone.

Holy Christ.

Gideon turned and sped in the other direction.

Made it halfway up the stairs just as the grenades detonated.

The blast threw him into the wall, smoke and debris flying all around him. He hit hard, felt the burn of random shrapnel peppering his back. But he was alive. He was still in one piece. Relief washed over him...until his nostrils filled with the alarming scent of his own blood.

A lot of it.

He shifted from where he had fallen on the stairs and looked down to assess the damage. Hundreds of lacerations and singed skin where the hot shrapnel had hit him. Nothing his Breed genetics couldn't heal on their own in a few hours' time.

But it was the other wound that gave him pause.

The catastrophic rip in his left thigh, which had nearly severed the limb and was currently gushing like a geyser with each heavy pound of his heartbeat.

Blood seeped out of him fast and hard.

His body could mend itself from injury. It had, more times than he'd ever bothered to remember.

But this was bad.

This was deadly bad, even for one of his kind.

CHAPTER 14

A heavy thump hit the front door, drawing Savannah up from the chair with a start.

Gideon?

It seemed like she'd been waiting forever, concern for him and distress over being left alone in the sorrowful old house making time drag endlessly.

Another loud thump sounded from outside the door.

She crossed the room, feeling a surge of relief. "Gideon, is that you?"

She wanted it to be him.

Prayed it was...until she heard the metallic snick of the lock, then the door opened and a large, blood-and-sweat-soaked body slumped in onto the floor.

"Oh, my God. Gideon!"

Savannah raced to him. She dropped down beside him, horrified at his condition. His hair and face, his hands—every exposed inch of him was covered in black ash, sweat and blood. So much blood.

He tried to speak, but all that passed his lips was a rasp of sound. "Keaton," he wheezed. "Minion...he's dead...can't hurt you now."

She blew out a curse that sounded more like a sob. "I don't care about him, damn it. All I care about is you."

He tried to sit up, only to slump back down onto the floor in a heap. Blood was pooling under him, pulsing out from scores of shrapnel wounds and a very severe injury in his thigh.

She glanced down at his leather weapons belt, cinched as a makeshift tourniquet around the upper portion of his leg. She could see muscle in the open gash on his thigh. Holy shit. She could see bone in there too.

"Gideon," she cried. "You need help. You need a hospital—"

"No." He snarled the word, his voice sounding unearthly, lethal.

His eyes were on fire, swamped completely in bright, glowing amber light. His pupils had thinned so much they almost weren't there. His fangs filled his mouth, stretched sharp as daggers between his parted lips as he struggled to drag air into his lungs.

"Get away," he gasped when she reached out to smooth away the soaked hank of hair plastered to his brow. His skin was pale white and waxy. His face contorted in pure agony. "Stay away."

"You have to let me help you." She leaned over him to try to lift him up.

Gideon's eyes rolled hungrily to her throat. "Stay back!"

The hissed command made her flinch, recoil. She stared at him, unsure what to do for him and half-afraid he was already too far gone.

"Gideon, please. I don't know what to do."

"Order," he said thickly. He recited a string of numbers. "Go now...call them."

She tried desperately to remember the sequence, repeated them back to him to be sure. He gave a vague nod, his eyelids drooping, skin growing ever more dangerously pale. "Hurry, Savannah."

"Okay," she said. "Okay, Gideon. I'll call them. Stay with me. I'm gonna get you help."

She flew into the bedroom to retrieve her wallet from her purse and a pen to frantically scribble the digits onto the palm of her hand. Then she raced out of the house and down the street, praying the battered pay phone on the corner wasn't out of service.

Fumbling change into the slot, she then dialed the number Gideon had given her. It rang once, then silence as someone picked up on the other end.

"Um, hello? Hello!"

"Yeah." A deep voice. Dark, arresting. Menacing.

"Gideon told me to call," she blurted in one panicked rush of breath. "Something's happened to him and I—"

Click.

"Hello?"

The dial tone buzzed in her ear.

~ ~ ~

It wasn't even ten minutes later that Savannah found herself standing beside an unresponsive Gideon, staring up into the hard face and unreadable eyes of a massive Breed male dressed in black leather and pulsing with lethal power.

He hadn't knocked, simply strode right in without a word of greeting or explanation. And he'd arrived on foot apparently, from where, Savannah could only guess.

Since she'd met Gideon and learned about his kind, she was coming to simply accept some things as simply part of the new reality.

Still, she could hardly curb the impulse to scrabble out of the disturbing male's way when he came farther inside the house.

The place was his, there could be no doubt about that.

He was the one who put the box of ashes in the hidden room below the kitchen.

It was his wrenching sorrow Savannah had glimpsed when she touched the reliquary.

He stared at her now without any emotion whatsoever. His green eyes didn't so much look at her as through her.

He knew. He knew she'd been down in his private cell filled with death.

Savannah could see the awareness of her breach all over his grim face, although he said nothing to her. Did nothing, except grimly go to Gideon's side. He bent his big body and went down in a crouch on his haunches beside Gideon. A low curse hissed out of big male.

"He won't wake up," Savannah murmured. "After I came back from making the call, I found him like this, unconscious."

"He's lost too much blood." The voice was the same deep, threatening growl that she'd heard on the other end of the line. "He needs proper care."

"Can you save him?"

The tawny head swiveled to face her, bleak green eyes raking her. "He needs blood."

Savannah glanced down at Gideon, recalling his sharp reprimand that she not come near him. He'd been furious, desperately so, even though it had been obvious that he wanted to drink from her— needed to. "He didn't want me. He told me to stay away from him."

That unsettling stare stayed locked on her for a long moment before the vampire returned his attention to his fallen comrade. He inspected Gideon's leg wound, snarling as he assessed the damage. "So, you're the girl."

"Excuse me?"

"The Breedmate my man here hasn't been able to stay away from since he saw you on the TV news earlier this week, talking about the sword used to kill his brothers."

Savannah felt a twinge of confusion. An odd niggle of dread. "Gideon saw me on the news? He knew I'd seen the sword?" She shook her head. "No, that's not right. We met at the library where I work. He didn't know anything about me before then."

The other warrior glanced over at her once more, a flat look that made her discomfort deepen even more.

"Gideon was looking at some of the library's artwork. It was just before closing, and..."

Her words drifted off as an unwanted realization began to settle on her.

Right. He just happened to be at the library, not looking for books, but browsing artwork outside her office. Flirting with her. Quoting Plutarch and practically charming her pants off under the Abbey Room murals.

Pretending he knew nothing about the fact that her roommate had been murdered the night before by a goddamn vampire—one of his own kind.

Savannah felt oddly exposed. Like a fool who had arrived two minutes after a punch line.

"Are you saying he sought me out that night?"

The warrior swore, low under his breath, but he didn't answer her question. There was no need. She knew the truth now. Finally, she supposed.

Gideon had seen her interview on the news and pursued her to get information on someone he was determined to find. Someone he believed was his enemy, perhaps connected to the murders of his brothers.

He'd used her.

That's why he knew where she lived, why he was always in the right place at the right time with her.

He was tracking her the way he would any other prey...or pawn.

God, was everything between them just part of some plan? Some private vendetta he meant to pursue?

Savannah staggered backward a pace, feeling as if she'd just been slapped.

He was still using her today, encouraging her to touch Rachel's bracelet so he could learn more about Keaton and the vampire who'd attacked him.

Now Gideon was lying there at her feet, wounded and weak, unconscious and bleeding—maybe dying—because of his damned quest.

And she was standing over him like an idiot, feeling helpless and afraid...terrified that she had let herself fall in love with him, when all she'd apparently been to him was a means to an end.

It was easier to accept that he was Breed—something far other than human—than it was to realize she'd been played this whole time. The hurt she felt was like cold steel in the center of her being.

One other person had used her to get something he wanted more, but Danny Meeks had only taken her virginity. Gideon had taken her heart.

Savannah took a step back. Then another, watching as Gideon's comrade from the Order adjusted the tourniquet around his savaged thigh and prepared to carry him back to where he belonged.

She felt cool air at her back as she edged out the open door and into the night.

Then she pivoted and bolted, before the first hot tears began to flood her cheeks.

CHAPTER 15

Savannah.

Gideon jolted back to wakefulness on a shout, his sole concern, his every cell, honed in on a single thought...*her.*

He sat up and felt the sharp stab of pain answer from all over his body, the worst of it coming from the deep gash in his thigh. He was in a bed. Lying in the Order's infirmary. He breathed in, and didn't smell any of the ash or sweat or blood that had crusted every square inch of him following his ordeal at the Minion's house. Someone had gone to the trouble of cleaning him up after patching him back together.

"What time is it?" he murmured out loud. How long had he been unconscious? "Ah, shit. What day is it?"

"It's okay, Gideon. Relax." A gentle female hand settled on his bare shoulder. "You're okay. Tegan brought you back to the compound last night."

Last night.

"Danika," he rasped, peeling his eyes open to look up at Conlan's Breedmate, who stood beside him, a roll of white gauze bandages in her hand. "Where is she? Where's Savannah?"

The tall blonde gave a sympathetic shake of her head. "I'm sorry, I don't know."

Damn it. Gideon threw off the sheet and swung his legs around to the side of the bed, ignoring the hot, spearing complaint of his wounds. "I need to see her. I need to find her. Keaton's Master is still out there somewhere. She's not safe—"

"She's gone, man." Tegan stood at the threshold of the infirmary room. His face was grim, barely an acknowledgment as Danika quietly slipped out and left the two warriors alone. "My fault,

Gideon. I didn't know—"

"What happened?" A spike of adrenaline and dread shot into his veins. "What did you do to her?"

"Told her the truth. Which is apparently more than you'd done."

"Ah, fuck." Gideon raked a hand through his hair. "Fuck me. What did you tell her, T?"

A vague shrug, although his green eyes stayed unreadable. "That she's been your personal obsession since you saw her on that newscast the day of the attack at the university."

Gideon groaned. "Shit."

"Yeah, she wasn't exactly happy to hear that."

"I have to go to her. She could be in danger, Tegan. I need to find her and make sure she's all right. I have to make sure she knows that I love her. That I need her."

"You're not in any condition to leave the compound."

"Fuck that." Gideon heaved onto his feet, grimacing at the agony of his wounded leg, but not about to let something as trivial as a recently severed femoral artery keep him from going after the woman he loved. "She's mine. She belongs with me. I'm going to tell her that, and then I'm going to bring her back."

Tegan grunted. "Kind of figured you might say that. And I'm way ahead of you, my man—for once, maybe. Got the Order's charter jet on standby, fueled up and waiting for you at the private hangar. You just need to tell the pilots where you want to go."

"Louisiana," he murmured. "She'll have gone home to Louisiana."

Tegan tossed him a stack of fresh clothing that had been set next to the bed. "What are you waiting for, then? Get the fuck outta here."

~ ~ ~

With the thick shadows of the Atchafalaya swamp looming up ahead, Gideon hopped off the back of the old pickup truck he'd hitched a ride on outside the Baton Rouge airport. His leg wound ached like a son of a bitch with every mile he ran, deeper into the dense vegetation and drooping, moss-laden cypress trees of the basin.

Savannah's sister, Amelie, lived on a remote road in this sparsely populated stretch of marshlands. Gideon knew precisely where to find her; after waking in the infirmary, he'd lingered at the Order's compound only long enough to run a quick hack on the IRS databases, which coughed up her address in no time at all.

He crept off an unpaved road to stalk up on the modest, gray-shingled house with its covered porch and soft-glowing light in the windows. There were no cars in the unpaved driveway out front. No sound coming from within the small abode as he stole toward it.

He climbed up the squat steps leading to the porch and front door, his thigh muscle protesting each flex and movement. His talent reached past the thin walls of the house, searching for telltale life energy. Someone sat in the living room, alone.

Gideon knocked on the front door—only to discover it wasn't closed all the way.

"Savannah?"

A muffled groan answered from inside.

"Savannah!" Gideon had his gun in his hand now, storming into the place, his body filled with alarm.

It wasn't Savannah. Her sister, no doubt. The early middle-aged black woman was bound and gagged on a kitchen chair in the center of the living room. Evidence of a scuffle were all around her, toppled furniture, broken knick-knacks.

But no sign of Savannah.

Amelie Dupree's eyes went wide as Gideon approached her with the pistol gripped in his fist. She screamed through the gag, started to flail in panic on the chair.

"Shh," Gideon soothed, working past his terror for what might have happened to Savannah. He tore Amelie's bonds loose and freed the cloth from around her face and mouth. "I'm not going to hurt you. Where's Savannah? I'm here to protect her."

"They took her!"

Gideon's blood ran cold. "Who took her?"

"I don't know." She shook her head, a sob cracking in her throat. "Couple of men came here, showed up about an hour ago. Tied me up and they took my baby sister away at gunpoint."

Gideon's growl of rage was animalistic, lethal. "Where did they take her? What did these men look like?"

Amelie sagged forward, her head in her hands. "I don't know, I don't know! Oh, God, somebody gotta help her. I gotta call the police!"

Gideon took the woman's shoulders in a firm grasp, compelling her to look at him. "Listen to me, Amelie. You have to stay put, call no one. You have to trust me. I'm not going to let anything happen to Savannah."

She stared at him, doubt swimming in her anguished eyes. "Are you the one? Are you the one who broke her heart back there in Boston, sent her back here last night like her whole world was falling apart?"

He didn't answer to that, even though the blame settled heavily on him. "I'm the one who loves her. More than life itself."

"Don't let them hurt her," she cried. "Don't let those men kill my sweet Savannah."

Gideon gave a solemn shake of his head. "I won't. I swear my life on that."

No sooner had he said it, a vehicle approached, pulling up alongside the house outside. The dull rumble of the engine went silent, followed by the crisp thump of two car doors closing a moment later.

Gideon lifted his head, every battle instinct coming alive inside him. He whirled around to head out the front door, his gun at the ready.

There she was.

Standing on her sister's front lawn in the darkness, caught in a headlock by a human man—a Minion, Gideon realized at once. The big thug held the nose of his pistol jammed up against Savannah's temple. She'd been crying, her face streaked with tears, lips ashen from terror.

All the blood rushed out of Gideon's head, started pounding hard in the center of his chest.

It was then he noticed the second man, a Breed male, standing at ease in the shadows of a cypress tree nearby. He was dressed in a tailored navy wool overcoat, his brown hair impeccably cut, and swept back elegantly from his face. Held in a loose grasp in front of him stood a gleaming length of polished steel. The long blade glittered in the moonlight.

Gideon didn't need to see the hilt to know there would be a bird of prey—a falcon—tooled into the handcrafted grip.

Hugh Faulkner's blade.

But this was not the Gen One sword smith Gideon killed back in

London all those centuries ago. He'd never seen this vampire before, he was certain.

"Drop your weapons, warrior."

Gideon glanced from the Breed male to the Minion holding Savannah, calculating which of the two he should kill first to give her the best odds of getting away unharmed. Neither was a guarantee, and he was loath to risk making a mistake that carried such a high cost.

"Put them down now," the vampire drawled. "Or my man will blow her pretty head off."

Gideon relaxed his hold on the pistol, then stooped to set it down.

"All of them. Slowly."

He took off his weapons belt and put it on the ground at his feet. The bandaged gash on his thigh was bleeding again, seeping through his pant leg.

The other vampire sniffed the air dramatically, lips peeling back in an amused smirk. "Not so untouchable, after all."

Gideon watched the Breed male turn Faulkner's sword on its tip in the moist earth of Amelie Dupree's front yard. "Do I know you?"

The vampire chuckled. "No one did. Not back then."

Gideon tried to place him, tried to figure out if, or when, their paths might have crossed.

"You wouldn't have noticed me. He hardly did, either." There was an acid resentment in the tone, but something else too. An old, bitter hurt. "His unacknowledged bastard. The only kin he had."

Gideon narrowed his gaze on the other male. "Hugh Faulkner had a son?"

A thin, hate-filled smile stretched the polished facade of his face into an ugly sneer. "A teenage son who watched him die at your hand, slaughtered in the open with less regard than might be shown common swine. A son who vowed to avenge him, even thought he had no use for me in life." Hugh Faulkner's bastard smiled a true smile now. "A son who decided to take from my father's killer the only family he had left too."

Gideon bristled, fury spiking in his veins. "My brothers were innocent children. You arranged for those three Rogues to go in and murder them?"

"I thought it would be enough," he replied evenly. "I thought it would settle the score. And it did, for a long time. Even after I came to America to begin a new life under a new name. A name I built into something prestigious, something respectable: Cyril Smithson."

Gideon vaguely recalled the name from among those of the Darkhaven elite. A wealthy, socially important name. One that could be destroyed within the Breed's civilian circles, if word of its patriarch's ignoble, murderous past were to come to light.

"Knowing I took your last living kin might have been enough, even after I found myself in Boston and watched you carrying out your missions as one of the Order," Smithson went on. "But then my do-gooder Breedmate foolishly donated some of my private things to the university, including my father's sword. When I went to retrieve it, Keaton was in his office pounding into a young slut. She saw me and screamed." The Breed male clucked his tongue. "Well, I couldn't be blamed for what happened next. The girl saw my fangs, my eyes."

"So you killed her too," Gideon said.

Smithson shrugged. "She had to be dealt with. Her roommate, here too."

Gideon followed the vampire's glance toward Savannah. She was breathing hard, breast rising and falling rapidly in her fear. Her eyes locked on to Gideon's, pleading, praying.

Smithson spun the sword idly with his fingers. "This blade was never supposed to leave my possession after the Rogues brought it to me with your brothers' blood on it. You were never supposed to know the truth of what happened that night. Now that you do...well, I suppose it's all come back around to the beginning again, hasn't it?"

The vampire lifted the sword, testing its weight. "I'd never been much good with blades. Crude weapons, really. But effective."

"What do you want, Smithson? A contest to the death with me, here and now?"

"Yes." He met Gideon's seething gaze across the yard. "Yes, that's precisely what I want. But I won't underestimate you the way my father did."

He slanted a look at his Minion. Two shots rang out in rapid succession, a bullet for each of Gideon's shoulders.

Savannah screamed. She struggled in her captor's hold now, her eyes tearing up as she looked at Gideon and the barrel of the Minion's pistol came back to her temple.

He barely felt the pain of the new wounds. His focus was rooted wholly on her, and on the wild, desperate expression in her gaze. He gave a faint shake of his head, unspoken command that she not do anything to risk her own life.

"That ought to level the playing field," Smithson remarked as the gunshots continued to echo through the bayou. "On second thought, another for good measure," he told his Minion. "The gut this time."

The Minion's hand started to move away from Savannah's head. Gideon saw it in agonizing slow motion—the twitch of muscle as the human's wrist began to pivot from its primary target to the new one at his Master's command.

Savannah, no!

Gideon didn't even have time to bring the words to his tongue. She seized the opportunity to shift her weight as the Minion's attention flicked away from her. Savannah knocked the man's arm up, just as he pulled the trigger. The shot went wild, up into the trees, and Savannah broke loose of the Minion's hold.

"Kill her," Smithson ordered.

And in one awful, shattering instant, another bullet blasted out of the Minion's gun. It hit her in the back. Dropped her like dead weight to the ground.

Amelie shrieked and flew off the porch behind him to race to her sister's side.

Gideon roared. Horror and rage bled through him, cold and black and acrid. "No!" he howled, racked with an anguish unlike any he'd ever known. "No!"

He leapt on Smithson, took him down in a hard crash to the ground.

He pounded and beat him, the pair of vampires rolling around in a savage hand-to-hand struggle in the wet grass. Gideon was vaguely aware of the Minion racing toward them, the barrel of his pistol aimed down at the scuffle, but hesitant to shoot and inadvertently snuff his own maker.

Gideon ignored the threat and kept up his punishment of Smithson. They tore at each other, gnashing with fangs and teeth as they wrestled on the ground. Gideon's fury was a hungry beast, waiting for the chance to deal the final blow.

When Smithson turned his head to reach for his lost blade, Gideon pounced with lethal purpose. He grabbed hold of the other male's throat with his teeth and fangs, sinking them deep.

He bit down hard into Smithson's neck, ripping out flesh and larynx in one savage shake of his head.

Smithson jerked and flailed in agony, blood spurting everywhere.

His Minion stood in stunned silence, a brief hesitation that was all the time Gideon needed to finish them both in one strike.

He picked up Faulkner's sword and drove it into Smithson's chest.

The vampire convulsed around the blade, eyes going wide and bulging in their sockets.

Gideon heard another round of gunfire somewhere close to him. Felt a sudden, hard knock in the side of his skull, before his vision began to fill with red. Blood. His blood, pouring into his eyes from the hole now bored into his skull from the Minion's final shot.

Smithson's chest rattled with a wet, gurgling breath as death took him under. His Minion dropped lifeless to the ground at the same time, the mind slave's life tied inexorably to his Master's.

"Savannah." Gideon dragged himself over to where Amelie hovered at her side. Savannah wasn't moving. Her back was covered in blood. The gunshot wound a dark hole burned through her pale gray sweater, up near her ribs.

"She's dying!" Amelie wailed, not looking at him, but focused completely on her sister. She petted Savannah with trembling hands, her face stricken with sorrow. "You promised to save her. You swore on your life."

"Move aside," he rasped thickly, his voice unearthly, ragged from injury and anguish and the crowding presence of his fangs, which filled his mouth. "Let me help her."

It was only then that Amelie turned to look at him. She sucked in a sharp breath and recoiled. She scrabbled backward with Savannah held close to her as if she thought she could protect her from the monster, bleeding and hideously transformed from the man he'd been just a few minutes ago. "Oh, my God. What kind of devil's spawn are you?"

"Please," Gideon hissed. His vision was fading, his pulse hammering heavily in his temples, bringing excruciating pain to his skull. He had to act quickly. There wasn't much time to do what was needed before one or the other of them died. He reached for Savannah's hand, gently took her limp form out of Amelie's grasp. "Please, it's the only way. Trust me in this. Let me save her."

He didn't wait. Couldn't let another second tick by without feeding the power of his blood to Savannah's wounds.

He bit into his wrist and held the opened vein over her parted lips.

"Drink," he whispered thickly. "Please, baby...drink for me."

Deep red droplets splashed down into her slack mouth. The stream picked up speed, pulsing out of him with every labored beat of his heart. "Come on, Savannah. Do it. Please take this gift from me. It's all I have to give you now."

Her tongue began to flick softly. Her slender throat began to work, taking the first swallow from his vein. She drank again, then another. Her eyelids started to lift slightly, just a hint of response, but enough to wring a sigh of naked relief out of Gideon's chest.

She would survive.

He felt it with a certainty that humbled him. His blood would save her.

She was alive. Smithson was dead, unable to harm her.

Gideon had kept his promise to her, after all.

His vision faded from dull gray to black, a numbness creeping over his scalp. He had to struggle to remain upright, invisible tethers dragging him down.

He fought the heavy pull of his injury and cradled Savannah's head in his arm, centering himself with the steady rhythm of her mouth working softly at his wrist, drinking from him, healing because of him.

For now, that was enough.

CHAPTER 16

Savannah was resting in a chair in the back bedroom of Amelie's house when Gideon woke for the first time since the shooting.

It had been nearly eighteen hours of waiting, of hoping.

Of praying that by some miracle, he would come back to her.

She had tended him as best she could, fully recovered from the ordeal herself and having never felt stronger in her life.

Thanks to him.

She went to his bedside as his eyelids began to twitch. Leaning over him, she stroked his face, smoothed back the soft spikes of his blond hair. He leaned his face into her touch, moaning quietly. His eyes opened narrowly, squinting in the dim light of the shaded bedroom. "Where are we?"

"My sister's house," she answered gently.

He wheezed slightly, anxious now. "Are we alone? Does anyone know I'm here?"

"Just Amelie. It's okay, Gideon. She knows about you. I helped her understand what you are. She'll keep our secret."

"Where is she?"

"In the other room, watching television."

He turned his face toward the hallway wall, and Savannah guessed he was searching for Amelie through the extrasensory ability he possessed. "I can't see her. My talent...it's not working. It's gone."

Savannah could feel his agitation. His pulse spiked with it. He brought his hand up to shield his eyes. "So bright in here."

She glanced to the window blinds, which were drawn down and blotted out all but the most scant illumination from the afternoon sunlight outside. "I'm sorry. I thought it would be dim enough for you."

She walked over to the dresser and brought back a pair of bug-eye sunglasses. "Here," she said, carefully slipping them on his face. "Try these."

He opened his eyes and gave a mild nod of approval. "Better. Probably not my best look, though."

"You look pretty good to me." She smiled and sat down next to him on the mattress. "I wasn't sure you would wake up again. I wasn't sure it would work."

At his frown, she went on. "That night when you came back in such terrible shape from Keaton's place, your friend from the Order said you needed blood. And Amelie told me what you did for me last night, after I was shot. You saved me with your blood, Gideon. So, I had to try to save you with mine."

He blew out an oath. "The blood bond, Savannah...it's permanent. Unbreakable. It's a sacred thing." His frown deepened. "This isn't the way it's supposed to be."

She sat back, feeling hurt. Feeling she'd done something wrong and he was disappointed. "I'm sorry if it wasn't what you wanted."

Gideon pushed himself up off the bed, and groaned in pain.

"Be careful," she said, trying to ease him back down. "You shouldn't be moving around, and I shouldn't be saying things that upset you. You were shot last night too. The one that hit me passed cleanly through my lung and ribs, but the one inside you..."

"Still in my head," he guessed grimly. "In my brain."

Savannah gave him a sober nod. "Amelie wanted to take you to the hospital—"

"No." He said it firmly, the same way he'd insisted the other night in Boston when she wanted to get him medical help for his injuries then. "Human doctors can't help me, Savannah."

"I know," she said. "So, I did the only thing I could think of."

He reached out, took her hand in his. "You saved my life." He swore again, more roundly this time. "When I realized you'd left...when I knew Keaton's Master was still out there somewhere, I couldn't get to you fast enough, Savannah."

She heard the rage in his voice for the enemy he'd wanted so badly to root out and destroy, and she nodded sadly. "I'm glad he's dead. For what he did to Rachel and your brothers, even to Professor Keaton. For what he did to you, Gideon, I'm glad Smithson is dead.

I'm glad you got what you came here for."

He scowled. "I came for you, Savannah. I love you. I should've said it before. I should say it a thousand times now, so you'll know what you mean to me."

She felt a warmth blooming in her breast, seeping through her veins. Not her own emotion, but Gideon's. Flowing through their bond.

"I know you feel it," he said, his grasp warm on her hand. "I know you can feel my love inside you now, in your blood. Tell me you love me too, Savannah. Tell me you'll let me prove it to you. Be my mate. Come back with me to Boston. Let me try to be the hero you deserve."

She slipped her hand out of his and gave a small shake of her head. "I don't want a hero."

She thought about how he almost died last night—in combat, now with a bullet buried deep in his brain. A bullet that could dislodge anytime and wreak more damage, maybe something her blood wouldn't be able to fix.

Maybe the bullet already had taken things from him: His ESP talent. His eyes.

"I couldn't bear it," she murmured. "I can't stand by while you go out to war every night. I'm not strong enough to give you permission to fight and bleed and maybe never come back."

Gideon was silent for a very long while, his face downcast. "I've been killing Rogues nearly all my adult life, trying to even a score. Trying to atone. It was an empty quest. But the Order is my family, Savannah. The warriors are my brothers now, the only ones I'll ever have. I can't give them up, not even for you."

Her heart breaking, she nodded mutely. Struggled to find her voice. "I understand. It wouldn't be fair for me to ask that of you."

He lifted her chin on the edge of his hand. "You didn't. You asked me not to go out and fight. Maybe that I can do. Maybe there are other ways—non-combat ways—that I can serve the Order's missions, yet keep a pledge to you...my woman. My Breedmate. My forever love."

Savannah wanted to let her elation flood over her, but she was still stung by the way they'd left things back in Boston. "You hurt me, Gideon. You weren't honest with me. Without that, we'll have nothing."

"I know." He stroked her cheek. "I know, and I'm sorry. Let me make it up to you. Let me love you." He caught her nape in his big, strong hand and pulled her to him for a brief, tender kiss. "Say you love me, and let me start being the man you make me want to be."

She let out a sigh, unable to resist him or refuse him. "I do love you, Gideon."

"Then let me bond with you properly, the way I want it to be for you, for us. Be mine, Savannah."

"Yes," she whispered against his lips. "Yes, Gideon. I will be your mate."

He pulled her against him, letting her feel his arousal. "Let's make it right, now."

She reached out with her index finger to push the ridiculous sunglasses down on the bridge of his nose. Amber sparks shot through the pale blue of his eyes. "You're only a few hours out of death's doorway, and you want to make love?"

He grinned. "Oh, I want to do more than that."

"My sister is in the other room," she reminded him, whispering on a scandalized laugh.

Gideon was still for a moment, time during which the bedroom door quietly closed on its own volition, the lock softly clicking into place.

He kissed her, then trailed his lips along the side of her neck. Savannah's heartbeat throbbed in response to the subtle grazing of his fang tips at her pulse point. He dragged her farther up alongside him and rolled toward her, grinding his rigid length into her hip in invitation and demand.

"You're very bad," she said, as he opened his mouth over her carotid.

And then gently, sensually, she felt those razor-sharp points pierce her delicate skin. Her veins lit up, electric and hot with power, as Gideon drew the first deep swallow from her vein.

"Oh, God," she gasped, pleasure flooding her. "You are very, very bad."

And as her body melted into him, Savannah was thinking how a lifetime with Gideon was going to be very, very good.

~ * ~

CHARACTER REFERENCE

GUIDE

CHARACTER REFERENCE GUIDE
(alphabetical order by first name or most common name)

-A-

Alexandra "Alex" Maguire   Breedmate of Order member Kade. Alex was born and raised in rural Florida swamp region. When she was nine years old, her mother and little brother, Richie, were killed one night in a brutal attack by Rogues (though at the time, she didn't realize what the attackers truly were). Alex and her father, Hank, fled as far as they could, settling in a small Alaskan town.

Alex's best friends are her wolf dog, Luna, and a former Alaska State Trooper named Jenna Tucker-Darrow. At twenty-seven, and her dad dead from Alzheimer's, Alex ran the family bush-piloting business, until on a supply run to the interior, she discovers a horrific crime scene that resembles the attack on her family. This discovery brought her into the center of an investigation being conducted by the Order—and into the arms of Alaskan-born Breed warrior, Kade.

Hair: warm blond
Eyes: brown
Breedmate mark: on the front of her left hip
Bloodscent: honey and almond
Unique ability: internal gauge that tells her with a touch if someone is being honest
Mate: Kade
Heroine in: Shades of Midnight (Book 7)

First mention in series: Appears in Shades of Midnight.

~ ~ ~

Alexei "Lex" Yakut (d.)   Breed male, second generation. Son of a corrupt Gen One named Sergei Yakut. Living at his father's rustic but expansive woodland hunting lodge outside Montreal, Quebec, Lex served as right arm to his father, commanding Sergei's security detail, which included a female Breedmate bodyguard (see Renata).

Lex's arrogance and lust for power proved his undoing when he arranged for his father's murder by Rogues and attempted to frame the visiting Order warrior, Nikolai, for the crime. In an attempt to insert himself into Dragos's inner circle, Lex arranges to hand over Niko to one of Dragos's lieutenants (see Edgar Fabien). Lex augments his bargain by offering up a child seer (see Mira) to Fabien for a sum of two million dollars. In the end, Lex himself is double-crossed by Dragos and his associates, duped into thinking he was to be escorted to a VIP meeting and is instead slain by a group of Enforcement Agents sent on Dragos's command.

First mention in series: Appears in Veil of Midnight.

~ ~ ~

Amelie Dupree   Human. Older half-sister to Gideon's Breedmate, Savannah. A former midwife, Amelie has lived at the Atchafalaya swamp for seventy years. She is widowed with two daughters and a son, and eight grandchildren. Her eyesight is gone now, leaving her with clouded, milky eyes, but she copes very well on her own. In contact with Savannah only occasionally since Savannah became mated to Gideon. Amelie is fond of Gideon, and is aware of the Breed's existence due to an incident that occurred outside her home three decades ago, when Savannah and Gideon were shot and nearly killed. Amelie saw Gideon save Savannah's life by giving her his blood, a secret Amelie has kept all the years since.

First mention in the series: Appears in Deeper Than Midnight.

~ ~ ~

Ancient, the (d.)   The last surviving alien and grandfather to Dragos. The Ancient was believed killed during the Order's war against their otherworldly forebears, but Dragos's father (also named Dragos) secreted the Ancient to a mountain cave in the Czech Republic, where the Ancient remained in a hibernation chamber until modern day. The Ancient was later removed by Dragos to his breeding lab, but then escaped to Alaska, where he was killed by the Order in Shades of Midnight.

First mention in series: Referenced in Kiss of Midnight as part of original group of Ancients who crash-landed on Earth thousands of years ago; referenced specifically in Midnight Awakening; first actual appearance in Veil of Midnight.

~ ~ ~

Andreas Reichen   Breed male, mate of Claire Samuels Roth. Born more than three hundred years ago in Germany, Andreas Reichen was leader of a Berlin Darkhaven. Reichen is smooth and sophisticated, cultured and cool—the ultimate charmer.

Although not formally trained as a warrior, Reichen has been long-acquainted with Tegan, who assisted the German Darkhaven leader with the elimination of a band of Rogues who'd been preying on civilians in his area in 1809. Reichen and Claire had been in love about fifty years before the timeline of Midnight Awakening, but the couple was betrayed (see Wilhelm Roth) and they endured a long separation before reuniting in Ashes of Midnight.

During his time apart from Claire, Reichen took a human lover, sex club owner Helene. The relationship ended in tragedy when, during the timeline of Veil of Midnight, Helene was turned Minion and led Enforcement Agents into the Darkhaven to slaughter all inside. Reichen comes upon the aftermath and has to kill his human lover in an act of mercy. He then burns his Darkhaven to the ground with a massive fireball, conjured by the power of his ESP ability.

Reichen and Claire are now mated and reside in their Darkhaven in Newport, Rhode Island. Reichen is currently a member of the Order, serving primarily on covert overseas missions while he works to gain control over his pyrokinesis.

Hair: chestnut brown waves, generally worn loose
Eyes: hazel
Unique ability: pyrokinesis
Mate: Claire Samuels Roth
Hero in: Ashes of Midnight (Book 6)

First mention in series: Appears in Midnight Awakening.

~ ~ ~

Anna   Breedmate and old friend of Elise Chase's. Elise encounters Anna at Andreas Reichen's reception in Berlin. Anna's Breed son, Tomas, had been friends with Elise's son, Camden, when they were boys. Anna had not heard of Cam's death and is clearly uncomfortable with the news. Friendly to Elise, offers to show her around Berlin if Elise were staying for a while.

First mention in series: Appears in Midnight Awakening.

~ ~ ~

Annabeth Jablonsky   Human. Resident of Harmony, Alaska, and waitress at Pete's Tavern. Under the name Amber Joy, Annabeth used to dance at a strip club in Fairbanks, where Teddy Toms saw her perform and developed a crush on her. Annabeth was partying with friends and Teddy Toms the night Teddy and his family were killed by the Ancient. She also saw Kade at Pete's the night after Alex met him and thought he was sexy.

First mention in series: Appears in Shades of Midnight.

~ ~ ~

Arno Pike (d.)   Breed male, Deputy Director in the Breed's Enforcement Agency, secret lieutenant to Dragos and a loyal member of his inner circle. Pike had been mated, but his Breedmate was killed in a mugging about a year before the timeline of Darker After Midnight.

Pike is at the Agency's Chinatown sip-and-strip when Dragos arrives to bask in his victory over the Order, which had sent the warriors scrambling for new headquarters after Dragos helped expose the Boston compound to human law enforcement. Pike is anxious about a public appearance by Dragos, but capitulates when his boss insists on a private table and the best females in the club. Pike soon joins in, and the night ends in wholesale slaughter of all the humans in the club.

Later, Pike is captured by the Order and questioned about his connections to Dragos. Pike tells Lucan it's too late to stop Dragos, but he refuses to say anything more. Hunter is tasked with finishing the interrogation by reading his blood. But the first bite reveals that Pike has ingested poison, and Dragos's lieutenant takes the truth with him to his death.

First mention in series: Appears in Darker After Midnight.

~ ~ ~

August Chase (d.)　　Breed male, father of Sterling and Quentin Chase. August's Breedmate is neither present nor specifically named thus far in the series. The patriarch of the venerable Chase family, August groomed his sons to be morally pristine, accepting nothing less than perfection from them at all times. He had been Enforcement Agency Director for a couple of centuries before his death on patrol at an undated time prior to son Quentin's death, which was five years before the timeline of Kiss of Crimson. Although August never spoke the words precisely, Sterling Chase grew up feeling that his father already had the son he wanted in Quentin, leaving Sterling to feel redundant and never able to measure up to his older brother.

First mention in series: Referenced in Darker After Midnight.

~ ~ ~

Aunt Sarah (Fairchild) (d.)　　Human. Believed to be Tavia Fairchild's deceased father's sister, but is later revealed to be one of Dragos's Minions tasked with guardianship over Tavia since her laboratory birth. Working in concert with another of Dragos's Minions (see Doctor Lewis), Sarah makes sure Tavia takes her medications daily and sees her private medical specialist regularly. Both of these individuals, on Dragos's orders, have made Tavia believe all her life that she has a serious condition that requires constant monitoring and treatments. Sarah has also helped foster the lie that Tavia's odd pattern of skin markings (her Breed dermaglyphs) are burn scars from a house fire that killed her parents but that she survived. "Aunt Sarah" later killed herself after being unmasked as a Minion by Tavia, following Tavia's realization that she's been betrayed all her life about who, and what, she truly is.

First mention in series: Appears in Darker After Midnight.

~ ~ ~

Avery, Detective   Human. Middle-aged police detective with the Boston Police Department. Avery is first introduced to Tavia Fairchild at the station, when she's brought in to view a lineup and identify Sterling Chase as the shooter at Senator Clarence's holiday party. Avery is a likable man, tries to make Tavia comfortable and assure her that she's safe. Later, after Sterling Chase breaks loose from police custody and flees the station to go after Senator Clarence as a certain link to Dragos, Detective Avery meets Tavia at the senator's office building and arranges for her safekeeping at a Boston hotel under police watch (see Murphy). Chase then confronts Avery to find out where Tavia has been taken. Avery tries to resist putting Tavia in what he feels is mortal danger from Chase, but eventually relents and gives up her location. Chase mind scrubs the detective, but leaves him unharmed out of respect for the human's obvious care for Tavia's wellbeing. Detective Avery is seen again, after Boston is in the midst of the mass Rogue attacks. He is in shock over the situation, like the rest of the population, but relieved to see Tavia is alive and well.

First mention in series: Appears in Darker After Midnight.

~ ~ ~

-B-

Ben Sullivan (d.)   Human. Former chemical engineer and research development manager for a cosmetics company in Boston, fired for his staunch opposition to animal testing. Ben's views brought him into veterinarian Tess Culver's social circle two years before the timeline of Kiss of Crimson, and the pair were briefly romantic, although Ben remains possessive of Tess after the breakup.

Ben is not as ethical as he seems; uses his chemical engineering skills to manufacture drugs for the dance club scene on the side. When an anonymous patron (see Marek) approaches him to make one of his concoctions, a red-powder substance similar to Ecstasy called Crimson, Ben takes the offer. Ben does not realize that his patron is a vampire and that Crimson has a devastating effect on the Breed. After he witnesses one of those reactions in a club-goer (see Jonas Redmond), Ben phones his patron to warn him of Crimson's unusual side-effects. After a meeting is arranged between them, Ben downloads his recipe to a flash drive and destroys all other records of the drug on his computer. He hides the flash drive in Tess's office for safekeeping.

After a confrontation by Dante and Sterling Chase of the Order, Ben eventually is picked up by his patron and brought to undisclosed location where he is ordered to surrender the recipe for Crimson or make a new batch on the spot for analysis. When he fails both commands, Ben is turned Minion by his patron. With instructions to retrieve the flash drive he stowed in Tess's office—evidence Tess has since discovered and turned over to Dante and the Order—Ben abducts her and brings her to the office where her assistant has been tortured and is soon killed (see Nora). Dante and members of the Order arrive not long afterward, and during a violent struggle, Ben Sullivan is killed by Dante.

First mention in series: Appears in Kiss of Crimson.

~ ~ ~

Big Dave Grant (d.)   Human. Resident of Harmony, Alaska, frequent patron of Pete's Tavern. Loud-mouthed and combative, Big Dave instigates a wolf-hunting party with other men after the unexplained killing of the Toms family. On the wolf hunt, Big Dave instead encounters the Ancient hiding in a cave and is badly injured. Flown to the area medical center, Big Dave is later stabbed and killed there by Skeeter Arnold, who has been turned Minion.

First mention in series: Appears in Shades of Midnight.

~ ~ ~

Big Man (d.)   Human. Berlin-area pimp who tries to intervene when Rio needs to feed from one of his girls (see Uta). Big Man pulls a knife on Rio and Rio is too close to insane with thirst to keep from retaliating. Rio kills the pimp in the alleyway.

First mention in series: Appears in Midnight Rising.

~ ~ ~

Bill Keaton (d.)   Human. Art History professor at Boston University when Savannah was attending as a freshman student, circa 1974. Keaton had an eye for his female students, including Savannah's roommate, Rachel. Keaton and the girl are attacked by a vampire one night, after hours at the university, leaving Rachel dead and Keaton hospitalized. It is later revealed that Keaton was turned Minion during the attack and is working in league with one of Gideon's longtime enemies from England (see Cyril Smithson). Gideon kills Keaton following a confrontation that leaves Gideon severely injured.

First mention in series: Appears in A Touch of Midnight (novella).

~ ~ ~

Bobby Alexander   Human. Dylan's stepfather, husband of Sharon Alexander and father of their two sons, Morrison and Lennon. Bobby was a drunk and a scam artist, responsible for the car accident that killed Morrison as a teen and drove Dylan's other brother, Lennon, to cut all ties to the family and join the military. When Dylan was a young girl, Bobby read her diary and saw entries about the dead women she saw with her ESP gift. He tried to cash in on his daughter's talent, but Dylan couldn't control her gift on command. Bobby eventually abandoned the family when Dylan was twelve years old and never returned.

First mention in series: Referenced in Midnight Rising.

~ ~ ~

Boston Police Department file clerk, unnamed (d.)   Human. Working at the police station the night Gabrielle came in, already serving as a Minion for an unnamed Master (see Marek). Clerk calls his Master with Gabrielle's unlisted phone number and address after she makes her report about a vampire attack outside La Notte nightclub. He is later spotted by Gabrielle when he follows her in daylight hours while she is taking pictures. He took off and Gabrielle attempted to chase him, but lost him in the city.

The clerk is present at the station the next time Gabrielle arrives there looking for "Detective" Lucan Thorne. Clerk has a private altercation with another cop (see Officer Carrigan), during which time the clerk stabs the other man to death in a stairwell at the station. The clerk then goes after Gabrielle, after seeing her speaking to Lucan on the street. The clerk attempts to run Gabrielle down with his car, but Lucan intervenes. Realizing the human is Minion, Lucan kills him, tearing out the clerk's throat in front of Gabrielle, terrifying her and for the first time exposing Lucan to her as one of the Breed.

First mention in series: Appears in Kiss of Midnight.

~ ~ ~

Brent (d.)   Breed male who picks up Gabrielle's friend, Kendra, at the nightclub in Boston. Kendra and Brent become inseparable, and it later turns out that Brent has gone Rogue, presumably under the influence of Marek, Lucan's corrupt brother. Brent is responsible for the suicide bombing in the underground train stop in Boston that kills Conlan, his identity discovered by Gabrielle when she's at the

Order's compound and views video surveillance footage from the scene.

First mention in series: Appears in Kiss of Midnight.

~ ~ ~

Brock Breed male, Order member. Mate of Jenna Tucker-Darrow. Born in Detroit, Brock is 110+ years old. He was recruited into the Order along with Kade, a few months after Conlan's death.

In the 1930s, Brock served as security detail and bodyguard for the Bishops, a prominent Darkhaven family in Detroit, Brock being personally responsible for one of their adopted Breedmate daughters, Corinne. When she went missing in the city at eighteen years old and was presumed dead, Brock blamed himself, a burden of guilt he carried even as he joined the Order. Good-natured with his comrades, but merciless with those who cross him, Brock felt unworthy of being loved or trusted with another person's life, until he was tasked with protecting an injured human woman, Jenna, brought back from a mission in Alaska that left her transformed in ways none of the Breed could have ever imagined was possible.

Hair: black, skull-trimmed
Eyes: dark brown
Unique ability: can absorb and diminish human pain and suffering with his hands
Mate: Jenna Tucker-Darrow (human)
Hero in: Taken by Midnight (Book 8)

First mention in series: Appears in Midnight Awakening.

~ ~ ~

-C-

Camden Chase (d.) Breed male, only son of Quentin and Elise Chase in Boston Darkhaven. At age eighteen, Camden began to rebel and ended up leaving home. He was one of a growing number of Breed youth who began disappearing from their Darkhavens during the timeline of Kiss of Crimson. It is later revealed that Camden and his friends were becoming addicted to a new narcotic called Crimson, which induces blood thirst and feelings of euphoria and power. Camden in particular was in danger, because he was a test subject of Crimson's creator (see Ben Sullivan). Cam was held prisoner and fed large doses of the drug. He developed Bloodlust and soon turned Rogue, killing a human neighbor of Sullivan's and bolting when his uncle, Sterling Chase, shows up at the crime scene and attempts to reason with him. Cam later arrives home at his family's Darkhaven, fully Rogue. When the youth appears to be intent on lunging for his mother, Elise, Sterling Chase shoots him dead with a titanium-filled bullet in front of her.

First mention in series: Appears in Kiss of Crimson.

~ ~ ~

Carrigan, Officer (d.)   Human. Carrigan was the soon-to-retire officer at the Boston police station who took Gabrielle's report about the vampire attack outside La Notte nightclub. Carrigan did not believe her, and is annoyed when she returns a few nights later looking for "Detective" Lucan Thorne (the false credentials Lucan gave her at her apartment). Carrigan treats Gabrielle rudely, then turns his bluster on a clumsy file clerk who turns out to be a Minion. Carrigan is stabbed in the neck by the Minion, who kills the cop in a quiet stairwell of the station after their verbal altercation.

First mention in series: Appears in Kiss of Midnight.

~ ~ ~

Chad Bishop   Human. Resident of Harmony, Alaska. Chad was partying with Annabeth Jablonsky, Teddy Toms, Skeeter Arnold and others the night Teddy and his family were killed by the Ancient. Made fun of Teddy and his stutter. Chad is no relation to the Breed family named Bishop.

First mention in series: Appears in Shades of Midnight.

~ ~ ~

Charlotte "Lottie" Bishop   Corinne's adopted Breedmate sister, grew up together at the Bishop family Darkhaven in Detroit. Lottie is five years younger than Corinne, and currently lives in a London Darkhaven with her mate. Has two grown sons, one of which has his own Breedmate and son.

First mention in series: Referenced in Deeper Than Midnight.

~ ~ ~

Christophe Archer (d.)   Breed male from Boston, second-generation. Son of Lazaro Archer, father of Kellan. Christophe comes reluctantly to the Order with Lazaro, seeking help after Kellan's abduction. Christophe is the typical Darkhaven-bred vampire, wealthy, well-connected, looks down slightly on the Order and their aggressive methods. But when his son is in danger, Christophe is ready to do anything, give anything, to have him back. Christophe is killed by corrupt Dragos ally, Enforcement Agent Freyne, outside the building in Boston where Kellan was being held.

First mention in series: Appears in Taken by Midnight.

~ ~ ~

Claire (Samuels Roth) Reichen   Breedmate of Order member Andreas Reichen. Claire Samuels was born more than fifty years ago, the daughter of an American peace worker and a Zimbabwean village doctor. Raised by her mother's wealthy Newport, Rhode Island, family after violence in Africa killed both her parents, Claire, a gifted pianist, later attended university in Germany. She was attacked there one night by a creature that tried to bite her, but was spared by another of his kind, a Breed male named Wilhelm Roth. Roth, already mated, took Claire to his Darkhaven as his ward.

There she learned about the Breed and her place in their world as a Breedmate. She also fell in love with a charming, if reckless, Breed male from Berlin, Andreas Reichen. But while Claire anticipated Andreas's proposal to be his mate, instead he left her without a word.

Spurned and heartbroken, Claire later capitulated to Roth after his Breedmate was killed and he offered to take her as his mate. Years later, that choice would return to haunt her, when Andreas Reichen enters Claire's life again, on a mission of bloody-minded vengeance against the villain who is her mate.

Hair: soft black
Eyes: deep brown
Breedmate mark: right side of her neck, by the pulse point
Bloodscent: vanilla and warm spices
Unique ability: dreamwalker
Mate: Andreas Reichen
Heroine in: Ashes of Midnight (Book 6)

First mention in series: Appears in Ashes of Midnight.

~ ~ ~

Coleman Hogg   Human. Dylan's boss at the tabloid magazine, unpleasant man. He was unhappy about her last-minute trip to Europe in her mother's place, threatening that if she wanted to keep her job, she'd better come back with some big story ideas. Dylan later sends him photos and an outline of her Czech Republic vampire story, but further aggravates him when she is forced to extend her stay out of the country. He eventually fires her via voicemail. After the Order finds out about the story and photos Dylan sent the magazine, Lucan orders Gideon to infect the magazine's computers with a virus and sends Niko and Kade to mind scrub Coleman Hogg.

First mention in series: Referenced in Midnight Rising.

~ ~ ~

Conlan MacConn (d.)   Breed male, first mate of Danika for more than four-hundred years. The couple lived in the Scottish Highlands for centuries, before Con's sense of duty brought them to America about a hundred years ago, where he later pledged his sword to the Order. Red-haired, handsome, good-natured Conlan was a member of the Order in Boston until killed in action by a Rogue's suicide bombing (see Brent) on a Boston train.

Conlan was approximately five hundred years old at the time of his death, the son of a Scottish chieftan's (Breedmate) daughter and Breed male. Conlan and Danika had been mated for upwards of four hundred years and were expecting their first child (see Connor MacConn) together at the time he was killed. Conlan's funeral rite was the first to occur within the current timeline of the series.

First mention in series: Appears in Kiss of Midnight.

~ ~ ~

Connor MacConn   Breed male, Danika and Conlan's son. Connor was unborn when his father, Conlan, was killed in action in Boston. Danika relocated to Denmark to have her son, and during the timeline of Ashes of Midnight, the boy is a blond, blue-eyed toddler of less than two years when Andreas Reichen and Claire seek shelter with Danika while on the run from Wilhelm Roth and Dragos. Several months later in the series timeline, in the novella, A Taste of Midnight, Connor and his mother are visiting Conlan's family in Scotland for the Christmas holiday. Danika dreads that her son will grow up one day to become a warrior like his father.

First mention in series: Appears in Ashes of Midnight as an infant.

~ ~ ~

Corinne Bishop   Breedmate of Order member Hunter. Born the summer of 1917, Corinne had been abandoned at the back door of a Detroit hospital just hours after her birth. Adopted by a prominent Breed family, the Bishops, the infant Breedmate was raised in a life of luxury until her eighteenth birthday, when she went missing while out at a jazz club. Corinne was abducted while under the watch of one of her family's Darkhaven security detail (see Brock) and was eventually presumed dead, a lie perpetuated by the actions of her Darkhaven father, Victor Bishop.

After seventy-five years of imprisonment in Dragos's breeding labs, Corinne is rescued by the Order, along with several other captured Breedmates. It is discovered that she and the others were part of genetic and reproductive experiments, where Corinne gave birth to a son thirteen years ago, a boy she named Nathan. Her quest to find him, and to stop the villain responsible for her suffering, brings Corinne into the middle of the Order's war against their enemy—and into the arms of one of the most lethal members of the Order, the Gen One former assassin called Hunter. Corinne loves jazz music, particularly Bessie Smith.

Hair: long, sleek ebony
Eyes: almond shaped, greenish-blue
Breedmate mark: back of her right hand
Bloodscent: bergamot and violets
Unique ability: sonokinesis
Mate: Hunter
Heroine in: Deeper Than Midnight (Book 9)

First mention in series: Appears in Taken by Midnight.

~ ~ ~

Curtis (d.)   Human. Newer kid at Anna's Place (see Jack). It is later discovered that Curtis is a Minion of Edgar Fabien's, after Curtis spots the Order warrior, Nikolai, recuperating in a garage apartment at the halfway house with Renata. Curtis's report to Fabien results in a team of Enforcement Agents swarming Anna's Place. In the melee, Nikolai manages to get his hands on Curtis but before he can get the Minion to tell him who his Master is, the human has a knife in hand and slices his own throat open, killing himself.

First mention in series: Appears in Veil of Midnight.

~ ~ ~

Cyril Smithson (d.)   Breed male. Unacknowledged son of Gideon's long-ago enemy in London, Hugh Faulkner, the sword-maker. Cyril witnessed the duel where Gideon killed Hugh, and the young Breed male swore a secret vengeance. Cyril sent Rogues to slaughter Gideon's young brothers and retrieve the sword Hugh lost in the contest against Gideon. Soon afterward, Cyril left England to begin a new life of wealth and privilege in Boston under the name Smithson.

He crosses paths with Gideon again when the sword inadvertently ends up in a collection of Colonial artifacts donated to Boston University, where Savannah Dupree learns of its ignoble past through her ESP touch, which sets into motion events that bring Gideon and Cyril into conflict once again. Cyril Smithson later follows Savannah and Gideon to Louisiana, where he shoots both of them in front of Savannah's sister's house. Gideon kills Cyril before saving Savannah's life with his blood bond. To this day, one of Cyril's bullets remains embedded in Gideon's brain, crippling his ESP ability and preventing him from taking on combat missions.

First mention in series: Appears in A Touch of Midnight (novella).

~ ~ ~

-D-

Danika (MacConn) MacBain   Breedmate of Order member Conlan MacConn until his death. Current Breedmate of Malcolm MacBain. Danika was born in Denmark more than four hundred years ago, and mated to Conlan of the Scottish clan MacConn from the time she was eighteen, until his recent death on a mission for the Order in Boston.

At the time of Con's death, Danika was pregnant with their first child. She left Boston to return home to Denmark, where she gave birth to her son, Connor. During the timeline of Ashes of Midnight, Danika provided a safe house in Denmark for Andreas Reichen and Claire Roth. There, she reads Claire's mind and assures Claire that Andreas feels the same regret at having lost so much time without each other.

Later, during the timeline of A Taste of Midnight, Danika and Connor travel to Scotland to reunite with Conlan's family in Edinburgh for the Christmas holiday. While there, Danika crosses paths with a dangerous Breed crime boss (see Reiver) and his scarred, mysterious henchman named Brannoc—a Breed male Danika once knew very well, at a different time, when Brannoc was a different man (see Malcolm MacBain).

Hair: blond
Eyes: blue
Breedmate mark: on her abdomen
Bloodscent: fresh rain
Unique ability: mind-reading
Mate: Conlan MacConn, long-time Order warrior (deceased); Malcolm MacBain
Heroine in: A Taste of Midnight (novella, Book 9.5)

First mention in series: Appears in Kiss of Midnight.

~ ~ ~

Dante (Malebranche) Breed male, Order member and mate of Tess Culver. An only child, Dante was born in 18th century Italy two-hundred and twenty-nine years ago. Still has some of his Italian accent. Dante's father was killed by a political rival in Italy; his mother perished in a riptide while attempting to save a drowning victim sometime later.

The swaggering wise-ass of the group, Dante has adopted the last name of Malebranche for when he's forced to mingle among humans. Malebranche ("evil claws") is also what he calls his weapons of choice—a pair of curved, titanium blades that he uses in hand-to-hand combat against Rogues. Dante fights hard and plays hard, and despite his brashness, he is also fiercely loyal to those he cares about. His closest friend in the Order is Sterling Chase, although that friendship becomes strained and nearly broken when Chase begins displaying signs of Bloodlust and his actions start to jeopardize Order missions. Dante and Tess had intended to make Chase godfather to Xander Raphael, but they instead ask Gideon to take the honor. The relationship between Dante and Chase is on the mend again during the timeline of Darker After Midnight.

Hair: black
Eyes: whiskey-colored
Unique ability: cursed with premonitions of death
Mate: Tess Culver (couple has a newborn son named Xander Raphael)

Hero in: Kiss of Crimson (Book 2)

First mention in series: Appears in Kiss of Midnight.

~ ~ ~

Dmitri (d.) Breed male, Nikolai's deceased younger brother in Russia. About twenty years Nikolai's junior, Dmitri was bright and bookish, fond of philosophy and taking things apart to see how they worked. But he adored Niko, wanted to be more like his older brother. One night Dmitri overheard one of Niko's rivals from the Ukraine making harsh remarks about his brother. Dmitri called the Breed male out and cut him with a dagger. A lucky strike, but it infuriated the other vampire, who took Dmitri's head in retaliation. Niko later hunted down the Breed male from Ukraine and killed him. Niko brought the prize to his parents as an apology for Dmitri's death, but they shunned him, telling Niko it should have been him instead of Dmitri. Niko left his kin and never looked back.

First mention in series: Referenced in Veil of Midnight.

~ ~ ~

Doctor Lewis (d.) Human. Private medical specialist who has been treating Tavia Fairchild's "condition" all her life. Doctor Lewis is, in fact, a Minion under Dragos's command, along with another of Tavia's handlers (see Aunt Sarah). Out of his private, secured clinic in rural Sherborn, Massachusetts, Doctor Lewis is also secretly treating others like Tavia—Gen One Breed females created in Dragos's breeding labs.

Through Doctor Lewis's records, Tavia discovers information about herself (as Subject 8, Patient "Octavia") and others who were placed into various secret locations to live unwittingly among the humans as part of the mortal population, their Breed genetics medically suppressed, until Dragos feels the need to activate his creations for his own purposes. Tavia also discovers that Doctor Lewis was using her gift of photographic memory to supply Dragos with names and intelligence on various political officials and human government contacts while she lay in medically-enhanced debriefing sessions at the clinic. Tavia kills Doctor Lewis at the house she lives in with her "Aunt Sarah," after the doctor arrives and attempts to drug her following her realization that she is something other than basic *Homo Sapiens*.

First mention in series: Appears in Darker After Midnight.

~ ~ ~

Dragos, aka Gordon Fasso, aka Gerard Starkn, aka Drake Masters (d.) Second-generation Breed male, unmated. Son of a Gen One Breed father who bears the same name (see Dragos the elder) and mother named Kassia.

Born in secret in the mid-1300s, Dragos was sent away by his mother to live with a family by the name of Odolf for her child's protection. Kassia feared what might happen if word got out that Dragos's Gen One father, during the war between the Order and their alien forebears, had secreted away one of the Ancients to a hidden hibernation crypt in the Bohemian mountains. Dragos's father died at an enemy's hand (see Marek), taking his secret to his grave, and Kassia, in danger herself, took her own life. But Dragos was too much like his duplicitous father. When he stumbled upon the secret of the Ancient's location many years later, he decided to use the knowledge—and the sleeping Ancient's genetics—to his own personal advantage.

Retrieving the Ancient and imprisoning him in his breeding labs, Dragos spent decades growing his own army of Hunters and experimenting to create a branch of the Breed never seen before: Gen One females, like Tavia Fairchild. Over the years, Dragos wore many masks and assumed many names. He moved in human circles as Gordon Fasso and Drake Masters, and amassed power and allies within the Breed as Gerard Starkn, director of the Enforcement Agency.

Dragos's madness grew over time, culminating in one final, irreparable act of retaliation on the Order for all their efforts to thwart him. He freed hundreds of Rogues from captivity all over the world, turning them loose on unsuspecting human populations and exposing the Breed to mankind in the worst possible way. Dragos was finally killed by Sterling Chase, but the damage he'd done was immeasurable. The bloody aftermath of that pivotal night has come to be known as First Dawn.

First mention in series: Referenced in Midnight Awakening; appears in Midnight Rising.

~ ~ ~

Dragos, the elder (d.)   Breed male, Gen One. Father to Dragos the second, mate of Kassia. One of the original members of the Order at its founding in mid-1300s. Committed an act of treason during the Order's war with the Ancients when he aided the otherworlder who sired him in escaping death and instead hid the Ancient away in a mountain cave in what is now the Czech Republic. Dragos the elder made the mistake of confiding his secret in another Breed male (see Marek) and paid for that error with his head, taking the location of the Ancient with him to his grave.

First mention in series: Referenced in Midnight Awakening.

~ ~ ~

Dylan Alexander   Breedmate of Order member Rio. Born and raised by her single mother in New York, Dylan had two half-brothers, both also named after rock musicians: Morrison and Lennon. Thirty-two during the timeline of Midnight Rising, Dylan Alexander was born with a troubling gift for seeing the dead. Fearful of being taken advantage of or shunned for this ability, she's long tried to hide it, to deny it. As an adult, Dylan went on to make a career for herself in journalism, until she let a personal bias cloud her reporting. Demoted to a tabloid rag, she stumbles across a blockbuster story while vacationing in the mountains of the Czech Republic.

This story, exposing a mysterious crypt hidden in the caverns, brings her face-to-face with the existence of the Breed—and puts her in the middle of the Order's war with a dangerous enemy bent on world domination. It also draws her to scarred, emotionally-closed off Rio, and into a passion for which neither of them was prepared. Dylan later learns that the man she thought to be her father (see

Bobby Alexander) was actually her stepfather, and her true father is a man her mother met in Mykonos by the name of Zael. Through Jenna Tucker-Darrow's investigation, it is revealed that Zael is a likely Atlantean immortal.

Hair: long, curling flame-red
Eyes: gold-flecked green
Breedmate mark: nape of her neck
Bloodscent: juniper and honey
Unique ability: can see and hear the spirits of dead Breedmates, but cannot communicate with them
Mate: Rio
Heroine in: Midnight Rising (Book 4)

First mention in series: Appears in Midnight Rising.

~ ~ ~

-E-

Edgar Fabien (d.) Breed male, second generation. Around four-hundred years old, unmated, and leader of his Darkhaven in Montreal, Quebec, for a century and a half as of the timeline of Veil of Midnight. A wealthy Breed civilian, Fabien has ash-blond hair, bird-like facial features and a slender, muscular build. He is always meticulously dressed, typically in the finest custom-tailored suits. Fabien's connections reach deeply into the Darkhaven elite and the highest tiers of the Enforcement Agency. His wealth and connections help insulate him from any fallout resulting from the sadistic, criminal bent of his personal interests, which include a fondness for young girls.

Fabien is also secretly in league with Dragos, a lieutenant in his inner circle. Alexei Yakut makes the mistake of underestimating Fabien's power and attempts to strong-arm his way into the fold by orchestrating his father's murder and offering up Order warrior Nikolai as the perpetrator. Fabien ends up with Niko in his custody and the child seer, Mira, as his personal prize, purchased from Alexei for the sum of two million dollars. In exchange for his efforts, Alexei is killed at his father's lodge by Enforcement Agents, an attack arranged by Dragos and Fabien. Later on, Fabien presents Mira to Dragos as a gift at a gathering of Dragos's followers. When the gathering is raided by the Order, Dragos blames Fabien for the botched security and shoots the Breed male between the eyes, killing him.

First mention in series: Appears in Veil of Midnight.

~ ~ ~

Eleuterio "Rio" de la Noche Atanacio   Breed male, Order member, mate of Dylan Alexander. Born in Spain, sometime in the early 1900s. Never knew his father, a Rogue who raped Rio's sixteen-year old mother and left her pregnant with a child she would fear and despise as a monster.

Later, orphaned as a young boy after men from the village raided his mother's cottage and killed her, Rio was found around the age of five and raised by an area Darkhaven. They taught him what he was and how to survive. They also gave the boy who was given no name by his mother, and who thought of himself as an abomination because of his "manos del diablo"—his lethal, devil's hands—an elegant, meaningful name: Eleuterio de la Noche Atanacio.

Despite his tragic past and a more recent betrayal by his first Breedmate (see Eva) that left him terribly scarred and nearly destroyed him, Rio remains one of the most noble, honorable members of the Order. He is mated to Dylan Alexander, whom he encountered in the Czech mountains, after Eva's ghost led Dylan to the cave where Rio was hiding.

Hair: dark brown, thick and wavy
Eyes: topaz
Unique ability: cursed with power to kill with his touch, particularly when provoked
Mate: Eva (deceased); Dylan Alexander
Hero in: Midnight Rising (Book 4)

First mention in series: Appears in Kiss of Midnight.

~ ~ ~

Emma MacConn   Breedmate of James MacConn, a cousin of Conlan MacConn. Emma is a petite redhead, in her twenties. She and James live in Edinburgh, Scotland, and were both present at the holiday party in the novella, A Taste of Midnight, where Danika encounters a dangerous crime boss named Reiver and his bodyguard, Brannoc (AKA Malcolm MacBain).

First mention in series: Appears in A Taste of Midnight (novella).

~ ~ ~

Eleanor Archer (d.)   Breedmate of Lazaro Archer, mother to Christophe and other, unnamed sons. Eleanor was killed in the razing of the family Darkhaven in Boston, an attack ordered by Dragos. Eleanor ("Ellie") was beautiful and headstrong, and deeply loved by Lazaro.

First mention in series: Referenced in Taken by Midnight.

~ ~ ~

Elise Chase   Breedmate of Order member Tegan. A ward of the Darkhavens since she was a little girl in the slums of 19th century Boston, Elise was raised by a prominent Breed family, the Chases. Eventually she became the Breedmate of Quentin Chase, elder brother to Sterling Chase. Quentin died five years before the events in Kiss of Midnight, widowing Elise. More recently, their eighteen-year-old son, Camden, went Rogue after being exposed to a drug called Crimson and is since deceased, shot and killed by Sterling Chase when the Rogue might have lashed out at his mother.

After Camden's death, Elise wants vengeance on the individual responsible for creating the drug that poisoned him. Her quest brings her up against Tegan from the Order, and introduces her to a dangerous passion she cannot resist.

Hair: light blond
Eyes: pale lavender
Breedmate mark: on the inside of her right thigh

Bloodscent: heather and roses and fresh spring rain
Unique ability: telepathically hears the sins and negative energy of humans
Mate: Quentin Chase (deceased); Tegan
Heroine in: Midnight Awakening (Book 3)

First mention in series: Appears in Kiss of Crimson.

~ ~ ~

Ethan   Breed male, young Enforcement Agent in Boston. Ethan is the Agent who calls Mathias Rowan down to the aftermath of the massacre at the Chinatown Enforcement Agency strip club. Ethan is a good Agent, but new to his post. Rowan reflects that the Breed male is devoted to justice, a rarity within the Agency at that time.

First mention in series: Appears in Darker After Midnight.

~ ~ ~

Eva (d.)   First Breedmate of Rio. Betrayed him and the rest of the Order to Marek, leading the warriors to an ambush that left Rio gravely wounded and near death. His injury was not Eva's intention, and when the team returns with mass casualties, Eva reveals her duplicity and eventually kills herself after Rio publicly denounces her.
    Eva appears as a ghost in Midnight Rising, first acting as a guide to Dylan Alexander in the Czech Republic, leading Dylan to find Rio, who is wasting away in the mountain cave where the Ancient had once been located. Eva implores Dylan to "save him." Later, Eva appears again, this time to Rio, after Dylan is captured by Dragos. Eva helps Rio find Dylan at the Croton Reservoir dam in New York. Eva makes one final appearance to Dylan, after Rio and Dylan are mated and safe at the Order's compound in Boston. Rio burns Eva's remaining personal effects, and Eva sadly smiles to Dylan in understanding, acceptance, before fading away.

First mention in series: Appears in Kiss of Midnight.

~ ~ ~

Evran (d.)   Breed male, Lucan's older brother, the middle of the three siblings (Marek being eldest). Evran went Rogue soon after he reached adulthood. He was later killed in combat during one of the old wars between the Breed and the Rogues, Evran being on the wrong side of the conflict.

First mention in series: Referenced in Kiss of Midnight.

~ ~ ~

-F-

Fiona MacBain (d.)   First Breedmate of Malcolm MacBain. Fiona was gentle and innocent, just twenty-two when Malcolm met her. She looked at him like some kind of fairytale hero, helped the jaded Breed male remember what it was like to be carefree and open. Mal and Fiona were together less than a year when he realized he loved her. They mated and lived at his castle Darkhaven outside Edinburgh, then soon Fiona became pregnant.

She was only a few months along when she traveled alone to the city one day to pick up bedding for the nursery while Mal was home building her a custom rocking chair. Fiona was grabbed off the street by a pimp who supplied a local Breed crime boss's blood clubs (see Reiver). Fiona fought her abductor and was stabbed through the heart. Feeling her pain through their blood bond and sensing she was still alive, Malcolm defied the noonday sun to look for her. He arrived in Edinburgh burned and weak, too late to save his mate. But he found the pimp and killed him, then vowed to avenge Fiona and their unborn child by infiltrating the organization of the crime boss and destroying him from the inside. Although Breedmate funeral rites call for cremation, Malcolm instead brought Fiona's bloodied body home and buried her that same day.

First mention in series: Referenced in A Taste of Midnight (novella).

~ ~ ~

Fran Littlejohn   Human. Resident of Harmony, Alaska. Works at the town's medical center. Fran was present when Skeeter killed Big Dave Grant at the center. Kade later trances her, making her forget what she witnessed and has her tell a gathering of Harmony residents that Big Dave died on the table from his attack injuries.

First mention in series: Appears in Shades of Midnight.

~ ~ ~

Freyne (d.)   Breed male, Enforcement Agent. Freyne is present at a crime scene with Mathias Rowan when Sterling Chase and Brock show up to talk with Rowan. Freyne taunts Chase about his nephew Camden's death, inciting Chase to fight with him. Later, after Kellan Archer's abduction, Freyne is the Agent who receives a tip from a human informant about the location where Kellan is being held. Freyne is present on the Agency mission to rescue the Breed youth, led by Mathias Rowan. While there, Freyne's duplicity and alliance with Dragos is revealed when, left alone with Chase to guard Kellan's father, Christophe, and his grandfather, Lazaro, Freyne instead murders Christophe and Lazaro narrowly survives. Freyne is killed by Hunter, who comes upon the attack and intervenes.

First mention in series: Appears in Taken by Midnight.

~ ~ ~

-G-

Gabrielle Maxwell   Breedmate of Order leader Lucan. Orphaned as an infant in Boston twenty-seven years before the Midnight Breed series opens. Gabrielle's unwed teen mother was institutionalized, and later committed suicide, after claiming to have been attacked by a vampire. Gabrielle doesn't know who her father is, was raised in foster care until being adopted by local (human) family, the Maxwells, when she was twelve. Gabrielle had a troubled youth.

At twenty-eight, she was living on her own and had become a gifted art photographer whose images, unbeknownst to her, often featured Breed locations. Gabrielle knew nothing about the world of the Breed, nor her place in it as a Breedmate, until her path crossed with Lucan's one harrowing summer night in Boston.

Hair: auburn
Eyes: soft brown
Breedmate mark: behind her left ear
Bloodscent: night-blooming jasmine
Unique ability: can sense, and is drawn to, areas of Breed presence
Mate: Lucan
Heroine in: Kiss of Midnight (Book 1)

First mention in series: Appears in Kiss of Midnight.

~ ~ ~

Gideon   Breed male, Order member. Mate of Savannah Dupree. Born in England in 1602. Renown for his skill with a sword, Gideon had worked independently to eliminate Rogues, but sought out Lucan to join the Order after Gideon's young twin brothers, Simon and Roderick, were killed in a Rogue attack outside their London Darkhaven. Gideon is the Order's resident genius, responsible for all the technology and even performs as the compound's medic when needed.

No longer runs combat missions due to irreparable brain injury sustained during the rescue of his Breedmate, Savannah thirty-plus years before the timeline of Kiss of Midnight. Gideon still carries a bullet lodged deep in his brain after that confrontation (see Cyril Smithson), which has crippled his ESP talent and impacted his eyesight so that he must wear some form of sunglasses at all times.

Hair: blond, cropped/spiky cut
Eyes: sharp blue, usually glancing over the rims of pale blue or silver shades
Unique ability: power to see life energy through solid mass (talent lost due to injury)
Mate: Savannah Dupree
Hero in: A Touch of Midnight (Series prequel novella, Book 0.5)

First mention in series: Appears in Kiss of Midnight.

~ ~ ~

Goran   Human. Handsome young barkeep at the small-town pub outside Prague, where Dylan and her traveling companions go for a meal and drinks after hiking in the Czech mountains. Goran flirts with Dylan, and tells the women about area lore and his own grandfather's recent witness of a fanged creature (see Rio) that attacked one of his field workers a few months before the timeline of Midnight Rising. Dylan wants to question his grandfather for an article she plans to write for the tabloid she works for, but Goran informs her that the old man died of old age recently.

First mention in series: Appears in Midnight Rising.

~ ~ ~

Green (d.)   Human. FBI Special Agent, NYC office. Green is FBI partner of Phillip Cho and Minion to Dragos. Green Tasers Jenna at the NYC office after she arrives for a meeting with Cho. Green accidentally shoots Cho in the vehicle while they are taking Jenna to Dragos, crashing the car. Brock is in pursuit in a second vehicle, follows the crashed FBI car to rescue Jenna. Green comes out shooting, and Jenna eventually kills the Minion using Brock's pistol.

First mention in series: Appears in Taken by Midnight.

~ ~ ~

Gresa (d.)   Human. Albanian delivery man who is one of a pair of bad guys who pick up Jenna after she flees the Order's compound in Boston and falsely agree to take her to the bus station. Gresa and his partner instead take Jenna to a meat-packing plant in Southie, Gresa shoots her in the thigh during a struggle in the van, then they lock her in a refrigerated room. Brock bites Gresa, then kills him by breaking his neck.

First mention in series: Appears in Taken by Midnight.

~ ~ ~

Grigori (d.)   Breed male, Kade's uncle. Younger brother to Kir and Maksim. Grigori was the family's dark secret, a vibrant, reckless, charming youth who was too wild at heart. Grigori fell into Bloodlust and went Rogue. Maksim tells Kade that once Kir learned that Grigori's addiction had led him to kill, Kir wrote the boy off completely, even though Kir loved him dearly. Maksim tells Kade that Kir never so much as spoke of Grigori again, and he was never the same. Later on, after Seth's funeral at the family Darkhaven in Alaska, Kir explains to Kade that although Kade reminded him of the best in Grigori, Seth was Grigori at his worst. Kir confesses that Grigori didn't simply disappear from the family; Kir felt duty-bound to make sure his brother could never kill again. He took his beloved brother's life, and feared that he would one day see his sons suffer a similar impossible situation.

First mention in series: Referenced in Shades of Midnight.

~ ~ ~

-H-

Hank Maguire (d.)   Human. Alexandra's stepfather. Ran a seaplane charter business in Florida when Alex was a kid. After the murders of Alex's mother and little brother, Richie, by Rogues in Florida when Alex was nine, Hank relocated with her to Harmony, Alaska. Taught Alex to fly when she was twelve. Hank was dead from Alzheimer's Disease six months before the timeline of Shades of Midnight.

First mention in series: Referenced in Shades of Midnight.

~ ~ ~

Hans Friedrich Waldemar (d.)   Breed male, corrupt Enforcement Agent located in Berlin, Germany. First introduced at the reception for Elise Chase and Tegan hosted by Andreas Reichen in Midnight Awakening. Waldemar tried to monopolize Elise's attention, bragging to her with stories of his Agency exploits. He then later expresses his distaste for the Order and Tegan in particular, remarking that the warriors are vigilantes who deserve no respect. Elise puts Waldemar in his place, reminding him of how Tegan saved the Berlin Darkhaven from a Rogue attack in the early 1800s. Later, during the timeline of events in Ashes of Midnight, Waldemar is revealed to be part of Wilhelm Roth's (and by extension, Dragos's) corrupt inner circle. Andreas Reichen seeks out Waldemar and kills him by breaking his neck.

First mention in series: Appears in Midnight Awakening.

~ ~ ~

Harvard the dog   Canine. Mixed breed terrier, shelter dog. Spared from euthanasia at a Boston shelter when Dante purchased the dog as a means of getting close to Tess. As a private joke, Dante names the pitiful creature after Sterling Chase. Tess later uses her healing ability to cure the dog of its cancer and other ailments. After Tess is brought to the compound, Dante brings the dog to her, where it becomes a part of the Order's growing family.

First mention in series: Appears in Kiss of Crimson.

~ ~ ~

Heinrich Kuhn (d.)   Breed male, director of the Rogue Rehabilitation facility in Berlin, Germany. Antagonistic toward Tegan when the warrior and Elise arrive to speak with one of the facility's patients (see Petrov Odolf). It is later revealed that Kuhn has been approached and threatened by Marek, and out of fear of Marek, Kuhn arranges for his facility guards to drug Tegan with tranquilizers when the warrior returns to question Kuhn again in private. Tegan is given up to Marek for capture and torture, and Kuhn is swiftly beheaded by Marek after serving his purpose.

First mention in series: Appears in Midnight Awakening.

~ ~ ~

Helene (d.)   Human. Lover of Andreas Reichen (prior to Ashes of Midnight) and owner of Berlin sex club, Aphrodite. Aware of the Breed, but she kept their secret. Raven-haired Helene also provided information to Andreas Reichen, including details on the disappearance of a girl from her club. Helene collects a name of the Breed male last seen with the girl: Wilhelm Roth, Claire's mate and Enforcement Agency ally to Dragos. In Veil of Midnight, Roth turns Helene Minion and sends her to Reichen's Darkhaven to facilitate the slaughter of everyone inside by armed Agents. Reichen comes home to discover her in the blood-soaked aftermath and is forced to kill her.

First mention in series: Appears in Midnight Awakening.

~ ~ ~

Henry Tulak (d.)   Human. Native resident of Harmony, Alaska, lived alone in a small cabin ten miles out of town. Killed the winter before the timeline of Shades of Midnight, causes unknown, until Kade later deduces that Tulak was a victim of Kade's brother, Seth.

First mention in series: Referenced in Shades of Midnight.

~ ~ ~

Henry Vachon (d.)   Breed male, second generation. High-ranking Enforcement Agency member located in New Orleans and longtime secret ally to Dragos (aka Gerard Starkn). Henry Vachon was a participant in the 1930s abduction of Corinne Bishop and her transfer to Dragos's breeding labs. After Hunter and Corinne collect Vachon's name as one of her tormentors, they travel to New Orleans where Hunter later breaks into Vachon's mansion with the intent of gathering intel on Dragos. Vachon resists compromising his alliance with Dragos, and reveals to Hunter that both Vachon and Dragos raped her the night of her abduction. Enraged, Hunter attacks Vachon and kills him. During the slaying, Hunter's blood-reading ability shows him the location of stored records and materials from one of Dragos's breeding labs.

First mention in series: Appears in Deeper Than Midnight.

~ ~ ~

"Homeboy" (d.)   Breed male, Boston resident. Skin trader who trafficks women to sell to other Breed males or humans in the market for females. Has three human women bound, beaten and held captive beneath his club when Kade and Brock raid his place. Homeboy dresses in a long fox fur coat, tons of bling and guyliner. Keeps two white pit bulls, which Kade uses his talent on, turning the dogs on their owner during questioning.

First mention in series: Appears in Shades of Midnight.

~ ~ ~

Hugh Faulkner (d.)   Breed male, Gen One. Blacksmith and sword maker in London, England circa 1600s. Hugh was an arrogant, nasty individual who unwisely challenged Gideon to a duel about three-hundred years before the timeline of Kiss of Midnight. Gideon proved the victor, slaying Hugh following the smith's attempt to cheat by attacking Gideon from behind. It is later revealed that Hugh had an illegitimate son (see Cyril Smithson) who witnessed the contest and vowed to retaliate for his father's death by murdering Gideon's young twin brothers.

First mention in series: Referenced in A Touch of Midnight (novella).

~ ~ ~

Hunter   Gen One Breed, Order member. Mate of Corinne Bishop. Born August 8, 1956, Hunter was conceived and raised in a covert laboratory environment under the control of Dragos. Given no name at birth, like the rest of his lab-bred assassin brothers, this lethal Breed male answers to the name of the role he was created to fill: Hunter. After his rearing in Dragos's labs, Hunter's home base was a meager farmhouse in Vermont, where he lived in an unfurnished, bare-floored cellar, tended by a Minion handler assigned to him since birth. Like all others raised to be Dragos's personal army of assassins, Hunter had been fitted from childhood with a black electronic collar that contained an ultraviolet light source. This UV collar, if tampered with or triggered remotely by Dragos, would detonate and kill him instantly.

Hunter has a special affection for Mira, who, as a child, unwittingly prevented him from carrying out one of his assassination missions (see Sergei Yakut) when he looked into the young seer's gaze and saw the girl would one day spare his life. She made good on that vision later, during the timeline of Veil of Midnight, and because of her, Hunter joined the Order's fight against Dragos. Hunter was a virgin until he met and became involved with Corinne Bishop while charged with escorting her to her family's Darkhaven in Detroit. Hunter and Corinne are now parents to her son, Nathan, also a Gen One trained assassin.

Hair: close-shorn, brownish blond
Eyes: golden, hawk-like
Unique ability: blood-reader (Breed and Breedmates only, does not work on humans)
Mate: Corinne Bishop
Hero in: Deeper Than Midnight (Book 9)

First mention in series: Appears in Veil of Midnight.

~ ~ ~

-I-

Ida Arnold   Human. Resident of Harmony, Alaska, and Skeeter's mother. Unpleasant person, harangues Skeeter constantly and is nearly killed by him after he's been turned Minion.

First mention in series: Appears in Shades of Midnight.

~ ~ ~

Ilsa Roth (d.)   Breedmate, first mate of Wilhelm Roth in Germany. Ilsa was timid, a poor match for Roth. She and Andreas Reichen both earn Roth's ire when Ilsa contradicts her mate at a public event and is reprimanded by Roth. Andreas finds the Breedmate crying in the rain and gives her his jacket before sending her home with his driver. Roth finds out and seethes with hatred for both of them. It was purported that Ilsa died in a Rogue attack thirty years before the timeline of Ashes of Midnight, but Roth later reveals to Claire that he had his first mate killed in order to pave the way to claim Claire for himself.

First mention in series: Referenced in Ashes of Midnight.

~ ~ ~

Irina Odolf   Breedmate of Petrov Odolf. Elise and Tegan are introduced to Irina at a Rogue rehabilitation facility in Berlin during the timeline of Midnight Awakening. Irina is there for a supervised feeding with Petrov, whom the Order seeks to question about the Petrov family journal recovered from a Minion (see Sheldon Raines) who'd intended to deliver the book to his Master, Marek. Irina and Elise bond over the loss of their beloved mates, and Irina eventually provides Elise and the Order with additional clues to the past, including information that will assist them in finding the hiding place of the last remaining Ancient.

First mention in series: Appears in Midnight Awakening.

~ ~ ~

-J-

Jack   Human. Friend of Renata's. Former military, Texas drawl, gray buzz-cut hair. Jack runs a halfway house for troubled teens. House is called "Anna's Place" in memoriam to Jack's wife, who was killed years ago by a teen heroin addict. Jack gave Renata shelter when she was a runaway from an orphanage. Jack again provided safe haven for her, and for Nikolai, after Renata drove Niko to Jack's place following her rescue of Niko from a Rogue rehabilitation facility outside Montreal, Quebec, where he was being drugged and held by Edgar Fabien, an ally of Dragos's. Years ago, Jack gave Renata the four custom daggers she always carries, which bear the words, "faith," "honor," "courage," and "sacrifice"—the qualities he saw in her as a young woman, and what he hoped would serve as reminders of the qualities that would see her through any situation.

First mention in series: Appears in Veil of Midnight.

~ ~ ~

James MacConn   Breed male, cousin of Conlan MacConn's, lives in Edinburgh. Dark-eyed mate of Emma MacConn. James and Emma were present with Danika at the holiday party where she first encounters a crime boss named Reiver, and his bodyguard, Brannoc (AKA Malcolm MacBain).

First mention in series: Appears in A Taste of Midnight (novella).

~ ~ ~

Jamie   Human. Gabrielle's gay male friend in Boston. Newbury Street art gallery owner where Gabrielle's photo exhibit was displayed in Kiss of Midnight. It is Jamie who instigates going to a nightclub after the art exhibit, which brings Gabrielle, Jamie and their friends Kendra and Megan to the club La Notte, where Gabrielle first sees Lucan Thorne and witnesses a group of vampires attacking a human in the alley outside. Later in the timeline of Kiss of Midnight, Jamie is abducted by Marek in an attempt to lure Gabrielle to him, but Jamie escapes from the vehicle at a red light. After his escape and Gabrielle's rescue from Marek, Jamie is allowed to go free without a mind scrub, a kindness Lucan grants Gabrielle, permitting her to decide how much to tell her friend as she tells Jamie good-bye.

First mention in series: Appears in Kiss of Midnight.

~ ~ ~

Jane Doe (d.)   Human. Gabrielle's unnamed teenage mother. Leaving home in Bangor, Maine, twenty-seven years before the timeline of Kiss of Midnight, headed for New York City with an infant Gabrielle, where she hopes to become a Rockette. On the bus ride toward Boston, Gabrielle's mother encounters a Rogue who attacks her outside a bus station restroom. She is bitten, and narrowly escapes the death of herself and her child, rescued by the intervention of an unnamed, dark-haired man (see Lucan Thorne). Gabrielle's mother flees with her, hiding the baby in a Dumpster, in her shock believing she was putting the infant to bed. Scared and losing hold of her sanity after the assault, the teenager is later picked up and taken to an insane asylum as a Jane Doe with no ID. She eventually cracks and commits suicide, leaving Gabrielle to become a ward of the state.

First mention in series: Appears in Kiss of Midnight.

~ ~ ~

Janet Human. Friend of Dylan's mother, Sharon Alexander. Janet worked with Sharon at the runaway center in Brooklyn, New York. Janet is present with Dylan and two of Sharon's other friends (see Marie and Nancy) on the trip to the Czech Republic, which Dylan attends in her cancer-stricken mother's place. While in town for a meal, Janet attempts to match-make between Dylan and a Czech bartender (see Goran). Because the women received Dylan's photos of her time in Prague, including images of Rio and the Ancient's hiding place in the mountain cave, Janet and her two friends are later mind-scrubbed by Niko and Kade on Lucan's orders. Later in the timeline of Midnight Rising, Janet helps Dylan pack up Sharon's office at the shelter and shows Dylan a photograph of shelter benefactor, Gordon Fasso (see Dragos). Janet further assists Dylan during the timeline of Taken by Midnight, by providing old photographs of the shelter and some of the other women who once worked there (see Sister Margaret Mary Howland).

First mention in series: Appears in Midnight Rising.

~ ~ ~

Jenna Tucker-Darrow Human (originally). Mate of Order member Brock. Jenna is a former Alaska State Trooper and best friend of Alexandra Maguire. Four years before timeline of Shades of

Midnight, Jenna lost her husband and young daughter when a timber truck collided with the family's vehicle on the highway in Alaska. Jenna barely survived, waking a month and a half later to learn her loved ones were gone. She quit her job as a Trooper, even though police work and helping people is a big part of her nature.

Thirty-three-year-old Jenna is human, but an attack on her by the Ancient has left her changed in many ways—not the least of which being a growing *dermaglyph* that's appeared on the back of her neck. The Order brought her from Alaska to their Boston compound to heal, aided by Brock's calming effect on the human. As Jenna's stay lengthened, the Order discovered her human DNA was being dominated by that of the creature who attacked her, gifting her with unusual strength and abilities, and transforming into something never seen before.

Hair: shoulder-length, medium brown
Eyes: hazel
Breedmate mark: does not have one
Bloodscent: does not have one
Unique ability: superhuman speed and agility, unlimited language comprehension, adaptive regeneration (body learning to heal itself after injury), and other abilities yet to be revealed
Mate: Brock
Heroine in: Taken by Midnight (Book 8)

First mention in series: Appears in Shades of Midnight.

~ ~ ~

Joey   Human. FedEx clerk in Boston who had to deal with an abusive customer (see Sheldon Raines). Joey assists Elise the next day when she returns to the FedEx store to pick up her "husband's" delayed package (see Odolf family). She has no ID to prove her claim, but Joey agrees to give her the package in exchange for her son Camden's iPod, Elise's only memento of her deceased son.

First mention in series: Appears in Midnight Awakening.

~ ~ ~

Jonas Redmond (d.)   Breed male, Darkhaven youth from Boston and close friend of Camden Chase. Jonas was the Breed youth whom Ben Sullivan witnessed having a violent reaction to Crimson in a Boston nightclub. Jonas continues using the drug and soon goes Rogue. The civilian is killed in an altercation with Dante outside a club, when Dante's titanium-edged blade slices Jonas's arm and the poison of the metal ashes the Rogue youth in the street.

First mention in series: Appears in Kiss of Crimson.

~ ~ ~

-K-

Kade   Breed male, Order member and mate of Alexandra Maguire. Close friends with Brock. Born more than one hundred years ago, raised on his parents' 10,000 acre Darkhaven wilderness compound outside Fairbanks, Alaska.

Kade been with the Order for about a year when Shades of Midnight opens, recruited by Nikolai, whom Kade had met decades earlier. Kade is a twin, had an identical brother, Seth, back home in Alaska. The untamed nature of his homeland is in Kade's veins. He is quick and impulsive and loyal, but also haunted by a darkness that lives inside him. He is forced to confront that darkness when a string of human slayings—obvious vampire attacks—in the Alaskan bush send him back home to investigate for the Order.

Hair: thick, spiky black
Eyes: wolf-like silver, fringed with inky lashes
Unique ability: can connect psychically with predator animals, experience their senses, direct their actions with a thought
Mate: Alexandra Maguire
Hero in: Shades of Midnight (Book 7)

First mention in series: Appears in Midnight Awakening.

~ ~ ~

Kassia (d.)   Breedmate, Dragos's mother and mate to the Gen One and Order member, Dragos the elder. Kassia was the artist who hundreds of years ago stitched a tapestry for Lucan, commemorating the Order's triumph over the Ancients. Unbeknownst to Lucan, the tapestry, depicting him on a rearing warhorse in front of his family's burning castle, also contained clues to a riddle woven into the design that later would lead the Order to the hiding place of the Ancient in the Bohemian mountain cave. Kassia was very close to Tegan's first mate, Sorcha. After Kassia's mate, Dragos the elder, was killed by Marek, she committed suicide to avoid being tortured by Marek for the secret of the Ancient's hiding place.

First mention in series: Referenced in Midnight Awakening.

~ ~ ~

Kellan Archer   Breed male, third generation. Son of Christophe Archer, grandson of Lazaro and Eleanor Archer. Kellan is fourteen years old during the timeline of Taken by Midnight, where he is first introduced in the series as the Darkhaven teen of a prominent Boston family who's abducted and held for ransom by Dragos's men. Kellan's abduction was actually a ruse meant to give Dragos the chance to find the location of the Order's Boston compound, a goal achieved when the Order rescues the teen and brings him and his grandfather, Lazaro, into Order protection at their headquarters. It is soon discovered that Dragos embedded a GPS device in Kellan's stomach, which the boy vomits up, alerting the Order that their longtime secret compound has been compromised.

Kellan Archer is a sullen boy, bereft over the loss of his parents and all but one of his family members (see Lazaro Archer) in a Darkhaven explosion carried out at Dragos's command. Mira befriends Kellan immediately, deciding he will be her best friend whether he likes it or not (he doesn't). During his recuperation with the Order, Kellan continues to withdraw, refusing to feed until Lucan takes him out to hunt in Darker After Midnight. He wants to join the Order for revenge on Dragos, but Lucan denies him, telling him he's too young and wants it for the wrong reason. Later on in Darker After Midnight, Kellan takes part in a snowball fight with Nathan. When Mira gets hit with one of Nathan's volleys, Kellan reacts with swift, protective fury. The two teen vampires grapple, and Kellan, sensing Nathan's lethal skill and training, asks him to teach him everything he knows.

Although Kellan is only a teenager as of the timeline of Darker After Midnight, his full romantic story is told twenty years afterward in Edge of Dawn.

Hair: ginger as a teen; brownish-copper, the color of an old penny, as an adult
Eyes: hazel
Unique ability: can read a human's true intentions with his touch
Mate: Mira
Hero in: Edge of Dawn (Book 11)

First mention in series: Appears in Taken by Midnight.

~ ~ ~

Kendra Delaney (d.)   Human. Registered Nurse and friend of Gabrielle's who unwittingly becomes involved with a Breed male (see Brent) after meeting him in the Boston nightclub La Notte. Kendra is later picked up by Marek and brought to an orgy with a large number of Rogues under Marek's leadership. While with Marek, Kendra is turned Minion for him. Marek uses Kendra to lure Gabrielle to him, leading to a confrontation between Marek and his brother, Lucan. Kendra dies when she leaps to her death from the high floor of a building at her Master's command.

First mention in series: Appears in Kiss of Midnight.

~ ~ ~

Kerr (d.)   Breed male, one of crime boss Reiver's henchman. Kerr and another thug, Packard, are sent by Reiver to silence Danika after she crossed him. Malcolm MacBain kills Kerr at the small cottage where Danika and her son were staying on MacConn lands.

First mention in series: Appears in A Taste of Midnight (novella).

~ ~ ~

Kir   Breed male, Kade's father, and brother to Maksim, who lives at the family's ten-thousand acre Darkhaven outside Fairbanks, Alaska. Kir is mated to Victoria, who is heavily pregnant with twin sons during the timeline of Shades of Midnight. Kir and Kade have always been distant because Kir has focused all of his energy on holding Seth up, over-protective of him because he knows Seth is the weaker of his two sons. Kir's fears are rooted in his past, when he and his brother, Grigori, had a similar dynamic to that of Kade and Seth. Grigori turned Rogue and Kir had to kill him. Kir and Kade reconcile at the end of Shades of Midnight, at Seth's funeral.

First mention in series: Appears in Shades of Midnight.

~ ~ ~

Kiril (d.)   Breed male. Guard at Sergei Yakut's lodge near Montreal, Quebec. Kiril and three other Breed males are assigned by Alexei Yakut to guard Nikolai after Sergei's killing. Believing Alexei that Niko was responsible for Sergei's murder, Kiril expresses his opinion that they should torture the warrior before the Enforcement Agency shows up to take him into custody. Kiril is particularly nasty and aggressive, unaware that Niko is not unconscious as he appears, but awake and very pissed off. As a six-man Agency detail approaches the lodge and Niko's time to escape is running out, he attacks Kiril, snapping the guard's neck and then using his dead body to crash through a nearby window in his attempt to elude capture.

First mention in series: Appears in Veil of Midnight.

~ ~ ~

Klaus   Breed male. Andreas Reichen's driver and member of his Darkhaven. Klaus is present when Reichen picks up Tegan and Elise at the airport upon their arrival in Berlin in Midnight Awakening.

First mention in series: Appears in Midnight Awakening.

~ ~ ~

Krieger   Breed male, Enforcement Agent in Germany, reporting to Wilhelm Roth. Agent Krieger phones Roth, pulling Roth out of a dreamwalk visit from Claire, to inform him about Hans Waldemar's killing and Roth's country Darkhaven being destroyed. Roth orders Krieger to send a team in to have Andreas Reichen killed.

First mention in series: Appears in Ashes of Midnight.

~ ~ ~

-L-

Lanny Hamm (d.)   Human. Resident of Harmony, Alaska, and cohort to Big Dave Grant. Lanny was at the impromptu town hall meeting where Alexandra Maguire first sees Kade, and was supportive of Big Dave's call for a wolf hunt. Lanny was later killed by the Ancient while in the Alaskan bush hunting with Big Dave.

First mention in series: Appears in Shades of Midnight.

~ ~ ~

Lazaro Archer   Gen One Breed. Jet-black hair, dark blue eyes. Appears to be around thirty years old, but is close to one-thousand years old. Lazaro has many regrets, including that he did not join Lucan and the Order during the war with the Ancients in the mid-1300s, and that he again refused Lucan's call to act when it became evident in present day that Dragos was intent on eliminating the Gen One population. Lazaro and his kin have lived in the New England area for a century or so. Lazaro blames himself for the violence visited on his family by Dragos: the abduction of his nephew, Kellan; the slaying of Lazaro's son, Christophe; and the destruction of the Archer Darkhaven by Dragos, which killed Lazaro's long-time Breedmate, Eleanor, and the rest of their kin living in the Boston residence.

Lazaro begins working closely with the Order afterward, offering up one of his unused Darkhaven retreats in Maine as temporary headquarters after the Boston compound is compromised to Dragos and the humans. Lazaro also shares with Lucan some history about the Ancients, that Lazaro's sire attended secret gatherings with the other Ancients and taught Lazaro some of their language.

First mention in series: Appears in Taken by Midnight.

~ ~ ~

Lieutenant, unnamed (d.)   Breed male, second generation. Lieutenant of Dragos's, executed the planned attack on the Archer family Darkhaven in Boston, which killed Lazaro's Breedmate, Eleanor, and the rest of their kin who lived there. Lieutenant reports to Dragos that Lazaro and Kellan are alive after the joint rescue effort by the Order and Mathias Rowan. Also informs Dragos that Hunter is now working with the Order. Lieutenant is later killed by Dragos after telling him more bad news, that the captive Breedmates were found and rescued by the Order's Breedmates. Dragos rips out Lieutenant's heart. It is later inferred in Deeper Than Midnight that Enforcement Agents Freyne and Murdock both reported to this Lieutenant.

First mention in series: Appears in Taken by Midnight.

~ ~ ~

Libby Darrow (d.)   Human. Jenna Tucker-Darrow's six-year-old daughter, who died in a car accident in November, four years before the timeline of Shades of Midnight. Libby was in the vehicle Mitch Darrow, Jenna's husband, was driving when a timber truck hit their Blazer, killing both Libby and Mitch and putting Jenna in the hospital with severe injuries. Jenna finally says good-bye to her daughter, visiting the cemetery in Harmony, Alaska, for the first time at the end of Taken By Midnight.

First mention in series: Referenced in Shades of Midnight.

~ ~ ~

Lucan Thorne   Gen One Breed, leader of the Order and mate of Gabrielle Maxwell. The youngest of three brothers, the other two deceased (see Evran and Marek). Lucan is no less than nine hundred years old.

Founder of the Order in mid-1300s in Eastern Europe with Tegan, Marek, and five other Gen One Breed warriors. Led the uprising against the Ancients during same period, following the killing of Lucan's mother at his father's hands. The war against the Ancients resulted in the slaying of all but one, who was secretly hidden for centuries by Dragos. After the Order eventually dissolved in Europe, Lucan later established a Boston headquarters in 1898 with Gideon in an effort to combat Rogues in that city.

Lucan is considered one of the most formidable Breed males in existence. As a Gen One, particularly one who's seen firsthand the devastating results of what Bloodlust can do to one of his kind, Lucan's greatest fear is losing himself to blood addiction. It is a fear he hides behind his contempt toward Rogues, but deep inside he dreads turning into the monster his father was. Lucan drives a black Maybach and carries two titanium-edge swords, in addition to other weaponry.

Hair: silky jet-black, falls to near his collar
Eyes: piercing pale gray
Unique ability: hypnotic manipulation
Mate: Gabrielle Maxwell
Hero in: Kiss of Midnight (Book 1)

First mention in series: Appears in Kiss of Midnight.

~ ~ ~

Luna (dog)   Canine. Alexandra Maguire's gray and white wolf dog.

First mention in series: Appears in Shades of Midnight and later books.

~ ~ ~

-M-

Maksim "Max" Breed male, Kade's uncle, Kir's younger brother at nearly three hundred years old. Unlike Kir, Max is openly proud of Kade and his work with the Order. While Kade is in Alaska on Order business, Max tells him about their family's dark secret: that his other uncle, Grigori, went Rogue and Kir could not deal with the fact (it's later revealed that Kir killed Grigori). Max's loyalty to Kir shackles him to the family Darkhaven, but at heart, Max craves adventure, appreciates the concepts of risk and reward, courage and honor. Kir is deeply attracted to a Breedmate at the Darkhaven, Seth's promised, but unclaimed mate, Patrice.

First mention in series: Appears in Shades of Midnight.

~ ~ ~

Malcolm MacBain (aka Brannoc) Breed male, mate to Danika MacConn. Highlands-born Malcolm is more than four-hundred years old, lives in a fifteenth-century stone castle outside Edinburgh, Scotland. Mal was as close as a brother to Conlan MacConn, the pair of Breed males both neighbors and brothers-in-arms who rode into many battles together. They also saw Danika for the first time together, and both were mesmerized by the Nordic blond beauty. Malcolm tried to impress her, seduce her with his dark, cynical charm. But it was Con who won Danika's hand in the end. Malcolm harbored no ill will for his friend's lucky match, but he secretly loved Danika for a long time.

Mal remained unmated until very recently, when a young Breedmate named Fiona stole his heart with her innocence and sweetness. Mal and Fiona mated and soon were expecting a child, but Fiona met with tragedy in Edinburgh while shopping on her own. A blood club supplying pimp grabbed her off the street, intending to hand her over to an area crime boss (see Reiver). She fought back and was stabbed and killed. Malcolm raced to the city in daylight hours to find her, and suffered UV burns and a savage knife wound across his face when he confronted the pimp. Vowing to avenge his slain mate and unborn son, Malcolm adopts a new name, Brannoc, and covertly infiltrates the crime boss's organization with a plan to destroy him from the inside.

Hair: shaggy, chestnut-brown
Eyes: gunmetal gray
Unique ability: not yet revealed
Mate: Fiona (deceased); Danika MacConn
Hero in: A Taste of Midnight (novella, Book 9.5)

First mention in series: Appears in A Taste of Midnight (novella).

~ ~ ~

Marek (d.)   Gen One Breed, Lucan's eldest of two brothers. The most fearless, according to Lucan. Marek was part of the Order when Lucan first founded it in the mid-1300s, along with Tegan and several other Gen Ones. Less than a hundred years after that conflict, Marek was presumed to have fallen into Bloodlust and taken his own life by seeking the sun.

During the timeline of Kiss of Midnight, it is revealed that Marek is not dead, but is in fact leading a group of Rogues in Boston intent on destroying Lucan and the Order in a quest for world domination. In Kiss of Midnight, Marek creates Minions of several humans, uses Rio's mate, Eva, against the Order, and eventually abducts Gabrielle in an effort to lure Lucan into his hands. Gabrielle is rescued and Marek escapes, thwarted, but continues to cause problems in Kiss of Crimson by funding the manufacture and distribution of a Bloodlust-inducing drug (see Ben Sullivan).

In Midnight Awakening, Marek reveals to Tegan that it was he, Marek, who turned Tegan's first mate Minion (see Sorcha). Marek also divulges his role in the concealment of the last remaining Ancient and his belief that the Breed should enslave mankind and become the kings the Breed were meant to be. After taking Tegan captive in Berlin with the help of a secret ally (see Heinrich Kuhn) and feeding him Crimson, Marek is confronted by Lucan and Elise, who've come to look for Tegan. In a rare show of indecision, Lucan finds the thought of killing his brother too difficult to carry out. Marek is instead slain by Tegan and Elise working together.

First mention in series: Appears in Kiss of Midnight.

~ ~ ~

Marie   Human. Friend of Dylan's mother, Sharon Alexander; works with Sharon and Janet at the runaway shelter in Brooklyn, New York. Marie is present on the trip to the Czech Republic with Sharon's other friends (see Janet and Nancy), Dylan attending in her cancer-stricken mother's place. Because the women received Dylan's photos of her time in Prague, including images of Rio and the Ancient's hiding place in the mountain cave, Marie and her two friends are later mind-scrubbed by Niko and Kade on Lucan's orders.

First mention in series: Appears in Midnight Rising.

~ ~ ~

Martina   Breedmate, and friend of Claire (Roth) Reichen's in Germany. A gifted architect, Martina designed a small garden park at Claire's request, after Claire admired her other work around the Breed communities. Martina had assumed the park was for Claire's mate, but it was actually done in memory of Andreas Reichen, who had been presumed dead in the attack on his Darkhaven in Berlin.

First mention in series: Appears (via telephone call) in Ashes of Midnight.

~ ~ ~

Mason   Breed male, guard at the Bishop Darkhaven. Kind-hearted, trustworthy. Mason comes to the protection of Corinne's mother, Regina, when Victor Bishop threatens her life after she uncovers his betrayal of Corinne to Dragos and Henry Vachon. During the confrontation, Victor reflects that he had long suspected Mason had feelings for Regina.

First mention in series: Appears in Deeper Than Midnight.

~ ~ ~

Mathias Rowan   Breed male. Enforcement Agent in Boston, used to work with Sterling Chase at the Agency. In timeline of Taken by Midnight, Mathias has been covertly supplying the Order with intel on corrupt Agents and other issues of interest to the Order. While many in the Enforcement Agency are untrustworthy and self-serving, Mathias is one of the good guys. He is the first to inform the Order of Kellan Archer's abduction, alerting the warriors of a tip leading to Kellan's location. Mathias leads the Agency team in the rescue of Kellan along with the Order. When it turns out that Dragos is behind the abduction and the later destruction of the Archer Darkhaven in Boston, Mathias Rowan tells the Order that he is their ally in the fight and that Dragos is his enemy now too.

First mention in series: Appears in Taken by Midnight.

~ ~ ~

Megan   Human. Close friend of Gabrielle's. Megan and her cop boyfriend, Ray, come to check on Gabrielle while Lucan is there and Lucan has to scrub their memories before he takes Gabrielle away to the compound.

First mention in series: Appears in Kiss of Midnight.

~ ~ ~

Millie Dunbar   Human. 87-year-old resident of Harmony, Alaska. Present at the impromptu town hall meeting where Alexandra Maguire first sees Kade.

First mention in series: Appears in Shades of Midnight.

~ ~ ~

Mira   Breedmate, orphaned in Montreal and abducted at the age of eight by the same Breed elder for whom Renata worked (see Sergei Yakut). Mira is a Breedmate girl with a precognitive gift for showing someone an event fated to take place in their future. Her ability comes with a price, however: each vision she gives takes away some of her eyesight. To combat this problem, she wore a veil over her eyes during the timeline of Veil of Midnight. After becoming a resident of the Order's compound in Boston, Mira was given custom-crafted purple contacts, created by Gideon, to protect her eyes and mute her seer's gift to others who might look into her gaze. Mira was nicknamed "Mouse" by Renata, who's become a surrogate mother to the girl.

During the timeline of Veil of Midnight, several people saw visions in Mira's eyes: Nikolai, Hunter, Sergei Yakut, Edgar Fabien, and Dragos. During the timeline of Ashes of Midnight, Mira accidently showed Claire a vision of Andreas's death by flames and smoke. During events in Darker After Midnight, Mira inadvertently shows Lucan a vision of war and bloodshed that soon comes to pass. Mira's closest friends, aside from Renata and Nikolai, are Kellan Archer and Nathan. She has a special connection to Hunter as well, who is fiercely protective of her. Mira is also immensely fond of the Order's resident canines, Harvard and Luna.

Although Mira is a child through the timeline of Darker After Midnight, her full romantic story is told twenty years afterward in Edge of Dawn.

Hair: blond
Eyes: a white so pure they seem colorless, mirror-like
Breedmate mark: in her hairline near her left temple
Bloodscent: lily of the valley
Unique ability: precognition, but she does not see or interpret the visions, which play out for the observer as though in a mirror
Mate: Kellan Archer
Heroine in: Edge of Dawn (Book 11)

First mention in series: Appears in Veil of Midnight.

~ ~ ~

Mitch Darrow (d.)   Human. Deceased husband of Jenna Tucker-Darrow and former Alaska State Trooper. Killed in car accident along with their daughter, Libby, in Alaska four years before the timeline of Shades of Midnight.

First mention in series: Referenced in Shades of Midnight.

~ ~ ~

Moric Kaszab (d.)   Breed male, second generation. One of Dragos's inner circle, secret lieutenants. Kaszab was head of the Enforcement Agency in Budapest, Hungary. He was present via video conference with Dragos during the timeline of Darker After Midnight, when the decision was made to unleash the Rogues from their rehabilitation facilities around the globe. Kaszab was eager for the carnage to come, expressed his belief that it was time enough that the Breed rise up to rule the night as was their birthright. At the close of Darker After Midnight, Kaszab is among the lieutenants reported as having been tracked down and eliminated by the combined efforts of the Order, Andreas Reichen, Mathias Rowan, and other like-minded members of the Enforcement Agency in various parts of the world.

First mention in series: Appears in Darker After Midnight.

~ ~ ~

Mrs. Corelli   Human. Elderly client of Tess's veterinarian clinic who brings in her white Persian cat, Romeo, to be neutered. Tess is fond of the old woman and far undercharges her for the service, demonstrating the kind of tenderhearted care for her patients and their pets that is slowly putting Tess into the red financially.

First mention in series: Appears in Kiss of Crimson.

~ ~ ~

Mrs. Kennefick   Human. Works at the Boston Public Library; Savannah's supervisor when she was a university student in Boston, circa 1974.

First mention in series: Appears in A Touch of Midnight (novella).

~ ~ ~

Murdock (d.) Breed male. Corrupt Enforcement Agent and ally of Dragos, but not part of his inner circle. Claims to report to another Agent out of Atlanta who is one of Dragos's lieutenants (most likely, the unnamed lieutenant who appears in Shades of Midnight). Murdock is originally from Atlanta, Georgia, area but was transferred to Boston about fifty years ago due to conduct issues. Has a reputation for solicitation of minors among the human populations and excessive force on both human and Breed civilian populations.

Murdock was at the Enforcement Agency watering hole in Chinatown when Sterling Chase and Hunter arrived there looking to gather intel on Dragos and his Enforcement Agency allies. Murdock disliked Chase, incited his anger at the club, resulting in a brawl between Chase and other Agents. After the altercation, Murdock went into hiding, but was later found by Chase, hunting humans as game in an illegal blood club outside Boston. Chase intervenes, disabling Murdock and taking him to an old grain silo for interrogation and torture.

During the questioning, Murdock reveals that Dragos is trying to find the Order's compound via some kind of Trojan horse (see Kellan Archer) and that he is making lots of Minions, including targeting a new senator (see Bobby Clarence). Chase kills Murdock after collecting the needed intel.

First mention in series: Appears in Deeper Than Midnight.

~ ~ ~

Murphy, Officer (d.) Human. Uniformed Boston police officer who was posted outside Senator Clarence's office the morning after the politician's murder by Sterling Chase. Murphy is a big man, with facial scar that splits the dark slash of his left eyebrow. Detective Avery assigns Murphy and a couple other officers to take Tavia Fairchild to an area hotel for safekeeping, fearing she's in danger too, because of her ties to the senator. It turns out Murphy is a Minion, something Sterling Chase realizes when he sees the officer escorting Tavia on the TV news. Murphy is killed by Chase at the hotel, when Chase arrives to rescue Tavia from the Minion. Tavia witnesses

Chase breaking Murphy's thick neck as if it were nothing, and here she begins to understand that Sterling Chase is not merely a man.

First mention in series: Appears in Darker After Midnight.

~ ~ ~

-N-

Nancy   Human. Friend of Dylan's mother, Sharon Alexander, since high school. Nancy is present on the trip to the Czech Republic with Sharon's other friends (see Janet and Marie), Dylan attending in her cancer-stricken mother's place. Because the women received Dylan's photos of her time in Prague, including images of Rio and the Ancient's hiding place in the mountain cave, Nancy and her two friends are later mind-scrubbed by Niko and Kade on Lucan's orders.

First mention in series: Appears in Midnight Rising.

~ ~ ~

Nassi (d.)   Human. Albanian delivery man who is one of a pair of bad guys who pick up Jenna after she flees the Order's compound in Boston, falsely offering to take her to the bus station. Nassi and his partner instead take Jenna to a meat-packing plant in Southie and lock her in a refrigerated room. Brock finds her, killing Nassi and his coworkers.

First mention in series: Appears in Taken by Midnight.

~ ~ ~

Nathan   Gen One Breed, Corinne's son, fathered by the Ancient who was held in captivity with Dragos. Nathan has jet-black hair, but as a Hunter, his head is shaved, making visible the dermaglyphs that cover his scalp. He has almond-shaped greenish-blue eyes like his mother, and also has her ESP gift of sonokinesis. A Hunter (raised to be an assassin), Nathan was born in Dragos's breeding laboratory thirteen years before Corinne was freed by the Order during the timeline of Taken by Midnight.

Genetically, Nathan is the half-brother of his mother's mate, Hunter, and is also related to Tavia Fairchild and the other, undiscovered Gen One females birthed in Dragos's labs, who are each the product of DNA blending between the Ancient and unknown Breedmates. Nathan is quiet and remote, unreadable. Though just a boy, he is expertly lethal because of his upbringing and training.

During the timeline of Deeper Than Midnight, when Corinne and Hunter find Nathan in his Minion handler's keeping in Georgia and find a way to free him of his UV collar, Nathan at first runs away. He returns to them the next night because he realizes he has nowhere to go. The couple takes him home to the Order's relocated, temporary headquarters in Maine, where Nathan eventually becomes friends with Mira and Kellan.

First mention in series: Appears in Deeper Than Midnight.

~ ~ ~

Nigel Traherne (d.)   Breed male, second generation. One of Dragos's inner circle, secret lieutenants. Traherne was the only one of Dragos's lieutenants with no direct ties to the Enforcement Agency, but was instead a well-connected, wealthy Darkhaven leader from London, England. He was present via video conference with Dragos during the timeline of Darker After Midnight, when the decision was made to unleash the Rogues from their rehabilitation facilities around the globe. Traherne alone expresses deep reservations about Dragos's plan, warning that an act of such magnitude cannot be undone. He reminds Dragos of recent setbacks in his operation's missions and suggests that exposing the Breed forever to mankind is too rash a decision. He goes on to say that his mate is with child and due any day, and his two older sons have given him more than a dozen grandchildren. Traherne's attack of conscience enrages Dragos, who orders the Breed male killed on the spot by the Hunter standing watch behind the London civilian on camera. Traherne's neck is snapped, and Dragos continues the meeting as if the dead male never existed.

First mention in series: Appears in Darker After Midnight.

~ ~ ~

Nikolai   Breed male, Order member and mate of Renata. Born in Siberia approximately eighty years ago, no surname taken. Niko is a thrill-seeker and a gearhead. He loves weaponry, gadgets and things that go boom. Niko custom crafts a lot of the Order's specialty ammunition used for combat missions and killing Rogues. He is impatient and a little cocky, full of explosive energy, but far from reckless. Nikolai is the one you'd watching your back in the heat of battle, but you would more than likely find him ahead of you, blazing the trail clear of danger before you even got there. Together, Niko and Renata are parents to orphan Mira.

Hair: sandy blond
Eyes: glacier-blue
Unique ability: telepathically generates rapid growth in plant life
Mate: Renata (couple shares parental responsibility for Mira)
Hero in: Veil of Midnight (Book 5)

First mention in series: Appears in Kiss of Midnight.

~ ~ ~

Nora (d.)   Human. Employee at Tess's veterinary clinic in Boston. Nora is tortured and killed by Ben Sullivan in the vet clinic after he is turned Minion by Marek.

First mention in series: Appears in Kiss of Crimson.

~ ~ ~

Nurse Doublemint   Human. One of a pair of nurses tending Sterling Chase in the medical facility he was taken to after being shot and Tasered at the Boston Police Department lineup. Chase nicknames the female "Nurse Doublemint" on account of the big wad of minty gum she chews at his hospital bedside. The nurse mentions that the lab needed to run Chase's blood work a third time, because the results keep coming back messed up. She also remarks to her coworker (see Nurse Mike) on Chase's condition, expressing astonishment that he could have survived so much bodily trauma. After Nurse Doublemint leaves the room, Chase begins his escape.

First mention in series: Appears in Darker After Midnight.

~ ~ ~

Nurse Mike   Human. One of a pair of nurses tending Sterling Chase in the medical facility he was taken to after being shot and Tasered at the Boston Police Department lineup. Mike is a big man, booming Boston accented voice. He's working on Chase, reporting his stats and preparing his medications and sedatives when his counterpart (see Nurse Doublemint) leaves to attend other hospital business. Mike thinks his patient is unconscious, but Chase is awake, waiting for his chance to make an escape. As Mike sets up the IV bag, Chase jumps on him to feed, then trances him. Chase takes the nurse's scrubs, but the shoes are too small. Chase puts Mike in the hospital bed, scrubs his memory, then flees the medical ward on foot.

First mention in series: Appears in Darker After Midnight.

~ ~ ~

-O-

Octavia "Tavia" Fairchild   Gen One Breed and Breedmate genetic hybrid, mate of Order member Sterling Chase; daywalker. Born in Boston twenty-seven years before the timeline of Darker After Midnight, raised by her aunt Sarah since infancy, when Tavia survived a house fire that killed her parents. Highly intelligent and capable, Tavia works as an assistant to a rising star senator in Boston. On the personal side, Tavia's greatest limitations are the "scars" she bears from the accident, and a rare medical condition that requires frequent treatments at a specialized private clinic. What Tavia doesn't realize—until her life collides with that of Sterling Chase, embroiled in an ongoing conflict of the Order's—is that everything she's been raised to believe has been a lie. She is neither human nor pure Breedmate; she is something extraordinary.

Tavia later learns the truth of her origins, including the fact that her aunt is actually a Minion tasked with supervising her upbringing and reporting to Dragos. Tavia also discovers there are other females like her when she and Chase uncover secured lab records in her doctor's office. Together Tavia and Sterling Chase are the parents of fraternal twins, a son and daughter, Aric and Carys, born just after the close of Darker After Midnight.

Hair: shoulder-length, caramel brown
Eyes: spring leaf green
Breedmate mark: on her lower back
Bloodscent: sweet, like nectar from a forbidden vine
Unique ability: photographic memory (also has other unusual abilities that are awakened once she learns the truth of what she is)
Mate: Sterling Chase
Heroine in: Darker After Midnight (Book 10)

First mention in series: Appears in Deeper Than Midnight.

~ ~ ~

Odolf, the family   Breed family with long lineage, originating in Germany. The Odolfs were entrusted by Kassia to covertly raise her son, Dragos, upon her death. They also carried the secret of the Ancient's hiding place in the Czech mountains. This secret drove most of the Odolf family mad, nearly all of the Breed males of this line going Rogue from the burden of the knowledge they held. The Odolf family kept a journal of their lineage, which also contained a riddle pertaining to the Ancient's hiding place, and a clue about Dragos's secret upbringing. Eventually, that journal left the family and was en route to Marek (see Sheldon Raines) in Boston. When the journal goes missing, intercepted by Elise and the Order, Marek turns to torturing members of the Odolf family, burning one Breed male with UV rays at Marek's lair in the Berkshires. Only one Odolf male remains (see Petrov Odolf), a Rogue being held in a rehabilitation center in Germany.

First mention in series: Referenced in Midnight Awakening.

~ ~ ~

-P-

Packard (d.)   Breed male, henchman for Edinburgh crime boss, Reiver. Packard was one of a pair of thugs sent to harm Danika after she nosed into Reiver's business. Killed by Malcolm MacBain (aka Brannoc) at Danika's guest cottage on MacConn lands.

First mention in series: Appears in A Taste of Midnight (novella).

~ ~ ~

Patrice   Breedmate at Kade's family Darkhaven in Alaska. Patrice had long been promised to Kade's identical twin brother Seth for about six years, but he never made good on the arrangement. Patrice has been quietly fond of Kade's uncle, Max.

First mention in series: Appears in Shades of Midnight.

~ ~ ~

Petrov Odolf (d.)   Breed male. Mate of Breedmate Irina Odolf for fifty-seven years. Has been institutionalized at a Rogue rehabilitation facility in Germany for past three years, after going on night binges and later attacking Irina in a fit of Bloodlust. Petrov is one of the family whom Kassia entrusted with the rearing of her son, Dragos, and the secret of the Ancient's hiding place in the Czech mountains. The weight of this burden has driven most of the Odolf family males mad, Petrov being no exception. His sanity cracks completely during the timeline of Midnight Awakening, and he begins chanting a riddle that is also found in the Odolf family's journal. In a moment of clarity, Petrov blurts "that's where he's hiding," a clue that brings Elise, Tegan and the Order closer to finding the Ancient and unmasking Dragos as a true villain. Petrov Odolf dies after an apparent overdose of Crimson while he's in the rehab facility.

First mention in series: Appears in Midnight Awakening.

~ ~ ~

Phillip Cho (d.)   Human. FBI Special Agent, NYC office. Takes Jenna's call at the NYC office inquiring about TerraGlobal Partners, a firm Jenna and the Order privately suspect might have ties to Dragos, and agrees to have a meeting with her. After Jenna arrives at the meeting with Cho and his partner, Green, it is revealed that both are Minions of Dragos's. They forcibly remove Jenna from the FBI office, intending to take her to their Master, until Brock intervenes and helps her get free of the Minions. During a struggle in the vehicle with Jenna, Green accidentally shoots Cho in the head, killing him instantly and crashing the vehicle with Jenna inside.

First mention in series: Appears in Taken by Midnight.

~ ~ ~

-Q-

Quentin Chase (d.)   Breed male. Son of August Chase, elder brother of Sterling. First mate of Elise Chase and father of Camden. Attended Harvard University, as did most of the Chases. High-ranking member of the Enforcement Agency in Boston. Quentin, like much of the Enforcement Agency, considered the Order to be dangerous vigilantes. Quentin died five years before the timeline of Kiss of Crimson, killed in line of duty when attacked by a Rogue brought into Agency custody. It is later revealed in Darker After Midnight that Sterling Chase blames himself for the killing, as he was responsible for clearing the Rogue of weapons and missed a blade that was later used on Quentin.

First mention in series: Referenced in Kiss of Crimson.

~ ~ ~

-R-

Rachel (d.)   Human. Savannah's college freshman roommate at Boston University, circa 1974. Rachel is killed by one of Gideon's old enemies from England, when she and her date (see Bill Keaton) are attacked on the college campus during an after-hours tryst. Savannah sees the attack via her ESP talent, after picking up one of Rachel's bangle bracelets that had been on the girl's wrist during the killing.

First mention in series: Appears in A Touch of Midnight (novella).

~ ~ ~

Ray   Human. Boston police officer. Boyfriend of Megan, Gabrielle's good friend. Ray and Megan go to Gabrielle's apartment to check on her one night and the couple encounters Lucan there. Lucan mind scrubs the pair before taking Gabrielle with him to the Order's compound.

First mention in series: Appears in Kiss of Midnight.

~ ~ ~

Regina Bishop   Breedmate, Corinne Bishop's Darkhaven mother and mate of Victor Bishop. Regina was devastated by Corinne's abduction—and presumed death—seventy-some years ago. After her mate's betrayal of Corinne is exposed, Regina threatens to expose Victor's lies, but he is prepared to kill her to keep her silent. Regina shoots Victor during a physical struggle, but does not kill him. She is saved by one of the Darkhaven's security guards (see Mason).

First mention in series: Appears in Deeper Than Midnight.

~ ~ ~

Reiver (d.)   Breed male, skin-trader, blood club organizer and crime boss from Edinburgh, Scotland. Reiver is several hundred years old, first gained wealth and ill repute on the border marches, where he raided for livestock, lands, and loyalty at the end of his sword. Reiver has several bodyguards and security detail at his club (see Malcolm MacBain, Thane, Kerr, Packard). During the timeline of A Taste of

Midnight, Reiver is expecting a shipment of live cargo—humans—to supply one of his blood clubs when Danika MacConn, using her ESP ability, overhears the conversation at a Christmas party in the city. Unable to stand by and let the trade and slaughter of innocent people take place, Danika attempts to spy on Reiver and report back to the Order in Boston. Her efforts earn Reiver's fury, and he takes steps to eliminate the threat she poses to his business endeavors. One of his most trusted bodyguards turns out to be an old friend of Danika's (see Malcolm MacBain). Reiver later discovers the connection between his guard and Danika, and ends up taking her hostage to root out the betrayer. During the confrontation, Reiver escapes, but Malcolm tracks him down and kills him, along with Reiver's underworld associates.

First mention in series: Appears in A Taste of Midnight (novella).

~ ~ ~

Renata   Breedmate of Order member Nikolai. Left by her mother as an infant at the orphanage of the Montreal convent of the Sisters of Benevolent Mercy, Renata has no family and never knew her father. At the age of fourteen, Renata was living on her own.

As of the timeline of Veil of Midnight, she is a twenty-something street-smart scrapper who's used to taking care of herself. She didn't know she was a Breedmate, didn't know about her unusual ability, until two years ago when she was swept off the streets along with several other humans and taken to be live, illegal, game for a cruel Breed elder (see Sergei Yakut). She fought her abductors, and in the process unlocked her unique ability. Since that time, she was forced to serve as a bodyguard for her captor.

It was in this capacity that she crossed paths with a member of the Order, Nikolai, who was on a mission in Montreal involving Renata's employer. While serving her abductor, Renata also came into contact with another abductee, a young Breedmate girl named Mira, whom Renata took under her wing. Renata carries four custom-crafted daggers that each bear a quality that guides her life: courage, faith, honor, sacrifice. The blades were given to her by a human friend (see Jack) who gave her shelter when she was a young teen on her own.

Since her mating to Nikolai, Renata has become an integral player in the Order's missions, thanks to both her powerful ESP talent and her skill with weaponry.

Hair: glossy black, chin-length angled bob
Eyes: jade green, almond-shaped
Breedmate mark: inside of her right wrist
Bloodscent: sandalwood and rain
Unique ability: mind-blaster (only works on Breed)
Mate: Nikolai
Heroine in: Veil of Midnight (Book 5)

First mention in series: Appears in Veil of Midnight.

~ ~ ~

Robert "Bobby" Clarence (d.)   Human. Young, attractive Senator from Massachusetts, employed Tavia Fairchild as his personal aide for past three years. He lives in an elegant estate on Boston's North Shore, has Ivy League connections, friend of the United States Vice President, Clarence's former college professor. The ambitious, newly elected senator received major campaign contributions from a businessman named Drake Masters (see Dragos). The senator invites Drake Masters to a holiday party at his home—a party Sterling Chase stakes out, where he discovers that Dragos is masquerading as Drake Masters. By the timeline of Darker After Midnight, Bobby Clarence has been turned Minion by Dragos. Sterling Chase first notices this fact when he sees the senator at the Boston police station, where Chase is in a suspect lineup, waiting to be identified by Tavia. Realizing Tavia could be in danger from both Dragos and his Minion, the senator, Chase attempts to kill Bobby Clarence at the station, but is shot and subdued. Chase later breaks out of police custody and tracks the senator to his estate, where Chase kills the Minion and the security detail that tries to stop him.

First mention in series: Appears in Deeper Than Midnight.

~ ~ ~

Robert "Buddy" Vincent Human. Shopkeeper of a gourmet chocolate shop in the wharf area of Newport, Rhode Island, and former high school classmate of Claire Reichen's. Buddy was the conductor's assistant in the school symphony where Claire played the piano. In the timeline of Ashes of Midnight, Buddy Vincent encounters Claire and Andreas in his shop and assumes that Claire must be her own daughter, since decades have passed and she looks nearly as young as she did in school. Buddy's flattery and fawning over Claire makes Andreas jealous.

First mention in series: Appears in Ashes of Midnight.

~ ~ ~

Roderick "Roddy" (d.) Breed male, one of Gideon's young identical twin brothers. Roddy and his brother, Simon, were slain in a Rogue attack more than three hundred years ago outside their Darkhaven in London. It is later discovered that the boys were murdered on the orders of one of Gideon's enemies (see Cyril Smithson), a revenge killing following Gideon's slaying of another Breed male—his enemy's father—in a duel.

First mention in series: Referenced in A Touch of Midnight (novella).

~ ~ ~

Rose Human. Works at Eastside Small Animal Rescue in Boston; answers the phone when Dante calls to inquire about picking up a dog, which he secretly intends to use as leverage in getting to know Tess better. Rose informs Dante that the dog he wanted is no longer available, but sells him another one instead (see Harvard the dog).

First mention in series: Appears via telephone call in Kiss of Crimson.

~ ~ ~

Ruarke Louvell (d.) Breed male, second generation. One of Dragos's inner circle, secret lieutenants. Louvell is a longtime Enforcement Agency director from Seattle. He was present via video conference with Dragos during the timeline of Darker After Midnight, when the decision was made to unleash the Rogues from their rehabilitation facilities around the globe. Louvell expressed some remorse at the decision, but ultimately agreed it had to be done. At the close of Darker After Midnight, Louvell is among the lieutenants reported as having been tracked down and eliminated by the combined efforts of the Order, Andreas Reichen, Mathias Rowan, and other like-minded members of the Enforcement Agency in various parts of the world.

First mention in series: Appears in Darker After Midnight.

~ ~ ~

-S-

Savannah Dupree Breedmate of Order member Gideon. Born and raised in the swamps of Louisiana, Savannah has been blood-bonded to Gideon since 1974, when he saved her life at the age of eighteen while she was attending university as a freshman student. Savannah has an elderly human half-sister, Amelie Dupree, who still lives in Louisiana. Savannah never knew her father, a wanderer who was little more than rumor in the family. Savannah is a nurturing woman and is the heart of home for the Order's compound in Boston.

Hair: tight, short black curls
Eyes: dark brown
Breedmate mark: on her left shoulder blade
Bloodscent: magnolia
Unique ability: psychometry
Mate: Gideon
Heroine in: A Touch of Midnight (series prequel novella, Book 0.5)

First mention in series: Appears in Kiss of Midnight.

~ ~ ~

Sebastian Bishop (d.) Breed male, Corinne's brother in the Bishop Darkhaven in Detroit, and son of Victor and Regina Bishop. Sebastian was two years older than Corinne at time of her abduction at age eighteen in the 1930s. Sebastian was believed to have killed himself forty years ago in despair over his growing Bloodlust, but we learn in Deeper Than Midnight that he was extremely tormented after discovering his father betrayed Corinne and allowed her to be taken by Gerard Starkn (aka Dragos). Sebastian learned of his father's lies when he'd been transferring some of his Victor's guns into a cabinet Sebastian had made for him. In the old cabinet were receipts of dressmakers and jewelers who were paid to replicate what Corinne was wearing when she went missing—clothing put on another woman who was killed and made to resemble Corinne in an effort to conceal her true fate. After learning this, Sebastian fell into Bloodlust. He went Rogue, and after a savage killing spree, Sebastian committed suicide, shooting himself in the head in his father's study.

First mention in series: Referenced in Deeper Than Midnight.

~ ~ ~

Sergei Yakut (d.) Breed male, Gen One. One of the eldest, most menacing members of the Breed, Sergei Yakut answers to no one and serves only himself. Originally from Russia, during the timelines of Midnight Rising and Veil of Midnight, Yakut is based at his rustic Darkhaven lodge in the outskirts of Montreal, Quebec.

Nikolai first saw the nasty Gen One in Siberia when Niko was a youth. Nikolai is later tasked with going to Montreal to talk with Yakut and warn him of Dragos's apparent intent to assassinate all remaining Gen Ones within the race. While at Yakut's lodge, Niko meets Renata and Mira, both of whom are living under Yakut's control. Yakut rules with a punishing hand; has burned Renata with irons and drinks her blood whenever he feels like it, using his bond to her to further control her and keep her in line. Renata is never permitted to drink from Yakut in return, out of his fear for how strong a full blood bond might make her and her ESP talent.

While at Yakut's lodge, Niko also learns of his blood club activities and a recent failed attempt on the Gen One's life by one of

Dragos's homegrown assassins (see Hunter). Yakut's son, Alexei, in a grasp for power and influence with Dragos and his inner circle, later betrays his father and arranges for his killing in a Rogue attack at the lodge.

First mention in series: Referenced in Midnight Rising.

~ ~ ~

Seth (d.)   Breed male, Kade's identical twin brother, shares Kade's talent of psychic connection to predator animals. Seth's wildness is stronger than Kade's, it overpowers him. Although Seth is studious and cerebral, he is not the strong leader that Kade is. Seth resents that Kade was able to leave Alaska while he could not. Seth's wild nature tempts him into killing humans, which eventually leads to his Bloodlust.

Later, it becomes clear that Seth has gone Rogue and cannot be saved. In a final act of redemption, Seth sacrifices himself to help the Order kill the last remaining Ancient. After a bloody altercation, both Seth and the Ancient plummet off the side of a steep cliff, where the Ancient is buried under an avalanche of ice and snow, but Seth comes to rest on an outcrop below. Although Kade attempts to save him, Seth dies of his wounds. Kade and Alex bring Seth's body home to the family Darkhaven, where Kade reconciles with his father and attends Seth's funeral with Alex.

First mention in series: Appears in Shades of Midnight.

~ ~ ~

Sharon Alexander (d.)   Human. Dylan's mother. A free spirit, forever falling in love with a new man and getting her heart broken. Never married again after Dylan's stepfather (see Bobby Alexander) abandoned the family when Dylan was twelve. Sharon is in the midst of a cancer battle during the timeline of Midnight Rising, causing her to send Dylan on her trip to the Czech Republic in Sharon's place. Sharon meanwhile continues to work at the runaway shelter in Brooklyn, New York, where she is crushing on the shelter's chief benefactor, Gordon Fasso (see Dragos).

Sharon's work at the shelter, and particularly her connection to a young woman who recently went missing (see Toni) provides clues for Dylan and the Order to get closer to Dragos. Eventually, Dragos finds out that Sharon's daughter is involved with the Order and he confronts the terminally ill woman, threatening her for information. Sharon does not compromise her beloved daughter, not even after Dragos reveals himself to be a vampire. During the altercation with Dragos, Sharon defies him, deliberately tumbling off her condo balcony, where she dies in the fall. Sharon Alexander is buried in Queens, New York, her afternoon funeral attended by Dylan and the other Breedmates of the Order.

Later in the series, during the timeline of Darker After Midnight, it is discovered that Sharon Alexander had an affair while in Mykonos, Greece (see Zael), and Dylan was born the following year.

First mention in series: Appears in Midnight Rising.

~ ~ ~

Sheldon Raines (d.)   Human. Minion that Elise follows into a Boston FedEx store in opening scene of Midnight Awakening. He is a violent, belligerent individual, furious when he learns a package he's expecting on behalf of his Master (see Odolf family) has been delayed due to a snowstorm. Elise tracks the Minion to his apartment building and stabs him dead with a dagger in her mission to kill Rogues and the unknown commander they served (see Marek) in an effort to avenge her son Camden's death.

First mention in series: Appears in Midnight Awakening.

~ ~ ~

Sheryl   Human. Lobby receptionist at the Boston Police station the night Gabrielle came in looking for "Detective" Lucan Thorne. On Officer Carrigan's request, Sheryl calls a police psychologist to come down to the lobby and deal with Gabrielle, but Gabrielle leaves before the psychologist arrives.

First mention in series: Appears in Kiss of Midnight.

~ ~ ~

Sidney Charles. Human. One of Harmony's Native elder residents and the town's long-running, pony-tailed mayor. After events escalate in Shades of Midnight, bringing several members of the Order to Alaska to clean up the situation, Sidney Charles and several dozen other Harmony residents and two newly arrived Alaska State Troopers are gathered at the town's church, where they are all tranced and mind-scrubbed by Tegan, Chase and Hunter.

First mention in series: Appears in Shades of Midnight.

~ ~ ~

Simon (d.) Breed male, one of Gideon's young identical twin brothers. Simon and his brother, Roderick, were slain in a Rogue attack more than three hundred years ago outside their Darkhaven in London. It is later discovered that the boys were murdered on the orders of one of Gideon's enemies (see Cyril Smithson), a revenge killing following Gideon's slaying of another Breed male—his enemy's father—in a duel.

First mention in series: Referenced in A Touch of Midnight (novella).

~ ~ ~

Sister Grace Gilhooley (d.) Human. Nun who used to volunteer at the women's shelter with Dylan's mother, Sharon Alexander, twenty-plus years ago. Sister Grace has been turned Minion for Dragos, acting as guardian of a holding cell in her home on the coast near Gloucester, Massachusetts, where several Breedmates were imprisoned. When Dylan, Jenna, Alex and Renata arrive at her home, Jenna immediately recognizes the nun as a Minion. Sister Grace attempts to escape, but Jenna attacks her. The nun, being Minion, refuses to answer any questions, quickly poisoning herself to avoid betraying her Master, Dragos.

First mention in series: Appears in Taken by Midnight.

~ ~ ~

Sister Margaret Mary Howland   Human. Octogenarian nun living in a retirement home in Gloucester, Massachusetts. Dylan finds the sister's photograph in a twenty-year-old class picture type of pose in front of St. John's Home for Young Women in Queensboro, New York, while searching for information about dead Breedmates who seemed to have ties to Dragos. Dylan and some of the Order's other women decide to contact Sister Mary Margaret to see if the nun can help them find missing Breedmates. The nun innocently leads the women to Sister Grace Gilhooley, who secretly serves Dragos as a Minion and holds a group of Breedmates prisoner at her home.

First mention in series: Appears in Taken by Midnight.

~ ~ ~

Skeeter Arnold (d.)   Human. Full name Stanley Elmer Arnold. Stoner, unemployed drug dealer and resident of Harmony, Alaska. Makes money pushing drugs and alcohol on dry Native population and teens in area, covertly supplied by Zach Tucker. Skeeter took cell phone video of the Toms family's bodies after the killings by the Ancient and uploaded it to the Internet, where the video caught the attention of the Order. Skeeter was later turned Minion by one of Dragos's lieutenants. On a mission to eliminate witnesses to the Ancient, Skeeter stabs and kills Big Dave Grant in the medical clinic in town. Kade then kills Skeeter in front of Alexandra Maguire and dumps the body in a steep ravine outside town.

First mention in series: Appears in Shades of Midnight.

~ ~ ~

Sorcha (d.)   First Breedmate of Order member Tegan. They were mated during the period of the Order's founding, mid-1300s. Sorcha was an innocent young woman, gypsy-dark looks and a sweet, trusting smile. She was abducted while Tegan was on a mission, and returned to him sometime later turned Minion. She had been abused, violated, a soulless shell. Tegan tried to make her better, feeding her his blood and draining hers, but she was too far gone. Tegan fell into Bloodlust trying to save her. Lucan locked Tegan away to help him recover, then he took Sorcha's life to end her suffering. Tegan long held this act of mercy against Lucan. In Midnight Awakening, Tegan learns it was Marek who took Sorcha all those years ago and turned her into his Minion in an effort to extract information from her about Dragos and the hiding place of the Ancient.

First mention in series: Referenced in Kiss of Midnight.

~ ~ ~

Sterling "Harvard" Chase   Breed male, former Enforcement Agent, current Order member. Son of August Chase, brother of Quentin. Mate of Tavia Fairchild. Sterling Chase was born and raised in Boston more than a century ago. Part of the Darkhaven elite, Chase comes from a well-connected, political family with deep ties to the Breed's Enforcement Agency.

Bound by the Chase family motto, "Duty first." Like the rest of his family, he holds several degrees from Harvard University, and before joining the Order during the timeline of Kiss of Crimson, most of Chase's combat training was academic. This, along with his rigid, by-the-book attitude prompted Dante to nickname him "Harvard" the first time the warrior met him, although the two later became as close as brothers.

Chase's uptight nature disguises an inner turmoil that has plagued him for many years. Those struggles have cost him family and friends, and have become dangerously more apparent in the time he's been part of the Order. Chase's fight to resist Bloodlust nearly costs him his friendship with Dante.

Chase and Tavia are parents to fraternal twins, a son and daughter, Aric and Carys, born soon after the close of Darker After Midnight.

Hair: golden blond
Eyes: blue
Unique ability: shadow-bender

Mate: Tavia Fairchild
Hero in: Darker After Midnight (Book 10)

First mention in series: Appears in Kiss of Crimson.

~ ~ ~

-T-

Taggart   Breed male, Enforcement Agent. First introduced in the series during the timeline of Deeper Than Midnight. Taggart is a big vampire posted as guard at the door of an Agency watering hole and strip joint (known as a sip-and-strip) in Boston's Chinatown district. Taggart and Sterling Chase have a strong mutual dislike and mistrust of each other. Taggart permits Chase and Hunter to enter the club only after realizing how lethal Hunter is. Taggart appears again during the timeline of Darker After Midnight, when Dragos walks into the Enforcement Agency hangout in Chinatown and blatantly invites the Breed males there to feed from—and kill, should they wish—the humans working the club. Taggart takes part in the carnage, but goes missing afterward and does not appear again thus far in the series.

First mention in series: Appears in Deeper Than Midnight.

~ ~ ~

Teddy Toms (d.)   Human. Nineteen-year-old Native kid, resident of Harmony, Alaska. Teddy is partying with Annabeth Jablonsky, Chad Bishop, Skeeter Arnold and others the night the Ancient slaughters Teddy and his family in their rural settlement outside Harmony.

First mention in series: Appears in Shades of Midnight.

~ ~ ~

Tegan   Gen One Breed, Order member, mate of Elise Chase. Tegan is approximately seven hundred years old. He sees no need to attempt to blend in with mankind, so he's never bothered with a surname. One of the original members of the Order at its founding, Tegan has a reputation for being stone cold, merciless and detached, the loner of the group.

Centuries ago in Europe, his Breedmate, Sorcha, was kidnapped by a powerful Breed enemy of the Order. Bled to the point of no return, Sorcha was sent back to Tegan a Minion of the Breed male who drained her (see Marek). Tegan went mad with grief and rage, and would have been lost to Bloodlust if not for Lucan's brutal, but necessary, intervention. Tegan thought he had cut himself off from all emotion until he crossed paths with Elise, a widowed Darkhaven Breedmate he had no right to desire.

Hair: tawny-gold, like a lion's mane
Eyes: gem green
Unique ability: reads anyone's thoughts and emotional states with a touch
Mate: Sorcha (deceased); Elise Chase
Hero in: Midnight Awakening (Book 3)

First mention in series: Appears in Kiss of Midnight.

~ ~ ~

Tess Culver   Breedmate of Order member Dante. Born in rural Illinois, Teresa Dawn "Tess" Culver is twenty-six years old during the timeline of Kiss of Crimson. Tess's true father was killed in a car accident when she was fourteen. Her mother remarried quickly to a successful local businessman. Tess's stepfather sexually assaulted her on her seventeenth birthday, during which time he suffered a heart attack. Tess's mother berated her daughter instead of supporting her, commanding Tess to use her special ability to "fix" him. Tess halted the man's death, then later takes it back after discovering he has also accosted young children.

Tess flees home, staying with friends until she finished school and began a new life, eventually working as a veterinarian in her own practice. She always knew she was different, and thought moving far away from her past would keep her personal demons at bay. Late one Halloween night, however, she encountered a dark, dangerous stranger in her clinic—Dante, severely wounded in combat. When she tried to help him, he bit her in desperate need of her blood. A bond that began out of necessity soon became a deep and unbreakable love.

Dante and Tess are parents to a newborn Breed son whom they named Xander Raphael, signifying both the healer and the protector their child is destined to be.

Hair: honey brown, long curly waves
Eyes: aquamarine
Breedmate mark: between the thumb and forefinger of her right hand
Bloodscent: cinnamon and vanilla
Unique ability: heals with her touch; she can also rescind the gift of her healing with a touch
Mate: Dante
Heroine in: Kiss of Crimson (Book 2)

First mention in series: Appears in Kiss of Crimson.

~ ~ ~

Thane   Breed male. Massive, built like a tank, lethal. Black hair, worn in a short queue, with a sharp widow's peak and slashing ebony brows over hawkish green eyes. Thane is one of Reiver's bodyguards, but it is later revealed that he is also part of an elite Enforcement Agency team out of London, sent to infiltrate Reiver's organization with the blessing of a high-ranking Agency director in Boston, Mathias Rowan. Thane invites Malcolm MacBain to join his Enforcement Agency team at the close of A Taste of Midnight, but Mal declines in order to focus on his new Breedmate, Danika.

First mention in series: Appears in A Taste of Midnight (novella).

~ ~ ~

Tilda   Breedmate who works at the Bishop family Darkhaven in Detroit.

First mention in series: Appears in Deeper Than Midnight.

~ ~ ~

Toni (d.) Breedmate ghost in Goth attire, who appears to Dylan at the hospital while Dylan is visiting her mother there. Toni appears again with other dead Breedmates at the shelter and warns Dylan that Gordon Fasso is Dragos.

First mention in series: Appears in Midnight Rising.

~ ~ ~

-U-

United States Vice President, unnamed (d.) Human. Former university professor of Bobby Clarence's in Boston, longtime friend and mentor of the up-and-coming senator. As Vice President of the United States, this man is a high-value contact of Dragos. Dragos had intended to use the Minion senator to get close to the top government officials of the nation, but instead it's Bobby Clarence's death that offers the best chance of bringing the Vice President into Dragos's hands. When a last-minute security concern thwarts the plan, Dragos speeds up his operation and unleashes the Rogues soon after the slight. With the human population in chaos, Dragos arranges another meeting with the Vice President, this time at the politician's residence in Washington, D.C. There, Dragos turns the man into his Minion after the Vice President refuses to help Dragos lead the President into his trap. The Order soon arrives on the scene, and upon killing Dragos, all of his Minions—including the Vice President—die at the same time he breathes his last.

First mention in series: Appears in Darker After Midnight.

~ ~ ~

Uta Human. Berlin-area prostitute who is standing in a dirty alleyway when Rio is in the city in need of a feeding. She tells him she's off duty, nervous about her pimp (see Big Man). Rio quickly feeds from the woman.

First mention in series: Appears in Midnight Rising.

~ ~ ~

-V-

Victor Bishop (d.) Breed male, Corinne's Darkhaven father; mate is named Regina. Victor Bishop is wealthy, well-connected and powerful. Had been allied with Enforcement Agency director Gerard Starkn (one of Dragos's aliases) around seventy years ago, when Victor's adopted daughter Corinne was taken captive by Dragos and another of his associates (see Henry Vachon). Victor was aware of the abduction, even permitted it, to spare any harm to his son, Sebastian. After Hunter brings Corinne home to Detroit following her rescue by the Order, Victor Bishop's duplicity comes to light. He later contacts Henry Vachon to warn him and Dragos that they've been discovered. Regina overhears the conversation and confronts Victor. He is prepared to kill her to ensure her silence, but one of the Darkhaven's security detail intervenes (see Mason). The guard shoves the wounded Victor Bishop out of a window, where he dies in the sunlight.

First mention in series: Appears in Deeper Than Midnight.

~ ~ ~

Victoria Breedmate, Kade's mother. Mate of Kir. Very pregnant with another set of identical twin boys when Kade returns home to the family Darkhaven outside Fairbanks. She has not been aware of how her ESP talent, the ability to communicate and connect psychically to predator animals, has affected her sons.

First mention in series: Appears in Shades of Midnight.

~ ~ ~

-W-

Wilhelm Roth (d.)   Breed male, second generation. Corrupt Enforcement Agent, director of the Agency in Hamburg, Germany and lieutenant of Dragos. Wilhelm Roth was Claire Samuels's first mate. Prior to Claire, Roth was mated to a Breedmate named Ilsa. He killed her to make way for taking Claire as his mate. Wilhelm Roth is killed by Andreas Reichen during a confrontation between the Order and Roth.

First mention in series: Appears without being named in Veil of Midnight; appears later in Ashes of Midnight.

~ ~ ~

-X-

Xander Raphael "Rafe" Malebranche   Breed male, son of Dante and Tess. Born December 17, during the timeline of Deeper Than Midnight. His godfather was to be Sterling Chase, but conflict between Chase and Dante made the new parents look in another direction. During the timeline of Darker After Midnight, week-old Rafe is presented to the Order and to his godparents, Gideon and Savannah. Rafe enters the series again as a young adult and new member of the Order in Edge of Dawn.

First mention in series: Appears as a newborn infant in Deeper Than Midnight.

~ ~ ~

-Y-

~ ~ ~

-Z-

Zach Tucker (d.)   Human. Older brother of Jenna Tucker-Darrow, and sole police officer on Harmony, Alaska. Has known Alexandra Maguire for ten years, slept together once, but nothing came of it. Zach seems like a good guy, until it's revealed that he's been secretly supplying drugs and alcohol to Skeeter Arnold, profiting off Skeeter's dealing to the local Native residents and teens. Zach's corruption proves his undoing when Alex discovers what he's done and confronts him. Zach chases her on a snow machine, shoots at her, but doesn't hit her. Zach is later attacked and killed by the Ancient. To cover up the slaying, the Order makes it appear that Zach and Skeeter were both killed in a drug deal gone bad.

First mention in series: Appears in Shades of Midnight.

~ ~ ~

Zael   Atlantean male. Dylan Alexander's true father. Golden hair, shot with streaks of copper. Intense, tropical-blue eyes, and bronze, tanned skin. Zael's photo was recovered among Dylan's mother's personal effects after she died. The gorgeous, ageless man is wearing a leather band around his wrist that has a tooled silver emblem in the shape of a Breedmate mark dangling from it. The only identification written on the back of the photo is: *Zael. Mykonos. '75.*

First mention in series: Referenced in Darker After Midnight.

~ ~ ~

READER Q & A

READER Q&A

Why did Gideon promise Savannah he wouldn't participate in combat missions? What is Lucan's ESP talent? Will the books ever be made into a movie or television show? How many total books will be in the Midnight Breed series?

From the time the series first debuted in 2007, I've received questions from readers on just about everything you can imagine. There are distinct front-runners—the questions listed at the top of this page in particular. With this Companion book and the novella, *A Touch of Midnight*, I've attempted to address the most frequent reader curiosities, but I also thought it would be fun to invite readers to submit additional questions—to me or to the characters—on any imaginable subject they liked.

The call went out via my website, and after a couple of weeks, my staff and I collected nearly a thousand questions submitted for consideration. We read and reviewed them all, which was a task both daunting and highly entertaining. Midnight Breed readers are not only smart and inquisitive, but really funny too! It was incredibly difficult to narrow the entries down to just the sampling of questions included in this Companion. I wish we could have included them all!

To those of you who sent in a question (or a dozen!), thank you. To the reader holding this book now, I hope you enjoy this thought-provoking, silly—and just plain fun—peek into the series and my work as its humble, deeply grateful author.

Questions for Lara Adrian

If you were to date a member of the Order who would it be and why?

—Tracey A., Manchester, United Kingdom

Oh, so hard to choose! This would be a problem, since I gave each of the warriors individual qualities—not to mention, knockout physical looks—that I personally find irresistible. I would probably have to sample them all, one at a time and at great length (ahem), before I could ever make that decision.

How do you come up with the characters, as well as the areas they come from and the places they travel to?

—Lois D., Burlington, MA USA

A lot of times, the characters and their backgrounds—including where they're from—pop into my imagination as a complete package. Sometimes, all it takes is listening to the right kind of music or a particular song or lyric and I'm able to bring a character to life. But sometimes it takes a bit more work on my part to make sure I'm not populating the series with characters who are too similar to one another, or who don't bring anything exciting and new into the story mix.

I have a fairly extensive collection of books on character archetypes, names and their meanings, etc., which I rely on when I'm stuck and need help (see the *Appendix* of this book for more information). As far as deciding on where to set the books, if the setting inspiration doesn't come organically out of a particular character in the story, I'll choose someplace interesting that I've either traveled to myself, or feel would make an exciting or evocative place for the story to go.

Will Brock and Jenna have a child together?
—**Phyllis B., Tallahassee, FL USA**

I'm not sure! Many readers have told me they hope to see Brock and Jenna bear a child, and I think it would be a sweet reward for this couple after all they've been through, but as of now, they're happy together even without a baby in their future. If I get farther into the series and it feels right to me that they should (or even can?) conceive, considering the human/alien being that Jenna is becoming, then I would certainly be open to taking them down that road.

I am enthralled with Gideon and Savannah. Will we get to see their specific story any time soon? I would love to find out why he made the promise (to refrain from combat) and the situation surrounding their meeting and bonding.
—**Donna B., San Antonio, TX USA**

Thank you, Donna! And thank you to everyone else who's told me over the years how much you enjoy Gideon and Savannah and want to know the story of how they met and fell in love. That's the hands-down most frequent question I hear from readers. I truly appreciate the outpouring of the affection for this couple, and I'm delighted to tell you that all those questions and more are answered—at last—in *A Touch of Midnight*, the original novella included right here in the book you're reading now!

How do you think up of all of the special gifts the Breedmates have? It is so hard for me to think of just one that isn't silly.
—**Lawren B., Menifee, CA,USA**

Oh, it's hard for me too! Since the Breed inherits superhuman strength, speed, longevity, etc., from their alien fathers, I thought it would make for a nice balance if each Breed male inherited not only his Breedmate mother's hair, eye and skin coloring, but also her unique ESP or empathic power. Because I was only concentrating on world building for the plot of one book in the beginning, I wasn't thinking about what that decision would mean down the road.

I didn't truly grasp the impact of that problem until I was beginning the third book of the series and suddenly had an offer from my publisher for three more. Each Breed male I introduce must have a unique ability, and so must each Breedmate, and so must every other Breed male or Breedmate who populates the story world, even in a minor role. Gah!

I've since created a big list of psychic abilities, superhero powers and weaknesses, etc., from which I can pick and choose and adapt or combine to fit my characters and make them unique. I try to give each main character an ability that will either enrich their story somehow (e.g., Nikolai, Brock, Tess, Claire) or complicate it (e.g., Dante, Reichen, Kade, Elise).

Will you write a book for Conlan and Danika's son?
—Loren B., Tuckerton, NJ USA

I don't have a full novel slated for Connor, but I do expect him to be involved in the series going forward. If I find a good heroine and storyline for him, I'll likely feature him in a novella.

Is the Ancient really dead, or will he come back?
—Joni J., Grants Pass, OR USA

He's really dead and won't be coming back.

I want to know why you "killed off" the last Ancient. I was hoping you would make him have his own love storyline!

—Amber C., Rosharon, TX USA

It was so tempting to try to find a place for the last surviving Ancient in the series! Sadly, he had to go for a handful of reasons. First, I had already established in the series history that pairings with Ancients and Breedmates tend not to end well, even if there is love between them at one time (see Lucan's parents). The Ancients are a conquering, savage race of alien beings whose culture is one of domination and destruction. Like any other wild predator, Ancients are never fully tamed and it's very hard—if not impossible—for them to curb their alien side.

Another reason for the Ancient's demise was that if he had lived, then all of the Breedmates who bore his offspring in Dragos's labs would be unable to bond with other Breed males so long as the Ancient was alive. Ancients, being alien, do not blood bond to one mate like the Breed, but those Breedmates who were forced to drink his blood while in captivity each shared a blood bond connection to him until his death.

The Breed can only have children with their mates and they can only have one mate at a time. How is it the Ancient was able to have multiple Breedmates pregnant at the same time?
—Amy H., West Seneca, NY USA

The blood bond is an exclusive, non-breakable connection between a Breed (male) and a Breedmate (female). The Ancients are alien, something other than Breed. Unlike their Breed sons, Ancients do not need to be blood bonded to a female in order to reproduce. This is how the Breed first came into being on Earth—as the scattered offspring of raiding Ancients who tore through human settlements and populations after crash-landing on this planet. Occasionally, some of the women in the path of those marauding Ancients turned out to be Breedmates, and if they fought back—bit their attackers, or somehow ingested some of their alien blood while a rape was occurring—that alien seed took root and a Breed son would be born. But the Ancients were not bonded in any way to the Breedmates who carried their offspring.

This is sort of a dumb question, but do you get to decide what the title of your books will be or is that decided by someone else?

— Tonya C., San Angelo, TX USA

Not a dumb question at all! Most of the book titles are my original choices, but there are a few that were nixed by my publisher for one reason or another. For instance, *Kiss of Midnight* was originally going to be called *Kiss of Darkness*, but a few months before my release date, a best-selling author came out with a vampire book under that title and we decided to change mine. I was really bummed at the time, because I'd written the entire book thinking of it as *Kiss of Darkness*. We even had the cover art designed with that title and had to make a last-minute revision! In the end, it worked out for the best, because *Kiss of Midnight* helped define the branding of the series and set the pattern for the titles of the next nine novels to come.

Can Breedmates get pregnant by normal human guys, or just Breed?

— Cara C., Hopkinsville, KY USA

If a woman born with the Breedmate birthmark does not share a blood bond with a Breed male, she will live her life as a normal, mortal woman. So, yes, she could carry a human male's child.

If a Breedmate has a daughter from a human man, will she be a Breedmate, too?

— Bettina H., Maglod, Hungary

No. Any child a Breedmate has with a human male will be born human.

Why did the Ancient make Jenna choose life or death before implanting a piece of himself in her?

— Necole C., Suamico, WI USA

There is most definitely a reason behind that choice, and it will be revealed before the series ends.

Are there more "otherworlders" that did not come to Earth with the original Ancients, and could we possibly see them show up in future books?
—Linda M., Mentor, OH USA

The Ancients are part of an alien race from another planet. There are others like them there, including females of their kind, of course, but I don't have plans to bring any more of those beings into the series. I felt it was important for me, as a writer, to have an understanding of the world they came from and the society they inhabited, so I sketched out a lot of details early on, which don't necessarily have a place in the series itself, but do form the background for what the Ancients are and how they lived among their own kind.

Did any other series influence you in creating the world and characters that you created?
—Yvette C., Hialeah, FL USA

This may sound odd coming from the author of a long-running series, but I'm a fickle reader and I get bored too easily to follow any series for more than a few books before I'm wandering off to look for something shiny and new. Of course, as a teen I loved Anne Rice, but when I began writing *Kiss of Midnight* in the summer of 2005, I wasn't following any series in any genre.

I'd read dozens of paranormal romances and urban fantasies, but there really wasn't a lot to choose from at that time when it came to vampires in romance. *Twilight* hadn't come out yet (which I've yet to read!) and J. R. Ward's wonderful, genre-bending series debut was still a couple of months away too. I'd read a few of Sherrilyn Kenyon's novels, which I really enjoyed for the complexity of her world-building and the camaraderie between her daimon-slaying vampire heroes. I'd read one or two of Christine Feehan's early vampire books, some very early Nancy Gideon vampire romances (a terrific writer, by the way), and a handful of others, but my tastes ran a bit darker than what I was finding in the genre at the time. I also enjoyed Lynn Viehl's engrossing series debut, which satisfied my craving for darkness and intriguing characters, but left me longing for a bit more romance. So, I can't point to any one series as influencing the genesis of mine, but it was more a matter of creating something that spoke to my own personal wants as a reader.

Breed vampires heal from injuries, so why is Rio disfigured and never healed?

—**Nancy C., Hope Mills, NC USA**

The Breed can heal on their own from UV burns and basic injury, but Rio's wounds were severe—nearly fatal. If he'd fed during his healing, and particularly if he'd fed from his Breedmate, he probably could have healed almost back to normal. But his mate, Eva, killed herself very soon after he was injured, and Rio was weakened and didn't feed for quite a long time afterward. By then, the scars were set and could not be taken away.

When will we learn more about the Atlanteans and their relationship with the Breedmates?

—**Cameron J., Orange, CA USA**

The connection between the Atlanteans and the Breedmates was first hinted at in *Deeper Than Midnight*, when Savannah's sister tells Corinne that Savannah's birthmark (her Breedmate mark) is where she was "kissed by faeries." The Atlanteans aren't classic Fae, but they are an immortal race of beings gifted with supernatural, extrasensory powers.

Just as I've twisted traditional vampire lore to give it otherworldly origins, I've also given an "alien" twist to traditional Fae mythology with regard to the Atlanteans in my series. As for the relationship between the Breedmates and the Atlanteans, it truly came to light in *Darker After Midnight*, when Jenna began making the connections between the Breedmates at the Boston compound and their true birth fathers. This relationship will continue to unfold and expand as the series continues.

Why did you choose Boston (for the series setting)?
—Sara F., Funchal, Madeira Portugal

Simply because I love Boston! My dad is from the area, and my family roots in Massachusetts go back to the Pilgrims' arrival. I've also lived in various New England states for more than fifteen years, so Boston and its surrounds feel like home to me. Plus, I wanted a setting that was different from the usual places you'd expect to see in a vampire series. Boston has an historic richness and old-World character, yet it's also very contemporary, urban and gritty. The same could be said of the Breed, so it just felt right to me that the series would be based in Boston.

Will you be introducing the Atlantean aspect in the new series?
—Angila D., McMinnville, OR USA

Yes! The Atlanteans play a much bigger, and more complex, part in the series beginning with *Edge of Dawn*. You'll meet characters from their world—some good, some bad and some with a foot in both camps. You'll also discover how the Atlanteans came to be and how their history (and future) intertwines with the Ancients, the Breed, and man.

In Jenna's dream the Ancient and a warrior (the inhabitant of Atlantis) talk about a Queen. Who is she?
—Sara C., S.Albino-Montepulciano, Siena-Tuscany Italy

Heh, heh, heh. You'll find out very soon!

After reading and rereading your series, I am curious as to how you came up with such amazing ideas for the background of the Ancients.

—Tracy F., Watkinsville, GA USA

The original germ of the idea is all my husband's fault! *g* As I was constructing the story background for *Kiss of Midnight*, and deciding on the rules of my vampire world, I shared with John that as much as I loved traditional vampire lore, I didn't want Lucan and the rest of the Breed to be undead or damned. I wanted them to be living, breathing, top-of-the-foodchain, superhuman beings with vampire characteristics. He jokingly said, "Maybe they're aliens."

He laughed, but I grabbed my pen and notebook and started jotting down details as fast as I could. The entire background of the Ancients came to me in rapid fire—from the climate of their planet, their social structure, their physical traits, strengths and weaknesses, everything. I like to think of my vampires as something of a cross between (the movies) *Predator* and *Blade*.

Why haven't or can't the Ancients produce a female? I mean in all those generations resulting after them, why can't there be some female offspring as a result?
—**Tori R., Port Saint Lucie, FL USA**

Remember, the Breed is the offspring of the Ancients (alien) and Breedmate females (half human, half Atlantean). The Ancients' DNA is the stronger of this pairing, even down the line in later generations of the Breed, so their genes determine gender in their offspring. In the case of this story world, it's always produced males. Dragos was able to manipulate gender and breeding in his labs, but scientific interference in reproduction is frowned upon by Breed society as being unnatural. On the Ancients' planet, among their own kind, they produce both male and female offspring.

Why did you choose the Atlanteans to be the fathers of the Breedmates and as the new (old) enemies of the Breed?
—**Tamara K., Birkenau, Hessen Germany**

It was actually a happy accident that Atlanteans played into the series in any way at all. In *Kiss of Midnight*, I had mentioned that the

Ancients devastated entire civilizations after coming to Earth. One of those civilizations I listed was Atlantis. When I wrote that, it was nothing more than a throwaway mention, but later on, many books later, I realized I needed not only a way to explain the existence of Breedmates, but I also needed to find a bigger, more powerful enemy for the Order than Dragos as the series continued to grow. Making the connection between a mysterious, hidden civilization like Atlantis and the Ancients felt like a perfect fit—one that had been right in front of me the whole time!

Was it hard to get a publisher to pick up a story with "alien" vampires in it? It seems to me the alien/science fiction genre is a little harder to pull into mainstream.
—Amanda K., Littleton, CO USA

I'm happy to say it was no problem at all. From the very beginning, I've had wonderful editorial support on pretty much anything I wanted to do with the series. I think the alien element of the Midnight Breed world is subtle enough that it doesn't fall into space-y Science Fiction/Fantasy categories, which aren't really my personal reading interest anyway, and which might have been problematic from a marketing standpoint. But no one has ever asked me to tone anything down or avoid certain storytelling choices in any way, and for that I feel quite fortunate.

I am a huge fan of the Midnight Breed series. I have every book to date. I am not sure if anyone has ever asked this or not, but out of all of the Breed members that you have written so far, who is your favorite and why?
—Jennifer L., Euclid, OH USA

Thank you, Jennifer! I'm so glad you're enjoying my books. I don't have a personal favorite character in the series, and that's a deliberate choice. I try not to let myself fall too much in love with any one character in particular, but instead focus all of my attention—and affection—on the characters I'm writing at the moment.

I think as a writer it can be all too easy to lavish all the love on one series "star" to the neglect of the others. I want each character, and each book's romantic pairing, to be as special as I can make it, and let no one pale in comparison to another character. I feel I've done my job when readers tell me who they love most and there's no clear winner, but favorites across the board!

Are we ever going to read about the years between Darker After Midnight and Edge of Dawn? Or do you not feel they are essential to the story line?
—Amanda C. Dodge City, KS USA

I may set a novella or two in the twenty years between First Dawn, which occurs at the end of *Darker After Midnight*, and the start of the new series arc that begins in *Edge of Dawn*. I have one idea percolating now, and I think it could be interesting to see a story set against the backdrop of those dark years of war. I don't envision any full novels set during that period, though.

When the captive Breedmates were rescued in 'Taken by Midnight' they were taken to Claire and Andreas's. Did they stay there indefinitely or move on to some of the nearby Darkhavens?
—Lisa D., Raymore, MO USA

Andreas and Claire's Darkhaven in Newport, Rhode Island, provided temporary shelter for the freed Breedmates. The ones who were pregnant at the time stayed on to have their babies there, but most have either reunited with their own families or moved on to make new lives for themselves elsewhere. It's possible that we might see some of those women again, or their grown children, in the second arc of the series.

I have read all of the Midnight Breed novels thus far and I always wondered. Why did you decide to promote this series as romance novels and not as vampire genre? I feel that they are so much more than romance novels.

—Lori D., Warwick, RI USA

Thank you, Lori! Marketing decisions for the series are made by my publishers, not me, but I do feel that the books are romances first and foremost. Each story is centered on the evolving romantic relationship between a hero and heroine, and everything else going on in the novel is secondary to the focus on that relationship. But I've always loved books with high-octane, engaging plots and lots of adventure and suspense, so writing those elements into my romance novels just comes naturally to me.

Why do the elders of the Order have so few children? It seems Breedmates only have one pregnancy each.

—Margie E., Akron, OH USA

As Lucan would likely tell you, the Order's compound, like any other military headquarters, is not an ideal place to raise children. Although having a mate and kids may be fine for the civilian Breed populations in the Darkhavens, it's long been a conscious choice that warriors in the Order do not go willingly into a blood bond or family life. But then I came along several years ago and started messing with everyone's lives! I'm taking great enjoyment in showing Lucan and the others that resistance is futile. *g*

Has Jenna turned into the first female Breed?

—Miriam W., Aztec, NM USA

The first female Breed that we've met in the series is Tavia. Jenna is human, and she cannot turn into one of the Breed. She is, however, taking on some of the genetic qualities of the Ancient, with some differences. For example, although she has developed a fondness for Brock's blood (I mean, really, can you blame her?) she will not develop fangs and will not require blood for sustenance like one of the Breed or an Ancient. Her human biology means she can still consume human food and she is also unaffected by ultraviolet light. So, Jenna is a powerful, unique genetic being unlike any other we'll see in the series.

Will we ever learn more about the Breed members' families? For example, we met some of Kade's family in Shades of Midnight. I'd love to learn more about other extended families!
—Shannon E., Benson, NC USA

I find it's a tricky balance, trying to provide fully fleshed-out backgrounds and backstories for the main characters without overwhelming the current storyline or the flow of the text with a lot of names and details about people we may never meet. So, for that reason, usually, unless a character's family will play a part in the book, or if some detail is necessary for explaining part of the story—for example, a character's motivation for being a certain way or doing something good or bad in the current storyline—I tend to leave those details out.

Although several of the Order's members are parentless (Lucan, Dante, Rio, Gideon, just to name a few) it's reasonable to assume there are parents and/or siblings out there for many of the other major characters in the series. Whether or not those family members will have parts to play in the books still to come, I'm not sure. But if it makes sense to bring some of them into the storyline, I'm definitely open to it. I need to be a little careful there, or the series could easily explode into a cast of thousands, all demanding a turn in the spotlight!

If they have the same ability (like Kellan and Alex), does that mean they are biologically related? Or just nature repeating itself?

—Amber F., Monroe, GA USA

I try not to make any of the characters' ESP talents exactly the same as someone else's, unless the characters share a maternal connection somewhere down the line. If talents seem similar, as with Kellan and Alex, and Tegan as well, in this case, there are subtle differences that separate them. Alexandra has the ability to detect deception in humans with her touch. Kellan's touch gives him the ability to determine a human's intentions, good or bad. And Tegan's talent works on human, Breed and Breedmate alike, giving him the ability to read anyone's emotional state with his touch.

Will Jenna enjoy the same longevity as the Breedmates since she has the Ancient's DNA implanted in her?
—Christina S., Camby, IN USA

Yes, but unlike the Breedmates, Jenna will not require a blood bond in order to live longer than a normal, mortal human or an unmated Breedmate. She will easily live as long as any of the Breed.

Did you always plan to reveal the Breed to the humans and if so, why did you want them revealed?
—Manna G., London, United Kingdom

From just about the midpoint of the series—while I was writing *Midnight Rising*—I came to the realization that if the series was going to continue for any length of time, it needed some room to grow and evolve. One thing I wanted to avoid from the beginning was stagnation in the series, and it seemed to me that it all could get pretty boring unless something big was coming farther up the road. I knew I'd need a closing point for one part of the series—something monumental, which would also provide a good twist that could carry me into another storytelling arc.

I was never in doubt about what that twist needed to be, so from that moment on, I began writing toward the events that unfolded in *Darker After Midnight*. Bringing the Breed out in the open has given me a big new canvas to work with, exciting new conflicts, allies and enemies, while still allowing me to remain faithful to the core characters and the heart of the series. I'm having more fun than ever, and I hope readers will enjoy all the twists and surprises still to come.

Why wasn't Rio able to sense Eva's deception through their blood-bond?

—Bettina H., Maglod, Hungary

Rio would only have been able to sense Eva's heightened emotions and her physical presence through their blood bond, but it's not a mind-reading connection. If she were careful to keep her emotions in check while she was betraying him, Rio would never know. And his trust in her as his mate would only blind him further to any deception.

As an author, what's the biggest challenge that you have felt and how did you overcome it?
—Rohinee I., Mumbai, India

My biggest challenge as an author is the same one that's always held me back in other areas of life: Self-doubt. I'm not sure I'll ever totally overcome it, since it's been with me forever, but somehow you do find ways to get past it, at least temporarily, which is often all the push you need. For me with my writing, having a deadline helps! So does all of the lovely email and online messages I receive every day from readers. But in the end, every writing session begins with a fresh new hell of a blinking cursor parked on a blank page.

Fortunately, for every ounce of fear and self-doubt I have that my ideas are lame or my writing is flat, I've also got an equal measure of stubborn determination that refuses to let me give up on anything that's important to me. There's an old quote I used to keep in a frame on my desk to remind me to be courageous, and I still find myself referring back to it whenever I'm caught in the paralyzing trap of self-doubt about my writing or anything else in life: *"Do it trembling if you must, but do it."* (Emmet Fox)

Your male main characters have such strong alpha attitudes. How do you pair them up with their Breedmates?
—Vikki K., Palm City, FL USA

I *love* big, bad, dominating alpha heroes. But it takes a strong woman to hold her own against a guy like that. I don't necessarily mean physically strong (although that's good too—just ask Niko or

Brock) but a woman who won't be cowed by a lot of arrogant bluster or dark, broody scowls and growls.

Many times, I'll match up an alpha hero with a heroine who will be a source of constant friction for him, whether that's emotional friction or as an obstacle standing in the way of something he wants (or thinks he wants). Other times, I'll look for a heroine who will bring out a softer side of him that he's reluctant to admit he even has—the unwilling protector, or the unexpected savior. Or I might push him into a situation where the heroine becomes his partner in some way, forcing him to rely on her and see her as his equal, either by giving him no other choice in the matter or by simple necessity.

It really depends on the characters and what my instinct tells me is the right pairing for them. And when I say the right pairing, realize that very often that's the dead last person they *think* they should be with!

What character trait do you admire most in your characters and why?

—Lysette L., Moorpark, AL USA

The same trait I admire in anyone: Resilience. Life can be a challenge, and we all go through our own personal hells and torment along the way. The ability to spring back from adversity, or to rise above something that threatens to drag us down, is huge. Anyone can be courageous, especially if you've never been tested. But it takes something extra to be able to come back stronger after you've been kicked to the ground or made to feel "less than" in some way. Each of my characters has this trait, and I hope their stories help illustrate for my readers that no challenge is too great to overcome, and we are stronger for everything we endure in life.

When starting this series, did you ever envision Lucan as a father?

—Michelle N., Olmsted Falls, OH USA

No! In fact, when I started writing Lucan's story, I didn't imagine his life beyond that one book, let alone envision him growing into his current role ten books later, as both a father and the diplomatic leader he swore he could never be. It's been a very interesting journey, full of surprises for him and for me!

I was wondering now after I have read all the books up to Mira's was there ever a book or character that was hard for you to write emotionally?

—Nikki N., Marion, IN USA

None of the characters have been more difficult than any others, however, early on in the series I decided against writing a certain character because I felt it would be too difficult for me personally to go there. Originally, I had intended to pair up Tegan with a completely different heroine than Elise. My plan for him was a concert pianist who was dying from leukemia—except the doctors were going to be proved wrong, because Tegan was going take her away and save her life with his blood. That's how I proposed the story when the series sold as a trilogy in 2005. But before I even wrote the first word of Tegan's book, I realized the storyline would be cutting too close to home.

You see, at that time, my husband's eldest daughter, Leslie, was undergoing treatment for leukemia, which had come back after chemotherapy a few years earlier and had later required a bone marrow transplant. I'd thought it would be therapeutic somehow to write a happy ending for a heroine fighting a similar battle, but as Leslie got worse and eventually passed away in January 2006, I knew there was no way I wanted to relive any part of that storyline in fiction or otherwise. So, while I was writing *Kiss of Crimson* that same year, I decided to instead recast Tegan's heroine as Sterling Chase's widowed sister-in-law, Elise.

You receive plenty of fan letters and comments. Do your fan comments influence your idea/direction of a book storyline? If yes, please share a particular situation.

—Madeline P., Escondido, CA USA

I do receive emails with suggestions for storylines or characters, and although I appreciate the enthusiasm and the emotional investment some readers have in the series (seriously, I take it as a tremendous compliment!) I have to stay true to my own vision for the series. I'm the only one at the helm, for better or worse, and the control freak in me won't have it any other way. But...I did make one exception.

A few years ago, I had my first book tour in Germany. At one of my events, a reader in an audience of over 150 people really pressed me hard to explain what it was about the Breedmates that made them different from basic human women. She wanted to know *why* they had unique blood properties that allowed them to carry a Breed offspring, and *why* they were psychically gifted, insisting that there must be something more to it than my admittedly lame answer of, "Um, they're just different." In all of my story building and plotting, I never clearly defined the origins of the Breedmates.

I came home realizing that was some lazy writing on my part, and I was determined to fix it if I could. So, I combed through the early books, looking for a possible solution that would be organic to what I'd already written. And I found it, more readily than I ever would have guessed. I found more hidden truths as well, things that will be coming to light as the series continues to unfold. Whether it was my subconscious running miles ahead of me, or good old-fashioned serendipity, I don't know. But thank you, anonymous German reader from Dortmund! You taught me a wonderful lesson that day, and helped make the series stronger at the same time.

Are there gay members of the Breed? Because they seem to give me the impression that they are in love affairs quite human and for a man it is not unnatural to love a man.
                                        —Patircia P., Grimma, Germany

Yes, of course, it seems only reasonable that there would be some Breed males who are emotionally and sexually attracted to other males, or bisexual. And I imagine the same to be true of Breedmates and Atlanteans as well. My personal feeling is that love is love, and only the heart can decide who it belongs to.

Do you ever get writer's block and if so how do you push through that block?

—**Sabrina R., Newark, NJ USA**

I've learned over time that if I'm struggling with a chapter or scene, usually it's because I'm not writing close enough to the character(s) and/or the conflict. Sometimes I'm in the wrong character's point of view, and I have to recast the scene from another character's perspective instead—the best choice is always the character with the most at stake. Sometimes the characters and conflict of the scene are fine, but there's something else that just doesn't feel right, or isn't portrayed cinematically enough to bring the moment to life on the page. In that case, I might change the location of the scene, or alter the point at which the scene opens, or try to capture what it was about the scene that excited me the most as I was plotting it and strive to maximize the impact of that element.

With all Minions he created, why didn't Dragos turn Rogue?

—**Tori R., Port Saint Lucie, FL USA**

Dragos was a very controlling, exacting man. And he was patient. My God, decades of planning went into his operation—centuries, if you go back to the moment he and his father first placed the Ancient into hibernation in that mountain cave. Dragos would have been extremely judicious when it came to ingesting blood to create a Minion. He would have known his limits and been careful to avoid going over the edge into addiction. But that's a great question!

Will Mathias Rowan ever get his own story?

—**Janae G., Rock Springs, WY USA**

I have an idea for a novella for Mathias, and we'll also see more of him as the series continues.

Will we be seeing more Dragos bred "assassins" like Hunter?
Men bred for evil, but who turn their back on their training and
fight for the Order.

—**Renee S., Woodstock, IL USA**

Possibly. And I've also had ideas in the back of my mind for a while now about some of the Gen One assassin "lost boys" who were not so deeply indoctrinated into the program like Hunter was, being an adult assassin, but who would have been closer to Nathan's age at the time they were released from Dragos's control. I might find a place for them in the series somehow. We'll see!

My question is why you gave Lucan a last name (Thorne), but
none of the other Order members have one. I would love to
know the last names to them and how they got them.

—**Tami S., Hamilton, OH USA**

Because Lucan is 900 years old, his surname of Thorne is a name he acquired along the way, more so than a true family name. Surnames were uncommon in the Middle Ages and earlier, so many of the oldest members of the Breed would not have had them, but would have chosen a surname later on to help them blend in with the human world. Dante's occasional use of the surname Malebranche ("evil claws") is a made-up name he's adopted in reference to his favorite daggers.

Surnames are more common among the modern Darkhaven populations of the Breed. In cases where a last name hasn't been given to a more contemporary character in the series, it's either because they don't have one, or because a surname didn't make itself known to me as I was creating the character.

Have there been any discussions about turning The Midnight
Breed Series into a movie or television series?

—**Teresa A., Knoxville, TN USA**

Very early on, we had a nibble from a cable television channel that specializes in family dramas and women's films. To no one's surprise, they decided the Midnight Breed series was not right for them! *g* I'm asked by readers quite often if/when I might adapt the series for film or TV—in fact, it's the second most frequent question I hear, right after demands for Gideon and Savannah's story.

The simple answer is, it's not up to me. Adapting a book or series of books for live action drama is very expensive, and it takes the right studio with the right people on board to do it well. If a great team came along with a solid vision for the series, I would love to see the Order brought to life on cable or film.

How did you come up with the design of the Breedmate mark?
—Teodora K., Lukovit Bulgaria

The Breedmate mark just "appeared" as I was writing the scene in *Kiss of Midnight* where Lucan is looming over Gabrielle while she sleeps and nearly bites her. Sometimes little gifts like this happen, and you learn to accept them and figure out what they mean later. For the red teardrop-and-crescent-moon birthmark that all Breedmates are born with, the meaning seemed pretty clear to me right away. It represents the fertility cycle (Breedmates, and Atlanteans, being fertile only during the period of a waxing or waning crescent moon) and the power and sanctity of blood (the teardrop shape is actually a blood drop).

Can a Breed ever end up with more than one power?
—Jennifer K., Hampton, NH USA

Not unless the author screws something up (which happens, much to my chagrin). Breed talents are always inherited from Breedmate mothers. However, with the introduction of the Chase twins, Carys and Aric, being born of a Gen One Breed mother and a Breed father, things could get interesting!

Is Hunter also related to Nathan and Tavia?
—Carrie B., Las Vegas, NV USA

Yes. They all share paternal genes from the Ancient who'd been kept in Dragos's breeding lab.

(Translated) I am a fan of Lara Adrian from the first book and look forward to reading many more. My question is, will there be more story for Rio and Dylan?
—**Desiree D., Madrid, Spain**

I'm so glad you're enjoying my books, Desiree—thank you! I don't have plans to revisit or expand on any of the couples whose stories have already been told, but you will see more of Rio and Dylan and the entire cast of characters as the series continues. I try to keep all of the main characters present in some way, so long as it makes sense that they would be involved in the ongoing storyline of the series.

Will all Breedmates find their vampire match they are destined for? Do the vampires instinctively know how to find their Breedmate or does it just happen?
—**Karen G., Levittown, PA USA**

Soul mates and fated mates aren't part of the Midnight Breed series. I try to pair up couples so that in the end it feels like they've always belonged together and are absolutely perfect for each other, but within the story world of the series, there really isn't a destined mate for each Breed male or Breedmate. They meet and fall in love much like we do—by chance, by accident, by sheer good fortune, and sometimes they do it kicking and screaming the whole way.

Will you ever do signings in bookstores outside the US?
—**Debra G., Cork, Munster, Ireland**

Ironically, the only places I have done book tours are outside the United States! I've been to Germany and Italy so far, and just recently had to turn down an offer to come to France for a convention and book signing tour due to conflicts in scheduling (hopefully I'll be invited again another time). My international publishers have been amazingly supportive in this regard, and I hope to do more overseas book tours in the near future. The United Kingdom is one place I would very much love to visit!

Will you ever come to CT for a book signing? I would like to meet you. No author I like comes to CT for some reason.
—Nathasha G., Bristol, CT USA

Thank you, Nathasha! I would love to come to Connecticut for a book signing (and to all the rest of the states where readers have been asking me to come for years, as well). Unfortunately, my US publisher doesn't send me on book tours, even though I've made it clear that I would love the chance to meet readers in person. The lack of support in this area is frustrating, but the only way I've been able to meet with US readers is by attending conferences that host public book fairs, and by organizing events on my own, or with the help of book clubs who put together signings for me at their local bookstores. And in 2012, I decided to host my own reader conference, LAMB-Con, in Boston. It was a great time, and I really enjoyed hanging out with readers from all over the country for an entire weekend, not just a couple of hours at a signing.

I hope to do more events in the United States, like LAMB-Con and other types of gatherings, but please understand that my options are limited due to expense and opportunity. To get notified of any of my upcoming events and appearances, be sure to sign up for my newsletter at www.LaraAdrian.com.

How did you come up with the name Tavia for the character? My name is Tavia, so it was so cool to read your book and pretend it was me.
—Tavia H., White Plains, NY USA

Hi, Tavia! You have a beautiful name—one of my personal favorites. The meaning behind Tavia's name in the series is explained in her book, *Darker After Midnight*. She was originally named Octavia by Dragos, because she was the eighth successful live Gen One female birth in his breeding lab.

Do you intend to have only vampires in your series, or will you incorporate other creatures; such as werewolves/shape shifters. Newly discovered, of course.

—Jaynee H., Kelseyville, CA USA

The only supernatural beings you'll see in the series are the Ancients, the Breed and the Atlanteans. To add anything else into the mix so far after the fact would only seem tacked on and inauthentic, I think. I prefer to keep the series lore as faithful to its beginnings as I can, and if I have the urge to write something that includes other supernatural beings or paranormal elements (and I do!) then I'd rather begin something completely new.

This series is so amazing. Do you have any other series brewing in the back ground? Starting another?

—Olivia T., Griffith, IN USA

Thank you, Olivia! I do have plans for other series, actually. I've been thinking about one particular paranormal romance idea (dragons!) for quite some time now, and I'd like to write some non-paranormal thrillers and romantic suspense stories as well. So, yes—more to come!

What message do you hope fans get from your books?

—Lysette L., Moorpark, AL USA

At the core of all my romance novels, even those outside the Midnight Breed series, is the message that we all belong somewhere, that we are uniquely special and important, and that home and family is wherever your heart is happiest. Find that place, even if you have to walk through fire to get there. And when it comes to love, don't settle for anything less than the one person who will cherish and protect your heart like the precious gift it is.

Carys (Chase) is a female and Breed. How will this affect her ability to procreate? Meaning, since she is Breed will she be able to bond with a Breed male?

—Sheri B., Tampa, FL USA

Carys, one of a small number of Breed females, is able to share a blood bond with a Breed male. Although the Ancients do not bond, the Breed (their offspring) do because they have Breedmate genes somewhere down the ancestral line. In Carys's case, her mother Tavia is a genetically altered Gen One Breed. Unlike a Breedmate, Carys, being Breed, would not require a blood bond in order to have near-immortal longevity or to strengthen her ESP talent.

Will one of the warriors have their heart owned by a human woman? Is this a possibility?

—Larissa M., Londrina, Brazil

Of course, it would certainly be possible for one of the Breed to fall in love with a human woman. For instance, I think Brock would love Jenna and want her as his mate even without the alien DNA that's turned her into something more than mortal. But I don't think I'll write a book featuring a pairing between a true mortal and one of the warriors of the Order, because the sadness of knowing he'll lose his human mate to old age and death would always be a specter casting a dark shadow over the romance. I think a love story between a mortal and an immortal is lovely, but it's also inherently tragic and not something I have planned for the series.

If you were to be remembered for one thing, what would you like it to be?

—Sarah P., Tomah, WI USA

Wow, tough question! It's going to sound totally sappy, but I don't care. If I am to be remembered for only one thing, I hope it's kindness. Life is too short, too hard and too damned precious to live it with anything less than an open, loving heart.

How did you learn to write about sex, and how do you know when to fit it into the action?
—Heidi S., Munich, Germany

LOL! Years of practice and meticulous research, Heidi. *g* No, the secret to writing about sex is checking your inhibitions at the door and tuning out the fact that one day many thousands of eyes (including your parents and in-laws, God help them) will be reading every sweaty, moaning word. It's really hard to write a good sex scene if you're worried about what Aunt Mary will think when the hero does *that* to the heroine, or vice versa. So, ignore the future spectators and let it all hang out (ahem).

As for when to fit the "action" into the "action," it's really a matter of sensibility and good judgment. For instance, dropping a sex scene into the middle of a gunfight probably isn't a great choice. Nor, I would argue, is segueing from a near-rape of the heroine by bad guys into a hot love scene and neck-bite by a horny alpha vampire hero. A good sex scene needs to be erotic and exciting, but it also needs to make sense within the fabric of the story.

Which of all the stories was the most difficult one to write?
—Isabel P., Munich, Germany

Each story presents its own challenges, and there are times during the writing of every book that I want to pull my hair out or dissolve into a fit of tears. Fortunately, those moments never last very long! But there was one particular book that was more problematic for me than any other—not because of a difficult story or characters, but because of something that was happening to me health-wise at the time and I didn't realize it.

When I was writing *Ashes of Midnight*, I developed a sudden, acute food allergy problem. I'd never been allergic to anything but penicillin, and even then, it was never a big deal that made any foods off limits to me. Well, thinking I was eating healthy while on deadline, I began having a particular salad about three times a week. This salad had a variety of delicious things on it, including gorgonzola cheese…which, in case you aren't aware (as I wasn't) gorgonzola cheese is full of penicillin! I got very sick progressively over a period of several weeks, and had no idea why. Migraine headaches every day. Hives in my hairline and scalp. Severely bloodshot eyes and weird, sporadic facial swelling. Oh, I was a mess! And I started having trouble concentrating, feeling kind of disconnected and lethargic.

I turned in the manuscript for the book and my editor called me a few days later with a couple pages of revisions and questions about various things in the book. This might not seem alarming, but I hardly ever have revisions (I'm a perfectionist, and I hate letting go of any book unless it's the absolute best I can make it). I struggled through the reworking of the book, even the minor stuff seemed to take me forever to get right, but I still wasn't connecting the dots that something was going wrong with my health. It ended up taking a massive allergic reaction and a 3am trip to the emergency room before I understood I'd been slowly poisoning myself for more than a month! And by then I was so messed up, it's literally taken five years and a daily allergy pill the whole time to get myself somewhat back on track. The real bummer is, I'm still very allergic to any food containing mold or fungus, and that will likely never return to normal. No more cheese or mushrooms of any kind! :::cries:::

This may be a weird question. But since the Breed get their food, do they use the bathroom like humans do? Feel weird asking, but it came to me one day and I'm just curious.
—Ashley P., Newark, DE USA

It's a very logical question, actually! Members of the Breed do not consume food except in very minute amounts and only in those rarest instances when they're pressed to give the appearance of being human. So, although their bodies are equipped with the same basic plumbing as humans, their main diet 99.9% of the time is fresh blood.

The Breedmates, however, are total foodies. They eat for pleasure, not sustenance, since their mates' blood is all they need nutritionally speaking. And so it stands to reason that the Order's compound and the Darkhavens would have bathrooms. But you won't see me writing about bathroom habits, because…well, eww. I prefer to stick to the fantasy stuff, and leave the rest to the reader's imagination!

With their extra sensitive sensory skills, aren't they having problems with the women's periods? It's a question that pops into my head always when I read about or watch a movie about vampires…
—Marijke W., Julianadorp, Noord-Holland Netherlands

LOL! Allow me to refer you to the bit about "sticking to the fantasy stuff" from the question above. *g*

I guard my writing pen with my life no one is allowed to use it or touch it they can only look at it. Which leads to my question will you ever have a merchandise store?
—Mary P., Griffin, GA USA

LOL! We've had lots of requests to open a merchandise store, and I'm excited to report that it will be opening soon! The store will be part of my website redesign at www.LaraAdrian.com and will offer all kinds of fun Midnight Breed series merchandise, as well as signed (or unsigned) copies of all my books. Watch for a Grand Opening announcement in my website newsletter, likely sometime in Summer 2013.

How hard is it for you to come up with new Breed characters or to expound on the older ones to make them come alive for a new book due to its wide popularity that wants to keep the Breed alive?
—Jean R., Watertown, CT USA

Well, let me tell you, hearing from readers who never want the series to end is a very nice problem to have! And it's tempting to want to keep a good thing going. I'm having a blast writing these books, and there's nothing more motivating than knowing thousands of eager readers are dying to get their hands on the next Midnight Breed novel as soon as it arrives in stores.

But I also feel I have a responsibility to longtime fans of the series—and myself—to maintain the series' integrity and not draw it out endlessly just because I can. I'm a plotting writer, so the thought of an open-ended, meandering series with no clear direction or resolution makes me more than a little twitchy! I'd rather bring it to a satisfying, but finite, conclusion earlier than necessary, than risk letting the series jump the shark years after I should have ended it.

What are the funeral rites for Breedmates?
—Tori R., Port Saint Lucie, FL USA

Fortunately, we've not had the need to attend a Breedmate funeral within the series (yet...), but it's very similar to the rites performed for one of the Breed, except for the release of the body. With a member of the Breed, the sun claims the body of the deceased, turning it to ash. With a Breedmate, after rites are performed, her body is cremated and her ashes remain with her mate until his death, if she had a mate, or with her Darkhaven family, if she was unmated. You'll find the funeral ceremonies described in the *Rituals* section of this Companion book.

Before you wrote the Midnight Breed books you had the Dragon Chalice fantasies as Tina St. John. Was any part of the Midnight Breed partially inspired by the Dragon Chalice series, either a character that you would've liked to develop more or differently, or were any plots inspired off the other?
—Karen W., St. Catharines, ON Canada

Very astute observation, Karen! I wrote the Dragon Chalice trilogy (which I'd always intended would be a quadrilogy) a couple of years before I began the Midnight Breed books. In the Dragon Chalice series, Braedon, the hero of the first book is the son of a wolf shapeshifter mother from a hidden, mythical realm and a human father. Through his mother's lineage, Braedon is gifted with a knack for chasing down and locating lost people or objects, earning him the nickname of Hunter (though not at all related to Hunters in the Midnight Breed series). There is also a minor, but pivotal, character named Lara in that book!

But the character I think you're probably referring to is Draec les Nantres, henchman of the villain of that series and one-time friend of Braedon's. I loved that dark antihero (still do) and there are bits of him that ended up in the Midnight Breed series characters, Dante in particular. The Dragon Chalice series was never supposed to end where it did, but my publishing contract for those books got cancelled after I turned in the third book, and I've not yet had the chance to finish the best part of the Dragon Chalice story. I will one day, hopefully soon.

How many books will there end up being in the end for the Midnight Breed Series?
—**Rebecca D., Morristown, TN USA**

I've sketched out plans for seven more novels to complete the series, following Edge of Dawn, plus a handful of novellas along the way. It's possible the number could change slightly before all is said and done, but the series is moving toward a planned conclusion in the current, second arc that began with *Edge of Dawn*.

I just am dying to know whose book is next. Nathan, please?
—**Jamie R., Centennial, CO USA**

Nathan's book is, in fact, up next! Watch for *Crave the Night* in early 2014.

Lara, how does it make you feel knowing that the Midnight Breed series and all of the wonderful characters in it, have touched the lives of so many people, in so many different and profound ways?
—**Kathleen E., Mexico, NY USA**

In a word: humbled. Many people aren't aware that I actually began my career as a published author writing historical romances set in the Middle Ages. I wrote seven novels which, for one reason or another, never gained traction in the marketplace or with readers. So, I was accustomed to writing in obscurity, telling stories for just myself (and my editor!). I had no idea how incredible it could be to have readers all over the world enjoying my books and loving my characters as much as I do.

Every email I receive, every social network post and message, every reader I meet at a book signing or conference who takes the time to tell me what my books mean to them, or simply that they can't wait for the next one, is a gift that far outshines any other trapping of bestseller success. It sounds so cliché to say that I love my readers, but it's true. And I'm completely humbled and amazed by the love they give back to me.

~ ~ ~

Questions for the Characters

Actually to all the Breedmates: What is it like to really live with a Breed male? Do they have the same bad habits as human men? And do their special talents in the bedroom and being a warrior just make it worth it?
—Mendi O., Summerville, SC USA

:::amused glances and private smiles all around the room as the women of the Order wait to see who's going to tackle that loaded question:::

(Renata clears her throat) Yeah, that last part. Definitely. So worth it.

~ ~ ~

BROCK

How can you stand the fact not to "feel" Jenna in your blood?
—Cerstin W., Hueckelhoven, Germany

I feel Jenna in my heart and soul. I have everything I could ever want or need in her. Our bond couldn't be stronger, just the way it is.

~ ~ ~

CLAIRE

When you were first brought to Wilhelm's Darkhaven and then later became his mate, what was going through your mind as you remembered everything that you had gone through with Andreas when you two were together?
—Shauna R., Palm Bay, FL USA

Grief. Pain. Confusion. I felt betrayed by Andre, but more than that, I felt a terrible regret for how I pushed him away our last night together. I let my insecurity create a wedge between us. When he didn't come back that first night after we quarreled, or any of the long nights and months that followed, I didn't have any reason to expect I would ever see him again. I made a foolish, dangerous choice in Wilhelm Roth. I didn't realize how far he would go to keep Andre out of my life.

Andre and I were together just four months, then separated for fifty years. Fortunately, we have all the time in the world to make up for those missed shared moments, now that we're together again as mates.

~ ~ ~

DANIKA

Hello, Danika!!!! I realize we came into the story as it was already playing out. We didn't see much of your Conlan. I'm a HUGE fan of Highlanders. What's your favorite memory of you and Conlan together?
—Ginelle B., Caledonia, MI USA

Oh, there were many over the course of nearly four hundred years together. But none sweeter than the moment we made our son together. After so long without the place for a child in our lives, we'd become accustomed to the lack. But then Con and I both woke the same day, feeling an overwhelming urge to bring new life into the circle of our love. I wonder now if he might have sensed his end was coming. I wonder if I sensed it too, but didn't know to recognize it.

The night we made love and shared our blood to create Connor was the most tender, most vulnerable I'd ever seen my brave warrior, Conlan. And I had never loved him more. Not in four hundred years, had I loved him more than in that one precious moment.

Will Connor be joining the Order?
—**Phuong T., Angier, NC USA**

As his mother, I pray he'll choose a different path. But Connor is his father's son, and in my heart I know he is a warrior.

~ ~ ~

GABRIELLE

Do the Breedmates have days away? Do you girls get stir crazy? It seems like it could get claustrophobic or they could miss being out in the sun.
—**Lawren B., Menifee, CA USA**

We do go out for day trips, sometimes. But less often, as you can imagine, once the violence around Boston increased with Dragos in the picture. Lucan and the other warriors get twitchy when they're not there to protect us during daylight activities, so for their sanity more than ours, we've all decided to curtail our time outside the security of the compound. Thank goodness for Internet shopping and grocery delivery!

If you could re-do one thing in yours and Lucan's relationship what would that be?
—**Sandy S., Olathe, KS USA**

(Gabrielle smiles and sends a private, intimate look in Lucan's direction) Not one thing. I think we're doing everything pretty well so far.

~ ~ ~

GIDEON

Why do you wear glasses? Doesn't the Breed have good eyesight?
—**Edan E., Indianapolis, IN USA**

Correct. All of the Breed is born with impeccable eyesight. I was no different, until things went south for me around 1974.

(Dante snorts from across the room) Disco wasn't good for anyone, man.

(Gideon ignores him, looks back with a shrug) I had a bit of trouble down in Louisiana. If you want the blow-by-blow, Savannah and I spilled all the details just for that book you're holding in your hands right now.

This is something I have always wanted to know, Gideon...do you ever miss fighting Rogues with the others?
—**Kimberly M., Apopka, FL USA**

(Takes Savannah's hand in his, rubbing his thumb over his mate's smooth skin) Sure, I miss being in the thick of the action. But I made a promise to someone that means even more to me. Now I make do using my other considerable skills—if I do say so myself—to help the Order take out our enemies in other, more creative ways.

~ ~ ~

HUNTER

How has parenthood changed you?
—**Sandy S., Olathe, KS USA**

I can think of no way that it *hasn't* changed me. Any more than I can think of a single thing in my life that hasn't been changed because of the love of this woman. *(kisses Corinne unabashedly, in front of everyone gathered in the room)*

~ ~ ~

LUCAN

Why are the warriors so disrespected? I don't understand why the protectors of the race, not to mention some of the oldest, are looked down upon by the Darkhavens. Thank you for your service from this human who appreciates when somebody is out there trying to save our lives.
—**Liz F., Springfield, MO USA**

(Nods tightly, clearly uncomfortable with the praise or the gratitude) Let them disrespect us. We get the job done, and we do it our way. I don't hear anyone complaining about us when the bullets and blood are flying. If anyone disrespects our methods, let them come out to the front lines and take the heat alongside us.

Exactly how do you decide who can be part of the Order? Why did you decide on Kade and Brock and not some Darkhaven youth? Are there tests that must be passed to join the Order?
—**Diane Y., Toms River, NJ USA**

Darkhaven youth as a warrior? *(tries and fails to stifle a smirk)* The Order's not an equal opportunity employer, and I make no apologies for that. Our new recruits come in through recommendation by one of the warriors, or they're hand-picked by yours truly. We put them through some paces, take them out on a patrol or two, see what they're made of. The ones who're still standing come daybreak make it to another round. Sooner or later, the wheat separates from the chaff. Then I decide who stays and who goes.

Can a vampire be changed back to a human?
—**Tiffany M., Port Arthur, TX USA**

Can a cat be changed back into a frog? Different animal altogether. Same with Breed and humans. No changes, no returns.

Why does Lucan not utilize the Breedmates with active powers to help with the fight? I know they need to be protected but it seems that so many of them could be used to help their mates.
—**Tiffany S., APO, AE USA**

I'm not gonna be the one to call Niko's mate to the front lines of combat, but if Renata—or any of the other women of the Order—want to contribute to our missions, they can and do. They've got a pretty decent track record so far too. If you need a refresher, check out *Veil of Midnight, Ashes of Midnight, Taken by Midnight,* and *Darker After Midnight.*

What has happened in your life or continues to happen, Lucan, to make you so angry all the time? Even with Gabrielle in the beginning, you seem angry! You act as if you need her so much, but even that makes you seem angry!
—**Lynn K., Willards, MD USA**

(snarls) Why do you think I'm angry? Do I look angry to you? *(brow furrows deeper, growl curls up from back of his throat)* For fuck's sake, I am *not* angry all the time. *(glowers as Gideon barely suppresses a chortle)* What's the deal, asking about my feelings for Gabrielle, anyway? Do I need to come right out in front of everyone here and say I need her? Hell, yeah, I need her. I love her, damn it! And why the hell do I have so many questions when everyone else in this Q&A session only has one or two?

:::Lara hastily steps into the room now:::

Oookay, thank you for participating today, Lucan. Moving on! Who's up next?

~ ~ ~

MIRA

Did you ever wish that looking in your eyes didn't tell the future?

— Christian W., Keansburg, NJ USA

Yes. Almost every day I wished for that. But it's better now.

~ ~ ~

NATHAN

Did you meet with any of your half-brothers, e.g. the ones that were rescued along with your mother (and their mothers) by the Order?

— Julia H., Duisburg, Germany

No, I haven't met any of them. Pretty sure I've seen some of them around Boston and elsewhere, though.

How many people have you assassinated in your short life before your mother and Hunter found you?

— Shannon C., West Yarmouth, MA USA

A lot. Taking the time or attention to count them wasn't part of my training.

~ ~ ~

NIKOLAI

How did Niko get into designing cool weapons and ammo for the Order?

— Rachel S., Tampa, FL USA

Why is Rachel S. from Tampa speaking to me in third person? *(grins, showing his twin dimples)* Remember, I was born and raised in Siberia during the height of the Cold War era. Weapons and ammo were my teething toys.

~ ~ ~

RENATA

How does it feel to be the first female "warrior" member of the Order?

—Katy N., Alfortville, France

Pretty fucking awesome. And by that I mean, it's an honor.

~ ~ ~

RIO

Why could you only see your dead mate's ghost when Dylan was in danger?

—Lara B., Barrys Bay, ON Canada

Why did she lead Dylan to me that day in the Czech mountains? Did she want to save my life, or did she want me to find my true mate in Dylan? You'd have to ask Eva these things.

When Eva appeared to me on that highway, I suppose after she'd died, she'd never tried so hard to reach out to me, the way she did when Dylan had been kidnapped by Dragos. Maybe my blood bond to Dylan helped bridge the gap between this plane and the next, and allowed Eva to appear to me.

Whatever the reason, I am grateful for what Eva did for me that day. For us, Dylan and me. I thought I would despise Eva for the rest of my life. I can summon no hate for her now.

~ ~ ~

SAVANNAH

You have been mated to Gideon for a long time, what advice can you offer the younger Breed couples in keeping the love/romance everlasting?
—Madeline P., Escondido, CA USA

Be honest with your mate, even if it scares you. Share everything you are, and trust the love you have together will see you through anything.

~ ~ ~

STERLING CHASE

As a father of twins, what are your fondest memories of them as babies/toddlers? I bet you have plenty of adorable stories.
—Madeline P., Escondido, CA USA

(chuckles) Memories of my children as toddlers usually involves Carys getting into some kind of trouble and Aric rushing in to get her out of it. Come to think of it, not much has changed now that they're grown.

~ ~ ~

TAVIA

Being part Breed now, years later, can you still eat both blood and human food?
—Angela B., Hillsboro, OH USA

Yes. I'm lucky, I have the best of both worlds. Savannah and Dylan's amazing cooking when I want it, and Chase's carotid for dessert.

~ ~ ~

TEGAN

When you were in Elise's apartment after you found her hunting Minions, you cooked her breakfast. For someone that only drinks blood and is a Gen One more comfortable with a blade or gun in your hand than a spatula, where did you learn to cook?

—**Sheri B., Tampa, FL USA**

The Food Network. Hang out here sometime with the Breedmates. I figure they must have stock in the network or something, because it's on just about 24/7.

Why did you stay with Lucan and the Order after Lucan killed your mate and locked you up to cure your Bloodlust?

—**Victoria W., Northridge, CA USA**

Didn't stay long. I left for a while, spent some time in Germany and other places. Hooked back up with Lucan in Boston because being a warrior isn't something I chose; it chose me. 'Sides, I couldn't say it then—not for a long time—but I know he did the right thing. For Sorcha and for me, Lucan did the right thing.

I know you don't go there now that you have Elise, but where was your dark place that you used to go when you wanted to get away from the Order?

—**Lisa S., London, United Kingdom**

Savannah knows.

~ ~ ~

TESS

I myself have been in the veterinarian field for 15 years and an animal lover so if you can pick 3 warriors and tell me if the warriors were dogs what kind of dog would they be and why?

—**Vikki K., Palm City, FL USA**

First, congratulations and thank you for so many years spent devoted to caring for animals. It's not an easy job. There's a lot of cruelty and heartbreak that comes with it, sadly.

So, three dogs to represent three warriors...?

(Dante grunts) We all know Harvard's was chosen a long time ago. Ugly little runt, if I recall.

(Tess rolls her eyes at her mate) Okay, I have my three: For Lucan, a Pit Bull, because he's aggressive and fiercely protective, deadly so at times. But also because he's terribly misunderstood by those who don't really know him. For Hunter, a German Shepherd, because he's fearless and loyal, and he will stride calmly into any battle that's asked of him, and he never, ever cowers. And as for my Dante—

(Chase interrupts, grinning) Chihuahua? Gotta be something barky, without the good sense to know when to shut up....

(Tess shakes her head at both of them.) For Dante, a Rottweiler. Because he's robust and intelligent, defensive of the people he cares about. But also because he can be a big clown when he's around people he loves.

(Dante quirks a dark brow) That doesn't include you, Harvard.

(Chase chuckles.) Great. I'll remind you of that next time you need me to haul your Chihuahua ass out of trouble on patrol.

(Tess shrugs, laughing now) See what I mean? Love.

MIDNIGHT BREED SERIES

TRIVIA

MIDNIGHT BREED SERIES
TRIVIA

I'm always amazed at the depth of series knowledge my readers possess. While I need a reference bible (or a book like this Companion) to keep all the details straight, dedicated fans of the Midnight Breed series can pull even the most obscure character name or book fact from their memory alone.

I witnessed this myself at LAMB-Con 2012, the first official mini-conference we hosted for Lara Adrian Midnight Breed fans. More than sixty readers gathered in Boston from all over the United States to hang out together with me for a weekend of fun and food, parties and informal chat sessions. As part of LAMB-Con, my staff and I collected hundreds of trivia questions and facts from the books to be used in the many contests and games we played that weekend. What follows is a sampling of those trivia quizzes, as well as a few extras we put together especially for this Companion.

Test your knowledge of the Midnight Breed, then add up your scores to find out if you are fit to join the Order, or if you would be put to shame by the greenest of Minions.

Good luck!

Who Am I?

1. People are always telling me how they love my gem green eyes
2. My brothers' names were inspired by rock legends, too
3. My best friend is Kade
4. I used to love having a beer at Pete's Tavern with my brother
5. I play the piano
6. I love being the Godmother of Xander Raphael
7. I drugged someone with 1800 milligrams of animal tranquilizer
8. I love peanut butter and jelly sandwiches
9. I used to live on Willow Street in Boston
10. My whole life I thought I was very ill—because that's what I was told
11. I carry four special daggers
12. I'm a pilot
13. I'm a total gearhead
14. I always worried about the wildness in my twin brother
15. I was three months pregnant when I became a widow
16. My mother considered me a monster and gave me no formal name
17. I was born August 8, 1956
18. I was born December 20, more than 900 years ago
19. I had twin brothers who were killed by Rogues in London
20. I am still getting used to listening to my jazz on CDs instead of on records
21. I made a donation to my college alumni in the 1920s

Answers
1. Tegan 2. Dylan 3. Brock 4. Jenna 5. Claire 6. Savannah
7. Tess 8. Mira 9. Gabrielle 10. Tavia 11. Renata 12. Alex
13. Nikolai 14. Kade 15. Danika 16. Rio 17. Hunter
18. Lucan 19. Gideon 20. Corinne 21. Chase

Your Score: _____

Am I Dead or Alive?
(at the end of ten books and one novella)

1. Eva
2. Skeeter Arnold
3. Mathias Rowan
4. Sharon Alexander
5. Conlan MacConn
6. The Ancient
7. Jonas Redmond
8. Libby Darrow
9. Aunt Sarah
10. Jamie
11. Xander Raphael
12. Uncle Maksim
13. Kendra Delaney
14. Quentin Chase
15. Alexei Yakut
16. Malcolm MacBain
17. Marek
18. Amelie Dupree
19. Sorcha
20. Thane
21. Wilhelm Roth
22. Senator Bobby Clarence

Answers:
1. Dead 2. Dead 3. Alive 4. Dead 5. Dead 6. Dead 7. Dead
8. Dead 9. Dead 10. Alive 11. Alive 12. Alive 13. Dead
14. Dead 15. Dead 16. Alive 17. Dead 18. Alive 19. Dead
20. Alive 21. Dead 22. Dead

Your Score: _____

First Kisses

1. Our first kiss was in the Breedmates' mission command room, after he asked permission
2. Our first kiss was in the kitchen of her apartment on Willow Street
3. Our first kiss was in a jazz club in New Orleans
4. Our first kiss was near a lake outside Andreas Reichen's Berlin Darkhaven
5. Our first kiss was in his quarters in the Boston compound
6. Our first kiss was in his abandoned Darkhaven
7. Our first kiss was in a dog kennel
8. Our first kiss was at the Boston MFA in front of *Sleeping Endymion*
9. Our first kiss was in a parking lot outside Pete's Tavern

Answers:
1. Brock and Jenna 2. Lucan and Gabrielle
3. Hunter and Corinne 4. Tegan and Elise 5. Rio and Dylan
6. Chase and Tavia 7. Nikolai and Renata 8. Dante and Tess
9. Kade and Alex

Your Score: _____

Lost and Found

1. In what state does Corinne find her son?

2. Where does Andreas find Claire after losing her at the Boston airport?

3. Who does Rio have to fight in order to save Dylan after finding her on a bridge over a dam in New York?

4. Which Breedmate found a photo of her birth father bearing the inscription: Zael. Mykonos, 1975?

5. Who found Jenna after she was Tasered and put in a car by FBI Agents Cho and Green?

6. Who was found in a locked bedroom in Edgar Fabien's property in the woods north of Montreal?

7. Using their blood bond, who was able to find their mate being tortured in a house in Berlin?

8. Dante found Tess at a North End coffee shop on what day?

9. Where does Sterling Chase find Tavia when the police were hiding her?

10. Who found Elise hunting Minions on the streets of Boston?

11. Who finds Nikolai at a containment facility being held by Edgar Fabien?

12. Which couple lost 30 years together before being reunited?

Answers:

1. Georgia

2. At her grandmother's house in Newport, Rhode Island
3. Dragos 4. Dylan 5. Brock 6. Mira 7. Elise 8. Her birthday
9. In a hotel suite 10. Tegan 11. Renata 12. Andreas and Claire

Your Score: _____

What Book Am I In?

1. Ben Sullivan
2. Irina Odolf
3. Enforcement Agent Freyne
4. Reiver
5. Sergei Yakut
6. Big Dave Grant
7. Edgar Fabien
8. Camden Chase
9. Seth
10. Henry Vachon
11. Buddy Vincent
12. Toni the dead Breedmate
13. Mason
14. Dr. Lewis
15. Jack
16. Victor Bishop
17. Zach Tucker
18. Christophe Archer

Answers:

1. Kiss of Crimson 2. Midnight Awakening
3. Taken By Midnight 4. A Taste of Midnight
5. Veil of Midnight 6. Shades of Midnight
7. Veil of Midnight 8. Kiss of Crimson
9. Shades of Midnight 10. Deeper Than Midnight
11. Ashes of Midnight 12. Midnight Rising
13. Deeper Than Midnight 14. Darker After Midnight
15. Veil of Midnight 16. Deeper Than Midnight
17. Shades of Midnight 18. Taken By Midnight

Your Score: _____

Whose Breedmate Mark is Located Here?

1. On the inside of her right thigh
2. On the back of her right hand
3. Behind her left ear
4. Between the thumb and forefinger of her right hand
5. Inside of her right wrist
6. On the nape of her neck
7. On her abdomen
8. On her left shoulder blade
9. On her lower back
10. On the front of her left hip

Answers:

1. Elise 2. Corinne 3. Gabrielle 4. Tess 5. Renata 6. Dylan
7. Danika 8. Savannah 9. Tavia 10. Alex

Your Score: _____

True or False?

1. Some of the immediate effects of Crimson to the Breed include extreme thirst, fever-like chills and a burst of enormous strength and endurance.

2. Rio's name means *"he who is free and of the night everlasting."*

3. The complete verse of the poem Tegan and Elise discovered (the one that Petrov Odolf repeats over and over) is: *"Castle and croft shall come together under the crescent moon...to the borderlands east turn your eye...at the sword is the clue."*

4. Dante's mother drowned in an ocean riptide after she swam out to save a child.

5. In *Taken By Midnight*, Jenna, Renata, Gabrielle and Dylan find the captive Breedmates.

6. Gabrielle is making meatloaf when Lucan first comes to her door.

7. Tegan and Dante established the Boston compound with Lucan.

8. It took Tavia six full months to recover from the dose of Crimson.

9. For the Christmas spent in Maine, Gabrielle gave Lucan the tapestry from the Boston compound.

10. Rogues identified Elise from the FedEx store's security camera.

11. Danika is living in Paris when Andreas and Claire stay with her.

12. Lucan tells Gabrielle that flowers are missing in all of her photographs.

13. Tess's full maiden name is Teresa Dawn Culver.

14. Claire's maiden name is Smith.

15. Corinne was 18 when she was abducted.

16. Elise's gown at the reception Andrea Reichen hosted was bright fuchsia.

17. As a genetically altered female Gen One Breed, Tavia can eat regular food and walk in the daylight.

18. The Boston compound was established in the 1920s.

19. After Kellan was first brought to the compound, he became ill because of a GPS chip in his stomach.

20. The words engraved on the handles of Renata's daggers are: Courage, Honor, Faith, Sacrifice.

21. Rio's image is on the old tapestry at the Boston compound.

22. The Breed get their talent by inheriting their mother's unique Breedmate ability.

23. The Order moved its headquarters to Vermont after being discovered in Boston.

24. Breedmates are recognizable by their small red birthmark present somewhere on their body, in the shape of a teardrop falling into the cradle of a crescent moon.

25. Dante and Tess named their baby Xander Robert.

26. Jenna used to be a FBI agent.

27. Renata made a promise to Mira in Veil of Midnight to get her a dog.

28. The number 7 plays a significant role in Breed funeral rites.

29. Brock and Jenna have a very special blood bond.

30. *Athena* is the name of Helene's erotic club in Berlin.

31. The name of the 18th century sculpture Dante and Tess stand next to while talking at the Boston museum is *Sleeping Endymion.*

32. The location of the Ancient's hiding place was secretly hidden in the tapestry.

33. Tegan and Elise stayed in a hunting lodge while in Berlin.

34. The Boston compound was located 300 feet below ground.

Answers:

1. True 2. True 3. False (...at the cross lies truth) 4. True
5. False (Jenna, Renata, Dylan and Alex)
6. False (homemade manicotti) 7. False (Gideon) 8. True
9. True 10. True 11. False (Denmark) 12. False (people)
13. True 14. False (Samuels) 15. True 16. False (dark purple)
17. True 18. False (1898) 19. True 20. True
21. False (it is an image of Lucan) 22. True 23. False (Maine)
24. True 25. False (Xander Raphael)
26. False (Alaska State Trooper) 27. False (to never leave her)
28. False (8, symbolizing infinity)
29. False (they don't have a blood bond) 30. False (Aphrodite)
31. True 32. True
33. False (they stayed at Andreas Reichen's Darkhaven)
34. True

Your Score: _____

Where Did I First See My Mate?

1. At an impromptu town hall meeting
2. Outside Chase's Darkhaven
3. In a cave in the Bohemian hills
4. In a veterinarian clinic on Halloween
5. At a senator's estate
6. In a vision I saw in Mira's eyes
7. In Hamburg while studying abroad as a student
8. At a jazz club
9. At Reichen and Claire's Darkhaven
10. In a cabin
11. At a bus station

Answers:

1. Kade and Alex 2. Tegan and Elise 3. Rio and Dylan
4. Tess and Dante 5. Chase and Tavia 6. Hunter
7. Reichen and Claire 8. Nikolai and Renata 9. Corinne
10. Brock and Jenna 11. Lucan and Gabrielle

Your Score: _____

Good Guy or Bad Guy?

1. I broke into Gabrielle's apartment when she was sleeping
2. I kidnapped Dylan and brought her to Berlin
3. I abducted Tess off the street in Boston
4. I broke into Elise's apartment
5. I chased Alex on a snow machine
6. I bit Tess when she was trying to help me
7. I kept Dylan locked up in a room
8. I jumped off the roof of a building with Gabrielle
9. I killed the Ancient by taking him over a cliff in Alaska
10. I killed the human woman who was my lover
11. I killed Tegan's first Breedmate
12. I drank from Jenna Tucker-Darrow in her cabin in Alaska
13. Alex found me in the Alaskan woods with a pack of wolves, naked and covered in blood
14. I turned Tegan's first Breedmate, Sorcha, into a Minion
15. I killed my nephew in front of his mother
16. I took my father's head after he slaughtered my mother

Answers:

1. Good Guy (Lucan) 2. Good Guy (Rio) 3. Bad Guy (Rogues)
4. Good Guy (Tegan) 5. Bad Guy (Zach Tucker)
6. Good Guy (Dante) 7. Good Guy (Rio) 8. Good Guy (Lucan)
9. Bad Guy (Seth) 10. Good Guy (Andreas Reichen)
11. Good Guy (Lucan) 12. Bad Guy (The Ancient)
13. Bad Guy (Seth) 14. Bad Guy (Marek)
15. Good Guy (Sterling Chase) 16. Good Guy (Lucan)

Your Score: _____

Midnight Breed Talent Show
Which ESP Ability Belongs to Whom?

1. Telepathically hears the sins and negative energy of humans
2. Cursed with power to kill with his touch, particularly when provoked
3. Hypnotic manipulation; can make someone see or believe something that's not there
4. Can sense, and is drawn to, areas of Breed presence
5. Connects psychically with predatory animals, can direct their actions with a thought
6. Heals with by touch; can also rescind the gift of the healing
7. Reads others' emotional states with a touch
8. Can see and hear the spirits of dead Breedmates
9. Mind-blaster; can debilitate even the strongest of the Breed
10. Shadow-bender; can manipulate shadows to conceal
11. Dreamwalker; can enter someone's dreams and observe or communicate with them
12. Internal gauge that tells with a touch if someone is being honest or deceptive
13. Cursed with premonitions of death
14. Sonokinesis; can manipulate sound waves to deafening heights or mute them
15. Absorbs and diminishes human pain and suffering with his hands
16. Photographic memory
17. Telepathically generates rapid growth in plant life
18. Psychometry; can read the history of objects with a touch
19. Mind-reader; can hear others' thoughts through psychic focus
20. Blood-reader; siphons memories from blood when drinking from either Breedmate or Breed
21. Precognitive gaze; visions play out for the observer as though in a mirror
22. Pyrokinesis; can start fires psychically

Answers:

1. Elise 2. Rio 3. Lucan 4. Gabrielle 5. Kade 6. Tess 7. Tegan

8. Dylan 9. Renata 10. Sterling Chase 11. Claire 12. Alex
13. Dante 14. Corinne 15. Brock 16. Tavia 17. Nikolai
18. Savannah 19. Danika 20. Hunter 21. Mira
22. Andreas Reichen

Your Score: _____

Who Said This?

1. "Happily ever after. Only in myths and fairy tales."

2. "Last time I checked, I wasn't campaigning for any Mr. Congeniality awards."

3. "Too much gray in your black and white world?"

4. "I can smell you...and I want to...taste you. I want you, and I'm not sane enough to keep my hands off you if I were to see you right now."

5. "It's no easy thing, to kill a brother, no matter what he's done. Ask Lucan, he'll tell you."

6. "We are warriors. Brethren. We are kin. We will not let anyone scatter us in terror."

7. "It was Mira who gave me the courage to demand my freedom."

8. "If this was Siberia, our balls would be jingling like sleigh bells and we'd be pissing ice cubes. Boston in November is a picnic."

9. "If I speak it, then everything I've tried to put behind me ...everything I've worked so hard to forget...it will all become real again."

10. "You just promised me eternity, you know. I can make you live to regret it."

11. "No birthday is complete without a kiss."

12. "Don't make me want to stay with you tonight when you will only wish me gone tomorrow."

13. "Dust off your knees, because you may damn well end up walking on them before the night is through."

14. "I never knew what it was to crave a woman's touch. Or to hunger for a woman's kiss."

15. "Sweetheart, the only reason you had a chance to drop me was because you played dirty."

16. "You don't write, you don't call . . . Don't you love me no more?"

17. "I love you, and I could give a damn if you're human, cyborg, alien, or some mixed-up combination of all three."

18. "Never in a million years could I have guessed I'd wake up naked in a vampire's arms on Christmas morning."

19. "You've had your fun. Now I'm taking you to bed."

20. "When I look in your eyes, one word leaps to my mind every single time: Forever."

21. "I'm a wreck for this woman, my friend. She owns me now."

22. "Female, I give you fair warning: you are playing with fire."

23. "I would quit breathing for her, if she asked it of me."

24. "Thank you for bringing me home."

Answers:

1. Dante 2. Tegan 3. Kade 4. Rio 5. Tegan 6. Lucan
7. Hunter 8. Kade 9. Alex 10. Gabrielle 11. Dante
12. Gabrielle 13. Lucan 14. Hunter 15. Nikolai
16. Gideon 17. Brock 18. Tavia 19. Lucan
20. Nikolai 21. Rio 22. Tegan
23. Dante 24. Corinne & Hunter (both)

Your Score: _____

Dead People We Never Got to Meet
Who Am I?

1. Dmitri
2. Sorcha
3. Kassia
4. Grigori
5. Richie Maguire
6. Fiona MacBain
7. Sebastian Bishop
8. Evran
9. August Chase
10. Eleanor Archer

Answers:

1. Nikolai's brother 2. Tegan's first Breedmate
3. Dragos's mother 4. Kade's uncle
5. Alex's brother 6. Malcolm's first Breedmate
7. Corinne's Darkhaven brother
8. Lucan and Marek's brother
9. Sterling Chase's father 10. Lazaro's first Breedmate

Your Score: _____

Trivia Scoring: How did you do?

Calculate your overall score and see where you rank!

188 - 209
Congratulations - you are granted honorary membership in the Order!

162 - 187
Stay away from the sun because odds are good that you are Gen One Breed!

136 - 161
Got a peculiar birthmark you're not aware of? You are a Breedmate waiting to be discovered!

110 - 135
Your bestie is a Breedmate and she is constantly telling you secrets about the Order, but you are merely human.

84 - 109
You would like to be a Breed historian, but Jenna isn't sharing her journals.

58 - 83
Look out! You must be too busy running from Rogues to read the books.

0 - 57
It's very sad, but even a brand-new Minion knows more than you.

MIDNIGHT BREED SERIES

AROUND THE WORLD

Since its United States debut May 1, 2007, the Midnight Breed series has been published in more than 18 languages in countries all over the globe. The series is a #1 bestseller in Germany, selling in excess of one million copies as of 2012. In Italy, the series has also landed on numerous bestseller lists, with sales reported at nearly half a million copies.

United States	Random House
	Lara Adrian LLC (self-published)
United States (audiobooks)	Audible.com
	Tantor Media
	Random House Audio
Brazil	Universo dos Livros
China	King-in Publishing
Croatia	Stilus Knjiga
Czech Republic	Brana Publishing
Denmark	Forlaget Tellerup
France	Editions Bragelonne
Germany (novels)	Egmont LYX
Germany (audiobooks)	Argon (CD/MP3)
	Audible.de (downloads)
Hungary	Ulpius-haz Publishers
Italy	Fanucci Leggereditore
Japan	Oakla Publishing
Netherlands	Uitgeverij Luitingh-Sijthoff
Poland	Wydawnictwo Amber
Portugal	Quinta Essencia
Russia	Azbooka-Atticus Publishing
Spain	Terciopelo
Thailand	Grace Publishing
Turkey	Epsilon Yayincilik
United Kingdom/Australia	Constable & Robinson
Vietnam	Vina Books

For an updated list of translations, or for license inquiries about the series, please contact the author at **www.LaraAdrian.com**.

THE FUTURE OF THE

MIDNIGHT BREED SERIES

Edge of Dawn and Beyond

So, here we are, at the close of this first chapter of the Midnight Breed series. I hope you've enjoyed taking an inside look at the characters, the novels, and behind-the-scenes peeks at how Lucan and the Order, the Breed and the Breedmates, the Ancients and the Atlanteans—even Dragos—all came into being on the page.

Looking back on these ten books and the two novellas that now comprise the series, I can't help feeling a sense of pride for what I've created. But more than that, I feel immense gratitude to you, my readers, for embracing the characters, the books, and me as well.

By the time this Companion publishes, the series will have seen the February, 2013, release of the eleventh Midnight Breed book, *Edge of Dawn* (Mira and Kellan's story).

Edge of Dawn kicks off the new story arc featuring the Order's offspring and many new characters I can't wait for you to meet. Don't worry that you'll be missing Lucan, Gabrielle, Gideon, Savannah, Dante, Tess, Tegan, Elise, and the rest of the original cast. They play an active role in *Edge of Dawn*, and will continue to be a big part of the series as it moves forward. And I can assure you that as much as I loved writing the first ten books, I'm having even more fun with the new ones.

After *Edge of Dawn*, I have plans for potentially seven more novels and a handful of novellas. If you've enjoyed the first leg of the series, I hope you'll join me on this next adventure too!

Next up after Mira and Kellan is Nathan's story, *Crave the Night*, currently slated for hardcover release from Random House early 2014.

In the meantime, I want to thank you for embracing my work so generously and so enthusiastically. Writing books for a living is my dream come true, but none of this would be possible without you, my dear readers.

You honor me well!

LARA ADRIAN

BIOGRAPHY

Lara Adrian Biography

LARA ADRIAN is the New York Times and #1 internationally best-selling author of the Midnight Breed vampire romance series, with nearly 4 million books in print worldwide and translations licensed to more than 19 countries. Her books regularly appear in the top spots of all the major bestseller lists including the New York Times, USA Today, Publishers Weekly, Indiebound, Amazon.com, Barnes & Noble, etc. Her debut title, Kiss of Midnight, was named Borders Books bestselling debut romance of 2007. Later that year, her third title, Midnight Awakening, was named one of Amazon.com's Top Ten Romances of the Year. Reviewers have called Lara's books "addictively readable" (Chicago Tribune), "extraordinary" (Fresh Fiction), and "one of the best vampire series on the market" (Romantic Times).

Writing as TINA ST. JOHN, her historical romances have won numerous awards including the National Readers Choice; Romantic Times Magazine Reviewer's Choice; Booksellers Best; and many others. She was twice named a Finalist in Romance Writers of America's RITA Awards, for Best Historical Romance (White Lion's Lady) and Best Paranormal Romance (Heart of the Hunter). More recently, the 2011 German translation of Heart of the Hunter debuted on Der Spiegel bestseller list.

With an ancestry stretching back to the Mayflower and the court of King Henry VIII, the author lives with her husband in New England, surrounded by centuries-old graveyards, hip urban comforts, and the endless inspiration of the broody Atlantic Ocean.

Visit the author's website and sign up for new release announcements at www.LaraAdrian.com.

CONNECT ONLINE WITH

LARA ADRIAN

Connect Online with Lara Adrian

The websites and social network URLs listed here the only official Lara Adrian sites. If you'd like to interact with Lara or get notified of book news, promotions, events, etc., these are the places you should visit.

Websites

www.LaraAdrian.com

www.MidnightBreed.com

www.LAMB-Con.com

Social Networks

www.facebook.com/LaraAdrianBooks

www.twitter.com/lara_adrian

www.goodreads.com/lara_adrian

www.pinterest.com/LaraAdrian

www.wattpad.com/LaraAdrian

Other sites and groups you may find online, including social network pages, character role playing groups, or other fansites, message forums, RPGs, fan fiction, etc., are operated and managed independently of Lara Adrian, her staff and/or publishing imprints.

Although Lara appreciates fan interest and creativity with regard to the Midnight Breed series and her other writings, she has no affiliation or presence with any site other than those listed here on this page.

APPENDIX

RESOURCES FOR WRITERS

APPENDIX

RESOURCES FOR WRITERS

The following is by no means a complete list, but hopefully a good starting point for anyone interested in learning more about writing, or in reading more about the books and organizations that have helped me hone my storytelling craft, particularly as it relates to the creation of the Midnight Breed series. I've also included some links to self-publishing information and publishing industry resources that I've found particularly useful.

For those of you who are aspiring writers, I wish you much inspiration and success!

~Lara Adrian

Books

Cowden, T., LaFever, C. & Viders, S. (2000). *The Complete Writer's Guide to Heroes & Heroines: Sixteen Master Archetypes*. Hollywood, CA: Lone Eagle.

Kenyon, S. (1994). *The Writer's Digest Character Naming Sourcebook*. Cincinnati, OH: Writer's Digest Books.

King, S. (2000). *On Writing: A Memoir of the Craft*. New York, NY: Scribner.

Le Rouzic, P. (1994). *The Name Book*. Fairfield, IA: Sunstar Publishing, Ltd.

McKee, R. (1997). *Story: Substance, Structure, Style & The Principles of Screenwriting*. New York, NY: Regan Books.

Schmidt, V. (2005). *Story Structure Architect: A Writer's Guide to Building Dramatic Situations & Compelling Characters*. Cincinnati, OH: Writer's Digest Books.

Swain, D. (1982). *Techniques of the Selling Writer*. Norman, OK: University of Oklahoma Press.

Vogler, C. (1992). *The Writer's Journey: Mythic Structure for Writers*. Studio City, CA: Michael Wiese Productions.

Organizations & Conferences

Romance Writers of America (www.rwa.org) -- open to unpublished and published writers

International Thriller Writers (www.thrillerwriters.org) -- published only; not open to indies

Novelists, Inc. (www.ninc.com) -- published only; indie friendly

Websites & Online Groups

Publishers Lunch (http://lunch.publishersmarketplace.com/)

The Passive Voice (www.thepassivevoice.com)

Digital Book World (www.digitalbookworld.com)

A Newbie's Guide to Publishing (http://jakonrath.blogspot.com/)

Self-publish Group on Yahoo
(http://groups.yahoo.com/group/selfpublish/)

Complete list of titles by New York Times & #1 internationally best-selling author
LARA ADRIAN

Midnight Breed Series
Kiss of Midnight
Kiss of Crimson
Midnight Awakening
Midnight Rising
Veil of Midnight
Ashes of Midnight
Shades of Midnight
Taken by Midnight
Deeper Than Midnight
A Taste of Midnight (ebook novella)
Darker After Midnight
Edge of Dawn
Crave the Night (releasing early 2014)

The Midnight Breed Series Companion

NightDrake
A Glimpse of Darkness (ebook collaborative novella)

LARA ADRIAN writing as *TINA ST. JOHN*

Dragon Chalice Series
Heart of the Hunter
Heart of the Flame
Heart of the Dove

Warrior Trilogy
White Lion's Lady
Black Lion's Bride
Lady of Valor

Lord of Vengeance

Want to stay informed of new releases and be eligible for special subscribers-only exclusive content and giveaways?

Be sure to visit

www.LaraAdrian.com

and sign up for Lara's private email newsletter!